Please feel free to s
publisher filters the

MW01612485

Tara Declan - tara_declan@awesomeauthors.org

Sign up for my blog for updates and freebies!
tara-declan.awesomeauthors.org

About the Publisher

BLVNP Incorporated, A Nevada Corporation, 340 S. Lemon #6200, Walnut CA 91789, info@blvnp.com / legal@blvnp.com

DISCLAIMER

This book is a work of FICTION. It is fiction and not to be confused with reality. Neither the author nor the publisher or its associates assume any responsibility for any loss, injury, death or legal consequences resulting from acting on the contents in this book. The author's opinions are not to be construed as the opinions of the publisher. The material in this book is for entertainment purposes ONLY. Enjoy.

Praise for Love is Blind

When I read Love is Blind, I could feel the characters, they lifted off the page and attached themselves to my daily life. I'd dream about what each cliffhanger meant, how they would react, and I feel in love with them as they did with each other. Good job to you, Tara, for creating a real masterpiece that forces the reader to experience everything your characters experience, and for making us love every minute of it.
- Eloise, Goodreads

This story was one of the first ones that I read when I discovered Wattpad. I fell in love with the story instantly and I can't wait to be able to have a paperback copy of it. If you haven't read this story yet, you need to read it ASAP! It is a must read story that will make you have so many emotions at once and can even change your point of view on life.
- Samantha Zuniga, Goodreads

I started reading this years ago on Wattpad before it was even finished. Since then I re-read it minimum of 12 times. This was such an amazing book and I found something different and read it different every time. This is a book I am really proud to say I have read. It is so amazing to see it get published. It's not much of a surprise though lol.
- Lucero Hinojoza, Goodreads

I happened to run into this book in Wattpad. As soon as I started reading it I was hooked! The story it's truly touching and will bring tears to your eyes. So read it already! Lol. But you will seriously not regret it.
- Katherine, Goodreads

I enjoyed reading Love is blind and I can't wait until it gets published.
- Cathy Chillemi, Goodreds

Love is Blind

By: Tara Declan

BLVNP

ISBN: 978-1-68030-821-1

Table of Contents

FREE DOWNLOAD

Get these freebies and MORE when you sign up for the author's mailing list!

tara-declan.awesomeauthors.org

Preface

One minute. That's all it takes. One minute and your life can change forever, leaving you with no power to fix it. People say things are already destined to happen, and we are fated to live our lives in a particular way, the way God has planned it. However, they neglected to mention how cruel and mean fate truly is. Things happen for a reason. But why do bad things happen to the good? It makes us strong, but why must we be so weak before we can be strong? Why must these bad things happen?

Why am I poor? Why was my father abusive before he got up and left us? Why am I so unconsolidated? Why am I not pretty? Why must life be so hard? What did I ever do to deserve this? And last but not least, why did some boy choose to step into our school and open fire in our halls? I know his mind was elsewhere, and he was slowly losing grip of reality, but why target Reece Collins in hopes for his death. Reece, the most popular guy in school, the star quarterback, best pitcher and star track runner; he has money, the looks, and a perfect family. It's amazing in comparison to my life, and although he's a jock, I've heard he is one of the nicest guys out there. He volunteers at a soup kitchen and does many other kind things. Why would anyone want to kill him? Yes, people are jealous of him, but jealousy is no reason to take a life. I don't know how he is, though; no one tells me this type of thing. Last thing I remember he was being put in the ambulance with the paramedics trying to stop the bleeding and save him. Now, I have no clue. No clue if he's alive or dead.

I don't have a crush on Reece or anything of the sorts; I merely admire him and wish I had his life. I have never even spoken a word to him. I've only seen him when his pictures are all over school, or I catch a glimpse of him in the hall, the cafeteria, or the AP classes we have together. All I can say about him is he isn't ugly by any means. My life consists of school, work, volunteering at the hospital and home. What a brilliant life.

Chapter One

Nine hours ago

I stretch climbing out of my bed. My limbs ache from the crappy mattress on top of the box spring, which lies on the floor and frameless. The frame broke a long time ago, so now the twin bed rests on the floor. My floor is scattered with pieces of paper and articles of clothing from my lack of time to clean. I stumble into the hall and to the bathroom where I take in my awful appearance. My brown curls are crazy today. My hair is frizzy as it falls around my shoulders. I run my brush through it, but to no avail. My pale white skin looks even paler than usual. My big brown eyes are plain and boring, I don't wear make-up because I cannot afford it, and most of it are tested on animals!

I brush my teeth which have a small gap, but I cannot afford braces. I head back to my room and pull out a blue t-shirt and a pair of jeans. I slip on some worn out All-stars. I sling my book bag over my shoulder and grab my iPhone, a gift from my grandma. It was free. I hurry down the hall to the kitchen, where my mom is standing in her waitress uniform. Her brown hair is tied back in a bun, and her green eyes look tired, her skin is lightly tan. She looks worn out. Being a single mom is hard enough, especially after everything that has happened the last few years. It is extremely hard to go from not working then one day having to start from scratch getting a job, taking care of your children. My heart aches as I look at my mom who looks like an exhausted shadow of herself, destroyed from stress.

"Hey, sweetie," my mom says with a weak smile.

"Hey mommy," I say brightly as I skip over and kiss her cheek. I love her to death. She is the best mom ever. She would rather die to protect me and starve to feed me, and she is truly my world. The feeling of knowing she is there for me and proud of me warms my heart.

"I have to pull a double shift today," she says with a yawn. She works as a waitress at the diner while attending night school to be a teacher. That's why we don't have a lot of money. Before my father left, we were fine and plenty of money. Now, we are poor, which definitely takes a toll on you. His leaving is not the main reason for our money struggles, but it is easier to blame him. People so often think that being poor means that you are homeless. No. It is struggling to put food on your table and taking care of the necessities that you need to get from day to day.

"Aw, okay mom," I say forcing a smile. "I'm going to volunteer after school at the hospital today," I tell her, and she nods, kisses my cheek, and grabs her purse and phone.

"Want a ride to school?" my mom asks, and I nod and grab a banana heading to the car behind her.

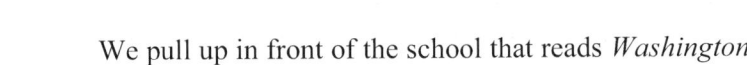

We pull up in front of the school that reads *Washington High,* and I turn to my mom. "I love you!"

"Have a good day. I love you too," she says, and I get out and walk up towards the schools doors past all the groups of students. I keep my head down. Still, no one pays attention to me like the usual. Heck, I don't even think anyone knows I actually go here! I make my way to my locker and exchange out my evening class books for my morning ones.

Shutting my locker, I continue down the hall unnoticed and to my first class, AP English. My teacher is sitting at her desk working on something, her blonde hair up in a bun with a nice shirt and jeans on.

"Morning, Miss Jennings," she says to me as I take my seat in the middle of her class and fish out my book, cracking it open.

"Morning, Mrs. Reed," I respond and begin reading the book. Mrs. Reed is my favorite teacher, and I feel comfortable around her.

The bell rings, and people slowly file in, but I don't really pay attention. Not until he walks in at least, with a bright smile on his face that brightens the room. He runs a hand through his cute brown hair and his stunning blue eyes glance over the room, and for a second, I think he saw me. I am probably wrong. I am invisible. No one ever sees me. My chest tightens a little and my stomach twists. He swiftly sits in the seat diagonal from me, and I take in his appearance. His varsity jacket over a white t-shirt and his dark blue jeans, it is Reece.

I sigh. I wish I had his life just for a moment. The rest my day carries on, as usual, going class to class being invisible, spending lunch in the library, and keeping my face buried in a book.

My second to last period of the day rolls around, and I round the corner and freeze as I see a shaky Erwin, our school's misfit emo kid, stalking through the crowd. My heart begins to beat faster, and the hair on the back of my neck rises. Something deep down in my gut tells me that something was wrong. My eyes land on what is in his hand as he stops. As soon as I see the shiny, silver weapon of death, it seems that others do too. Erwin slowly raises the pistol in the air and points it at someone. My eyes follow the trail of the gun as my heart feels like it's bursting out of my chest. I gasp slightly as my eyes land on the target, Reece, who looks like he has just seen a ghost. His face scrunched up in what looks to be a concern and my eyes scan the people around him, thinking someone would help. But his friends all look as though they are frozen in shock, much like some of the other kids, while others quickly push past each other in fear and fighting to stay alive. Fear — a deep, heart-wrenching fear is on everyone's face. The cries of some students can be heard. Where are the adults?

Gasping in another deep breath, I watch in fear as the scene unfurls in front of me. Reece extends his hand, and his lips are moving as he attempts to calm a shaking Erwin. A part of me hopes that a begging Reece will convince Erwin to think this through, but not a shot works. Erwin has a distant, scary look in his eyes, and the gun is shaking in his hand. It seems as though the world has stopped all that could be heard is frantic screaming and Reece's pleading.

Reece's pleading. I hear his voice full of worry and at the same time, a concern for Erwin. It's almost as if Reece is welcoming a death that Erwin wishes to give him, and I am just frozen where I stand watching it unfold.

Bang.

The sound of the gun firing shakes me to my core, and I fall to the ground in hopes of staying alive. As I lay on the ground and the earth-shattering sound of the gun firing stops, I hear voices in panic racing around. Prying my eyes open, I look along the floor seeing people on the ground, shaking, and some trying to stand. Then, the scariest sight ever reveals itself.

Reece Collins lying on the floor, a red puddle forming around him. His body looks lifeless. My stomach churns. It is an image that will stay with me forever. People rush to him and try to stop his bleeding head. The EMS workers rush in and begin working on him quickly before stabilizing him, and the ambulance hauls him off. Why did this happen to this school? I feel something hot and wet fall from my face and realize it is tears for a guy I do not even know.

Chapter Two

After the events had transpired at school, police escorted everyone out, EMS workers checked everyone, and parents were called. After that, everyone was released to go home. Almost everyone was shaken up, but one thing is for sure, today was a day that was going to stay in our minds forever. The images of what I saw play over and over in my head as I take the bus to the hospital since my mom is at work.

I am currently sitting in a recliner in Lila's room, here in the hospital where I volunteer; I have my hair pulled back in a ponytail and wears some blue scrubs that one of the nurses at the hospital handed me. Lila is asleep. Her brown eyes shut softly and a red bandana around her bald head. Her skin is extremely pale. Although asleep, sadness is written all over her face; it makes my heart ache.

Sighing out a deep breath, I slowly rise up and brush the back of my hand softly over Lila's cheek before weakly smiling down at her and walking out of the room to get back to work. As I walk down the hospital hall, I cannot help but look through the glass windows at all these poor people; each with a unique story. The reason I love to help out here is it keeps me from feeling sorry for myself because there is always someone out there who has it worse than I do.

Continuing past the rooms, I enter the waiting room in the ER surgery area because I am looking for my boss, May. I stop; however, when I see a woman in her late thirties with light blonde hair, baby blue eyes, and stunning looks sitting in a chair crying. My heart aches I know what it is like to sit in a waiting room unsure of what is happening behind the doors and what the outcome will be.

Across from her in a corner is a boy. Looking young and around twenty-one, his hair is dirty blonde and has chilling green eyes that also hold sadness in them. While looking also scared with what is happening, he tries to maintain a strong face for the girl beside him. She seems younger than me by a year or two, possibly sixteen or seventeen. Then, there is a man pacing across the waiting room with a worry and exhaustion on his face. He is in his forties and has dark brown hair and green eyes. A small girl about six is in his arms, her legs squeezing tightly around his waist and arms around his neck, her little head on his shoulder and her brown hair falling down her back. As the man turns sideways, I see her tear soaked face and cloudy blue eyes. I want to walk past them, but something is pulling me to them. There was a feeling deep down me urging me to do so. After the events that transpired today, I feel like I could use being a little good in the world today. So maybe I can soothe their fears.

Is it because I have been where they are? Or is it my crazy need to help people? Either way, I decide to make my way towards the crying woman and sit beside her. She does not seem to notice me, and as I take in her appearance, my heart aches for this poor woman.

"Hi, are you ok?" I say softly. I know, of course, that she isn't okay, but I still had to ask. What else was there really to say? I'm a complete stranger for Pete's sake!

"Um, not really," she says in a crackly, sweet voice as she looks up at me with so much pain in her eyes that my heart shatters into a million pieces.

Reaching over I rest my hand on hers. "What happened?" I ask her softly. The woman squeezes my hand and releases a heart-wrenching sob. At first, the feel of her hand was so foreign to me, but I told myself that she needs comfort.

"My son was shot today and is having surgery right now in hopes of saving him. But they are not sure if he will live," she cries as she grips onto my hand. "My... baby." She sobs. I rub her back hoping to calm her, the least thing I could do.

"I am so sorry," I say as I try to soothe her. "I'm sure that it'll all be okay," I softly say not because I believe it will but because I know what it is like to not have any hope.

"Thank you," she chokes as she seems to calm down, but honestly, I think she is just out of tears and tired. "What is your name?" she asks me trying to distract herself, I guess.

"I'm Payton Jennings," I say giving her a weak smile to let her know that I am here for her.

"Do you have family here?" she asks. I look away and shut my eyes for a moment thinking.

"Sort of, but I volunteer here too," I reply dodging her question. "Do you have any other family here?" I ask her softly hoping to take her mind off things that are happening in a room not too far away.

"Oh, yes," she says sniffling. "That man is my husband Leonardo, and that little girl in his arms is Rayne. Then, over in the corner is my other son and daughter, Conner and Juliet," she tells me as she looks around at them, and she cries a little bit more. She is a mother who doesn't know if she is ever going to see one of her children again. That is a pain that no one should ever have to experience.

"Tell me about them," I tell her, seeing as it will distract her.

She gives me a sad smile and sighs. "Well, Rayne is our miracle child; after I had Juliet, the doctor said I couldn't have any more children. Then, ten years later Rayne came into the world and was a blessing for all of us. She's the sweetest most amazing little girl I know. Then, you have Juliet, she's quiet and shy around people she doesn't know, but with her family, she's outspoken and can be a brat. Then, comes Conner he is in college and is really outgoing, wants to be a doctor, which is so amazing. Now, I just wish he would settle down. Then, you have my son that got shot," her voice cracks as she brings him up. "Since the day that boy could talk, he was all up in everyone's business trying to solve problems, or he was talking about sports. He has always been caring and has the power to lift anyone's spirits. He actually volunteers at the shelter," she says, and her voice is thick the whole time she talks about him. "I hope he'll be okay!" she cries and squeezes my hand.

"Everything will be okay," I say as I continue to rub circles on her back.

We sit in silence with her soft sobs and my mind turning on ways to help. A doctor comes into the waiting room with a nurse by his side. "The Collins?" he asks, and the woman's head shoots up as does the rest of her family's. She stands weakly. I slowly rise up beside her in shock.

"It was nice meeting you, but I have to get back to work. I hope everything will be okay," I say to her, smiling softly.

"It was lovely meeting you, Payton. Thank you so much for helping me. You are an incredible young woman," she says and pulls me into a warm embrace. "Please stop by and visit me." She gives me a weak smile then turns to her husband and kids walking to the doctor.

My heart is thumping against my chest. I just met Reece's mom, held her hand, and helped her while she was sad. I really hope he's ok; I don't want his mom to lose him. She seems amazing. Please, let him live.

Chapter Three

My eyes flutter open the next morning, and I roll over landing on the hard floor. Groaning, I sit up, rub my swollen eyes as I look around my room, and knock some papers away from my side.

I don't want to get up! I think to myself but stand up anyways and make my way to my closet grabbing some jeans and a long sleeve t-shirt. Dragging myself to my bathroom, I stare in the mirror. Did yesterday really happen? It felt like a nightmare then, looking in the mirror at my crazy hair that I quickly try to fix. I know it's no dream. If it had been, I'd be a little less ugly. I cannot believe it happened. Someone opened fire at my school. That only happens in movies, and TV shows. It never seems like it can happen here in my town. And Reece, God, I hope he is okay! His mom is too amazing to lose her child. No parent should ever have to bury their child. When someone kills someone, do they realize that they are killing someone's son or daughter or loved ones? And when you kill someone, you aren't hurting them because once they die, they're gone. They won't know the idiot, who killed them, but their family does, and it's they who gets hurt. So they might as well realize their plan is stupid, and killing people is uncalled for unless you're killing a killer or in war.

Once I have finished in the bathroom, I go back to my room, slipping on my shoes and throwing my bag over my shoulder. *I can do this,* I tell myself taking a deep breath and ascending the stairs. I hear a TV playing the news channel, which is all that we have. I go into the living room seeing my mom seated on the small couch and staring at the television. Pictures from yesterday flash on the screen and then some of Reece.

"Yesterday, a young man brought a gun to his school and took target on our town's all-American boy, the track star, baseball star, and quarterback, Reece Collins. At this time, the one possible reason as to why this happened is jealousy. Reece was shot and barely made it through the night and is now at the hospital in critical condition. Washington High will not be having classes until Monday, and any students that need to talk about this traumatic event can speak to the counselor. Once the police had arrived, the gunman then turned the gun on himself and killed himself..." The newsman is cut off by my mother as she turns and sees me.

"Oh, honey!" She silently sobs as she stands on her feet and pulls me into a bone-crushing hug.

"Mom," I say softly as I hug her back. Somehow, my mom's hugs always seem to warm my heart.

"I'm so happy you are okay. I cannot lose you. No, I cannot lose another child... well, almost," she mutters and at that, I cannot help but release the tears I have been holding back, especially not in her warm, motherly embrace. It hurts to know that she is close to losing a child, and I'm close to losing a sister. It kills me all the time.

"I know, mom. I'm okay, though," I say softly and hugging her closely. Is this how Reece's mom, dad, and family feel?

"How are you handling this, though?" she asks as she pulls away to look into my eyes. The concern is etched into her face.

"I'm okay, but that's probably because I didn't know him," I say honestly.

"If you say so, honey." She kisses my cheek and catches a glance at her watch. "Crap, look at the time. I got to get to work! Do you want a ride to the hospital?" she asks grabbing her things.

I nod. Walking to the door, the fall breeze hits me in my face as I hold it open waiting for her to shuffle out of it. Finally, she does, and we make it to her car. She drives quickly and drops me off at the hospital. I jump out.

"I love you!" I call to her blowing a kiss.

"I love you too," she calls, and she takes off. Running my hand through my hairs or well yanking it through, I walk towards the automatic glass doors. The sterile smell of the hospital hits me in the face as I make my way in.

Digging in my purse, I grab my ID and clip it onto my shirt as I walk into the back, looking around for Mays. I walk through the plain white walls, thinking of how bare and empty this home away from home for some is as I spot May's figure walking into a room. Her black hair is tied up in a ponytail, and she is in some dark blue scrubs with a stethoscope draped around her neck. Slight wrinkles are etched into her forehead, and she turns around facing me.

"Hey, Payton. How are you?" she asks as I walk to her. Her dark brown eyes are sad and worried. Working in a hospital is definitely not an easy job, and I know that it leaves an effect on the nurses, especially May.

"I'm fine, May. I don't have school today. So I am just going work here if that's okay?" I ask, and May just nods allowing this answer to be all that she needed.

"Of course, it is dear we could always use the help. Plus, you are great with the patients," she says with a smile.

"Alright, I am just going to see Lila first. How is she?" I ask glancing past May down the hall to where her room is. My stomach twists slightly always afraid for a bad answer to my question.

"She is still in the coma, but the doctor said she is doing a little better," she says and gives me a weak smile.

Sighing, I walk past her down the white hall, passing windows with blinds up and down, and kids sitting in beds with family around them and supporting them. Finally, I reach her room and walk inside. The TV is playing softly, and Lila is laying in the hospital bed. Her bald head is exposed, and she is still, eyes closed gently and rests peacefully. Walking over to the chair beside the bed, I sit down and look around the room. It's so silent and sad. I just want to hear her voice. I miss it. I miss the laughter and the jokes; I just miss her.

A soft knock comes from the door which slowly opens. "Payton?" a familiar voice asks, and I look up seeing Reece's mom peeking in at me. "I'm sorry for disturbing you." She apologizes, and I stand up waving her apology off. Honestly, I needed an interruption to distract me from my hope slipping away.

"It is okay, ma'am," I say as I stand in front of her and take in her appearance. Her blonde hair is all messy, blue eyes tired and swollen, and big bags are below them. She is still in the same clothes from the night before so they're wrinkled. She looks miserable.

"Oh, I forgot to introduce myself, silly me dear. I'm Georgia Collins," she says with a weak smile and outstretches her hand. Slowly, I take it into mine, and hers is so soft and cold.

"Nice to meet you, how is Reece?" I ask her as we step outside of the room.

She smiles weakly at me and asks, "Can we get some coffee?" Quickly, I glance around at the empty hall and look back at her almost pleading face, and it seems as if she's begging for someone to talk to.

"Sure," I say, and she nods. We begin walking to the cafeteria; it's not too busy right now.

We walk over to the coffee machine and get one before paying and taking a seat at one of the hard, plain chair and tables.

"So how is Reece?" I ask as we sit down. I fold my hands around my cup resting on the table.

"You know Reece?" she asks curiously and raises an eyebrow.

"Not personally, but I know of him. I've never really spoken to him. He probably doesn't even know that I am alive," I say in a rush hoping she does not get any crazy ideas.

"Oh... I am sure he does, dear," her face falls, and she says with a sly smile, "Even if that was true, there's always now."

"But... why?" I ask raising an eyebrow.

Her smile disappears. "He is yet to wake up, but he is okay. However, I don't think he's ever going to be the same again. The doctor has informed us that when he wakes up... well... I haven't truly said this aloud before. He is blind now," she says softly, and I suck in a breath in shock. "When he wakes up, he's going to have so much trouble and won't be able to do a lot of things he's used to, like sports. I am afraid to say I don't think his friends will stick by him, dear. I'm just asking you to attempt to be his friend. Just come by and see him. You don't have to be his friend. Be my friend and just visit him and meet him. I truly believe there is something about you that would be good for him when he wakes." Tears cloud her eyes.

She just asked me for my help with Reece. Am I going crazy? Did she just say he is blind? What is going on with the world? It's official; I am going crazy. So what am I going to do now?

Chapter Four

Why am I such a nice person? Why can I not say 'no' to anyone?

This was the stupidest thing you ever agreed to Payton. My little voice in my head scolds me causing me to release a groan of aggravation.

Shut up! I mentally yell back at the annoying voice. "Stupid voice," I mumble under my breath as I sit Ms. Rose's food down on her dinner tray.

"What's that you say, dear?" she asks in her crackly, frail voice. Her short, blonde-gray curls are kind of flat, and her blue eyes, though surrounded by wrinkles, are so alive and happy. Her name is Rose Daylin, but I call her Ms. Rose because it suits her beautiful personality better. She is a widow. Her husband passed a couple years ago to cancer. That sick, awful cancer is always taking good people away. Ms. Rose has heart problems and just had another surgery due to it.

"I was just talking to myself," I say giving her a smile.

"Aw good! You had me a little afraid my hearing was leaving me, and I'd have to buy an aid," she teases with a smile revealing her shining dentures.

I chuckle at her and shake my head. "Well, I'm sure you'd look stylish with one," I smile at her jokingly.

It's sad to say, but Ms. Rose is like my only best friend.

Payton, you're so pathetic. Your only friend is an 80-year-old woman. The annoying voice says, and I sigh. Heck, the voice is right I am pathetic. I look at Ms. Rose and give her a sad smile while she begins to eat her Jell-O.

"Ms. Rose, I really want to stay and chat, but I have something I have to do." I walk to her side and rest my hand on her shoulder.

"Alright, dear, do what you need to. Then come back and see me, we'll have a talk," she says to me as she reaches up and pats my hand. I smile down at her and nod. Taking a deep breath, I walk away only turning to wave bye. In the hall, I take a deep breath and try calming my crazy nerves. Stupid nervous disorder; it's like I get nervous over anything and freak out about it.

I am crazy. Why on planet earth did I agree to do this? Oh yeah, because I am a nice person who lacks the ability to just say no!

Oh, grow a pair and get this over with! My voice in my head yells at me and I seriously want to slap it.

Shut up! I am going! I think back to it as I force my feet to move forward and walk down the almost empty hall. I make a turn and down another hall until I reach the elevator and walk inside hitting the circle with a two on it causing it to light up. I lean against the back wall resting my head on it and shutting my eyes.

This is going be awful! What if he wakes up? Oh God, what if he thinks I am some crazy stalker who likes him? What if he honestly has no clue who I am? Stupid what ifs? Why do what ifs have to be so scary? What if there were no what ifs? Hmm... Now, that's a good question.

The door slides open with a *ding*, and I walk out of the elevator and down the hall until I find the room. Taking a deep breath, I knock on the door lightly and wait for it to open. Finally, it creaks open, and Georgia stands before me.

"Hi, Payton, I'm so glad you are here! I sent my husband to take the kids home to get a shower and some rest," she says as she opens the door for me to walk in, and I look around the room. No flowers or get-well cards or anything were in there as I was expecting. Then my eyes land on him, and I am amazed at how good looking he still is even in a hospital bed.

His brown hair is messy, and his face is a little bit pale. He has a large white bandage wrapped around his head. His blanket is pulled up to his shoulders, only showing the top of his gown and covering his arms. He is so still, and it breaks my heart to see him like this, knowing what happened. Flashbacks from that day go through my mind — the screaming, the fear, and the blood that surrounded Reece's still body.

"Thank you, dear. I just need to go home quickly and shower, change clothes, and I will be back. I've just been worried sick. You have my number if anything happens. Thank you so much you're amazing," she says with teary eyes as she walks over to Reece and kisses his forehead and whispers something to him. Then she smiles sadly down at him with teary eyes and grabs her purse walking over to me. She wraps her arms around my neck and hugs me.

"Thank you," she whispers and squeezes me. I reach up and pat her back until she releases me. "I'll be back soon," she says glancing at her son and blinking her teary eyes.

"Alright, take your time," I tell her because I know how it feels to stay at the hospital in the same clothes and no sleep.

She nods and leaves. I look around the room and then walk over to the chair by his bed and sit down staring at him. His chest is slightly rising and falling, and I glance at his heart monitor to see that it's normal.

"Hi, Reece," I say softly looking up at him. I know people say talking to them helps. I just hope he doesn't remember this.

"Well, I know you definitely don't know who I am, but that's okay. I'm Payton Jennings. Who's that? Well, we have AP English together and a few others. Still no clue? Didn't figure," I say as I nod my head, feeling like a crazy person. What the heck? I am crazy! Here I am, sitting and talking to a boy who has not a clue who I am or cannot hear me. I am talking to him!

"Maybe if I describe myself, it may help. Well... I have frizzy, brown, curly hair. Ugly, plain, muddy brown eyes, pasty, pale, white skin. Chubby cheeks. I have no friends because I am shy and a loner. I dress plain and cheap because I can't afford a lot, basically just food. I hide in the library at lunch time. I'm not bullied because like I've said, no one knows I'm alive. I'm smart; get good grades and volunteers at the hospital since I already spent all my time outside of school here. Yep, that's me. No clue who I am? I figured," I say still feeling stupid talking to myself. I stare at his face in boredom.

Then, I see his lips move slightly upwards, and my eyes almost bug out of my head. Holy crap! I think he just moved! Oh my gosh, is he waking up? Oh no... I hope he didn't hear me.

Go get a doctor, dummy! The voice in my head yells, and I don't even argue back because it's right. So I leap up and race out of the room and to the nurses' desk panting. What? I am not an athlete.

"Everything okay, Payton?" the nurse behind the desk asks me.

"I think Reese Collins is waking up! His mouth moved!" I say quickly to her.

"I'll go have a look," she says in shock and gets up racing down the hall with me hot on her tail.

Holy cow! What if he wakes? What if he heard me? This is awful!

Chapter Five

Reece's POV

Day of the Shooting

"Reeceeee, Reeceeee, wake up!" a small voice says as a finger pokes my cheek. Groaning, I open one eye and see Rayne looking at me smiling. Her little blue eyes are shining. Waking up to her in the morning isn't so bad, probably because she has me wrapped around her little finger. Her brown hair is in curls, and she is wearing a cute dress. I attempt to hide my smile. She is going to be a heartbreaker one day, and I know she'll make my big brother job hard.

"Morning, monkey," I say with my raspy, morning voice. I open my other eye, sit up, and stretch. The blanket falls down to my waist revealing my shirtless chest, tan and ripped. I am not trying to sound cocky. It's just I worked hard to look like this so I am just appreciating it.

"Morning, Reece! Bye!" Rayne says as she pats my head as if I were a dog and skips away. I shake my head and smile. I throw my legs out of the bed, walk to my closet and grab some dark blue jeans and a white shirt taking them into my joining bathroom. I brush my pearly white teeth and slip on my jeans, buttoning them. I reach up in my cabinet and grab my deodorant and put it on my pits. Smelling good is important, especially when you are me. Then, I pull on the white shirt and look into the mirror. My blue eyes are shining, and my face was smooth from shaving last night. I place some hair jell on my hands and run them through my hair giving it a messy look.

I walk out of the bathroom and back into my room. I grab my black leather wallet and put it into my back pocket then grab my keys, placing them in my front pocket. I grab my Varsity jacket from the chair at my desk, which is across my large room and put it on. Lastly, before I leave, I walk to my dresser and grab some Axe for today spraying it on and placing it back alongside my row of colognes. Running my hand through my hair, I smile and walk out my room shutting my door behind me. I walk down the long spiral staircase and through the living room into the kitchen.

Laughter fills my ears as I enter to see Rayne, my little sister, sitting in her chair kicking her feet back and forth as she eats her eggs and bacon. To her left is Juliet, my other little sister, who is sixteen. Her blonde hair is in curls, and her blue eyes are twinkling. She has light makeup on and is wearing her school uniform since she goes to a private school. She slowly picks at her eggs laughing with Rayne at my older brother, Conner. He is nuts and supposed to be in college. His dirty blonde hair is messy. He is still in his PJ bottom and no shirt, and even though, I cannot see his green eyes I know they probably have dark bags under them. My dad is seated at the end of the table with a paper in front of him and coffee on the table.

"Morning, everyone!" I say with a smile as I sit beside my brother. My mom is by the stove and cooking away, she is wearing high heels with a black pencil skirt and blouse.

"Morning, honey!" my mom says looking over her shoulder and smiling at me. Her blonde hair is up in a bun. My mom is amazing and every day she inspired me by all the work she does while raising us hooligans.

"Morning," Conner says with a mouthful of his breakfast as he looks over at me. Under his eyes are the think bags that I suspected must've been a wild night partying.

"Good morning," Juliet says with a bright smile briefly before returning her attention to Rayne.

"Reecee!" Rayne says with a smile. If Rayne is in the room, she will demand the attention that the entire room has to offer.

"Morning, son," my dad says glancing over his paper, smiling. My dad can be explained in a few words which are, hardworking, stern, kind, and smart.

"What are you doing after school today, Reece?" my mom asks as she sits my plate in front of me and sits at the other end the table. Momentarily, I think of how appreciative I am of her.

I take a bite of my food and then look at her. "I plan to go to the shelter and volunteer," I say after I swallow my food nodding appreciatively.

"Oh, that's sweet, honey. You should be going," she says as she looks at her diamond encrusted watch.

I glance down at my watch and groan. Crap, I need to go! "Bye, I love you guys!" I say as I leap up and kiss my mom's forehead and then my sister's. I give my dad a hug and then pat Conner's back as I pass him.

"I love you too!" they all reply as I race out of the room. I walk through the house, out the front door, and down the large front porch to my black *2013 Chevy Camaro*. I retrieve the keys from my pocket and unlock the doors as I slip inside and start it. Pulling around the round driveway, I get onto the road and begin towards the school.

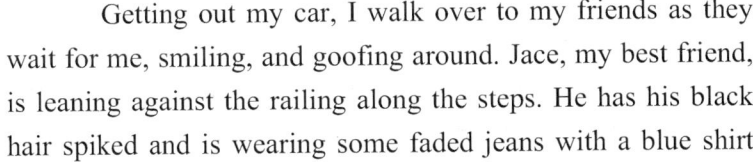

Getting out my car, I walk over to my friends as they wait for me, smiling, and goofing around. Jace, my best friend, is leaning against the railing along the steps. He has his black hair spiked and is wearing some faded jeans with a blue shirt and his varsity jacket. Beside him are some of our other teammates. They are my friends but not my best friends.

Joining them, we do the man hug and Kyle, one of the guys, is talking about his latest hook up while I stand and pretend to listen. I mean, I hate how they play girls! It's stupid! They treat girls as if they are animals. They are people as well, incredible people. Now, I'm sure the hell am no virgin, not even close, but I still think of them as women and not toys. Surprising as that is, seeing as I am Mr. Popular.

The bell rings. I nod to the guys and walks off with Jace.

"Man, I feel bad for Kyle, bro," Jace says shaking his head as he walks alongside me. I look at him with a raised eyebrow. Why would he feel bad for Kyle? He just had sex. That's not a normal thing to feel bad for someone who just had sex. Needless to say, I am a little confused.

"Why?" I ask with a chuckle. I have known Jace for a long time, and I know the words that will follow are bound to be funny.

"Cause the girl he slept with was one of my leftovers," he says with a laugh as we turn a corner and continue to our class. I contain my distaste for how he referred to a girl as a 'leftover.' But it is Jace I am talking to, so it is expected nonetheless.

"Wow..." I say as we reach our AP English class. I still yet to figure out how Jace is in it. Not saying he's stupid or anything it's just he's an idiot and does not try.

We walk inside, and everyone is sitting down. I look around the room, and my eyes fall on Payton. Gosh, she is pretty, Even though she has crazy brown hair, brown eyes, and pale skin, she still is pretty because of this glowing light around her. She also is very intriguing because she never talks to anyone!

I sit down in one the front rows, and the class begins. After class, the rest of my classes and lunch go normal, just hanging with the team and girls hitting on me — the usual. Finally, at the second to last class change of the day, I stand at my locker with some of my teammates while Jace is on the other side the school. I hear something behind me, and I spin around facing Erwin. Then, my eyes slowly fall onto the gleaming pistol, pointing my way. My heartbeat quickens and sweat begins to form on my forehead. Come on, brain, work. Is this real? I can feel everything flash before my eyes. My adrenaline begins pumping as I try to process how to get out of this situation.

"Erwin, put the gun down. You don't want to do this. Please just put it down before you hurt someone or do something you regret. Please," I plead with him, not worried about my own life but of those around me. I couldn't care less if I died right now because I have lived and have change lives. Others aren't that lucky so at least spare them. There are so many people here, so maybe I can help him calm down and think we can get out of this situation in one piece. My heart thumps as fear pulses through me.

His hand shakes the gun, and I continue to plead. The word, "please," just continue to fall out of my mouth, then I watch as his finger inches the trigger back, and a *bang* fills the air.

"Reece, no, give me back my doll!" Juliet says as she races across the backyard after me.

"Never!" I scream like a warrior and head for my treehouse jumping one-handedly onto my rope ladder. I reach the top pulling the ladder with me and look down at my six-year-old little sister Juliet. Her blonde hair is in a braid down her back, and she is wearing a white dress. Her thin arms are folded over her chest. Being the eight-year-old boy that I am, I stick my tongue out at her.

"Reece! Give it back, or I will make you!" she says angrily.

"You are a crazy kid," I laugh and shake my head.

"Really? Come down here and we will see whose crazy!"

Rolling my eyes, I drop the ladder and climb down standing in front of Juliet. She takes an angry step forward and glares at me.

"Conner!" she screams at the top of her lungs, and an eleven-year-old Conner races out of the house to Juliet.

"What?" he asks in a panic. His eyes search her to find any injuries.

"Beat Reece up for me! He took my Barbie!" she says to him giving him her puppy dog eyes.

Crap, no one can say 'no' to those. So being clever, I take off running to a mud puddle and hold Barbie by her hair over it.

Juliet grabs Conner's arm and drags him with her. "Reece! Put her down now! Or I will stick Conner on you," she says glaring at me.

"Put her down? Alright," I say with a shrug, and an evil smirk pulls onto my lips as I slowly release her hair sending her tumbling into the mud.

"Conner, attack!" Juliet shrieks as she runs to save her Barbie rolling in the mud and becoming covered in the wet earth.

Next thing I know, Conner has me in the mud, and we are wrestling.

"Children what are you doing?!" an angry mama bear yells. We all freeze and slowly sit up looking at our mom with her hands on her hips.

"He started it!" Juliet tattles as she tries to look all innocent dripping with mud.

Lies! That little brat. She is the one that used our brother like a dog.

Mom knows her game, though. That is why I smile with triumph when she says we're grounded, as long as Juliet got in trouble too.

"Alright, Reece, this is all on you! Do not let them hit the ball," Coach says, and I nod adjusting my team ball cap and taking the pitcher's mound. My eyes connect with Jace's, the catcher, and I watch his fingers and finally nod. I pull back and raise my knee in the air and pitch. It sails past the batter, and Jace catches it, standing up and throwing it back to me. Catching it, I get ready and throw another.

Finally, I'm on one of the last batters of the game, and it all rides on this pitch. Sweat falls down my face as I bring my knee up and launching it. Strike. I smile and catch the ball preparing another pitch. I let it rip. Strike. My heartbeat speeds up, and I am so nervous. Preparing the last pitch, I release it and watch as it zooms by the batter. "Strike, you're out!"

Yes! Yes! Fuck yeah! I holler, and Jace and I run to each other hugging. We just won states!

I bend down at the starting line making my butt go up little higher. The gun sounds and I take off running. Sweat falls down my face as I take the lead and run. My legs pick up speed and move faster and faster. I feel free as the wind hits my face, and I push myself harder as I run the track. I see someone beside me and smile as I push my legs harder and take off faster. Finally, I see the finish line ahead and increase my speed more. It gets closer and closer and then I feel my waist break through it!

The crowd roars as I drop to my knee panting and having a hard time breathing. "This year's State Track Champion in the 3-mile is Reece Collins!" An announcer says, and I smile while they hand me a *Gatorade*. The crowd cheers.

This is unbelievable.

Seeing my State football winning play flashes through my head next but, then I hear a voice. It sounds like heaven.

"Well, I know you definitely do not know who I am, but that's okay. I'm Payton Jennings. Who's that? Well, we have AP English together and a few others. Still no clue? Didn't figure," this mysterious voice comes from.

"Maybe if I describe myself, it may help. Well... I have frizzy, brown, curly hair. Ugly, plain, muddy brown eyes, pasty, pale, white skin. Chubby cheeks. I have no friends because I am shy and a loner. I dress plain and cheap because I can't afford a lot, basically just food. I hide in the library at lunch time. I'm not bullied because like I've said, no one knows I'm alive. I'm smart; get good grades and volunteers at the hospital since I already spent all my time outside of school here. Yep, that's me. No clue who I am? I figured," the voice continues but is still fuzzy, yet I cannot help but smile at its cuteness. Suddenly, my head begins to hurt bad, really bad actually! I cry out in pain and move around. The pain is unbearable.

Suddenly, it begins to fade. Everything begins to fade, and I return to my dreams or well memories. That was weird. What the hell was that about?

Chapter Six

Payton's POV

"Payton what happened again?" Georgia asks as she stands in front of me, outside of his room. I gave her a call explaining everything. She then rushed down here and now, here we are.

"I was talking to him then his mouth moved! So I ran to get a nurse. We came back, and he was waking up. He was in so much pain, though, so they had to knock him out. He should wake up again soon," I tell her once again, and tears fall down her cheeks.

"Thank you so much!" she says as she hugs me.

"Not a problem," I say smiling.

I hear feet coming towards us, and I look over her shoulder to see her husband, Leonardo, walking up behind her. He wraps his arms around her waist with a sad face.

"Is he okay?" he asks his wife, and she nods as she uses the back her hand to wipe her tears away and then smiles.

"Honey, this is Payton. The nice girl I told you about," Georgia says looking at me proudly and winks.

He looks up at me with his green eyes. "Hello, a pleasure to finally meet you. I'm Leonardo, but you can call me Leo," he says as he nods to me and I smile.

"You too," I say politely and smile at him. "I better get back to work," I tell Georgia with a smile.

"Alright, dear. Come back or I will hunt you down again!" she says with a teasing smile, and I laugh nodding.

"Yes, ma'am, I will be back tomorrow morning," I turn around and walk back to the elevator and walk back to Ms. Rose's room.

"Ahh and she returns," she says as I walk in and sit in the chair beside her, laughing.

"I do," I say as I look up at her TV to see the news on. A picture of Reece pops up, so I know what it's talking about since Rose has the volume off.

"Payton, why didn't you tell me about this?" she asks taking on her grandma persona.

"I did not see a point in worrying you when I am fine. I'm alive, I'm fine," I say rolling my eyes.

"Did you see it?" she asks bluntly, and I look away from her prying eyes down at the end of the bed.

"Yeah," I mumble not making eye contact.

"What? I am an old woman, Payton. You have to speak up," she says as she reaches down to her remote and pulls her bed up to sit.

"Yes, I was there," I say a little bit annoyed with having to repeat it.

"Oh, dear! You must be so traumatized!" Ms. Rose says with sad eyes.

"No, I'm fine I didn't know the boy, and I didn't see a lot," I lie and slowly look back at her sad eyes.

"Payton, it could've been you. You saw someone get shot," she says with sad eyes. My stomach churns at the thought. It could have been me.

"I know," I say softly looking down at my hand folded in my lap. "But it wasn't," I say biting my lip to hold back my tears.

I haven't spoken to anyone about this, and it's kind of hard to.

"I'm glad for that," she says, and I look up to see a small smile appear on her face.

"Me too," I say and then I feel my phone buzz, and I pull it out. It shows a text from my mom.

"Mom: I am outside the hospital."

Shoving it back into my pocket, I smile and stand up. "See ya, Ms. Rose. I will be back in the morning," I tell her as I walk to the door and smile.

"Alright, dear. Take care of yourself," she says, smiling. I nod and leave.

I slip on my shorts and tank top; then, drop onto my small bed and curl up under my covers. My body feels exhausted and overwhelmed by the events of the day as they go through my mind. I shut my eyes and try to fall asleep.

I see the shining pistol pointing at Reece and watch as Erwin's finger pulls back on the trigger. My body is frozen, and my heart is pounding. Reece falls to the ground, and blood is everywhere. Tears stream down my face as I fall to the ground shaking.

"No!" I scream as the *"Bangs!"* continue to echo around the hall.

"Payton! Payton! Wake up!" my mom's frantic voice says as she shakes me. "You're ok," she says as I open my eyes and look at her face full of worry.

"Mom, I saw it," I cry, and she wraps me in her warm embrace, and I sob on her shoulder. Why does this bother me so much?

Chapter Seven

Reece's POV

My dreams slowly fade away again. Pain doesn't engulf my head, but I still do not wake. Instead, I feel like I am in a very light sleep. I am asleep, but I can hear.

"Juliet, I know you and Conner will just love her when you meet her. She is a truly amazing girl. She is mysterious and quiet, yet she is beautiful inside and out and so sweet. She is just so kind and nice," my mom's voice says and sparks my curiosity. Who is she talking about?

"What'd you say her name is again, mom?" Juliet asks, and I can just see my mom smiling.

"Payton Jennings."

Payton Jennings? I know that name. Wait, I know her. She was cute, but a total loner. I never spoke to her before. She probably likes me. I just don't know! What does she have to do with anything?

"She is so nice and helps in every way she can, but I feel as if I am missing something about her," my mom says softly trailing off into silence. She probably is thinking.

Suddenly, a small ache begins in my head, but it's not too bad. I feel a hand wrap in mine and squeeze it. I try my best to squeeze back.

Come on, stupid hand, work! I yell to myself and finally squeeze back. I hear my mom squeal in joy.

"Reece!" she yells in a happy tone. "Juliet, go get a doctor!" my mother says.

What? Why a doctor? Slowly, I peel my eyes open, expecting to see the shining light or my mom's beautiful smiling face. Instead, I am met by a cruel darkness. I blink thinking maybe it's just my eyes needing to adjust. I reopen them and nothing, just plain nothingness.

"Mom?" I ask my voice raspy from not talking for a while. How long, though?

"Yes, sweetie? I am right here," she says to my left, and I can hear things so much clearer now.

"W-why can't I see?" I ask choking back a dry lump in my throat.

"Sweetie, you were shot..." my mom pauses, and I hear a few sets of feet enter the room. "The doctors were able to save you," her voice cracks and I reach out searching for her face. My hand touches her nose, and I slowly move it over to feel cool liquid on my fingers, tears. My mom is crying. That is never good. "But they could not save your sight."

At those words, my world falls out from under me. You know the feeling when someone tells you something and your earth literally crashes. Everything about me falls apart. I have to be able to see! How am I supposed to run track? Play baseball or football? Drive a car? I can never see anything again. If I have kids, I will never get to see their smiling face... never get to see my daughters grow into beautiful women, go to her prom or get married. I will never get to see my son play football or any sport for that matter. I will never get to see if he grows to look like me. Worst of all, on my wedding day as I stand at the end of the aisle, I will never get to see my beautiful bride walk towards me in a white dress and breathtaking looks.

I will never get to see my mom smiling at me, and my dad frown creased head when he scolds me. I will never get to see the woman who finally tames Conner. I will not get to see Juliet dress in her prom dress or wedding dress. Worst of all, I will never get to see Rayne as anything other than her happy six-year-old self. I will not get to see the girl she becomes.

ure, I will be there. But I will not be able to see it. How will I support my family and myself? What kind of job can a blind man get? I know jobs are not supposed to discriminate on disabilities, but let's face it, they do! What kind of women wants to be with a blind man? What people want to be friends with one? I refuse to be a burden on anyone!

How is this fair? I am nice to everyone. I never take girls virginities, I do not do drugs or get drunk, and I volunteer at homeless shelters and help others. Why did this have to be me?

"Reece, I am Doctor Grey," a rough male voice says. "I am going a check on you and see if you're ok." My anger boils to its top.

"Of course, I'm not ok! I cannot see!" I scream as loud as my dry, raspy voice allows then begin to cough. Each cough causes my head to ache more and more.

"Conner, hand me that water," my father's voice commands, and I hear shuffling then a straw touches my lips. "It's water, son, drink," my father says, and I begin to slowly suck in. Cool water attacks my burning throat, and I stop using my hands to try to push the cup away. After a few tries, I find it and do.

"I cannot do anything without my sight," I mumble shutting my broken eyes tiring to contain the tears.

"Son, just like everything else in life, you can learn to adapt and exceed. Sweetie, in no time, you'll be able to do things and take care of yourself," my mom says, and I feel her hand touch my arm and squeeze it. I know it's her because of her motherly touch.

"Mom, I don't want to be blind. I don't deserve this. Why?" I say softly but my voice cracking.

"I don't know, son. Things happen for crazy reasons. Sometimes to take us to something greater. This is just a hill in your path, and you can cross it. You have our support, and we will always be by your side. Maybe, this is your destiny, and something great and beautiful will come from it," my mom says. She is always the voice of reason but just this once it doesn't help. I just had my world torn from under my feet, and honestly, I feel like I am still falling, and I just cannot help being angry that this happened.

Chapter Eight

Payton's POV

Quack! Is that a duck? Why do I hear a duck? Quack! What the heck? Sitting up, I look at my phone to see it is flashing. Oh, it's my phone! I reach over and answer it without looking at the screen. Looking at it would have been pointless; my eyes haven't opened up yet.

"Hello?" I say as I rub my eyes.

"Good morning, Payton. This is Georgia. I'm sorry to wake you. I thought you'd be up getting ready for the hospital," she says, and you can hear the guilt in her voice. I feel bad it's not her fault I sleep in by accident.

"Oh! It's ok! Besides, I needed to get up. I overslept. What can I do for you?" I ask as I stretch and run my fingers through my brown hair, or at least, try.

"Reece woke up last night. It was difficult for him and emotional. He is depressed, angry, sad, and confused because of being blind. It's just a hard time and extremely long night. Leonardo had to go to his office to work on some business so he can miss more and be with Reece. Conner has Rayne trying to keep her from asking questions about Reece that are pretty hard to answer. Juliet had to go to school today to get makeup work. I was wondering since you are always here if you would mind sitting with him for an hour or two tops this morning while I run around quickly and do things I need to?" she asks then it sounds like she's holding her breath and is nervous.

Crap! Well, we all know my answer, dang; I need to grow a darn spine. This is going be an interesting morning. He's awake. She wants me to babysit him. He doesn't know me. Conclusion: he'll think I am a stalker.

Just say no dummy! "Sure, yeah, I'll do it. I should be there in half an hour. I have to take the bus," I say with a sigh as I stand up and stumble to my closet tripping over papers and articles of clothing.

"Payton, do you not have a car?" Georgia asks in shock.

"No, my mom does, and she's at work," I explain trying to make it sound like it's nothing because it truly means nothing to me.

"Do you at least have your licenses dear?" she asks, and I shake my head. Why is she so curious?

"Yeah, I have mine," I tell her as I look for something to wear.

"Oh, hmmm… well, dear, I will save you the trouble of catching the bus. Conner and Rayne have to go by Conner's school to pick up some work so he could swing by and pick you up then drop you off here. He will not mind, and it will give you a chance to meet them. Just give me your address," she says, and I know she is just trying to be helpful. Honestly, though, it will be a little awkward riding in a car with a guy I don't know.

That would be so weird, but I have to meet him eventually, and I really hate taking the bus. It's scary. "Um... okay," I say after a few moments and tell her my address. She says he'll be here in fifteen minutes, and I hang up my phone.

In my closet, I pull out some of my faded blue jeans that are actually kind of form fitting and my blue, V-neck, cute scrub top. I quickly head to the hallway and inside my bathroom. Pulling off my shirt, I clip on my bra then pull up my jeans. I put on my deodorant and brush my teeth. Grabbing my brush, I force it through my hair until I have most of the knots out leaving it in curls and a little frizz.

Sighing at my stupid pale plain reflection, I leave the bathroom and go back into my messing room and grab my phone and purse turning to the kitchen where I grab a water and green apple. A car horn beeps outside my house, and my stomach flips. I am about to meet the most popular guy in school's brother... great. Taking a deep breath, I walk out of my front door and down the path to a black Escalade waiting for me. My legs shake as I near it and my nerves are awful. I am shaking like a dryer. I try to calm myself by taking calming breaths. I reach the passenger door and grip the handle taking one last deep breath and pull it open.

In the driver seat sits the dirty blond hair boy from the waiting room. "Hey, you must be Payton. I'm Conner," he says with his deep, hot voice and smiles at me. I climb inside and hook my belt.

"Nice to meet you. I'm Payton, but you already know that." I ramble but smile at him. Normally, I would be a mess, but for some crazy and mind-boggling reason, I feel calm and fine with him like he's my best friend. I mean, don't get me wrong, this guy is hot but not my type and too old. Okay, not really that old but still.

"Nice to meet you too. We better go," he says as he puts the car in drive and pulls away.

A light tap touches my shoulder, and I turn to look over my shoulder to see a small, pretty, little girl. Her blue eyes are so captivating like Reece's.

"I'm Rayne," she says as she outstretches her hand to me. I take her small hand in mine and shake it, smiling at her.

"I'm Payton. It is lovely to meet you," I say to her, and she smiles widely up at me.

"You too!" she says happily back in her seat, and Conner chuckles.

About ten minutes into the drive, it was a not too awkward silence, and Conner finally speaks up. "You know, I am so glad my mom met you. You have helped her a lot with handling the whole Reece thing. I must say you are an amazing person to help a stranger," he says as we pull up to the hospital.

I feel the blood rush to my pale cheeks, and I shake off his kind comment. "I'm just me," I say as I hop out of the car. "Thank you for the ride. Bye, guys!" I smile and wave at Rayne.

"Bye," they reply, and I shut the door. I pull my purse up on my shoulder, walk to the slide doors, and retrieve my ID card from my purse, clipping it to my top.

"Morning!" I say to the girls at the desks and walk to the elevator and heading up to Reece's floor. I walk down the hall and head to Reece's room. I peek at the door, and Georgia looks up at me from a sleeping Reece and smiles, her face washing with relief.

"You're here!" she whispers with joy as she walks over and hugs me tightly. "Thank you so much for doing this. You've been such a help, and I will never be able to repay you. But if you ever need anything just ask," she says as she pulls away and walks back to Reece and kisses his cheek, then grabs her bag and walks to me.

"Please do not let him scare you off. He is not as bad as he may seem now. He is usually a pleasant, happy boy, but that's gone. All he is now is angry and bitter, so don't take anything he says to heart. He's napping now he should be out for a while. If anything happens, call me. Thank you again,"

"No problem. I am happy to help you. You're a great person," I say, and it is true. She is amazing.

She smiles and says thanks. She looks at Reece's sleeping form and heads to the door. "I'll be back in two hours tops," she says and waves bye to me. I nod approaching Reece's sleeping form. His eyes lightly shut and his face full of peace. Slowly and softly, I sit down in the chair by his bed and retrieve a book from my purse, which is a pretty big one. I crack it open and begin to read. I get through the first paragraph when a shocking voice startles me.

"You don't have to be here. You can just go. I'm fine. I don't need anyone's help." His voice is deep, and I can hear the agitation in it. I look up to see his blue eyes staring right at the ceiling.

"How'd you know someone was here?" I ask curiosity getting the best of me.

"You and my mother talk so damn loud. You woke me." He grunts, and his voice is nowhere near pleasant or what I expected his mood to be.

Payton! Remember his mom said he's not himself. I tell myself as I take a deep breath.

"We weren't talking loud. We were whispering," I tell him annoyance clear in my voice. He doesn't reply. Good, at least, he shuts up now. If he kept talking as he was, I swear I would lose my nice girl-*ness* and slap him.

I return to reading my book and get to the next page when a grunt interrupts me. I look up to see Reece feeling around his sides and around the bed and cursing under his breath. "Stupid ass remote," he mumbles still searching.

"Um... Reece?" I ask clearing my throat and biting my bottom lip, afraid he may yell at me.

"What?" he snaps angrily, but I can tell his anger is not meant for me.

"W-what are you looking for?" I ask him a little nervous. I hate it when people are hateful with me.

"I want to sit up. I'm sick of lying," he says as he continues his search and swearing.

Turning the edge my page down, I mark my spot and lay the book on my bag. I stand up and step beside his bed. Taking a deep breath to calm my nerves and build my courage, I reach down and grab his right wrist, the one closest to me. Slowly, I guide it down the bed to the remote then I change my hold to where his pointing finger is. I guide it around the remote and push it on the button to sit him up. All the while, I ignore the sparks that shot through my hand, through my arm and onto the rest my body.

"Thanks," he grumbles and lays his head back and stares off into space. I nod my head stupidly and blush because of how dumb I just was.

"No problem," I say and sit back down picking up my book and return to reading it.

Two pages later his voice breaks the silence. "What are you doing, Payton? I hear a paper noise," he asks, and my breath catches. He knows my name. Holy crap! Is this a dream? I reach up and pinch my arm, and when pain shoots through my arm, I rule out that it was a dream.

"You know who I am?" I ask in confusion.

"Yeah, my mom talks about you," he says as his eyes look over at me, and his face drops and looks sad. "So what are you doing?" he asks with a sad sigh.

"Reading a book," I say simply at that he rolls his head away from me.

"Lucky, that's another thing I will never enjoy again," he says having a little pity partying which bugs me. At least, he is alive! Besides, it strikes me that he use to enjoy reading, anyway.

"There's this thing called Braille," I say sarcastically and shock myself. What the crap? I never have the balls to say something like that, especially not to him.

"Like I know Braille," he says angrily and chuckles dryly.

"You could always learn," I say as I toss my hands in the air, quite annoyed with his own closed mindlessness. He is nothing like I expected.

He's not himself right now. My voice says in my head.

Shut up. I groan back at it, knowing it is right.

"And who would teach me?" The edges of his mouth turn up a bit.

"Me," I say simply, but a minute later, what I just said sinks in. Oh crap, what did I just agree to? This is sure to be hell. Why in the world did I say I would? I don't think I will ever know.

Chapter Nine

Reece's POV

I can hear her breathing and the sound of paper moving. This morning my mother talked about Payton. She wants her to sit with me, and I plainly told my mother that I do not need a babysitter! I am not five! I can take care myself. What does she do? Goes ahead and calls her! So I wake up to them yapping loudly. I tried to get Payton to leave, but the girl is stubborn. Maybe if I don't talk to her, she'll get bored and leave.

My back is starting to hurt from lying down. I really need to sit up. Normally there's remote for that by the bed, I think. Stretching out my hand, I search for the remote. I run my hands around my sides and come up blank. What the hell? Where is the damn thing?

"Stupid ass remote," I mutter as I release a string of colorful words.

"Um… Reece?" a weak, feeble voice asks me, and I will admit it is kind of cute.

"What?" I snap, but my anger is not towards her. I am just so aggravated that I cannot find this damn remote.

"W-what are you looking for?" her cute voice asks stuttering at first. I can honestly sense some fear in her voice, not that I blame her. I am an ass. Oh well, it doesn't matter she probably thinks I am some blind, incapable freak.

"I want to sit up. I am sick of lying."

I hear the sound of movement and someone stands up, then footsteps approaching me. A soft, warm, little hand grabs my wrist, and I am startled by the sparks that shot through my arm. The hand slowly guides mine down to a cool plastic object which I guess to be remote. Then the hand moves to my hand, folding all of my fingers down except for my pointer then runs it over the buttons to the one that sits me up. She pushes my finger down on the button, and I feel myself sitting up from the stupid lying down position. She releases my hands, and all the sparks leave me. I hear some movement as she sits back down and the sound of paper returns.

"Thanks," I mumble as I lean my head back. I listen to her breathing and all these little sounds I can hear now. This is so boring! I feel like I should twiddle my thumbs.

"What are you doing, Payton? I hear a paper noise," I say after hearing the paper noise again and again.

"You know who I am?" she asks me confused. Is she crazy? Of course, I do. I cannot tell her that, though. It will probably freak her out.

"Yeah, my mom talks about you," I say as I move my eyes to look over at her. Stupidly enough, I cannot see, and it made me sad. "So what are you doing?" I ask with a sad sigh.

"Reading a book," she says simply and at that, I roll my head away from her.

"Lucky, that's another thing I will never enjoy again," I say feeling awful for myself. I love reading books, finding a new world. Now, I can never do that again.

"There's this thing called Braille," she says sarcastically, and I am shocked. Holy crap, did that just come out of her mouth? I never thought she would ever say anything like that to anyone or that she could be sarcastic.

"Like I know Braille," I say angrily and chuckle dryly. She's dumb, why would I know how to do that?

"You could always learn," she says I hear some sort of movement. She is right. I could learn. But how?

"And who would teach me?" I ask her the edges of my mouth turning up a bit.

"Me," she says simply, and I am shocked. She just offered to help me. She wants to spend more time with my cranky ass. Is she nuts?

"You're going teach me? Do you even know it?" I ask as I chuckle dryly. This is actually kind of fun to talk to her and mess around, but I will never tell anyone that.

"Um... well, no, but I can learn. It wouldn't hurt to learn," she says as if it is nothing.

"Fine then, looks like we are going to be learning some Braille," I say as I fight back a small smile and turn my head towards the ceiling and shutting my eyes.

"Goodbye, Payton. Thank you! I'll see you soon," I hear my mom's voice again, causing me to wake up. I open my eyes and face the darkness. I just want to see again.

"Bye. Yeah, I'll see you tomorrow," Payton replies with her sweet voice filling my ears.

I hear a set of footsteps leaving and another set that comes towards me. My mom, I assume, sits down beside me. "How was your time with Payton?" she asks me grabbing my hand and holding it.

"Fine, but I do not need a babysitter every time you leave," I grumble and then hear a set of feet enter the room.

"Hello there, Dr. Grey," my mom says in an upbeat tone.

"Hello. How are you feeling, Reece?" he asks, and I can hear his feet coming closer to me. My back is really starting to ache, and I wiggle around trying to move.

"Good, but sore. Can I move?" I ask really wanting to get out of the bed.

"Actually, yes, you can. I was just going send in a nurse to help you walk." I feel him do something to my arm.

"Thank you," my mom says, and I hear footsteps leave the room. Finally, I am going to get out of this bed! A few minutes later, another set of feet enters the room.

"Hi, Reece! I'm Tia, nurse and physical therapist." A woman greeted me nicely.

"Hi," I mutter as I try to be kind. I mean, she is going help me walk so I cannot be mean to her!

"So are you ready to stretch those legs and get moving? I know you want to get out of that bed," she jokes and walks over to my side.

"I sure am," I tell her, getting excited about getting back on my feet. I love walking and any movement. I love to be active. This is going to be great. I can finally get out of this bed and move. I am just really worried about how this will proceed, given I'm blind and all.

Chapter Ten

Payton's POV

"Lila, please wake up. I just want to hear your voice one more time. When you went into surgery the last time, I never thought you would slip into a comma. I know there are always risks with surgery, especially ones that were that big, but I just want you to wake up so I can hear that sweet voice of yours," I whisper as I sit down next to Lila, holding her hand and tears stream down my face. She has to wake up. I cannot take not having her in my life. She is another reason why we don't have very much money. The hospital bills are expensive.

I remember before she got sick how she would wake me up by blaring One Direction. She always loved the blonde, Irish one, Niall. Honestly, I would never admit this to her before, but I like the black-haired one, Zayn. Now, I wish I would have told her because she could never wake up. Funny how little things you never say can be so painful when you never get the chance to say them.

A knock comes from the door, and I sit up sniffling and whipping away my tears. The door opens, and Georgia walks in with a sad smile.

"Hi, Payton," she says as she comes over to me.

"Hey, how's Reece?" I ask involuntary, and she smiles a little larger.

"He's fine. The nurse took him out for his first walk. I just wanted to say thank you for your help and give you this."

She pulls out a set of some sort of car keys and hands them towards me. "It's one of our many extra cars. You can borrow it," she says, and I hold out my hand. She drops them into it. Why would she do this? It's way too kind.

"No, I can't use your car. That's way too kind." I try to give the keys back.

"No, dear, use it. I know you need it. Don't worry about anything. I know you'll help me a lot more in the future." She insists.

I release a sigh and nod. "Thank you," I stand up wrapping my arms around her neck. My heart bursts with joy, how can someone be so nice? This feels like an unbelievable dream.

"You're welcome. I better get going. He may be back by now," she says as she releases me from our tight hug and walks towards the door. "Do you mind sitting with him a little tomorrow morning?" Well, I cannot say 'no' to her for sure. She just gave me one of her cars to use.

"Sure, I will be there," I say with a smile, and she nods walking out the door.

What have I just gotten myself into? *Spending more time with the grumpy butt,* the annoying voice in my head interjected.

I lean over and kiss Lila's head as I roll my eyes at myself. "Bye, Lila. I love you," I say softly as I turn and walk out of her room.

I head down the hall and to the elevator, heading to Ms. Rose's room. When I get to her room, I lightly knock before walking inside. She is sitting up on her bed and flipping through channels on the TV.

"Payton!" I smile at her.

"Hey," I reply and sit in the chair by her bed. "How are you?"

"I'm good. Or as you, kids, these days say, 'chill.'"

"We don't say that these days." I laugh at her, shaking my head.

"What have you been up to this morning?"

"Just helping out a new friend."

"New friend? Do tell," she responds sounding intrigued.

"The other day I met this woman whose son was shot, Reece's mom. I was there for her and all. Well, she needs my help sometimes with watching him, so I sat with him this morning. He is having a really tough time since he lost his sight," I explain. We spend the rest of the time talking about that and some other stuff that is silly. Finally, it's time for me to go.

"I have to go," I tell her as I stand up and pat her shoulder.

"Alright, dear. See you tomorrow!"

"See you then," I say as I head for the door. I walk out going to the elevator. I grip the keys in my hand as I enter the parking lot, and I pull out the keys, hitting the unlock button in hopes of finding the car. I see the lights flash in front of me. I walk towards them and find a black Chevy cruise. I hit the unlock button again and hear the clicking sound of unlocking again.

I walk to the driver's side, open it, and slip inside. Smiling, as I slip the key in the ignition and start the car. I clip my seat belt and take off towards my house.

Walking into my house, I head for the kitchen looking for something to eat for dinner because my mom is pulling a late-nighter. Opening up the fridge, I see that there is nothing but some green apples and a little milk. I grab the milk and sit it on the counter. I grab a bowl from one cabinet and some cereal from the cabinet beside it. At least, we have a bowl of Reese's Puffs left. I pour the cereal in and then the milk. I carry the empty box and empty gallon of milk and drop them into the trash can. I have to scrounge up some money and go to the grocery store tomorrow.

I look around the small kitchen and eat a spoonful. I become tired as I eat, and once I finish, I dump my bowl into the sink and head up the stairs to my bedroom. I get a large baggy, gray t-shirt from my closet and some black panties from my dresser. Carrying them to the bathroom, I lay them on the back of the toilet. Stripping my clothes and starting the warm water, I lay out two towels and step into the shower. The warm water covers me, and I let the heat relax me and think about everything.

When I'm done, I shut off the water, get out dry off, put my hair in a towel, and get dressed. I head to my bedroom and curl up in a ball under my blanket and drift off to sleep.

My eyes slowly open when my brain decides it does not want to sleep anymore. I sit up in my bed and look around my messy room.

I really need clean it, I think to myself.

You don't say! The annoying voice in my head says sarcastically back to me.

Shut up, voice. It's too early for this; I argue back silencing the voice.

Standing up, I stretch and crack my back. I make my way to my closet and grab a gray long sleeve V-neck and dark blue jeans. I go ahead and change into them and then walk down the hall to the bathroom, brushing my unperfected teeth. I brush my hair with force allowing me to get knots out. I decide to braid my hair so I quickly divide it into threes and braid it over my shoulder. I twist a hair band around the end and return to my room fetching my purse and shoes.

On my way out, I swing by the kitchen, grabbing a green apple and out to the car as I take a bite of my apple. I slide inside the car and start it. I pull onto the road and head towards the hospital munching on my apple the whole way. I pull into the parking lot and park. I get out and lock the car. I carry my apple's core up to the front the hospital and drop it in the trash, and the search my purse for my ID card then clips it to my top like every day. I walk inside the doors and head to the elevator, and I get on it riding up to Reece's floor. My nerves are not too bad today because I have realized Reece is an ass. Yeah, I get it. He's blind, but at least, he is alive and healthy. Not everyone is that lucky, so he doesn't need to be grumpy. I get it. He had it all, but still, he shouldn't be mean to me for just trying to help!

I reach his door and tap softly. Georgia swings the door open, and a smile spreads on her face. "Come in! I am going head out now. I already gave him a kiss. I love you, Reece," she calls to him and the as she walks past me. "Good luck, he's a little crabby today," she whispers.

"Thanks for the warning," I whisper back, and she nods.

"I will be back as soon as I get these things taken care of."

I shut the door, walk over to the chair, and sit down. Reece is staring at the ceiling with a small black ear bud in one ear and the other falling loosely at his side. I can see his iPhone resting on his hard, stone-like stomach.

"Payton, you probably have more important things to do than being here so you can leave," he says in a dull, monotone voice.

"Well, Reece, contrary to popular belief, I have absolutely nothing better to do," I say rolling my eyes, even though he cannot see that I did. I shift in the chair and pull out my book.

"So more or less you have no life?" he asks in accusing tone.

"I have a life. Thank you very much." I groan and return to reading my book.

"Oh, yes, of course, Your life is spending the day in a hospital," he states in an arrogant, rude tone.

"Has anyone ever told you are an insensitive jackass?" I ask. My anger is growing, and I think I am going to punch. I clench my jaw, and my eye begins to twitch.

"No," he says simply as if it's nothing.

"Well, you are," I say, grinding my teeth.

"Well, leave then! I do not need a damn babysitter!" he says angrily, and I look up at his face to actually finally see a motion. Not a good one, but hey, we are making progress.

Shutting my book for a second, I look at him where he lies halfway down. His hair is messy, his eyes are shining, and he has a cute five o'clock shadow from not shaving.

"Oh, no, buddy boy. You are not pushing me away. You may push away the rest out the way, but you can't push me. I will push back. So get over it because I am going nowhere. And it's not that you need a babysitter, but you need company. So take the stick out of your butt and lose your attitude," I say, and when I am done, my breathing is kind of hard, and I have my face set.

"You are annoying," he mumbles, and I smile to myself as I see the edges of his mouth turn up.

"Thank you," I say happily and reopen my book to resume reading.

"That was not a compliment," he mutters shaking his head.

He shuts his eyes listening to his music, and I return to my reading. Peaceful silence covers us. Every once in a while, I would sneak glances up at him, and his head is turned in my direction and almost looks like he is staring at me. But I know that's impossible, and he is probably just thinking.

After a good thirty minutes, the silence is broken. "Payton…" Reece says drawing out my name.

"Yes?" I ask as I glance up from my book.

"Can we go for a walk?" he mumbles. I look around for a second thinking about it and sigh.

"Sure, one minute," I reply as I stand up and walk down to the nurses' station and see Tia.

"Hey, Payton," she says smiling.

"Hey, Tia. Can I take Reece for a walk?" I ask with a smile. She looks at me with a raised eyebrow and shrugs.

"Sure, I see no reason why not? Just unhook everything and he'll be okay. Swing by on your way back and I'll reattach him," she answers, and I nod.

"Thanks," I tell her with a smile and skip back to Reece's room. I walk over to his bed. "We have the green light," I say as I begin to unhook him.

He softly chuckles under his breath trying to hide it. "Alright," he says, and I can see a smile sneak onto his face.

My hand accidentally brushes his arm, and sparks shot through it, leaving little tingles. I pull back his covers revealing his gown which is riding up mid-thigh and his medium hairy legs are exposed, but they are actually muscled and toned from sports, I guess.

"Reece?" I ask rolling my lips into my mouth.

"Yeah?" he asks in an almost kind voice.

"Do you have boxers under your gown?" I ask hoping he says, 'Yes!' I so don't want to see his butt. Well maybe I…

no, I don't... it would be a nice sight, though. Wait, what did I just say?

"Why? You want to see my butt?" he asks with a real smirk which causes me to smirk and my heart to beat faster.

"No, I do not want to see your buttocks." I shake my head furiously.

"Yes, I am wearing boxers so sadly you will not see my rear," he says still holding his smirk.

Once again, I roll my eyes. "Swing your legs over to my voice." He does as I had instructed, and I hold his arm to help him stand. "Ready? Stretch your legs?" I ask, and he nods his head. I slip my arm through his arms, guiding him. I carefully lead him out of the room and try to ignore the sparks traveling through my arm.

"You don't have to lead me," he mutters sadly.

"Really, you think you can do this by yourself?"

"Why not?" he shrugs his shoulders.

"Go for it then," and releases his arm, gesturing my arms to go forward. Stupid, he can't see that.

Reece proudly takes a step forward and another and begins walking straight... towards a trash can.

"Reece! Watch..." But he cuts me off with his hand. I bite my lip and shake my head. I guess there's only one way to learn. He nears it more, and I shut my eye. Oh, gosh! What happens next causes me to hold back my laughter. Mister-I-can-do-this-without-your-help crashes into a trash can and falls on his butt.

I skip over to him. "That was a trash can."

"Shut up," he grumbles, and I laugh. I slip my hand into him and help him stand up, ignoring the sparks. He rises in front of me as I pull.

"Want to do it by yourself still?" I ask looking up into his amazing blue eyes.

"No," he grunts, and I nod slipping my arm back through his.

"Glad you see it my way," I say with a proud smile, and I can hear him laugh lightly. Maybe, just maybe, this won't be so bad. And maybe, just maybe, he isn't an ass.

Chapter Eleven

Reece's POV

I will admit. Saying that I do not need her help was not the best idea, and I will not do that again. It was dumb, and it seriously hurt. On the bright side, I have slowly been gaining back the ability to look on the bright side. At least, it's as bad as the first time I tried to walk. That went bad, and I felt pretty awful.

"Alright, Reece, you can do this," Nurse Tia tells me as she holds my arm, leading me as I walk forward. My brain is fighting with my legs. I'm trying to stay balance and get them to keep moving. The feeling is fear. What if there's something in front of me? I try shutting my mind off so my legs will work and my fear will dissolve. After a few minutes, I get my legs processing again.

There is a feeling of wanting to walk but not knowing where to go, where you're at, or what's around you. Not being able to see is like being stuck in a lifetime of playing Pin the Tail on the Donkey. It sucks and is kind of scary.

"Now, we are going turn," Tia says as she guides me around a corner. "Here." She grabs my hand and lays it on a cool wall. "This is one wall," she adds, and I nod. "Try by yourself now. This hall has nothing in the way as long as you walk along the wall. Let it lead you and all of your other senses." Her hand slips from my arm.

Taking a deep breath, I step forward trying to use my hearing and touch as I slide my hand down the wall, and I feel confident taking steps forward. I allow it to lead me down the wall, and I start to get the hang of it. My hand suddenly falls, and I move my hand to the edge and realize I've reached the corner.

"Corner?" I ask turning my head where Tia's feet stop walking.

"Correct," she says. "This hall is tricky there are things in the way. Do you want to try it on your own?" It wasn't that hard last time so why not?

"Sure, I'll give it a go," I say as I shrug my shoulders. Taking a deep breath, I take a step forward with my arms stretched in front of me as I try and feel around.

I take another step forward and then a sharp pain hits my waist causing me to groan. A hand grabs my arm and pulls me back and to the left.

"That was a bed," she says simply, and I groan cussing under my breath. She carefully guides me and then lets me take the lead until trip over my own feet.

She holds me steady. "I'm done for today." I am so sick of this. I cannot do anything by myself. Heck, I cannot even pee by myself! When I try to walk, I run into walls.

So that is how my first walk went — good until I began walking into things. When I walked with Payton, it was actually kind of fun. To be honest, Payton is actually nothing like I thought she would be. She is really feisty and sarcastic, but she is also really nice and kind.

I kind of like her even though I don't exactly know what she looks like. I remember little hints of what she looks like, just a bit. That's all. Yesterday with her was really fun, I love fighting with her it's the only entertainment I get. Everyone walks in freaking egg shells around me.

'Don't hurt the blind boy.'

'Don't hurt the blind boy feelings.'

No one ever gives me attitude or their real opinions, at least, not like they used to.

So now, I lay here in this stupid, uncomfortable hospital bed, waiting for Payton to come to my room and sit with me. My mom and dad had to go to work, and my brother and sisters have school work today.

That leaves me sitting here listening to music waiting for her to come inside. I hear the door creak open with the one ear that I have earplug-free. Then it shuts and footsteps near my bedside.

"Hey, Reece." Her sweet, innocent voice sings and I can hear her sit down in the chair beside me.

"Hey there Payton," I say as I smile slightly. I hope she doesn't see that. It may hurt my depressed, jerky reputation.

"What you listen to?" she asks, and I can tell she's not reading because I cannot hear the sound of the pages flipping.

I shut my eyes for a second thinking about it. "*Stop and Stare* by the One Republic," I mumble slightly as I listen to the song and let it flow through me.

"Oh, that is a good song," she says simply, and I can hear a smile in her voice. I really wish I could see it. I know she doesn't know how much it means to me that she doesn't worry about my feelings or what is going on with me.

"Indeed, it is," I say as I reach up running my hand through my messy hair, I can feel its roughness with my hand. After a few moments, I hear Payton unzip her bag and then a book being cracked open. "You know you do not have to stay, I'll be okay. I am getting better," I say not wanting to burden her or make her feel like I'm using her or anything. Also, I don't want her to be here. I want her to want to be here.

"Reece, we already figured out that I don't have a life, so I am just going stay here," she says, and I can hear the sarcasm in her voice. It's truly crazy how over the past few days I have learned little things in people's voice and the different tones, like angry, sarcasm, and things like that.

"Whatever," I mumble and turn my attention back to my music.

"Oh, stop being so grumpy! If you don't I won't give you your present," she says with a teasing tone. What in the hell is she talking about a present?

"Present?" I ask curiously. What would she of gotten me?

I hear some rustling and then she places a book on my lap. "Here, open," she says, and I hear her sit down. Taking a deep breath, I feel the present. I lift it up and begin to slip my hand around it, and I start to unwrap it. I feel the cool hard cover, and I flip it over and slide my hand over the top of it feeling slight bumps.

"A book?" I ask confusion etched in my voice.

"It's Braille for Dummies," she says with a chuckle. God, her laugh is so freaking cute! How could I just realize this? It is so cute and hard to explain. My heartbeat speeds up as I chuckle along lightly with her.

"Really, I'm a dummy? I was number two in our class," I say with a cocky smile.

"And I am number one," she says with a cocky tone this time.

"Of course." Her laughter fills my ears again, and my heart beats a little faster.

"Oh, let's just start learning Braille," she says, and her voice seems agitated, yet her voice has a sweet happiness to it.

"Fine... I have nothing better to do," I say with a slight smirk. This will be fun and probably, difficult. This will give me more chance to bug the crap out of her. That's becoming my new favorite hobby.

Chapter Twelve

Payton's POV

I know that I have little money, but I knew the store keeper. She gave me a deal on it. The money that I did spend on it was so it was worth it because it was funny seeing his face. I stand up and scoot the chair closer to his bed. He reaches over and grabs the remote, setting himself up further.

"Are you ready?" I ask as I flip the page open.

"I guess. Do I have to write in Braille?" he sighs and asks sounding a little nervous.

"No, I mean, you can if you want and if you can still write normal, then you can do that," I tell him because I honestly see no reason why not.

"I don't know if I still can," he says with a thinking face.

"We will try that soon anyways. Ok, now, to chapter one," I say with a slight smile, and he groans. I look at his blue eyes and feel so close to him. His brown hair is slightly messy and is so darn cute. I clear my throat lightly and begin to read what it says. "These letters are arranged so that you can see how it all goes together. W is the only letter that does not fit this," Then I slowly left his hand and place it on the 'A' for him to feel. He closes his eyes and feels the one dot and nods.

"Alright, I got it. One dot is A," he says with a slight proud smile.

"Now, this is B," I move his hand to it so he can feel it. He shuts his eyes again feeling.

"Two dots going down is B," he says, and I nod. "I feel like I am playing with dice."

"Hardy-har-har. Be serious for once," I say and reach up lightly to push his shoulder.

"I am serious."

"Oh, hush! Now on to C." He shoots me a fake mad face and then shuts his eyes and feels it.

"Two dots sideways is C. I understand Miss Party-pooper," he says with a smirk.

"Oh hush, grumpy butt," I say as I move his hand to D. He feels it and then shuts his eyes.

"Over two and then down one is D," he says sticking his tongue out at me. "This is actually pretty easy."

"Look who's getting a little cocky."

"Oh hush, what's next? A, B, C, D, E. E?" he asks, and I start laughing.

"You had to say your ABC's to figure out its E?" I smirk.

"No…" His face is clearly guilty.

"You did!" I say laughing and lay my head down beside him because I am laughing so hard.

"Shut up," he mumbles with a pouty face.

"Make me," I joke and he smirks.

"I will later," he says and winks. My face burns as the blush rises. One good thing about him is that he cannot see when I get embarrassed. I take in a deep breath and then grab his hand and place it upon the next letter. He feels it and shut his eyes remembering it.

"Two dots diagonal is E," he says with a smile.

"Yep. Now to F." We continue until we reach J at the end of the row.

"Two down on the far side and over one left is J," he says smiling a genuine smile.

"Good job!" I reach up and pat his head.

"Can we please stop for today?" he begs and gives me a pleading look. I stare at his amazing face and still captivating looks. His five o'clock shadow has turned into slight bread. He still looks hot, but I think he needs a shave.

"Fine. Let's see if you can still write," I say, and he shuts the book. I fetch a pen and paper from my purse and place it on top. "Here. Try." I hand him a pen and position it above the paper.

"What do I write?" he asks with a look of confusion, and I cannot help but smile. Gosh, sometimes, I forget this boy is blind. If he weren't blind, we'd never be talking.

Stop thinking of that, Payton! My voice inside my head yells, and I listen to it because I am just depressing myself.

"Whatever you want," I say trying to make my voice sound normal as if he didn't affect me but we all know it did.

"Ugh, fine," he says squishing up his face and trying to concentrate. His hand slowly begins to move a little, and he groans. Then he shut his eyes and tries again, this time, more confident. "There. I think I just need a lot of practice, but I'm sure I will be able to do it," he says as he lifts the paper and hands it to me in my direction.

I take it from his hands. At first, it is really messy and bad, but his second time was actually and surprisingly good.

Payton has no life.

His big dramatic sentence; the first one he writes since he went blind. And it's about my having no life.

"Funny! Really funny! Aren't you so nice?" I shoot him a fake glare even though I realize he can't see it.

"Oh, I know," he smirks, and I just shake my head laughing. He is crazy, and it's crazy how we get along.

"You're so cocky," I say, rolling my eyes and grabbing the things off his lap. I accidentally touch his leg which sends waves of sparks through me.

"No, I'm not," he says with a smirk that makes me smile.

"Reece, you need to shave." I stare at his sexy yet annoying bread. He reaches up and strokes his chin.

"I cannot shave, though," he says in a sad voice and looks away from me.

"I'll shave your face for you," I say as I shrug my shoulder and scoot back the chair and then sitting back into it, staring at him. Gosh, he is so cute, and I still cannot believe he is talking to me.

"Can you even shave?" he asks looking at me with a raised eyebrow.

"Well, I shave my legs," I say simply, and he chuckles, shaking his head and running his hand through his hair. I mean, it's the same thing practically. How hard could it be?

"Alright. I will call my brother and have him bring the stuff." He grabs his phone, hits a button, and raises it to his ear.

I sit there and watch as his perfect lips move as he speaks into the phone and how his eyelid lightly flutter over his blue eyes. His eyelashes are so black and thick. I honestly never notice that before. Pieces of his hair are falling on his face, and he looks so cute. He lays the phone down, and my stomach growls. Crap, I haven't eaten.

"Want to walk to the cafeteria and grab a bite to eat?" he asks me, and I groan.

"No, it's okay," I lie as I grip my stomach.

"Come on. I can tell you're hungry. I will pay. It's the least I can do. I owe you for helping me. Besides, I am also starving," he says as he removes his blankets.

I feel horrible letting him pay, but he did offer. I groan and lay back my head for a second before sighing and standing up. "Fine! I guess so." I shake my head.

"Grab my wallet from my bag." I nod grabbing it and turn back around to see him carefully standing on his wobbly legs. He turns his neck both ways cracking it, and I watch his amazing biceps pop out as he reaches forward making sure he is not going hit anything. He uses the bed to lead him to the end of it, and he stands there and waits.

"Do you want your wallet or…?" I ask slowly, and he cuts me off.

"I don't have any pockets," he mumbles, and I nod placing it inside my pocket. "So I am trusting you with it," he finishes, and I roll my eyes.

"Good job on how far you walked," I tell him with a smile as I loop my arm through his. Sparks dance through me causing me to smile. This is crazy weird that I am walking with this freaking sex god, and here, I look like a *Looney Tunes*. I wonder what people say when they see him and me together.

That you're his sister. The mean voice says inside my head. Haha. I am not even pretty enough to be his sister. We reach the elevator, and I hit the down button, stepping inside with him right beside me.

"Payton?" He asks, and I turn to him looking up.

"Yeah?" I reply leaning my head on the wall behind me.

"Why are you be quiet?" he asks eyes looking in my direction, and I stare up into his blue orbs, causing my heart to pick up speed.

"I am a quiet person," I respond to him, and the elevator doors pull open as he burst out laughing.

"You... quiet?" he laughs, and I groan yanking him forward with me. "Ow! My arm!" he whines, and I smirk.

"You'll be ok, you big baby!" I roll my eyes and pull him along with me. He groans as I lead us down some halls and into the cafeteria. We walk up to the counter, and I hand Reece his tray and grab my own. "What would you like, Reece?" I ask as we stand at the start of the thing.

"Is there any pizza?" he asks me, and I glance around. Finally, I spot the pizza and lead us to it.

"What kind?" I look up at him. He keeps his head facing forward. His face wrinkles as he thinks as if he is scared they won't have what he asks for.

"Pepperoni," he says and I nod to him. I look up at the young lady standing behind she smiles at Reece.

"What can I get you?" she asks in a flirty voice staring at Reece, checking him out. How stupid is she? I say as roll my eyes.

I bite my lip to hold back my laughter and clear my throat. "We'll have two pieces of pepperoni and two pieces of cheese," I say, giving her a kind smile. As she serves up the food, I look at Reece's tense stance, and I realize how hard this must be on him. I turn back to the girl with black hair in a bun and tan skin with green eyes. She is really pretty. Good thing, he cannot see her. She sits two plates in front of us, and I place them on our trays. I hold my tray in one hand and use the other to lead Reece to the drinks.

"What do you want to drink?" I ask him with a smile.

"Water," he says, and I am slightly taken back. Everyone these days like pop and all those sweet drinks. I am a big fan of water for one because it's cheap. I smile at him and fill a cup of water and sit it in his tray. I also grab me a cup of water and continue to the paying area.

"That'll be ten dollars, dear," she says with a sweet smile. I grab Reece's wallet and open it, seeing it stuffed with 50 and 100 dollar bills. I quickly find a ten and hand it to the women placing the wallet back into my pocket. Picking up my tray with one hand again and using the other, I guide Reece to a table.

"Here," I say, taking his tray and sitting it down. I watch as he finds his chair, pull it out, and sit nicely. I smile and sit across from him. "You are getting really good at that."

"Thanks. It takes a lot of practice," he says as he smiles at me, picks up the pizza and bites a piece off. I am so shocked. Reece has come far, and I am so impressed with him. He is really smart, and it's impressive. I am really scared he will realize how ugly and a loner I am and quit being my friend and talking to me. There is something about him I never thought I would find in someone, and he is just so amazing. I even like his grumpiness because that is a fun side to play with.

Chapter Thirteen

Reece's POV

"Is there any pizza?" I ask as I grip the plastic try tighter.

"What kind?" her sweet voice asks from beside me.

"Pepperoni," I say and stare straight ahead. This is the first time I have been in a public place.

She loops her arm through mine sending a spark wave through my body. "What can I get you?" a girl's voice asks, and it seems kind of flirty. I just keep a blank expression on my face. This is freaking crazy. I hate this. I cannot see anything. I want to see what people look like or my food.

Payton clears her throat, and I am curious to why. If I could see, I would be able to know why. "We'll have two pieces of pepperoni and two pieces of cheese," she says by my side.

I am so tense. It's just I cannot help but think of what people are thinking and saying about me. Probably, that I am a freak. I hear plates, and Payton's warm hand return to my arm, and she leads me somewhere. I feel like a dog being lead everywhere.

"What do you want to drink?" her sweet voice asks, and it warms my insides. *Reece, stop! No girl will ever like a blind boy!* I tell myself.

"Water," I reply simply.

"That'll be ten dollars dear," An older lady's voice says, and I hear Payton set her tray down and make some shuffling sounds. A minute later, her hand guides me again to a table. She stops.

"Here," she says, taking my tray from my poor hands and setting it down. She disappears, and I reach out finding the cool metal bar of the back of the chair. Pulling it back towards me, I allow my hand to slip down the back of it and land its seat. I angle my butt to sit where my hand is. Once my butt rests safely into the seat, I allow a small smile to stretch upon my face. "You are getting really good at that," she tells me, a smile in her voice.

"Thanks. It takes a lot of practice," I say as I smile at her and pick up my pizza to my lips taking and bite of it. Honestly, I kind of want to prove to her that I don't need help, and I can still do some things on my own. You know trying to impress her even though she will never like me. I honestly would give anything to just be able to look at her one last time and drink in her looks. I release a sad sigh and take another bite from my pizza.

"What's wrong?" Payton asks me, and I can hear the concern in her voice.

"I just wish I could see some things again just for a second," I say softly and take another bite from my pizza.

"Didn't you use to say you read a lot of books?" she asks me, her voice had a 'duh' tone to it.

"Yeah," I mumble taking another large bit.

"Well then, you must have some kind of imagination," she says simply, and I am totally confused with where she is going with that. Do I have an imagination? I don't know. I guess I kind of do.

"I guess I do. What is your point?" I ask really confused and waiting to hear what she has to say. She has officially sparked my curiosity.

"Well, you are used to seeing pictures and seeing with your eyes. You have yet to try touching and feeling something and turning that into a picture," she says, and I start thinking. Is that even possible? I am so confused.

"Is that possible?" I raise my eyebrows and taking another bite off my pizza.

"I don't see why it's not," she says and then I hear shuffling coming from her. I turn my head around and hear a slight chatter of the few other people here, and I can catch good bits of what they are saying. "Here," Payton's voice says, bringing me out of my focus on the other people I hear. I hold out my hand, and she places a kind of heavy piece of plastic it feels like.

"What is this?" I ask furrowing my eyebrows.

"You tell me," she responds, and I can hear the smirk in her voice.

Shutting my eyes, I bring my other hand to the object and begin to feel it. It is kind of heavy. One side dips into what I think is glass, and there are little bumps along the edge. On the other side, there is a dip, round as a quarter and another one a centimeter above. To the left is oval. I paint this picture with my mind and see an iPhone.

"*iPhone*," I tell her confidently.

"See. It works," she says, and I can hear the happiness in her voice that she was right. I hand the phone out to where I hear her.

"Here," I say giving her my winning smirk.

"Thanks," she mumbles, and she takes her phone from my hand, and her fingertips brush my palm, causing sparks to shot through my body. We finish eating our food she stays silent, and I listen to other people around us talking. Finally, we finish, and she takes my tray to the trash I assume and then we walk back to the elevator and to my room. Silent the whole way so I just listen to her breathing.

"Reece! There you are!" Conner says as we enter my room. "Hey, Payton," he says calmly, and I chuckle. I find the end of the bed and Payton leaves my side which kind of makes me feel very lonely. I use my hand to lead me up my bed and sit down where I feel the bed and kick up my legs, returning to my sitting position. "Wow, bro! Improvement," Conner chuckles by my side and I roll my eyes. He is always so happy when he is around me. I just do not get it! It pisses me off that he's so happy around me while I suffer in the pain of the dark. Besides, Conner has never been this happy. Yeah, he has always been upbeat, just not this much.

"Did you bring the razor and cream?" I ask in an annoyed voice.

"Yeah, want me to shave you?" he asks, and I hear a bag rattle.

"Nope, Payton said she will," I say with a light smile.

"I am going to go and get some water to use," Payton says, and I can hear a smile in her voice. Her footsteps leave the room.

"You like her!" Conner's annoying voice says from beside me as he pats my arm.

"No, I don't," I mutter, and he laughs at me.

"You do!" he says teasing me as he pats my cheek.

"Where's Rayne?" I grumble, and he chuckles. I hear him sit down into a chair.

"With Juliet. They'll be here soon."

"I am stuck with you until then?" I groan, and he laughs.

"Oh, I love you too, little brother," he says, and I can hear him faking hurt by the sadness in his voice.

"What about mom and dad?" I ask, ignoring what he said.

"They love you too," he says, and I know he is joking with me, and he knows what I meant.

"I meant, what they are doing," I say as my frustration builds.

"Dad is bringing home the bacon, and mom is getting some things," he says with a chuckle, and I shake my head at him.

Footsteps re-enter the room, and Payton sits a bowl of water on my lap. "Okay, ready?"

I take a deep breath. "I am trusting you with my beautiful face," I joke, and I hear her laugh lightly. Then the sound of the shaving cream fills my ears, and the cool, smooth cream touches my face, giving me a light chill along with the sparks from her hands touching my skin. I hear a splash of water, and it coolly touches my faces as she begins to shave it. I hear her breathing and her warm breath on my face. Gosh, she is awesome.

Once she is done, she removes the bowl from my lap, and I reach up and stroke my chin. My face is as soft as a baby's bottom. "Reece, I have to go and visit other people now." She steps to my side again, and my heart falls.

"Oh, alright," I say sadly and run my hand through my hair. "Payton? Will you come back before you leave?" I ask her. Please, let her say yes! I am so worried! I just want to spend more time with her for some crazy reason.

She is quiet for a second and then sighs. "Sure, why not? I put your wallet back up," she says, and I smile at her.

"See you later," she adds, and I smile as her feet carry her out of the room.

I really enjoy spending time with her! Oh, how I cannot wait to spend more time with her. I don't like her. It's just she's my only friend I have right now, and she lights up my dark world. I wish there is a way she would like me. I feel close to her, and it's been barely a few days. I don't know what's happening.

Chapter Fourteen

Payton's POV

I sit beside Lila's bed and hold her hand in mine. I have already visited Ms. Rose, and now, I am sitting here with Lila.

"Lila, I don't know what to do," I whisper to her. "The more time I spend with Reece, the more I begin to like him. But I can't like him! If I like him, I am going to get hurt because there is no way in hell he would ever like me. He could never like me. What do I do? I still want to be his friend," I say as I shift in my seat. A ripple shoots through my stomach, and I realize that I am hungry.

"Lila, I just want you to wake up. Life has been so tough, and I just want you back," I say softly as tears slowly begin to leak out of my eyes. I reach up quickly and use the back of my hand to whip away my tears. I take a deep breath trying to calm myself. I tighten my grip lightly around her hand. My phone beeps and I retrieve it from my pocket looking at it.

Mom: I am bringing home dinner. I will be home in an hour. XOXO

I smile at the text and see the time, 7:00 PM. I better go swing by Reece's room and say bye. I cannot believe he wants me to stop by! That is just freaking crazy! Standing up, I lean down and brush my lips against her pale, cool forehead.

"I love you, Lila Bug," I say as I stroke her cheek. I slowly walk to the door and hold it open while I spare a last look over my shoulder at her sad sleeping form. A single tear falls from my eye, and I whip it away. I shut the door behind me and breathe in a deep breath of the hospital, the smell of cleaning supplies and disinfectant spray. Taking a step forward,, I begin my slow walk back to the elevator.

The elevator begins to move, and I try to cheer myself up as I head for his floor. *Ding!* The elevator chimes as the doors slide open. I begin to walk down the hall and to his room. Why did he want me to come back by? Does that mean something?

Oh, of course, it doesn't mean anything! My voice inside my head laughs at me.

Shut up! I mumble! Gosh, it is so annoying. I stand outside his room and take a deep breath. *I can do this,* I tell myself as a sea of butterflies erupts in my stomach. Stupid nerves! I softly knock on the door, and it creaks open. I see Georgia in front of me, smiling.

"Payton! My dear!" she says happily as she pulls me into a bone-crushing hug. "Reece said you were going stop by.

I am so happy to see you," she tells me as she pulls me into the room.

As I step inside, she shuts the door behind me. I see a curly blonde hair girl, Juliet, with stunning blue eyes like Reece, sitting in the chair by Reece's bed. She is wearing a blue sweater dress with black leggings underneath and a pair of converses. She is beautiful, and I wish I looked like her just a little bit. She seems preppy, yet she seems like a rebel. I am not sure anything about her. I will figure it out.

Sitting on the couch near the window is Conner. His dirty blond hair is sticking up, and he has a smile on his face. He is smiling down at Rayne, and her brown hair is in a braid and her blue eyes are shining.

His dad is sitting on the other side of Rayne with his brown hair neatly styled and his bright green eyes also shining. Reece is sitting up in his bed and staring at the ceiling with a blank look on his face. His brown hair is all stylish, and his blue eyes are glistening, and his face looks so much better without his facial hair. I say I did very well at shaving his face.

"Hey, Conner, Rayne, Mr. Collins… and Hi, Reece," I say as I smile at everyone.

"You haven't met Juliet yet have you, dear?" Georgia asks still smiling. "Juliet, this is Payton. Payton, this is Juliet," she introduces us, and Juliet smiles at me.

"Hi! It is nice to meet you, Payton," Juliet says. Her voice is nice and pretty.

"It's nice to meet you too, Juliet."

I just stand there, smiling. "You came back," Reece says, and a slight smile appears on his face as his eyes look in my direction.

"Payton, if you want you can sit on my lap?" I look at his joking face rolling my eyes.

"Why would she sit on your lap?" Reece asks from his bed, confused.

I laugh lightly and look at Conner and raise an eyebrow. "Because there is nowhere else to sit," he says, and a cocky smile rises on his face. I may not have known him long, but that smile makes me think he is up to something. Reece is quiet for a second and then shifts in his bed. He reaches down with one of his strong arms and pats the bed beside him.

"Here, Payton. You can sit by me," he says, and I feel the blood rise to my cheeks. Sadly, I am in a room full of people who can notice. I try not to meet anyone's eye, but I do know, I want to kill Conner's sneaky ass.

Slowly, I walk over and sit down beside him. His side brushing against mine and I feel sparks through me. Stupid hormones always flaring up around him.

"Happy?" I ask with a smirk, trying to hide the blush.

He turns his head to me, and I stare into his eyes. "Ecstatic," he says as his lips turn up into a smirk. "Did you go see everyone else you needed to?" he asks me in a soft voice. I look up and see everyone staring at us, but once I caught them, their heads snap the other direction and begin talking among themselves.

"I did," I say as I look in his eyes and quickly pry mine away in fear of the feelings that were bubbling up within me. "But I have to leave soon."

I stare at his perfect lips. That was a bad idea, almost as bad as staring at his eyes. I wonder what it is like to have those lips pressed against mine, and his arms wrapped around me.

No! Bad Payton! I tear my eyes from his lips and look at his forehead. That is a safe place to look.

He'd never kiss you! The voice in my head laughs, and I groan.

"Ok, well, guess what?" Reece says in an upbeat tone, and I cannot help but smile.

"What?" I ask with a light laugh.

"I get to go home the day after tomorrow!"

My smile falls, and I try to stay happy. If he goes home, he won't be my friend anymore. "That's great," I say in a fake tone.

"Yeah," he says softly, and I feel his hand touch my arm, and his fingers brush my skin sending sparks to me. "I was wondering…" he trails off nervously. "Would you come over and visit me when I am out? Spend time with me and stuff?" he asks me as his hand still rests on my arm.

He wants me to come over! Oh, my gosh! "Sure," I say as I nod my head.

"Great!" he says with a smile, and we sit in silence for a few minutes.

My phone beep and I look at the time. 7:45 PM, it reads.

"I have to get going," I say as I scoot off the bed.

"Oh, alright," he sighs, and I almost think that he is sad for me to go.

"I will see you tomorrow morning for Lesson Two," I say with a smile, and he nods his head.

"Bye, everyone!" I say as I head for the door, and they all reply with byes. I go to the care and drive home.

Clank! Bang!

"What the…?" I sit up straight on my bed and rub my eyes. The banging and clanking continue. I roll out of my bed and pull on a pair of shorts off of the floor. I look at my window to see the morning sun peeking through. I groan, tug at my hair as I walk to my door and to the kitchen. I squint at my mom who is bouncing around the kitchen fixing something.

"Mom?" I mumble in a sleepy voice. She freezes and turns to look at me.

"Yes?" she says in a chipper voice.

"What are you doing?" I groan as I walk to the table and sit down, placing my elbow on the table top and resting my head on my hand.

"I was going to make you breakfast," she says smiling.

I pull my eyebrows together giving her a suspicious look. "Why?" I ask confused.

"Can I not make a meal for my lovely daughter?" she asks with a fake hurt expression. I give her that 'are-you-serious?' look, and she sighs.

"No, you *cannot*," I say stressing the 'cannot.' "Why are you so happy, anyhow?" I add with an expecting look.

"Well, I have just one month left of school, and then I graduate. Finally, I can get a good-paying job, and we won't struggle as much with money," she says with a large smile.

A frown appears on my face if only it were that easy. I really don't want to burst her bubble. "Mom, that still won't take care of the hospital bills," I say glumly.

"I know, but I won't have to pay for school anymore," she mumbles with a frown.

My heart cracks seeing my mom sad, so I force a smile on my face. "I am happy for you, Mom," I say and stand up hugging her. Well, at least, I am now awake.

"Thank you." She hugs me back, and I feel so warm and safe in my mom's arms. She pulls away and returns to the eggs she is making, and I go sit back at the table. "Payton? I have been meaning to ask you, whose car do you have?" she asks with her serious mom voice.

"You know, Reece Collins, the boy who was shot?" I ask my mom, and she looks at me confused.

"Yes..." she says slowly.

"Well, I met his mom at the hospital and helped her. Then she had something to do and asked if I would sit with him. I agreed, and we became friends. Well, we are kind of each other's only friends. Anyhoo, I am teaching him Braille. I stay with him and talk. So Georgia, his mom, had an extra car. They're rich and let me use it so I don't bother you with bringing me every day," I say and smile as I think about Reece.

"Oh wow! What nice people! I would love to meet them! And you have a friend. I am happy for you," she says and then pauses. "One question, why are you teaching him Braille?" she asks me confusion all over her face.

"He's blind," I state sadly, and her face falls.

"Aw, I'm sorry I asked," she says and drops some scrambled eggs on my plate and gets water from the fridge. She places both on the table, in front of me.

"It's fine," I say as I begin to eat, and she gets her own plate and water, sitting across from me.

"Payton, I just want you to know that I am so proud of you, and you are an amazing person for looking on the inside of people, and you have such a kind heart. I love you so much," she says with tear-filled eyes.

"Aw, thanks, Mom, I love you too. I learned from the best," I say to her, and she smiles then eats her food.

After ten minutes, I am done, and I stand up. "I have to go get dressed for the hospital."

When I reach my locker, I pull out a t-shirt and black zip hoodie and change into them. Then I switch out my shorts for a pair of navy blue sweat pants. I go to the bathroom and brush my teeth and pull my hair back into a bun. I return to my room, grabbing my purse and keys and slipping on shoes. I race to the kitchen where I tell my mom I love her and head to the car. I want to see Reece. It's weird, but I feel this pull to him, and I want more. Especially, if I look in his eyes, I am a goner. Too bad, he will never see me that way. If he weren't blind, we would have carried on never speaking, and thinking of that kills me. I like him, and he can never like anyone as ugly as me.

Chapter Fifteen

Reece's POV

I hear Payton's footsteps exit the room and my smile fades.

"Aw!" my mom cries, and I release a groan.

Please, God. No, don't let her say any—

"You two are so adorable!" I grumble 'too late.'

"She is nice and shy," I hear Juliet, say.

"I like her," Rayne says in her small, cute voice, and I cannot help but smile. I love my little sisters, especially Rayne.

"She's a good kid, a little mysterious, though," my dad's rough voice says, and I can hear a smile in his voice. He is happy most of the time. We get that from our parents, not as much for Juliet and me, though.

"I think she is—" my mom begins, but we all cut her off saying, "Amazing!"

She just laughs, and I can hear her standing from her seat and digging through something. I hear her grab something like a bag and make her way to my side. Something lightweight is placed on my lap, and I raise my eyebrows towards her direction.

"What is this mom?" I ask slowly dragging my hand across on side of it. It is slick and glossy feeling, kind of like those Victoria Secret bags. Don't ask me how I know that.

"It's a present, goofy," she says with a chuckle, and I feel her ruffle my hair lightly.

Sliding my hands up the side of the bag and reach inside pulling out what feels like stuffing paper, I reach the bottom, and my fingers latch onto a cool metal, square object. Pulling it from the bag, I hold it in my hands and try to create a picture of it. Shutting my eyes, I imagine a metal or hard plastic, square. As I continue to feel, I can tell one side is glass, and it feels like a phone.

"Mom, I have a phone," I say simply. Honestly, why would she buy me a phone when I have one?

"Sweetie, this is no regular phone. This one is completely voice control. You tell it your message and whom to send it, and it will. You can tell it what music you want to hear, and you will hear it. Same with everything else," she says, and I hold the phone tightly in my hand.

This is really cool! "Thanks, mom," I tell her as a smile spreads across my cheeks.

"No problem!" I then feel her press her lips to my forehead lightly in a motherly kiss. The bag then disappears from my lap, and I hear her footsteps return to her seat.

We sit in what is mostly a silence for a while until I decide to finally break it after hearing quiet chatter between Rayne and Conner.

"Can I ask you guys something?" I ask as I turn my head lightly and slowly back and forth.

"Sure," a few voices say, relaxed. "Yeah," the others say at the same time, a little more upbeat.

"Umm… well…" I pause as I shift awkwardly in my bed. "I was wondering. What does Payton look like? I mean, I remember her, but my memory is kind of foggy. I was hoping you guys could be of some help and use," I say nervously and as I tangle my fingers together.

"She has really pretty, past the shoulder length, brown curls," Juliet says with an amused tone in her voice.

"She also has these really beautiful big, chocolate brown eyes," Conner says, and a pang hits my chest as he calls her beautiful. What the hell was that about? I ask myself.

"Her skin is pale white but looks good with her brown hair and eyes. Her face is heart-shaped, and she never wears any make-up," my mom adds.

Hmm… never wears make-up. That's rare for this day and age. I start to see the fogging image I have more clearly. I see her innocent face and brown curls. Her brown eyes were so pretty, especially since she doesn't even wear make-up.

"She dresses very modestly, loose clothing and kind of old clothes too. I still say there is way more than meets the eye with her," my dad's strong voice says and my image of her grows. As I remember, her body always being covered from prying eyes every day. Her clothes were old and never new or fancy. Maybe my dad is right. Who am I kidding? My dad is almost always right! So, what could someone as great as her be hiding?

"I think she is really, really pretty!" Rayne's adorable voice calls, and I smile.

"Thanks, guys," I say as I see her bright smile at me. I think she is too. I say to myself.

After about twenty more minutes of me sitting here silent and listening to my families silly chatter, I hear someone stand followed by everyone else, apart from one person.

"Well, son, we better get going," my dad tells me as he walks towards me with his loud footsteps. His strong hand rests on my shoulder, and I sense him getting closer and finally hugging me. I pat his back, and he pulls away. "I love you, Reece," he says and then messes up my hair, which probably cannot get any messier.

He walks away and maybe to the door. Suddenly, something heavy falls on my bed beside me, and I jump slightly startled. Small, thin arms cling tightly to my hard chest, and I slowly lower my arms around Rayne's small body and pull her close to me. She snuggles her tiny head in my chest, and I smile.

"I love you, Reece. Please, never leave me," she whispers, and I smile softer. I use my other hand to reach for her head, and once I find it, I stroke her silky hair gently.

"I love you too, monkey, and never," I whisper back to her, and she squeezes me tighter, and I do the same.

She kisses my cheek lightly before crawling off my bed. Another set of heavy footsteps approach my side, and a tough hand holds onto my shoulder. "I love you, brother. See you tomorrow."

"Love you too, and sadly," I reply tossing in a joke for good sakes.

Lastly, a set of arms cling tightly to my neck, and I breathe in my mom's perfume. "I love you so much, baby boy!" she says as she holds me tighter, and I groan lightly.

"I love you too, Mom," I say and reach up finding my way to hug her back. After another minute, she pulls away and leaves me with a kiss on my forehead. She walks to the door as I hear her heels click.

"Bye," they say, and I hear them all leave. I release a sigh of relief and then remember one is left for the night. This is our basic normal night routine.

"Juliet, you don't have to stay. I am fine," I tell her, and she laughs.

"Whatever. I will be here on the couch if you need me," she says, and I hear her shift around. That girl is a fireball inside in an innocent-looking body. See, Juliet attend Adams Private School, and Rayne attends Roosevelt Prep School, while Conner and I attended Washington Public High School. Juliet's school is for smart people, which I could have gone to, but they are all about the education and no sports, so I choose public school. Our parents let us choose where we go which I think is a very respectable thing to do.

I lie back in my bed and try to go to sleep.

I am back there again. In that hallway with a gun in Erwin's shaking hands. However instead of the gun being pointed at me as I expected, it wasn't. No! This time, the

gleaming pistol was pointing straight at the brown hair, brown eyed beauty. Her eyes are dark with fear as she stares at the barrel of the gun. I walk as a single tear rolls her angelic cheek. She is not just some girl! That's Payton! I watch as the gun shakes more as his finger inches the trigger back.

It all happens so fast as I race in front of her at impossible speeds and the bullet goes through my shoulder and lands in her chest. We both collapse and I see her, a puddle of blood surrounding her. No! No!

"No!" I yell as I force myself on my knees and use my hands to cover her bleeding chest. "No!" I yell again as a tear runs down my face as I stare into those dead, glassy eyes.

Then, I hear more shots, and I look around to see my family all on the floor with puddles of blood around them. How'd they get here? I begin to ball and scream as I look into each of their dead faces.

"Reece! Wake up!" A frantic voice calls. I try opening my eyes and hoping to see a light, but instead, it's just the darkness. "Wake up! It was just a bad dream!" the voice says shaking me and finally, my eyes open, and my cheeks are damp.

"Reece!" Juliet says, and I nod, happy to hear her voice. "Good, I told you that you would need me. Want to talk about it?" she asks trying to help as she holds my hand, but I just shake my head. Sighing, she gets up and walks away to the couch.

I can never, ever tell her the truth to anyone. These nightmares haunt me. Mainly, it's his face, and I can never sleep. I just wish this was all a nightmare, but I know it isn't. I guess that's good, though, I have a new friend now.

Chapter Sixteen

Payton's POV

"Good morning, May!" I say with a bright smile. She turns to face me as I walk towards the elevator.

"Good morning, Payton!" she says back with a kind smile. The elevator doors slowly slide open, and two doctors in white coats along with two nurses step out of it, giving me a smile. Stepping inside, I hit the number, and the doors slowly shut. I cannot wait to see Reece. For some reason, I just feel drawn to him, and it feels like we've known each other forever. *Ding!* The doors slide open, and the nervous tingles shot through me as I adjust my bag higher on top of my shoulder. No matter how many times I see Reece, I still get nervous. I hate my nerves!

I reach his door and lightly tap on it, not wanting to barge in or anything. "Come in!" his voice calls, and I smile slowly open the door.

Reece is sitting up in his bed. The top of the blanket is collected at his waist. His brown hair is wet and falling onto his face and almost to his eyebrows. His blue eyes are sparkling, and he looks so clean, and the large smile on his face tells me he is at least in a good mood.

"Hi, Reece. You seem in a good mood this morning," I say with a smile as I pull my normal chair up beside his bed and sit down dropping my bag to my side.

"Morning, Payton," he says with his dazzling smile as he turns his head to the side so his face is in my direction. "I am in a great mood! I took a shower this morning..." he says and pauses for a second, so I speak.

"That's good you took a shower. You were developing an odor," I joke, and he lightly chuckles, causing his chest to vibrate and shake.

"I took a shower by myself!" he says ignoring my comment and smiling proudly. I sit in shock! He was able to take a shower by himself! He is improving so much!

"Reece, that's great!" I exclaim as I leap up and wrap my arms around him hugging him. Crap! What am I doing, hugging him? I slowly begin to pull away awkwardly as blood pumps to my cheeks. Then, I feel his strong arms wrap around my back hugging me back. I smile as the fireworks take off, and I then bit my lip. Finally, a minute later, we pull apart, and I am blushing. I sit in the chair and try to pretend nothing happened. Reece is in his bed with a construed face that looks like he is in deep concentration.

A couple awkward, silent minutes pass and I shift uncomfortably in my seat. Clearing my throat, I bend down to retrieve my book from my backpack.

"Lesson time," I say breaking the silence as I place the book upon his lap and crack it open to the alphabet again.

"Yay," he says sarcastically, and I roll my eyes. He reaches up and runs his hand through his hair.

"Let us review real quickly," I say as I take his hand and place it on one of the letters in the first row. He closes his eyes for a second before opening them and smiling.

"J," he says, and I smile nodding my head.

"Correct," I say happily. "This one?" I ask as I move his hand to a different letter.

"Um... four dots together. G?"

"Yep," I say as I then take his hand and move it to another one ignoring the feelings. "How about this one?"

"D," he says proudly, and I smile at his happy face. I know he is looking at me, but it is crazy to think that he can actually not see me at all. Then again, I guess he has never seen me before. I force that thought aside and continue to quiz him.

"Alright, I'm done!" he says turning his neck back and forth cracking it.

"Not so fast sucker. We have to learn one more row," I instruct, and he groans out.

"Dang it!" he complains, and I shake my head as I move his hand onto the K starting the second row.

"One dot on the top and bottom left to your hands is K," I say, and he feels it, shutting his eyes, and thinking.

"Alright!" he nods like a bull rider signaling the time to release the bull from the chute.

"Three dots straight down is L... Two top across one bottom left to your hands is M," I say, and he waits for a second before nodding to continue on the next letters

Once we reach T, we stop, and he smiles as he feels around on the top of the book and flips it shut.

I laugh as I remove it from his lap and replace it in my bag. "We will finish this tomorrow!" I say, and he laughs.

"I will be home tomorrow!" he tells me excitedly, and I nod.

"Yeah, I know. I will swing by when I get out of school." His body stiffens, but he nods his head.

"Good," he says with a more force smile and reaches to something pulling it out from his side. It looks like an iPhone but cooler.

"What is that?" I ask him as I raise my eyebrow and reach up and mess with my hair in a ponytail.

"My phone," he says simply, and I sigh. "Speaking of which what is your number?" he asks me, and I just smile and shake my head at his randomness and the fact that Reece Collins is asking me for my number! Every girl's dream!

"304-542-9962," I inform him, and he nods smiling.

"Create a new contact. Name: Payton Jennings. Number: 304-542-9962," he says, and the phone makes a *ping* noise.

"New contact has been saved," says a robotic women's voice. Like the one you can get to read you book on your *Kindle*.

"That is cool!" He chuckles, and I smile.

"I know!" he says as he replaces it back beside his side. A few minutes past in a peaceful silence, and I hear Reece move. "Do you want to play twenty questions?" he asks as he seems bored.

"Sure," I say, knowing even if you play twenty questions it never last twenty questions. Then I yawn from the lack of sleep I got last night. I had a horrible dream so I could not go back to sleep.

"You tired?" he asks me, and I sigh as I stifle another yawn.

"A little," I say, and he nods his head.

"How come?" He wonders, and I look down to the ground for a second before taking a deep breath and answering.

"Nightmare."

"Same here," he says, and I look up in shocked. He has nightmares? I hope it's not about the shooting. I look up when I hear the sound of movement in the bed and see that Reece has laid the bed back some and is now laying on his side facing me. "Come, lie here, and we'll play twenty questions," he says, and my nerves suddenly take off like a thoroughbred in the Kentucky Derby.

With shaky legs, I stand up and climb into his bed facing him. I smile rests lightly on his face, and I stare into his amazing blue orbs.

"Hi, there," he says as his cute lips pull up into a side way smirk. There are about 6 inches in between us, and I can feel his warm breath brush against my face.

"Hi," I say back quietly, and his smile lifts higher revealing the cutest dimple on his left cheek.

"Let's start," he says and takes a deep breath. "What is your favorite color?" he asks, and I chuckle at his silly thinking face he had. It was all serious looking.

"Turquoise, What's yours?" I reply, and he groans.

"You cannot re-ask my question! But this time only I will answer, though," he says with a goofy smile. *Dang!* He is really in a good mood, and it is spreading to me because when he smiles, I cannot help, but smile too. "It's blue," he says with a smile. "What is your favorite food?" he asks.

I twist my lips a little as I think. That is hard. I love all food, and it shows! That's why my body is not a perfect and flat. "Hamburgers," I say as I smile large. "What is—? Never mind. What is your favorite sport?" I have always wondered because he plays so many and he is good at almost all of them, so I am curious to what his favorite is.

"Hmm…" he says for a second and then frowns a little. "I love all three. In football, I love the feeling of being in charge and leading. Also, the moment when the ball snaps back into my hands, and I have to find an opening quickly, the adrenaline starts to pump, and it's great. I love baseball because the moment I step on the pitcher's mound all eyes go to me, and I feel unexplainable as I strike out batters. Lastly, I love track. It was my escape just being able to run as fast as my legs would carry and the moment I feel the ribbon break across my stomach that I won is amazing. I love them all but will never be able to play them again," he says frowning a little, and I feel so bad for bringing it up.

"I am sorry," I mumble looking from his face.

"No, it's fine," he says with a sigh. "Who is your best friend?" he asks me, and I sigh.

"Our age? I don't have one," I say shyly, and he nods.

"I thought I did, but you know how you can be wrong about people," he says, and I am shocked. He doesn't have friends now. How mean do people have to be?

Without thinking, I ask my next question. "What happen to all your friends? You were popular," I ask, and he sighs shrugging his shoulders.

"No one I guess wants to be friends with a blind person," he says feeling pity for himself.

"You are still you. Being blind is not who you are. It is just a part of you that makes you stronger," I say in annoyance.

"I know," he sighs and shakes his head. "Who else do you know in the hospital?" he asks me, and I sigh taking a breath.

To tell him or not? That is the question remaining. I could take him with me and tell him, or I could lie. Lying is bad so that leaves just one option. This is going be hard. I have never really spoken about it a lot out loud. I guess there is always a first for everything.

Chapter Seventeen

Reece's POV

Once that stupid question slips from my lips, and I feel presence change. I realize that was an awful question, and I feel like a total ass. It's just, her question was personal for me, and I wanted to ask her a personal question too. I never meant to upset her. Great! This morning has been great until just then. This morning I got up and was able to take a shower all by myself just by using my hands to feel around me. That made me so happy because I honestly thought I would never be able to do anything on my own again no matter how bad I wanted too! Now, knowing I can is a fear lifted from my shoulders, and it makes me so happy. My morning got better when Payton got here; being around her cheers me up. Then I had to go and open my mouth and insert my foot. If she wanted me to know, she would've told me! But she didn't, and I want to get to know her better! Stupid, stupid me!

"Reece?" her voice says softly, and I can feel her body moving. "Do you want to come on a walk with me?"

Still feeling like crap, I nod my head and pull the cover off me and stand up. I allow my hand to lead me to the end of the bed, and I wait.

An arm slips through mine, and I feel the explosion inside of me and know it's Payton. Her heart is beating loudly, and her breathing is speeding up. Could she be nervous? "Let's go," she says as she tugs me along with her. I have no clue where she is dragging me.

"Where are you taking me?" I ask as I hear the '*Ding*' of the elevator door, and then I am brought inside. I hear the doors close tightly.

"To whom I always go see," she says softly and then the door opens again. She begins leading onto another floor. I can feel people walk past me and talking through the quiet hall. I feel her move and the sound of a door swing open. She then pulls me into the room I assume and shut the door behind me with a click.

"Where are we?" I ask as she slowly leads me somewhere.

"Here sit on the couch," Payton tells me, and I sigh using my hand to feel the leather back of the couch and the seat of it. Then I place my hands on the seat behind me and lower myself onto the couch. The room is silent for a moment, and I shift making myself more comfortable. The leather on the back of the chair is cool and sends chills through me as it brushes the skin of my back that is revealed through the robe. Payton sighs as she sits down beside me.

"We are in my sister's hospital room," she says with a weak voice. Her sister? She has a sister? Why is she in the hospital? How come she's not talking? I am truly confused.

"Is she asleep?" I ask trying to get more information from her.

"Yeah, she's been asleep for the past few weeks," she says in a low, shaky voice, and I reach over to where I hear her and feel her hand. Once I find it, I take it tightly into mine and softly scoot over a little.

"How old is she?" I ask in a light voice. I want to know what happen. Why she is in here? But, those are hard questions so I will start with easy ones first because that is what I would want people to do for me.

"Ten," Payton replies, and I can just imagine her big brown eyes becoming cloudy with tears, just by how thick her voice is becoming.

Ten years old? Holy crap? Why would a little ten-year-old girl be in the hospital instead being out, living life, and growing up?

"What is her name?" I ask swallowing a lump, building in my throat. I have this feeling in the bottom of my stomach that this is a bad and hard situation, especially for Payton.

"Her name is Delilah, but I call her Lila."

Delilah? That is a beautiful name. I am sure she is just as beautiful as her sister is.

"Payton, what happen to her?" I ask. Maybe if she talks about it, it will help her, and she'll feel better.

She releases a deep breath and shifts slowly in her seat. "When she was eight, she started getting really sick, and we took her to the hospital and waited all night. My mom was in tears as she sat beside the bed. I was in the bed holding Lila while she cried. She was so afraid of what the doctor would say. The doctor came in at six the next morning and told us that Lila has Leukemia and Lila fell apart. I kept myself together for her. My mom fell apart too. I have never seen my mom cry so hard. The doctor started her on chemo," she stops for a second, and she releases her tears. Letting go of her hand, I wrap my arm around her neck and pull her close. My cheeks are cool from the light tears that fall down my face.

"It was gone, and she was doing. She was so happy and alive, dancing around, and returning to school. She was so much happier and fine. Then, suddenly she relapsed, and her weight began to melt off of her she was sick and bleed a lot. The Leukemia made a comeback, and we had to start everything again. She ended up having surgery, and something happened with the anesthesia, and she didn't come out of it, at least not yet. So we have been waiting on for. I volunteer here to be closer to her and remind myself, 'No matter how hard my life gets, someone has it worst.'" She cries, and I hold her in my arms. "I just want her to wake up!" she sobs.

She cries into my chest as I hold her, and tears slide down my cheeks too. God, I am an ass! Her sister could die, and I pity myself for being blind. At least, I am alive! I rub slow circles on her back in hopes to sooth her.

"Shhh... it'll be ok, Payton. I am here. It'll be ok," I whisper to her as I begin to rock her slowly back and forth. "I'm sorry," I say as I continue whispering.

I feel her shake her head in my chest, and my heart slowly breaks for her. She is so much stronger than I thought. Payton is truly an amazing person and sister.

Chapter Eighteen

Payton's POV

The tears ski down my face as I think about it. I shift in my seat as I hold his hand tightly. My eyes shut as I think about it.

FLASHBACK

My eyes jerked open as I heard the sound of someone throwing up. I looked at the time, twelve in the morning. Groaning, I got up and went to the bathroom, the heaving and puking sound continued. I slowly pushed the door open and found Lila on her knees in front of the toilet and vomiting into it. I quickly went to her side and scooped back her long, brown waves out of her face. I felt her forehead, and it was on fire!

She stopped puking for a second and I heard her crying and her body shaking.

"Shhh... it's okay! I'm here, sweetie," I said in a calming voice. "Mom!" I screamed, hoping to wake her.

"Sissy, I don't feel so good," she said to me as she looked up at me with her dark green eyes. Her face is white as a sheet and is covered in sweat and tears. She turned back to the toilet again and threw up.

"Mom!" I screamed as I hold back the tears. Something was seriously wrong with her! I knew it. I felt it!

"Honey, what is—?" my mom began but stopped once she saw Lila's condition.

"I am going call a doctor!" she said quickly as she took off running to get the phone. Lila's vomiting continued until she finally stopped and leaned her head on the side of the toilet seat.

She released a groan and grabbed her stomach with her hand. "It hurt!" she cried, and I bit my lip to keep myself from crying too.

"I know, sweetie!" I said as I rubbed her back.

"The doctor said it's probably just a bug and to give it a day," my mom panted as she stood back in the doorway.

"It's not a bug, mom." I looked at Lila's innocent face.

"I know. Let's give it a few hours then we will take her to the ER," my mom said as she walked over to Lila's other side and put her arms around her. I reached up and flush the toilet. Normally, vomit made me sick, but I knew right that being sick would be the wrong thing.

She looked up at my mom with teary eyes, and I saw a drop of blood on her lip. "Is that blood?" I asked, and my mom opened her mouth and then gasped.

"Her gums are bleeding," my mom said softly.

I looked at her arm and saw blue and green bruises that were scattered all over her arms. "Lila? How long did you have these bruises?" I asked, brushing my fingers lightly across her skin.

"A while," she cried.

"Mom, this can't wait," I said, and my mom nodded her head in agreement.

"I'll get the car, and you bring her out."

"It's going be okay, Lila," I carried her out of the bathroom, out of the house, and to the car. I sat her in the back seat with me. My mom sped to the hospital as I held Lila tightly to me.

Once we got to the hospital, I carried her into the emergency room with my mom right beside me. My mom rushed to the nurse. The nurse took one look at Lila's shaking and seriously sick body. She did something quickly, and I noticed nurses and doctors rushed to us and took her from me. They ran tests to determine that she had Leukemia after that everything about our lives changed.

I tell Reece about it all as I cry, and he holds me in his arms. I feel so safe and protected. The rest of that day carries on like this. I stay in his arms as we sit in my sister's room, and I cry. Finally, once I know it late, I walk Reece back to his room, and Conner is there waiting. I leave him with his brother and decide to head home as I have to go back to school tomorrow.

The morning sun wakes me from my dreamless somber, and I throw my blankets off of me knowing I need to get ready for school. So I force myself to climb out of my bed and stumble to my closet. I groan as I flip through my clothing that all looks pretty much the same.

I don't want to go back to school. Actually, after having a long break, no one wants to. I settle on some gray sweatpants and a black t-shirt. I am too tired to want to wear jeans. All that crying and emotions yesterday really wore me out. I take my things to the bathroom where I get ready and tie my hair in a messy bun. I look at my appearance and see the large black circles underneath my eyes from crying.

Taking a deep breath, I walk back to my bedroom, slipping on my shoes, and grabbing my purse and backpack. I stop almost forgetting a hoodie and tug it over my head and walk to the kitchen. I find that my mom has already left, so I grab an apple and water. I take a bit as I head to the car and set the water down in the cup holder. I start the car and pull onto the road, still munching on my apple. I arrive at school and park. Getting out, I grab my things and then shut the car door locked. As I walk to school, I am shocked to see most of Reece's friends acting all normal. I am sure the shooting is in the back of everyone's mind, and we are all scared. But still, they seem as if it is nothing.

Jace, Reece's best friend, seems a little different, however. He is wearing a black shirt and jeans, a worn-out look on his face, messy hair and seem like he has something bugging him. I wonder if he is feeling guilty for ditching his friend.

I drop my apple core in the trash can outside of the school. The hallway is full of gloomy faces, and I slowly make my way to my locker. I can do this! I tell myself repeatedly. I open the door, change out my books and head to class. I sit there, and it feels so different and lonely knowing when that bell rings Reece will not be strutting in that door. The bell rings and class begins just like any other day, but you can feel it in the air. Everyone know Reece is not here, everyone remembers the shooting, and that will never change and the fact that Reece is not here, well that Reece is truly no longer alive.

Reece before the shooting was nice, and he gave off a slightly cocky attitude and was always happy. That Reece is not who he is anymore, not because he cannot see but because this Reece is still nice and caring, but he is shy now. He values life and is more depressed than he is happy, not that he let anyone see.

The rest of my class continues like this and I hide in the library at lunch. Before lunch is over, however, I decide to go to my locker. I change out my books, go to the restroom because I drank too much water, and really need to pee! As I am in the stall, I hear a couple people enter, and I don't mean to hear their conversation, but it's kind of hard to miss with their high pitch voice.

"OMG! Did you hear about Reece Collins?" girl one asks the other.

"Yeah! He is like blind now!" girl two says in a dramatic voice.

"It totally sucks. He was so hot!" girl one says, and I peek through the door and see two blondes at the sink doing their make-up. Are they freaking kidding me? He is still hot!

"I know, and now, he is just weird. Being blind is just so creepy. He's like special now," girl two says and my anger keeps rising.

"I know. I hear that not one person outside his family visits him!"

I visit him you... you bitches! If only I were brave enough to say that to their faces.

"Well, I got to go to class." Then, they both leave the restroom. I step out of the stall, face red in anger, and I wash my hands before going to my next class. What kind of sick people think that way? People like that should become deaf or blind to learn a freaking lesson.

The last bell rings, and I hang around the classroom like I normally do, allowing the halls to clear, and once they do, I gather my things and walk down the hall. I grab my things from my locker and shut the door and head to the main door. I keep my head down as always. Suddenly, I feel something slam into me, and a hot liquid covers my hoodie. I stumble backward and look down at my hoodie which is soaked. Groaning, I look up at the stupid person who spilled what I am guessing is coffee on me. I am greeted by a sorry look, Jace. His black shirt is a little wet and his cup in his hand is pretty much ruined.

"Shit! I am so sorry. My mind was somewhere else, and I wasn't paying attention," he says. He tilts his head back and rubs his face.

"It's fine. I understand," I say a little stunned. He sees me.

"I am so sorry about your hoodie."

"It's fine. I have more," I lie and shrug, not wanting to make a big deal, but this is my only hoodie.

"Alright, but I still feel awful." He shakes his head.

"It's okay," I say with a fake smile. I just want to get in the car already and go see Reece! I am still ticked about what those stupid bimbos said early.

"At least, let me make it up to you. Where are you headed?" he asks with a small smile, and I roll my eyes.

"To my car," I tell him. Even though it's not my car, it sounds better when saying that rather than to a car if you know what I mean.

"Well, I will walk you," he says, and I begin shaking my head. "Nope, it's the least I can do." His face is set, and I can see kindness in his eyes.

"Fine," I groan and continue the walk, and he quickly catches up walking with me.

"I am Jace Higgins." he walks alongside me.

"I know," I say simply, and I can sense his cockiness.

"Well, what's your name?" he asks as we walk through the parking lot.

"Payton," I say. This is so weird talking to him. Thankfully, we reach the car. I stop, pulling out the keys and opening the door to throw my bags in the backseat. I then tug the wet hoodie over my head and toss it back there too.

"Are you new here?" he asks me, and I laugh, rolling my eyes and slipping inside.

"Not even close," I say, and he begins staring at the car in confusion. Everyone thinks I'm invisible always.

"Where'd you get the car? It's nice," he raises an eyebrow, and I know why he is interested in it because he has probably seen it at the Collins' home. So now, he probably wonders why the hell I have it.

"A friend. Speaking of which, my friend is expecting me so bye," I say as I shut the door and start the car and pull onto the road heading to the Collins' house. Everyone knows where their house is, one because it's the biggest house in town and two because the house is commonly used for our small town celebration.

As I course down the road, I cannot get the thought of what those girls said out of my mind. Glancing up, I see the long driveway, driving down a road surrounded by trees as I enter the Collin Plantation, in other words, a huge house with lots of lands.

I see the large three-storey house come into my view as I pull in front of it and park the car I get out and the cool air sends chills through me. I grab my things and head up the large stairs to get to the large black door. With a shaking hand, partly from the cold and partly from the nerves, I knock on the door. A few minutes later, it swings open revealing a smiling Reece, who is wearing a white tank top and some sweatpants. I can see his large biceps, and his chest and abs indents can be seen through his top.

"Payton?" he asks double checking.

"Hey, Reece, ready for the next lesson?" I ask smiling at him, and he nods and steps sideways. He is not special or anything, those girls don't know him and as for his friends they are not true friends. I walk inside, and he shuts the door turning around.

"Let's do this," he says with a smile, and I cannot get over how amazing he looks. I don't care what anyone says about him. They are all stupid, but they are right about one thing — he is not the same Reece. No, this one has me as his friend, and that is something the old him did not have.

Chapter Nineteen

Reece's POV

"Reece! Wake up!" a girl's voice says in my ear, and I am confused. I know that voice. As my brain starts to work again, I begin to process whose voice that was. "Wake up," it repeats. Now that my brain is on, I realize it is my mom.

I peel my eyes and am met by the ever unfriendly darkness. "Yes, mom?" I ask tiredly.

Yesterday wore me out, and I couldn't sleep well last night. I kept thinking about all the hell that Payton has been through and all the suffering that she was put through. I cannot fathom the thought of one of my little sisters being that sick. Payton is one the strongest people I know for handling it all, and it also makes her beautiful.

"Did you forget what today was?" my mom asks, and I can hear a chuckle in her voice. Today? Wait, what is today?

Then it hits me! I was so caught up in what Payton had told me that getting to go home slipped my mind!

"I get to go home!"

"Yeah, and we have someone who is coming in to teach you how to use a stick to walk," she tells me, and I feel her grab my hand lightly in her warm one.

"Great," I say sarcastically. I feel so incompetent when other people try to help me. I'm the person who helps others, and it feels weird when I am now the one who is being helped. And I don't like it.

"Oh, be happy! This is for the best!" my mom says in a slightly scolding tone.

"Fine." I groan in defeat. It would be nice to learn how to walk without running into things. I think that if I run into one more thing, I am going have a concussion. "What time does the person get here?" I ask because I just want to go home! This stupid bed is killing my back, and I just want the feeling of my home around me.

"Ten minutes at the most," she says with a smile, and I nod my head. I always did wonder if the sticks really work. Finally, I hear a door creep open and footsteps that have a different beat to them enter the room.

"Hi!" my mom says with a happy voice.

"Hello, are you the Collins?" a deep male voice asks. Is that who's going to teach me? I wonder and hear my mom stand up.

"Yes, are you Carter?" she asks, and I hear him come closer.

"Yes, I am Carter Alexander," the boy says, and he sounds like he is in his early twenties.

"Well, this is Reece, and I guess, I will leave you two to get to it," my mom's sweet voice says as she exits the room. The other footsteps approach my bed, and I throw the blanket off of my body and sit up.

"So you're Reece?" the guy asks, and I roll my eyes. Obviously, I am!

"Yeah, are you blind?" I ask bluntly. I know that may seem kind of rude, but I haven't seen someone who can see teach someone how to use a stick.

"No, not anymore," he says, and my ears perk up. Did he just say not anymore? What in the heck does that mean?

"What do you mean not anymore?" I ask. I will be honest, I am happy about going home, but my mood is not the greatest seeing as I had only a little sleep. If only Payton were here. I know she could cheer me up; she has that power.

"You see, I had a motocross accident ten years ago, and it more or less made my optic nerve quit working. So I ended up blind. Back then, they didn't know surgery could fix it, and I went on living blind used a stick and everything. About a year ago, I went to the doctor, and they told me I could have surgery done, and it would restore almost all my sight. And I went for it. Now, I have 85% of my sight back," he says, and I can hear his tone change into a happier one. So there is surgery? I wonder if I could get it.

"So now, you help other blind?" I ask with a sigh, and he chuckles.

"Pretty much. Plus, I know, some need friends and people who understand and that's what I am here for." I hear him walk around the bed. I pick my legs out of the bed and sit on the edge. Did he just say I need friends? Not that it is not true, but… that is kind of, well, hurtful! I stand up and walk to the end of the bed.

"I have friends," I lie, trying to sound less pathetic.

"If you say so, I am still here for you," he says to me, and I nod. "Let's begin. This is the stick, feel it and become best friends with it." He steps in front of me, grabs my hand, and place a thin metal thing into my hand. I slide the cool metal rod in my hand, and then gently grab its plastic handle. I tighten and release my grip on it, getting the feeling.

"Ok, now what?" I ask as I hold it in my hand and have it pointing in front of me.

"Use it to feel the ground ahead of you so you know when something is near and can avoid it," I nod, moving the stick across the ground and tapping it around. I step forward as I continue and then it hits something in front of it, and I stop. "That's the door," he says, and I just nod again as I hear his footsteps go past me and the click of the door opening. "Now continue." I release a sigh. I must admit, this guy is pretty cool.

I continue to use the stick to guide myself down the hall. And I don't hit anything! Go me!

Half an hour later

"Here's my number. I'm here if you ever need a guy to talk to," Carter says, and I smile. He is actually a pretty cool dude.

"Thanks, man, for the help," I say as I hear him walk to the door.

"Not a problem, I'll chat with you later," he says as he leaves, and I sit up to wait for my mom. I just want to get changed so bad so I can go home! Then, see Payton!

"Mom, hurry up," I mutter and then I can hear the sound of her clicking heels enter the room.

"Oh, calm down," she says as she makes her way to my side. "Here are some clothes," she adds as she places a soft pair of cotton-feeling long things, which my guess is sweatpants and a T-shirt. "What are you waiting for? Your dad's signing the release forms so get changed," she says, and my face brightens with a smile, and I stand up quickly. I shut my eyes and feel my bare back searching for the bow once I find it I rely on my memory to undo it. I allow the stupid hospital gown to slip off my arms and fall in a pile at my feet. I slowly turn around and run my hand across the crumpled bed sheets until they run onto the pile of clothes. I grab the sweats and try to pull them on slowly and carefully, visualizing what I am doing. I then grab the tank shirt and pull it on.

My mother's light chuckling confuses me, and I raise my eyebrows in question. "What?" I ask and wish I could see what was so funny.

"Oh dear, it's nothing just you have your shirt backward. I am only chuckling because it reminds me when you were little and wanted to be different so you wore your shirt backward."

"I was such a backward child," I state, shaking my head.

"Was? Honey, you still are." I chuckle; then, strong, powerful set of footsteps enter the room, and I can tell they are my dad's.

"Ready to go, champ?" he asks, and I smile at his old nickname for me.

"Ready," but am stopped by my mom's voice.

"Here," she says as she comes behind me and slips a jacket over my arms. "Now, let's go," she says a smile in her voice.

I just nod and grab my stick, knowing they will get everything else and slipping my cell phone into my pocket I had to search for. Finally, I use my stick to follow my father's footsteps, and soon, my mother is by my side.

Ding Dong!

The doorbell chimes over my headphones. Since I have been home, all I have done is lie on the comfy, large leather couch and listen to music. I pull my ear buds from my ears and reach for my stick, knowing it's Payton. My mom is upstairs in her home office, working on some design, and dad had to return to his office. I rise up and use my stick to lead myself out of the den and to the door. This whole stick thing is taking a lot of practice and is a little tricky, but I just need time.

I reach the door and place my stick beside it. Sliding my hand over the wood, it finally lands on the cold metal handle, and I twist it pulling it open and am greeted by a cool breeze that carries Payton's strawberry sent with it.

"Payton?" I ask, wanting to make sure even though my body is aware of her presence.

"Hey, Reece. Ready for the next lesson?" she asks, and I can hear a smile in her voice. I nod my head and gesture her inside. As she passes, I can smell her amazing scent and warmth.

"Let's do this," I smile and feel around the door before I finally find my stick. "Follow me," I tell her as I shut my eyes and use my stick to lead me to the den.

I really hope I don't run into anything because that would not be impressive. I really want her to see how far I have come. I just don't know why, though. Ever since she told me about her sister, I feel closer to her, and it is great. I really want to know more because I have a gut feeling that there is.

Chapter Twenty

Payton's POV

I watch as Reece grabs one of those canes and begins walking with it, and I am shocked. Since when could he do that? I follow him through their beautiful house. He leads me into a large room with a huge flat screen TV, three large, black leather couches, a big stone fireplace, and a big bookcase on one wall that is filled with movies and games. I look around in awe, and the walls have family pictures hung on them.

"You can have a sit," Reece's voice says sweetly, and I cannot help but smile as I look back at him.

He is leaning his cane against the back of the leather couch and using his hand to feel his way around to the front of it. "Do you need help?" I ask him, kind of worried for him.

"No, I can do it," he insists, and I nod as I watch him feel his way to the front of the couch with closed eyes and use his hand to sit down. I smile at how he did it even though it took him a little bit. His blue eyes pop open, and I cannot help but stare at them.

"Are you going to sit down?" he asks me with a raised eyebrow even though he was looking a little over to my right.

"Yeah," I say. His eyes flicker to where I stood, and I begin walking towards him and sit down on his left side, dropping my bag at our feet. "When did you learn how to use the cane?" I ask him not being able to handle my curiosity.

"This morning. That's why I am not that good at it yet." He turns his head in my direction.

"I thought you were pretty good," I say to him while I pull the Braille book from my bag.

"Thanks!" he says and then turns his head away from me. "Let's start this lesson," he adds with a smile that seems kind of forced, but I choose to ignore it.

"Alright," I say, cracking the book open. "Let's review first," I instruct as I place the book on his lap, and I quiz him on the letters A to T.

He gets stuck on a few of them but finally, gets them all down.

"Now, onto U," I say as I run his hand over the letter.

"One dot right top, two dots on the bottom," he says as he shuts his eyelids, hiding his blue eyes and feels the dots.

"Correct." I give him a feel more seconds until he stops moving his hand. "Now with V," I say as I place his hand onto the V.

He runs his hand over it; eyes still shut and feel the dots. "Three downs on the right and one on the bottom left," he says as he feels over it. "Now, to the next one," he adds with a smile.

"X." I place his hand on top of it.

He returns to feeling it, and I watch his face in concentration. "Two dots, two on the bottom," he says as he feels them.

"Yeah," I say as he opens his eyes and looks at me with this cute half-smile that makes me smile back. We continue with Y and Z and then lastly W because it's so different.

Once we are done, I quiz him on them, and he begins to get the hang of it. Finally, he sighs and sits back on the couch.

"I am so done for today! Please let's do something else," he says stretching, and I laugh lightly.

"Alright, fine," I groan with a smile, and I shut the book, returning it inside my bag. "Where are your mom and dad?" I ask him as I look around the silent house.

"My mom is in her home office, and dad is at his work," he says and sighs as he shuts his eyes.

"What will we do then?" I ask as I look at him happily.

"Hmm… twenty questions?" he asks smiling, and I groan at his stupid suggestions.

"No, I don't feel like it," I say and look around the room. My eyes go to the TV and movies. "Why don't we watch a movie?" I ask but then stop, feeling like a total idiot. What a bitch I am? I feel so bad. I reach up and place my hand onto my face to rub it.

"Okay, you can watch a movie, and I will listen as long as it is one I know really well," he says calmly, not seeming bothered.

"I am so sorry! I didn't mean to say that! I forgot. It's just I forgot," I say, slumping down and placing my elbows on my knees and my head in my hands.

"Payton, it's fine. I want to try this," he says simply. He says as I feel his hand touches my back, and slightly rubs it. Sparks shot through me, and I begin calming down.

"Okay," I swallow my pity and say as I stand up and walk to the movie case, looking through them. "What's *The Notebook*?" I ask him, turning to look at him.

"You have never seen *The Notebook*? Are you sure you are a girl?" he asks me with his eyes open.

"No, I have not, and yes, I am very sure that I am female."

"Well, it's just my mom and sisters watch that movie a lot so I know it very well. Put it in. We will watch it. Everyone should see it," he says, and I laugh. I walk to the TV and place the DVD into the player.

I walk to the couch, sitting back down beside him, and turning the TV on. Reece has his head still resting against the back of the couch and eyes shut. I feel suddenly cold, and my body shakes.

"Are you cold?" he asks me, opening his eyes.

"A little; my hoodie got ruined by some idiot who ran into me," I say, and he nods as he feels around and then hands me a cotton jacket that I had not noticed before.

"Here," he says, and I take it from him. I slip my arms through the sleeves while looking at the TV and hit play. I snuggle into his jacket which is loose on me and smells like him. It smells like cotton candy, and I love it. I shut my eyes and breathe it in.

"What are you doing?" he asks with a hint of laughter in his voice.

"Nothing," I say quickly as a blush rises on my face.

"Uh-huh, okay," he says with some more laughter.

The movie begins, and I watch it closely. Reece has his eyes shut, but I can tell he is awake and listening. I begin to get a little tired and lean my head against his soft shoulder. His body stiffens a little and then relaxes. The intense sparks flow through me.

I smile as I watch the sweet movie. And I keep my head on his shoulder in a nice, friendly way.

Footsteps enter the room, and I look up seeing Georgia's smiling face. I quickly sit up and pause the movie. "Hey, Payton, would you like to stay for dinner?" she asks me. I think for a second as I look at Reece, who is now sitting up and his blue eyes are shining.

I can either go home or try to find food or eat some good food here. That's an easy one. "Sure, thank you," I say with a smile, and she nods.

"Not a problem dear," she says. "I am going start it now so you, kids, can finish your movie," she says, and I nod my head okay. She leaves the room with a smile, and I turn back to the movie.

"Is this too hard on you?" I ask, referring to the movie.

"No, I am okay. I can see what is happening in my head."

"Okay." I hit play again, leaning my head back onto the couch and holding the jacket close to my body.

The movie continues, and I watch it intently, and before I know it, the movie is over. My face is covered in tears as I try to wipe them fiercely.

"Are you crying?" Reece asks with a smile as his head is turned towards me.

"No! Of course not!" I argue as I wipe the tears away.

"Oh, you are," he teases. I bump my shoulder with him, and we laugh. Times like this, I forget he is blind. At times like this, everything is normal. He is just like every other guy; not blind, but a hot, fun-loving, funny, silly, a tad bit immature, and crazy guy. He's not blind to me right now. He's amazing and perfect. He is the guy I am seriously starting to like because I like spending time with him and can never wait to see him. When I am around him, it is like going to a different world, and I can never get enough of it. I wish he could like me, but that's impossible. He may be blind now, but he would still never date an ugly duckling like me.

Chapter Twenty-One

Reece's POV

I know, I know! What kind of guy watches *The Notebook* willingly? Technically, I am not watching the movie. I am just listening to it! See? I am so smart. Payton's head is resting gently on my shoulder, and I feel the tingles go through me.

I listen closely to the movie and remember the scenes of it in my head.

I hear footsteps enter the room, and Payton sit up quickly. I sit up straight, opening my eyes. I hear my mom's voice fills the room.

"Hey, Payton, would you like to stay for dinner?" she asks her, and Payton is quiet for a second.

"Sure, thank you," Payton says, and I cannot help but smile.

"Not a problem, dear," she says. "I am going start it now so you, kids, can finish your movie," she adds and then I hear her footsteps leave the room.

"Is this too hard on you?" she asks, and I know she is referring to the movie.

"No, I am okay. I can see what is happening in my head," I explain, knowing she probably wouldn't get it.

"Okay." She plays the movie because I hear the noise return. I wish she would lay her head on my shoulder again.

If Payton and I were ever in a relationship, it would be a lot of work. We would have to work 24/7, and it would in no way ever be easy. If I were to get a chance with her, though, I know I would be willing to try. I would do whatever it takes it to make it work because I think she deserves the best.

I shut my eyes and return to imaging the movie. Mostly, I am not paying attention; I just concentrate on Payton's close body heat and smell of strawberries.

Finally, I hear the end of the movie. I can hear some sniffling, and I know Payton is crying. It is impossible not to cry.

"Are you crying?" I ask with a smile as I look towards her.

"Of course not!" she argues, and I chuckle lightly.

"Oh, you are," I reply with a smirk.

I hear footsteps enter the room. They are light ones, so I guess it is a girl. "Hey guys, dinner's done. Come on," Juliet's voice says. I know what she is doing. She's waiting to lead us to the dining room because she doesn't think I will make it. Caring yes, but very aggravating.

I feel the couch moves as Payton stands and I do too. I know she is still beside me because I can hear her heartbeat. So I reach out for her hand but stop midway, feeling stupid. A warm hand connects with mine, and I smile softly as she begins to lead me behind my sister. I don't like being led like a puppy dog, but I honestly don't mind as long as Payton is doing the leading.

We enter a room full of chatter, and Payton places my hand on the chair, and I pull it back a little before feeling my way around so I can sit down. This is going to be awful! I am going to have problems because this is a new element for me. The chairs on both sides of me scrape against the wooden floor as they are pulled back and sat in. I wonder who is where.

"I will be right here the whole time if you need my help," Payton whispers to me, probably noticing my stiffness. I nod and smile likely and look in her direction.

I hear the sound of more people sitting down, and I turn my head back down to where the table should be.

"It's so nice to be here again," my mother's voice says with a crackly sound to it.

"Join hands," my father says, and I feel Payton hesitantly grab my right hand and another soft hand grab my other, which I am assuming is Juliet. I bow my head and shut my eyes, waiting for my dad to say the prayer. "Dear Heavenly Father, we thank you for the food you lay before us. We thank you for keeping us all together and blessing us through this hard time. Thank you so much, God, for looking over Reece and keeping him with us and thank you for leading us to Payton. Bless us and keep us safe. In God's name, we pray. Amen," my dad finishes, and we all say, *amen*.

I hear some sniffling from the left end of the table and look that way wondering what it is about.

"Mom, it's okay," Conner's voice says, and I swallow hard. I know I am a part of the reason she is crying, and it kills me to know I made my family cry.

"Excuse me for a minute," my mom says through sniffles, and I sigh. I want to go comfort her, but I can't. I don't even know which way she went or anything.

"Here, Reece. Eat some soup," Juliet says as I hear the sound of glass clinking. I slowly place my hand on the table and feel for silver wear. I finally touch something metal and run it through my hands, and it feels like a spoon. Next, I try to find the bowl, and I can only imagine how retarded I look. They are all probably staring at me. What an awkward moment?!

"Conner," I hear Rayne's voice whisper lightly. It would be unnoticeable for most people, but for me, it is loud like normal talking.

"Yes, Rayne?" he replies softly, hoping to avoid my ears I guess. It's too late now.

"What is Reece doing?" Rayne asks, and my chest tightens. I know Rayne is young and doesn't fully understand. At the hospital, there weren't a lot of issues with this because I could still seem normal and not face challenges, and she never saw me eat.

"Um... well..." Conner whispers lightly not know what to say. I place the spoon back on the table and close my eyes, holding back the sad feelings. "He was trying to find his bowl," Conner finally says.

"Silly, Reece! It is right in front of him," Rayne says lightly, and it hurts me. I know she's young, but it still hurts not being able to do what I use to and her looking at me like I am crazy and different. Just how everyone else will.

I hear my mother's return, and I sigh, feeling the awkward tension. "Rayne, he can't see that remember?" Conner says even softer, but I can still hear it.

"I f-forgot," she stutters sadly, and I sigh again. Great! I managed to upset someone else!

"Here," a soft voice says beside me and takes my hand, causing shocks and the placing the spoon back in it and then moving my hand to the bowl.

"Thank you," I mutter lightly to her and try to eat some. After some unsuccessful tries, I finally get the hang of it, and the table is full of casual talk.

We finally finish, and my mom and sisters clean the table. "I better get going," Payton's voice says.

"Alright," I say as I take her hand, and we walk to the door; more like she leads me.

"I have to go the hospital tomorrow after school, but I will come by after."

"Alright, be careful," I tell her. If I could still see and was the Reece that could see, I would have been all cute and crap, tucked a strand her hair, leaned down, and kissed her perfect lips, which I can't see let alone locate. I would probably end up kissing the air. Wait! Where did all this kissing talk come from? It's not as if I am seriously starting to like her, is it? Impossible! Well, more impossible she'll like a blind guy. She probably thinks I am weird! I feel her hand still in mine and slowly guide it to my lips. I lightly kiss them and then smile a half-smile up to where I think her head is and then dropped her hand, imagining her disgusted face.

"Good night," I tell her softly. Even though I seriously have an urge to kiss her, I can't, though.

"Good night."

I hear the door open, and she leaves. A small smile stays on my face for a few seconds before reality hits me. I am blind, and my life is different. I am not the guy that girls dream of anymore. I am the freak now.

Chapter Twenty-Two

Payton's POV

His dark eyes glow a dark anger at me. One step at a time, he nears my body, curled in a ball on the floor.

"Get off the ground, you worthless piece of crap! You are spineless! Get up!" His harsh voice bellows and my body shakes as he towers over me.

"P-please, don't," I beg as he glares down at me, and I swallow hard, choking back the tears and knowing what was going to happen next. He bends down and grabs my small body by my shirt and lifts me up onto my feet. He draws back and hits me in my face. I cry out unable to prevent it.

"You ugly, cry baby! I wish you were never born!" he yells in my face, and some spit lands on it. With all the strength I have left, I hold back the tears. He begins hitting me, and each hit hurts until I feel my world darkening and my mom's

voice in a distant screaming. They begin fighting, and then all I see is darkness and his haunting face.

"NO!" I scream as I wake up and realize it had all been a nightmare. Then the haunting truth faces me, it was not a nightmare. It was my past.

I get out of bed and look at the clock, 5:50 AM. Good enough; time to get up I guess. I think as I toss my blanket and get out of my bed fully awake this time. I go to my closet and withdraw a black t-shirt and some jeans along with underwear. I carry them into the bathroom, strip my PJ's and step into the warm shower. I try to wash all the memories away but end up crying. Finally, the tears stop, and I am clean, so I climb out of the shower to get dressed.

I look down at a few fading scars on my arms and a couple on my face that are not noticeable, but I see them. Today is probably not going to be my day.

I brush my hair and leave it hanging around my shoulders. I finish in the bathroom, return to my bedroom, pull on Reece's hoodie jacket on, and then slip on some shoes. I grab my things and head downstairs, knowing my mom is still asleep.

In the kitchen, I grab a banana. I know what you're thinking, why not an apple? Nope, thought I would change it up. Plus, I am out of apples! I peel the yellow skin from the banana and begin eating it and sip my water. I leave the house and walk to the car and climb inside, starting it up and turning the heat on high. It's really chilly this morning. Sitting in the car, I finish my banana and place the peel in the cup holder beside my water. I unscrew the plastic cap of the bottle and take a long drink before recapping it and placing it back down. I shift the car into drive and set out on the journey to school.

I arrive at school and do the same invisible routine of going my locker and then to class. In class, everything goes as normal, and I still remain the same nobody as always. The bell rings, dismissing us to lunch, and I gather my things. In no hurry, I walk casually to my locker, changing out my things. I sling my full back on top of my shoulder and shut my locker door and walk away to the library.

Walking through the library doors, I look to see the librarian's desk empty, so I just shrug and walk through the back case towards the tables and take a seat in one of the hard wooden chairs. I look around the empty, silent room that is until my eyes fall on the slumped shoulders of a hard at work Jace.

Should I talk to him or not? Nope, I think I will just stay here. I decide as I retrieve a book from my bag and crack it open. As I begin to return the time ticks by and I pull Reece's jacket closer to my body without knowing.

"Well, Hi there, Payton," a stupid voice says, interrupting my reading and causing me to look up. I watch as Jace pulls back a chair and then plops down into it.

"Hi," I mumbled, not wanting to deal with him.

"Aren't you just so friendly?" he jokes and gives me one of those charming smiles.

"Totally." I roll my eyes. He bugs me because he has yet to make an effort to see Reece!

"Why do I get this strong feeling you do not like me?" he asks with a raised eyebrow, and I cannot help but snort.

I slam my book shut and look up at him with a slight smirk. "I'm not your biggest fan," I state bluntly. I am not trying to be rude, but this boy just caught me on a bad day.

"How come? I am not a bad guy." Once again, I roll my eyes and place my book back inside the bag.

"Let me ask you one thing. How is Reece? You know your 'best friend'?" I ask him with a raised eyebrow. His face quickly changes along with his attitude.

"He's fine," he obviously lies, and I laugh dryly as I stand up and pick my bag up.

"You honestly have no clue," I state, shaking my head, spinning on my heels and marching away. A tight hand quickly grasps my wrist.

"Wait! How'd you know?" he asks with a confused look on his face.

"Because he's my friend," I say bluntly in anger and tear my wrist from his hand and walk off quickly.

"Ms. Rose?" I say, forcing a smile as I enter her hospital room.

"Payton, is that you? 'Bout time you come visit me!" she scolds playfully, and I smile for real.

"I am sorry, Ms. Rose," I say as I walk over and sit in her chair beside her bed.

"You better have a darn good excuse to where you have been," she says with her warming smile.

"I guess I do. I have been with Reece," I say as I bite my lip, trying to hold back the grin that comes with thinking about him.

Ms. Rose is hair is flat, and her skin is wrinkly. Her eyes look downer than normal. She must not be feeling well. "How is he?" she asks seeming a little more alert.

"He seems good, but different. I feel like he is suffering on the inside and just not talking about it. I am afraid he will blow up soon," I tell her honestly.

Her face twists as she thinks. "Try to get him to open up dear. Get him to talk about it. I see the look on your face as you talk about him, and I know you like him. And he would be crazy not to like you. You are an amazing person and beautiful. So promise me that you will give it a shot."

"I promise. Thanks," I say, swallowing and trying to smile back the tears.

"Good," she smiles, and we continue to talk for the next half an hour. Then I decide to go see Lila. I tell Ms. Rose goodbye and promise to stop by and see her tomorrow.

I leave her room, head down the hall to the elevator and go see Lila. Once I reach Lila's room, I slowly push the door open and hear soft cries. Whose cry is that? I wonder as I walk further inside. I see a brown hair lying in the bed, and she looks up with green, tear-filled eyes.

"Mom?" I whisper softly as I walk towards her crying figure. "What's wrong?" I add once I reach her and place my hand on her back, rubbing small circles on it.

"I'm an awful mom! I missed so much time with her! Her life was not always that great! That is my fault too. I have failed you." She sobs.

"Mom, that's not true at all. You didn't miss anything! Mom, you protected us when he abused us or well me. You shielded us from it as much as you could," I tell her as I scoot in front of her and take her hands into mine.

"I should have done more. I should have made sure you never got hit, and Lila never had to see or hear that," my mom says as tears ski down her checks.

"Mom, listen to me," I instruct her as I stare into her eyes. "There was nothing more you could do. If you did, you'd be dead, and that'd have done us no good. You could not protect us 24/7, and you did your best. What happened was *not* your fault. It was his fault! He is the reason I don't do bad things. He's the reason for all my fears. He is why I cannot trust and why I think so little of myself, mom. It was *him,* not you! Mom, you have always been a great mother and perfect. It is he who was not a father to us. He is to blame definitely, not you! You are a hero to us and one the strongest persons I know. Mom, because of you, I still have a chance." Tears slip down my cheeks.

My mom would try to protect us as best she could. Sometimes she even ended up seriously hurt. I never knew that she blamed herself. It was nowhere near her fault.

"I should have been there more. It's like it is too late now. I feel like I have let you all down," she says as the tears continue to fall. The worst pain I can ever feel is seeing my mother cry. It is an awful, sickening feeling to see your mother cry, or at least, it is for me.

"Mom, it's not too late for me! I am still alive and breathing! Look, Lila is still alive, and there is still time! Mom, you are the best, and I truly love you," I say to her as I have her look at Lila and then back at me.

She sniffles and uses the back of her hand to whip her face. "How about from now on Sundays are our day together? We will come in and see Lila and things like that." My mom offers with a hopeful smile.

"Sounds good, mom." She smiles at me and pulls me into a tight hug that was just so warm and welcoming.

I arrived at Reece's about an hour ago after leaving my mom to head to work. Since I have been here, Reece and I have reviewed the alphabet and started learning words.

"Okay done! No more, Payton," Reece begs just like always, and I laugh lightly.

"Reece, you are such a complainer," I say as I shake my head and then remember he cannot see that. The moment I saw Reece, my mood brightened some, but other than that, I have just decided to fake my happiness.

"I'm not complaining. I just am tired."

"If you are tired now, how will you ever survive school?" I ask him with a raised eyebrow, and his face falls.

"I'm not going back to school," he says simply and looks down at his rough hands.

"Why not?" I ask slightly anger that he does not plan to return to school.

"I don't want to," he says simply, and I can feel his mood shifts as he leans back on the couch.

"You don't want to?" I snort. Why is everyone catching me on my bad day? "So do you honestly think 'I don't want to' is enough of a good reason?" I ask in an 'are-you-serious' voice.

"Going back is just too hard," he complains crossing his arms across his chest. He sounds like a little kid.

"Too hard? Whoever said life was easy, Reece? Have some courage and face your fears! Just because you think it will be too hard, doesn't mean it will. So the only way to truly get over it is to face it. Giving up is like quitting and letting your blindness win. Don't let that happen." I more or less lecture him. He needs to wake up and smell the freaking coffee. The shooting took his sight not his courage.

"Amen, Payton! You tell him," Juliet smiles as she walks into the room and sits down in the chair across from us. She crosses her leg over the other, and I take in her shocking look. She is wearing ripped skinny jeans, vans, and a red tank top with a black jacket over top.

Reece suddenly sits up quickly and his face changes to an unrecognizable face. "Juliet, have you been smoking again?" Reece asks in a scary tone. Juliet looks caught off guard and nervous.

"No, it was my friends not me. If you don't believe me, smell my breath," she says simply, and he just shakes his head.

"Good, because it will kill you," Reece tells her and leans back on the couch.

"Yes, dad," she says with sarcasm and smirks. "Anyhoo, Payton what are you doing Friday?" Juliet asks me with a friendly smile.

"Absolutely nothing," I say after thinking for a second.

"Great! Come over for family movie night," she says with a smile, and I look at Reece, who just smiles and shakes his head as if he knows something.

"Sure," I say with a shrug of my shoulders. It is now official. I cannot wait until Friday! Movie night with this amazing family and the guy I like. Like? Do I like him? Yeah, I think I just may. Now, if I tell him or not or act on it is a different story and is honestly not likely. What an emotional day today has been and now I just cannot wait for Friday. Who knows what it has in store for me? But I do know I get spend extra time with Reece!

Chapter Twenty-Three

Reece's POV

"Sweetie, I can have someone stay with you," my mom says to me as I sit on my comfortable bed. She is getting ready to go to work and is being all motherly and freaking out.

"No, mom, I am a big kid. I don't need a babysitter," I groan as I lean against my headboard.

"Well, Conner only has one class today so he will be home in an hour or two. Keep your phone on you at all times and call if you need anything. Your cane it still beside you." I nod my head. I am a little annoyed by the fact that she is treating me like I am five!

"Got it, mom. I am fine. I can handle it." I grunt, and I stare straight ahead.

"Okay, okay," she says, giving up. "I will see you later. I love you, son," my mom says as I hear her step closer to me and then I feel her lips press against my forehead in a motherly way.

"I love you too, mom." I hear her heels click against the floor as she leaves the room. I don't hear the door shut so I figure she left it open.

I slide down my bed until my head rests on the pillow and pull the headphones from around my neck. I then place them in my ear as I lay back on my bed facing the ceiling. "Play music," I command, and the music begins to feel my ears.

Slowly, my eyes drop shut, and my mind just hears the music as I near sleep. I haven't been able to get a lot of sleep lately. Nightmares have been haunting me dreams.

I see the track lying ahead of me, and the stands are full of supporters. I scoot down in starting position with my rear end in the air. I glance to my left, seeing the turf with my teammates standing on top of it. Then I glance to my right to see the other runners lined up on their spots. I rock on my heels as I wait for the gun to fire.

Bang! The gun sounds and I push off my weight and begin to run, taking the lead. As I round the first turn of the track, I take a nice lead from the others. I shut my eyes gently and let my feet carry me around the track that is imprinted into my brain.

Lap after lap, I allow the cooling air to brush my face as I continue to run. I look to my side and see a guy a good distant back. So I keep running and see the blue ribbon ahead of me and push my legs harder. Finally, it breaks across my waist, and a large smile stretches across my face as I hold my arms in the air. Arms wrap around me, and I look around into the faces of my cheering teammates.

"Great job, Reece!" one says, and that is followed by many other "Congratulations!" on winning states again.

"Awesome job, man," Jace says as he hugs me. He is in his uniform too.

"Thanks, buddy," I reply as I smile like a madman. I cannot. I just won Indiana State Track Champion again.

"Reece!" A sweet, girly voice screams and Jace step away, giving me a wink. I roll my eyes but still smiling as I watch Clair comes bouncing and bolting towards me, her blonde curls flowing behind her. She flings her thin arms around my neck and hugs me tightly. She then pulls away from me and smiles up at me with her gorgeous gray eyes. "Baby, you were amazing!" she says with a big smile.

"Thanks, sweetie," I tell her as I smile down at her. She leans up and connects her lips with mine, sending my body into an even greater happiness. The kiss is sweet and perfect. I really love this girl. We pull apart resting our foreheads on each other, and I watch as she slowly opens her gray eyes. I smile at her, and she smiles back.

"I love you so much," she says with her loving eyes.

"I love you more," I reply as I kiss her lightly and then just hold her against my chest.

Clair is the greatest girlfriend ever. She is sweet, innocent, nice, gorgeous, and she is a softball player along with track runner. We met started dating the first day of freshman year, and this is our second year together. Nothing was going tear us apart.

My stomach growling wakes me from my memories. I sit up in my bed and ignore the unpleasant darkness.

"When did I get so hungry?" I ask myself. Reaching over to the side of my bed, I feel around for my stick and finally, find it. I use it to steady myself. Once I did, I then begin to search my path, making sure there is nothing in front of me. I tap around finally making it out the door and down the hall as I continue to tap to avoid everything in my way. I enter another room and then a dilemma hit me. I don't know where the stupid ass cabinets are! Heck, I am not even sure where I am! My brain is so cloudy from trying to think.

Crap! Where am I? This sucks now what do I do? I cannot stay here, but I cannot call my mom because then she will never leave me alone again. I can't call my dad. He's busy. Juliet is at school, and Conner is in class, and I am lost in my own home! Freaking great! I don't even know what time it is. If I kept walking, I would just end up lost more. What to do? *What to do?*

Sighing, I gently sit down and then proceed to just lie down, shutting my eyes and waiting for someone to come home.

"Reece, I'm home!" Conner calls through the voice, causing me to shot up straight and run my hand through my hair. Finally! It has been forever!

"In here!" I call back still, sitting on the floor. I can hear footsteps walking through the hall and then finally enter the room.

Conner lightly chuckles as he nears me. "Why are you on the ground?" he asks in confusion, and his footsteps stop beside me.

"Well... I am kind of lost," I tell him honestly as I scratch the back of my head.

"How long have you been here?" he asks, and I smile sheepishly.

"A while," I reply with a slow nod.

"And where were you headed?" he asks as I feel him grab one of my hands and tug me up.

"Kitchen. I am hungry," I reply, and he chuckles again.

"Alright, come on, little brother. Let's get you something to eat," he says, and I groan.

Could my life get any worse? Oh no, I'm trusting him to make my food. Crap! He will probably make me sick. On the other hand, I really want food. I am starving. Oh, I will eat anything he makes me, I don't care it's not like I can see it.

I thought this would be a little easier than it is. This is actually totally hard, and I just hope it will all get better. I need it to. Maybe I

Chapter Twenty-Four

Payton's POV

The next couple days play out similar to Tuesday. I go to school, then to the hospital to see Lila and Ms. Rose, and then I go to Reece's house and do a lesson before coming home doing homework and going to bed.

Now, it is finally Friday morning, and I am flipping through my clothes stupidly. I want to look nice, but it's not like he would actually see what I am wearing. You can't blame a girl for trying. I just really want to look nice since I kind of like him. This is so darn stressful! I groan as I tug my hand through my hair and stare at what clothes that are hanging in my closet.

I choose a black and gray V-neck with some dark fitting blue jeans. I carry them to the bathroom and change into them. The shirt actually fits me nicely, and the jeans hug all the right places. I smile as I brush my teeth and then brush my curls untangling them. Once I am done, I look at my reflection satisfied because this is as good as it will get. With that, I head back to my room, pulling on Reece's hoodie and as I do, a smile spreads on my face. Then I slip on my shoes and grab my things as my stomach does a nervous flip flop.

I really don't want to eat anything so I just quickly grab a banana and walk towards the door already starting to shake, and I have to still get to school.

I slip into my seat in English just like every morning and bounce my foot up and down with nerves. The bell rings, and the kids poor in. Mrs. Reed begins teaching when a knock comes from the door, and everyone looks up. Mrs. Reed walks over to the door that is locked and opens it slightly, sticking her head out to speak with the person. She shuts the door and walks back to the broad.

"Payton, you need to go see the counselor, Ms. Payne," Mrs. Reed says, and I sigh as I put my things into my bag and stand up heading for the door.

Why does she need to see me? I can't be in trouble! Great, this really helps my already nervous nerves.

I slowly walk down the hall, shaking as I see her office near ahead of me. I reach her office door and knock on it, waiting for her to open it. Once it opens a smiling woman in her twenties with blonde hair in a bob cut gestures me inside. Her eyes are dark green, and she's wearing one of those skirt suits.

"Payton, how are you?" she asks with a large smile as I walk towards the leather chair across from her desk. She walks towards her desk after closing the door shut.

"I am good. How are you?" I ask being polite to her.

"I am good. Thanks. Have a seat dear," she says as she sits down in her rolling chair. I smile, sit down, and fold my hands in my lap, nervously fiddling with them. "Well, dear, you know it's almost February, and you are close to graduating. I have this big thing to talk with you about. The way it is looking, you are going to be Valedictorian. So I just wanted to give you the good news," she says with a large smile.

Valedictorian? No! Good news? Is she crazy? That's awful news! That requires speaking in front of a lot of people. My two biggest fear, public speaking, and being the center of attention.

I mean, don't get me wrong, this is a wonderful honor but all those people.

Hope you don't puke, my stupid voice says inside my head.

"Do I have to?" I ask with a sick-looking face. If I was nervous before, there is nothing to compare to this.

"Yes, you should be happy! You worked hard for this, and it's a big honor! Are you afraid of speaking?" she asks me with a frown.

I look at my trembling hands and nod shyly.

"Aww, dear, don't be afraid. But just for a second, forget about the speech and think about being Valedictorian itself," she says, and I shut my eyes, forgetting everything about the speech.

Payton Jennings, Valedictorian of her Senior Class. It has a nice ring to it! I cannot believe the work paid off! This is so unreal! What is crazier is I am graduating soon! Time has flown by!

"You are right. It is an honor," I say with a smile.

"It is, and don't worry about the speech for now. I will help you with it in March. Now, get back to class and enjoy the news, Miss Valedictorian."

"Thank you," I say with a bright smile and stand up quickly. I walk to the door and head back to my class.

My visit at the hospital was kind of quick. Ms. Rose and I talked for a while and then I went to see Lila for a little and then I headed to the Collins. I told Reece yesterday that I am giving him a day off from his Braille lesson.

I stand on their front porch as I knock on the door. No answer. That is strange. I slowly creak open the door just a crack and hear a banging and swear words echoing through the halls.

I step inside and follow where I hear the angry voice was coming from. I turn a corner into a room that I remember is the game room and see Reece sitting up and rubbing his head. His brown hair is messy, and his eyes look frustrated.

"Reece, are you okay?" I ask with a weak voice almost in fear.

"Yeah! I am just freaking peachy! I can't do anything myself! I can't make it through my house! I run into walls! I can never see anything ever again! I have lost everything! I have lost football, track, baseball and my friends! My mom treats me like a five-year-old! I can barely do anything on my own! So yes, I am okay," he shouts in anger and frustration.

I have never seen Reece like this. He is usually so sweet and caring and makes it seem like he is ok. This time is different. It's as if he has been holding this all in and now, exploded.

As he stands, I see a tear fall down his cheek, and he shuts his eyes, walks forward and touches the wall, uses his hand to find the doorway and then disappears. I am frozen in my spot and speechless. *He didn't mean to yell at me,* I tell myself and quickly follow behind him and into another room. I look around taking in all the trophy's, ribbons and pictures hanging on the blue walls as a sign of this being his room.

Reece is sitting on the edge of his bed with his head in his hands. I take a deep breath as I near him. "Reece," I whisper his name once I reach him. His body stiffens, and I sit down next to him.

"Payton, I am sorry. I snapped," he mumbles, and I reach over grabbing his hand.

"It's okay. I just wasn't expecting it. I guess I never realized how hard this must be on you. But Reece, I'm your friend, and I will be here for you no matter what," I tell him as I squeeze his hand.

He lifts his head up so that his eyes are facing my face, and I am staring at him. "You know one of the hardest parts about all of this?" he asks me with a frown.

"Not being able to see?" I guess, and he chuckles lightly as he shakes his head.

"Not being able to see how beautiful you are," he says with a serious face, and I am taken back. Did Reece Collins just say that to me?

"I am not beautiful, though." I disagree with him.

"Yeah, you are." he tightens his hand around mine. My hormones kick into overdrive.

"You don't know that," I argue, and he sighs.

"I want to try something. Just trust me and sit still please," he says with a voice sounding desperate, clinging to any hope it can.

"Alright," I say, shutting my eyes and holding still.

Reece's hand slips from mine and slowly slides up my arm over my shoulder and up my neck to my face. His almost rough warm hand travels softly over my cheek bone. His fingers lightly brush my eyelids lightly, and then his hand moves over my forehead gently and back down my face. His hand rests under my chin while his thumb runs gently over my lip.

My body is on fire from all the sparks that are shooting through me at his touch. His thumb continues to move slowly over my lip. I felt his warm breath beating on my face, and it smells like wintergreen.

I feel a tingle erupt through my lips and a soft, warm pair of lips on mine. His hand rests on my cheeks as he kisses me. It's so sweet and caring. This is my first kiss, and it is with Reece Collins? I have died and gone to heaven because this is the perfect first kiss. It is so innocent and sweet. He pulls away pressing his forehead to mine.

"See, you are so beautiful," he whispers, and I smile as I open my eyes and stare into his perfect blue ones. Does this mean we are dating? No, it was just a kiss — a kiss that means the world to me.

"We're back!" Juliet's voice screams, and Reece and I pull apart. I stand up and so does he.

"Let's go! It's movie night!" I say, and he nods as he reaches over and takes my hand so I can lead him to the kitchen.

Once we get there, I am greeted by a smiling Juliet in some black skinny jeans and a white T-shirt. She looks at me with a bright smile. Georgia is already pulling things from the cabinet to make for dinner and Rayne is sitting on one of the counters, swinging her little legs back and forth. A smile is stuck on my face as I can still feel the kiss. I glance up and look up at his face which has a smile on it too.

"Movie night! Are you guys ready?" Juliet asks as she walks over to us. Movie night this is going to be so much fun! I just cannot wait. Reece and I may not be dating or anything, but I think there could be something there. Or at least, I hope there is. I just want this movie night to begin so I can forget my stress and have fun! I nod my head excitedly.

Chapter Twenty-Five

Reece's POV

The rest of the week carries on like normal. I made Conner swear to not tell my mom about me getting lost. However, luck is not on my side because Wednesday I got lost again and this time, it was my mother who found me, and now, no one ever leaves me home alone which is so freaking annoying. Conner has helped me surprisingly. He told me to shut my eyes and imagine our house, and if I know exactly where I am, I can use the image to find my way. I also have my stick to use. Slowly, I am making progress. It is not big or great, but at least it's something. For the rest of the week, I also have this excitement inside of me for Friday, not for movies because I can't exactly watch them, but for seeing Payton!

I open my eyes as I hear Rayne's little feet running down the halls. I sit up in my comfy bed, swing my legs off on one side, and reach my hand out to feel around my cane. I stand on my feet as I stretch, cracking my back, and then using my cane to steer me over to my closet. Once I reach the wall, I gently press my hand against it and allow myself to feel around the wall for the handle. Finally, my hand grasps the cool, metal handle. I twist it, opening my closet door and feel the inside from left to right. I run my hand over the clothes and feel the different types of fabrics. I feel a cotton shirt sleeve shirt and pull it out. Then I move my hand to the right side of my closet and feel the denim material of jeans. I pull out a pair that is thin. I lay it over the shirt on my arm and step back and use my cane to get myself back over to my bed.

As I reach the bed, I lay the clothes on it and feel for the cotton material of my shirt. Once my fingers find it, I move it around until I feel the opening at the bottom, and then I reach up and find which side has the tag. Once I figure that out, I pull it over my head the right way and down covering my bare chest. Then I feel down to my waist and grab my pajama bottoms and slowly push them off. I sit down gently on the edge of my bed and hold them jeans with the buttons and pull them up to my knees before standing up again and pulling them to my waist and buttoning them.

I smile at my success. See, I am getting better at this? I grab my cane and use it to find my way to my bathroom adjoining my room. Once I feel my feet leave the carpet and step onto the tiles, I know I enter my bathroom. I turn to my left where the stick should be and grab my comb that I feel resting on the counter. I hold it and use it to brush my hair that is starting to get a little bit longer than normal. I then reach out and grab a hold of my toothbrush and the tube of toothpaste, feeling around and trying to figure them out. With my right hand, I reach up finding the knob and twisting it, and the sound of water pours from the faucet. I place the toothbrush under it and then brush my teeth. Once I am done, I return to my room and sit on my bed.

Knock, knock

I turn my head to where the knocking it coming from. "Come in," I call as I wait for whomever it is to enter.

The door creaks open and footsteps enter. "Hey, honey, you got yourself all dressed by yourself?" my mom's voice asks in a caring yet annoying tone.

"Yes, mom, believe it or not, I am capable of things like that," I mutter in response. I know it was rude, but I cannot help it. Her clinging is just too much for me. She is suffocating me.

"Sorry. I am getting ready to take Rayne and Juliet to school. Conner is still here and your father's already at work," my mom says.

"Alright then," I respond.

"Let Conner know if you need anything," she says, and I nod. "I love you, sweetie," she says, and I nod.

"I love you too," I sigh and then hear her footsteps leave. Picking up my phone, I fall back on my bed.

"Call Carter," I say and then hear my phone ringing.

"Hey, man!" Carter says in a happy tone.

"Hey, what's up?" I ask as I run a hand through my hair.

"Nothing, how are you doing?" he asks me, and I sigh.

"Not too good. This cane fucking sucks!" I complain to him, and he chuckles lightly.

"Guessing you ran into things?" he asks, and I groan. "That would be a yes," he then says.

"I wish there were another way."

"There is. What are you doing tomorrow?"

What am I doing tomorrow? Nothing just like every other day, my life is so boring now! "Nothing," I reply.

"Alright. Now, you are," he says, and we talk about our plans for a little longer until he has to go.

I decide to practice my Braille with the cards Payton left for me. Man, I cannot wait for Payton to get here! I am really starting to like her as crazy as it seems.

The doorbell rings, and I stand up from where I am sitting in the game room. Conner had to go pick up Rayne, and my mom and Juliet went by the store on their way home, leaving me here by myself. The doorbell ringing makes me so excited because I know it can only be one person, Payton! So I quickly and, may I say, stupidly get up and rush towards the doorway forgetting my cane. My body slams into a hard object, and I fall backward on my butt. I hiss in pain. "Shit! Fuck that hurt, stupid ass wall!" I swear up a storm as I sit up rubbing my head frustrated! I am so freaking stupid for running into that dang wall!

"Reece, are you okay?" a voice asks that I automatically know as Payton's. I didn't hear her enter because of my annoyance.

"Yeah! I am just freaking peachy! I can't do anything myself! I can't make it through my house! I run into walls! I can never see anything ever again! I have lost everything! I have lost football, track, baseball and my friends! My mom treats me like a five-year-old! I can barely do anything on my own! So yes, I am okay," I yell at her. And I know it's mean of me, and I am being an ass, but I can't help it, it slips. My frustration builds, and everything piles up, and I explode. I push myself off the ground, and a tear slips from my eyes.

Closing my eyes, I hold out my hand to touch the wall and then use it to lead me to the hallway and to my room. Once in my room, I stumble to my bed and sit down on the edge resting my head in my hands. I hear footsteps enter the room a few seconds later.

"Reece," Payton whispers my name as she walks softly towards me and my body stiffens slightly as she sits down next to me. How can she do that? Why doesn't she hate me? I was a complete ass to her! Why didn't she leave like everyone else outside my family would? She didn't leave. That says something.

"Payton, I am sorry. I snapped," I mumble. I seriously do feel bad for it. She didn't do anything but tried to help. Her warm and grabs a hold of mine and warms up my whole body.

"It's okay. I just wasn't expecting it. I guess I never realized how hard this must be on you. But Reece, I'm your friend, and I will be here for you no matter what," she says to me as she squeezes my hand.

I lift my head up in the direction I know she is sitting and ask, "You know the hardest part about all of this?"

"Not being able to see?" she says unsurely, and I cannot help the light chuckle that leaves me and shakes my head. Of course, that's what she thinks it would be.

"Not being able to see how beautiful you are," I tell her honestly. I would give anything to have one more look at her. To see her brown eyes, her brown hair, and her lips.

"I am not beautiful, though," she says in a serious voice. How can she not see just how beautiful she really is?

"Yeah, you are," I say as I tighten my hand around hers in hopes to get my point across.

"You don't know that," she argues with me, and I sigh. I wish there were some way I could show her. Just then an idea hits me.

"I want to try something. Just trust me and sit still please," I say this is a chance I need her to agree.

"Alright," she says to me, and I smile.

I let go of her hand and move my hand up her arm to her shoulder and up her neck to her face. Her skin is so soft like velvet. I run my hand gently over her cheekbone, memorizing each piece of her face. The feeling of my hand on her skin has shocks going through me, and I would be lying if I said there wasn't a desire building inside of me. I feel her soft eyelashes brush my fingers as I go over her eyes. Then, slowly I move my hand to her smooth forehead and then back down the other side of her face drinking in her features.

I place my hand under her chin and rub my thumb over her lips. Her lips are soft and perfect like to clouds that I want to get lost in. The desire inside of my just keeps building, and all I can think about is what it would feel like to have her lips on mine. If I kiss her, though, she may pull away in disgust; this could risk everything. I feel my head lower to where my thumb is. Gently, I replace my thumb with my lips and kiss her softly. To my surprise, she doesn't retreat. She continues to kiss me. This kiss wasn't about lust. There was a lot more to it than that. Her lips were so innocent and tasted like a delicious sweetness. This is the best kiss I ever had. I pull away slightly and lean my forehead on hers. This kiss was so much better than any kiss I ever shared with any other girl. That includes my first love, Clair. We had dated freshman and sophomore year before she left for the summer, and we grew apart ending. This kiss was a million times better than that, and it has me talking like a sap now.

"See, you are so beautiful," I tell her. I know one kiss doesn't mean we are dating, but she didn't pull away or freak out so maybe I can actually stand a chance with her.

"We're back!" Juliet calls, and I groan lightly. Curse you, sister, for ruining the moment! We pull apart, and I feel Payton stand up so I do too.

"Let's go! It's movie night!" she says to me, and I nod reaching over to take her hand, partly because I lost my stick and partly because I need her touch. She leads me off to where Juliet must be.

I can hear pots and pans once we enter a room so I take it that we are in the kitchen. A smile is stuck on my face as we stand together; I can't stop replaying the feeling of her lips on mine. It was addicting.

"Movie night! Are you guys ready?" Juliet asks as I hear her footsteps near me.

"Yeah!" Payton says happily.

"Kids, it's dinner time!" my mom yells, saving me from having to listen to another moment of my sister's and Payton's chatter.

I stand up and feel Payton grab my hand, and I know it's her from the tingles. She leads me to the dining room and places my hand on the back of the chair allowing me to feel my way and sit down. Taking a deep breath, dinner begins, and we have hot dogs. My mom had already fixed mine for me. Subtle, I know.

I reach to my plate and carefully lift my hotdog up to my mouth and take a small bite of it. Once I get it down, I continue to eat it.

The conversation continues around the table. "Payton how is school?" my mom asks her, and I stiffen a little with the mention of it.

"It's good. I am actually Valedictorian this year. Just found out today," she says, and I smile. That's so great for her. I am truly proud. I would have been Salutatorian if it wasn't for the shooting.

"That is so wonderful, dear!" My mom exclaims happily.

"That is very good, Payton," my dad says to her in his kind, fatherly tone.

"That is good," I tell her as I lean over to where she should be and whisper to her.

"Thanks," she whispers back. After we finish eating, everyone is so excited for the movies so we all retreat to the den.

Payton leads me to a couch, and I sit down on it and feel the leather beneath my hands. Payton sits beside me, and I can feel her body's warmth. "I am going sit beside you, bro," Conner says, and I feel the other side of me sink. I hear people sitting down on the other couches.

"What should we watch?" my mom asks.

"*A Walk to Remember*!" Juliet shouts, and I groan, not another Nicolas Sparks movie.

"*Fast and the Furious*!" Conner shouts back from beside me.

"How about a vote guys? Who want to watch *A Walk to Remember*?" my mom asks and then I hear her counting.

"Majority rules. Sorry, guys," my mom says, and I groan. Here goes another crying fest. I reach up and wrap my arm around Payton's shoulders and lean my head back shutting my eyes so I can picture what's happening. I haven't got it to where I can do that with my eyes open yet.

I hear the music start and know its beginning. This is a good movie, but so unmanly. On the bright side, at least, I have my arm around a gorgeous girl's shoulders. I wish I could call her my girl. Maybe someday, I will.

Chapter Twenty-Six

Payton's POV

This movie is really good so far, and the actor who plays Landon is mighty fine! I have honestly never seen this, and I only voted for it because the girls did. At first, I was not sure if I would be able to actually be able to concentrate on this movie because of the wonderful, perfect arm that is around my shoulders. How can anybody be so amazing? Isn't there a law against that? More importantly, why me?

Back to the point, I didn't think I would be able to pay attention, but it turns out this is a really good movie so far and is hard not to pay attention to! Who knew? I rest my head lightly on his shoulder and smile. I steal a peek up at his face to see a cute little grin resting on it. My smile grows a little larger as I look back on the TV. I never thought I'd be sitting here with my head on Reece Collin's shoulder. If someone had told me this would happen, I would have laughed in their faces and ask what they've been smoking?

The room is quiet as the movie continues, and I smile. Is this what real families are like? It is really nice. For the next half hour maybe, I'm not sure; I sit there against Reece and feel so comfortable and safe.

A big smile stretches on my face because of something during the movie. I have never really been a fan of romance, but I quite like this one. A smile spreads across my face even bigger this time. I wish Reece, and I could be like Jamie and Landon. It's so sweet. Not too long later, I feel Reece's body stiffen, and I look up at him in question, but his face is blank and gives away nothing.

The part that he must have been dreading came on, and as it finished, I cannot help but cling to Reece's chest and hold him tightly. The tears come pouring out of my eyes. Reece's hand finds my back and begins to gently rub it as I sob into his chest.

"Shhh... it's okay, sweetie," Reece whispers, and I continue to cry. This just brings up my sister to me and how she must have felt, and what my mom and I had to deal with.

I am not going to lie. I lay there and cry as memories of my sister goes through my mind. Reece holding me tightly to his chest, I calm down and finish the movie which has a happy but horribly sad ending! I find myself crying all over again in fear of that actually happening to me.

I look up at Reece with teary eyes to see the light from the TV showing shining tears falling down his cheek. I look around the room, hearing, seeing, sobbing and find that Georgia is curled up in Leonardo's arms also crying. Rayne and

Juliet are holding each other crying. I peek over Reece and find Mr. Manly, Conner, sitting with his arms crossed firmly over his chest with a face of concentration, but my eyes catch a small tear falling from his eyes.

I sit up from Reece's chest and whip my face off with the back of my hand. His arm is still draped over my shoulder. Finally, the rest of the sobs come to a stop, and I try my hardest not to think about the movie because if I do right now, I will cry again.

"Oh! Payton, dear it's so late! I would hate for you to drive home in the dark! Would you like to stay the night here?" Georgia asks as she whips her eyes. She then smiles at Leonardo and kisses him lightly on his cheek before standing up with a small, sincere smile on her face.

I really hate leaving my mom by herself. It kills me, but I am just too tired to drive, which I blame on all the dumb crying. "Sure, thank you. I will just call my mom," I say as I stand up and walk to the hallway.

"If she wants, I will talk to her!" Georgia calls. I know she would. Georgia is the talker in the family and so nice and sweet. It's hard not to love her. She is like the idea mom. Leonardo, on the other hand, is a man of a few words. Very few. Yet, he gives off this vibe of being the "sheriff" if you would like and enforcing the rules. He seems really nice and kind though just like the idea father.

I press Number Two on speed dial, and it rings. "Hello?" my mom says on the third ring.

"Hey, mom," I say with a smile. I love my mom's voice it makes me feel so safe and loved.

"Oh, sweetie! Hey! I have to pull an all-nighter," my mom says to me, sounding sad as she refers to her work.

"Oh, it's okay. I was calling see if it was okay if I stay the night here with Reece and the Collins'?" I ask biting my lip.

"That would be great. I always worry about you when you are alone," she says with a soft voice. I then hear someone shout her name. "I got to go, sweetie! I love you so very much! Have a good night! Talk to you in the morning!"

"Okay, I love you too mom." We say goodbye before I go back in the room. "It's fine with her," I say, giving Georgia a weak smile.

"Great, well, off to bed we go! You can sleep in Reece's room if you want," she says and then kisses all her kids a goodnight and even me too. Then, Ms. Bouncy Georgia disappears up the stairs.

"Night, kids. Behave," Leonardo says, hugging all the kids and even me, which shocks me but makes me happy. He's so fatherly. He leaves and disappears behind Georgia.

"Well, I am going to take munchkin up. Night, y'all," Conner says as he scoops a droopy-eyed Rayne into his arms and walks off with her.

"Well, I am off. You two behave yourselves and try keeping it down," Juliet jokes and shoots me a wink.

I laugh, rolling my eyes, and she trots off.

"Sorry about my family. They can be a bit... much," he chuckles, and I laugh too. I grab his hand and lead him to his room. His hand slips from mine, and he walks to his bed. "If you want, you can get a shirt from my dresser," he says.

"Okie Dokie," I say as I walk to his wooden dresser and pull out a white shirt.

Turning around, I see Reece shirtless undoing his jeans revealing his mouthwatering abs. I mean I have never seen a body that amazing before. It's indescribable. They are tan, not too much but not too little. Just perfect! Once his jeans are off, he is just in his blue boxer that is a little low, showing his hot V that leads down to, yeah, you know where. My heartbeat picks up, and I blush lightly as he runs his hand through his hair.

He turns around, giving me a nice view of his butt and feels around his bed before pulling back the cover and crawling inside and looking my way.

"Could you... um... shut your eyes?" I ask, biting my lip.

"May I ask why? I am blind. I cannot see you." I feel the blood rush to my cheeks. *Whoops.*

I quickly change into his shirt which smells like him, and it is amazing. The shirt is big on me and falls mid-thigh, which doesn't matter since he can't see. But I swear, sometimes, I forget that. Slowly, I walk on the other side the bed and crawl in.

Reece rolls over, and I stare into his blue eyes. "Payton?" he whispers, his breath fanning my face.

"Yes?" I whisper back, hoping I don't have bad breath! That would be embarrassing.

"Can you come with me tomorrow morning? Carter, my new friend, and I are going somewhere. I really want you to come with. Please?" he says, and his face is serious. Who is Carter and what are they up too? I wonder. Only one way to see.

"Sure," I say with a smile and kiss his cheek. He smiles back.

"Good night, Payton," Reece says to me with a smile and shuts his eyes, wrapping one arm around my waist.

"Good night, Reece," I reply as I snuggle close to his chest. This is the most amazing feeling in my life. I can definitely get used to this. I just cannot wait for tomorrow! I wonder what he's up to. With a smile and breathing in Reece's amazing scent and feeling his warmth, I drift into a great night sleep.

Chapter Twenty-Seven

Reece's POV

"Conner! Give it back now!" a girly voice shouts loudly, and I open my eyes to the darkness that I am beginning to get used to. I stretch slightly and feel a soft hand on my chest. I move my arms slightly, feeling that I have something warm and amazing smelling in my arms — Payton.

"Never!" Conner shouts as I hear loud footsteps run across the floor above me.

I wonder if Payton is asleep. Well, I don't see how she could still be asleep. They are so loud! Listening to her breathing, it sounds a little too fast for her to be asleep.

"Are you awake?" I whisper lightly as I listen to Conner and Juliet continues to fight.

"Conner, I warn you. If you do not give it back, I will cut you balls off in your sleep!" Juliet says quite loudly and, to be honest, if I were Conner, I'd give up now.

Payton moves a little in my arms. "Yeah, it's kind of hard to sleep," she laughs lightly.

"I apologize once again for my family." My family can be very, embarrassing at times.

"Don't be, they are very entertaining," she laughs again, and I smile. Her laugh is one of the most beautiful things I have ever heard.

"Want some breakfast?" I ask, figuring my mom's probably up making it.

"Sure," Payton says, and I feel her moving and sitting up. Slowly, I sit up to and swing my legs off of the side of the bed.

"Do you see my cane anywhere?" I ask not remembering where I left it. The den, I think?

"Um…" Payton says, and I feel her weight leaving the bed meaning she is standing up. "Yeah, there it is! Someone must have brought it back in here," she says as I hear her walking across my room.

"Can you bring it to me, please?" I ask her as I stay seated on my bed.

"Sure," she says kindly, and I hear her footsteps near me. "Here." I reach out, and she places my guide stick in my hand. "What time is your friend picking us up?" she then asks me.

"Well, what time is it now?" I ask wondering how long we have.

"It's… um… 9:00 AM," she says and walks a little.

"Okay, he'll be here at twelve, so we should eat and then get ready," I tell her as I stand up with my cane.

"Okay, wait, can I borrow some bottoms?" she asks me with a nervous tone in her voice.

"Go for it," I tell her and then hear her footsteps and my closet door opening.

A few minutes later, I hear her footsteps approach me. "Let's go," she says, and I smile and nod. Payton slips her warm hand into my left one, and I hold my cane in my right hand as we leave my room and head to the kitchen.

The sound of a frying pan sizzling feels my ears, so I take it as we are now in the kitchen. "Morning, Georgia," Payton says kindly.

"Good morning to you too!" my mom's happy voice says. "Breakfast is up. Have a seat," she says, and I can hear the smile in her voice. Payton leads me to the small table that sits in our large kitchen.

She does the usual, placing my hand on the back of the chair, and I sit down. I hear the chair beside me pull out, and I can feel her beside me.

"Here you kids go," my mom's voice says as I hear a plate set down in front of me as the glass contacts the wood.

The smell of bacon and biscuits feels my nose so I gently reach on my plate and pick up a crispy piece of food. I am going to say bacon from its bumpy feeling. I continue to eat, and I also hear Payton chewing her food. Yes, I realize just how creepy that is!

"Mom! I hate Conner!" Juliet complains as her footsteps enter the room.

"What's new?" my mom asks, and Juliet groans as she slides out the chair and sits at the table.

"Gee, thanks, mom," she mutters from near me, and I can just imagine her giving my mom a pouty face.

"You are welcome," my mom say sarcastically back at her, and I cannot help but chuckle. I must admit my family can be pretty entertaining in the morning time.

"Juliet, can Payton borrow some clothes for today please?" I ask her hoping she'd say yes.

"Sure, as long as I can help her get ready," Juliet says which is very typical for her.

"I don't know. That's up to her," I say shrugging my shoulders and pushing myself from the table a little.

Payton is quiet for a while and then finally replies. "Sure, let's get this over with," she sighs, and I hear Juliet clap happily.

"Let's go! We will be back, Bubby," Juliet says, and I can hear her and Payton stand and then walk away.

Sighing, I stand up grabbing my cane and begin to leave the kitchen. "Honey, need any help?" my mom's voice stops me.

"No, I am fine," I mutter and then continue my way to my room where I get ready.

"Are we almost there?" I ask Carter as I sit in the front seat of his car, and Payton is on the back.

"Five more minutes; tops," Carter say calmly, and I groan. We have been in this car for the past hour and to be honest, my butt is numb!

"Where are we going?" Payton asks us for the able hundredth time. It feels like it!

"You will see soon," I say as I rest my head back on the comfy headrest.

"Ugh!" she groans.

I just smile and shake my head.

"Don't worry, Payton, I am sure you will like it," Carter says with a chuckle.

A few minutes later, I feel the car come to a stop and shut off. "We are here!" Carter says, and I feel him pat my shoulder.

"Good. Now, Payton can lay off the nagging," I joke as I reach to my left side and unhook my belt.

"Bite me," she mumbles, and I laugh.

"Sorry, not in public, sweetie," I joke with her as I place my right hand on the door feeling around for the door handle. I open the door and the cool winter air swipes in. I get out and get my cane and then feeling where the door was. I shut it. While I do this, which is slow, Carter and Payton get out of the car.

Payton walks beside me as we follow Carter's footsteps inside the building. Once inside, I can hear the sound of puppies barking and dogs panting. With that, my excitement grows, and I wish I could see Payton face when she realizes we are here to get me a guide dog with the help of Carter, of course.

Carter told me this process may take a long day but I am ready, and I cannot wait at all!

Chapter Twenty-Eight

Payton's POV

"Conner! Give it back now!" Who is that female voice? I wonder as I open my eyes and stare up at an unfamiliar ceiling. Where am I? This isn't my room!

"Never!" A male shouts and then it hits me as I shift slightly and feel a warm, comfy body under me.

"Are you awake?" Reece asks, and I look at him from under my eyebrows look at his glowing blue eyes that are staring up, and his brown hair is messy from sleeping. I feel his bare chest under my arm.

"Conner, I warn you. If you do not give it back, I will cut you balls off in your sleep!" Juliet says in a very loud and serious voice.

I move a little bit more as I smile. This is actually an amazing way to wake up. "Yeah, it's kind of hard to sleep," I reply to him with a chuckle.

"I apologize once again for my family," He whispers softly to me, and as I stare up at his face, I see a slight blush cover his cheeks.

"Don't be, they are very entertaining," I chuckle again, and a smile rises on his perfect lips.

"Want some breakfast?" he asks with his sexy raspy sleep voice. That is just so amazing sounding.

"Sure," I say as I sit up on the bed and stretch my arms above my head like a cat.

"Do you see my cane anywhere?" Reece asks me as he sits up to and perches on the side of his bed.

"Um…" I say as I stand from the bed and walk around his room looking for it. "Yeah, there it is! Someone must have brought it back in here," I reply as I finally spot it resting by the door.

"Can you bring it to me, please?" he asks me kindly. I know he hates asking for help. It is written all over his face.

"Sure," I say as I walk over to it and pick it up. I then carry it back other to where he is seated on the edge of the large bed. "Here." he reaches his hand out, and I place it in his grasp. "What time is your friend picking us up?" I ask remembering that his friend, Carter, is supposed to be taking us somewhere.

"Well, what time is it now?" he asks me, and I look over at the clock on his nightstand.

"It's… um… 9:00 AM," I inform him as I walk closer to him.

"Okay, he'll be here at twelve, so we should eat and then get ready," he tells me as he holds out his cane and uses it to stand up.

"Okay, wait, can I borrow some bottoms?" I ask as I look down at the shirt that falls mid-thigh. There is no way I am going to go downstairs in this. I definitely do not want his family getting the wrong idea.

"Go for it," he says. I nod as I walk over to his closet and open it. I withdraw a pair of black sweat and pull them on.

"Let's go." I approach him. He smiles at me and nods his head. I slip my hand into his, and its warmness spreads through me. The feeling is a sense of caring and protection. Reece holds his cane in his right hand, and he looks so hot in only his boxers. Thank you, Georgia, for not caring if he wore a shirt. I can keep drinking in his body. We head for the kitchen.

As we walk into his kitchen, I see his mom at the stove with her blonde hair in a messy bun. She's wearing a gray, short-sleeve T-shirt and some plaid pajama pants. There is a frying pan in her hand that has the sizzling bacon in it and steam rises off of them. "Morning, Georgia," I say as she turns around and smiles at me. Her face is bare, and yet she still looks beautiful.

"Good morning to you too!" she replies to me with a smile. She does not seem to mind her eighteen-year-old son standing in her kitchen in nothing but his boxers, which is hot and holding a girl's hand, who by the way just slept in his bed. Is it a blind guilt thing for Reece? "Breakfast is up. Have a seat," she says nicely as she begins fixing two plates. I guide Reece over to the table and lightly place his hand on the back of the chair.

He slides his hand on it and sits down. I smile at him and sit beside him.

"Here you kids go," Georgia says as she sits a plate in front of both of us along with something to drink.

I watch as Reece takes a deep breath and then reaches out slowly touching his plate. He picks up a piece of bacon and takes a bite. After he eats it, he reaches back for more and continues to eat. With a smile stuck on my face, I begin to eat the bacon and biscuits on my plate, which are in fact very yummy! Georgia can really cook!

"Mom! I hate Conner!" Juliet's voice says all of a sudden, and she marches into the kitchen.

"What's new?" Georgia asks her with a smirk and shakes her head. Juliet groans as she sits at the table. She is wearing a pair of blue pajama shorts with a gray, spaghetti strap top, and her blonde hair in curls around her shoulders.

"Gee, thanks, mom," she mutters as she gives her mom a *"Really?"* look. I bite my lip to suppress my laughter.

"You are welcome," Georgia replies sarcastically back at her and Reece chuckles deeply. His family is quite entertaining in the morning, and I like it. I think as I continue to eat.

"Juliet, can Payton borrow some clothes for today please?" Reece asks Juliet, and my head shoots up not expecting that.

"Sure, as long as I can help her get ready," Juliet says with a smile. Juliet help me get ready? Do I trust her with doing that? I don't know why I wouldn't.

"I don't know. That is up to her," he tells her, shrugging his shoulders and pushes himself away from the table. I look to see that his plate is empty.

"Sure, let's get this over with," I sigh, and Juliet claps happily with a smile replacing her frown.

"Let's go! We will be back, Bubby."

I stand up and so does Juliet, and she leads me out of the room and to the staircase.

"Come on," she says as she jogs up the stair and leads me down the large halls. I have never been up here, and it is very pretty. She finally stops at a dark purple door and opens it. I walk into a really cool room.

The walls are a pretty maroon color, and she has a large bed in the middle bedside to glass doors that I guess lead to a balcony. On one side of the room is a large entertainment system with couches in front of it with a black rug. Behind the couches and against the wall is a desk that has books and papers all over it. On the other side of the room are two doors, I guess one is to a bathroom, and the other is to the closet. In between the two sits a beauty desk with scattered makeup and hair stuff.

"Your room is really pretty," I tell her with a smile as I look around.

"Thank you," she says, smiling. "Now, what should you wear?" she says as she strokes her invisible beard. "It's cool out so something warm."

I nod my head, and she smiles brightly as she skips over to her closet and swings it open. Juliet withdraws some clothes and then waltz back over to me.

"Here, put these on," she says handing me the clothes and pointing to the other door. I nod and walk inside the large bathroom.

I strip Reece clothes and wear the dark, boot-cut jeans she picked out. Since I am a tad bit bigger than Juliet, the jeans hung me lightly, which shows my curves. I then pull the red V-neck she handed me and pull it on. The shirt clings to me tightly and really shows off my breasts. I then pull on the black, leather jacket that has short fur on the inside which is really warm. I step out of the bathroom, and Juliet smiles really brightly as she grabs my wrists and tugs me to her makeup desk.

"Sit," she orders, and I obey as she begins putting makeup lightly on my face and irons my hair.

About a half an hour later, she makes a sound of satisfaction, and I hear the doorbell ring. "You are done!" she smiles, and I stand walking to her floor-length mirror. My jaw drops in shock; my brown hair is straight hanging down around my shoulders.

My face doesn't have a lot of makeup on it, but it looks really pretty and perfect. These clothes even make my body look decent.

"Wow," I say clearly impressed.

"Yes, wow. You look gorgeous."

"Thank you!"

"No problem. Now, go," she says to me.

I take off to Reece's room where I grab my shoes, put them on, and then grab my purse. I rush to the front door to see Reece standing there talking to a tall, dark-brown hair guy with chocolate eyes. He is actually really good looking and has muscles, but nowhere near as hot as Reece.

I walk to Reece's side, smiling. "Payton, this is my friend, Carter. Carter, this is Payton." The guy looks at me smiling brightly.

"Great to meet you, Payton. Shall we all leave?" he asks, and Reece nods. So, do I.

We get into his car and drive to wherever we are headed. Carter and Reece tell me how they met, and Carter tells me his story, which really was sad. Finally, we arrive at the place after a long while, and we all walk inside where I am shocked at what I see.

There are people in t-shirts that have "Guide Dogs for the Blind" wrote on them. There are a couple of doors around the room, and in the middle, people are walking dogs around that have a harness and a guide dog shirt. There are all kinds of breeds of dogs.

"Hi! Can I help you?" a middle-aged woman asks as she walks up to us. She is wearing one of those green shirts.

"I am Carter. This is Payton and Reece, and we are here to get Reece a guide dog," Carter says, smiling at the woman, and she nods.

"I'm Joy, and I will be helping you. Why don't you guys follow me and you can meet the dogs who are trained and ready for a partner," the women says. She has her black hair back in a ponytail, and she has tan skin with big green eyes. She leads us to one of the doors and swipes her card, allowing us all to enter. My heart melts as I see the dogs running around in what looks to be their playroom having a blast.

It means so very much to me that Reece brought me with him for this big moment! Why, though? I don't know.

"I really want you to help me pick one out," Reece's voice whispers in my ear, sending shivers down my spine and blush to rise in my cheeks.

"Okay," I whisper back, biting my lip to hide the grin that is trying to break across my face.

"These guide dogs are all serious and business when the harness is on, but when it's off, it's playtime," Joys says, and Carter smiles as he wanders off to play with a couple dogs. I take Reece's hand, and we walk farther into the room with all the happy looking dogs.

Suddenly, something bumps my leg, and I stop, causing Reece to stop as well. I look down to see a Golden Retriever sitting in front of Reece, staring up at him with its big brown eyes and panting happily.

My heart melts as I see just how adorable it is. The dog stands up and rubs its head against Reece's left hand. That's so cool. It's as if this dog can sense that he is blind. A beautiful smile spreads across his face as he scoots down and pets the dog. The dog begins licking his face, and I can see an automatic bond between these two.

"What does it look like?" Reece asks me, and I smile at him as he pets the dog's head.

"Well, the dog is a Golden Retriever and has kind of long hair that is more of a creamy, yellow color and is adorable."

"Do you like it?" he asks me, and I look at him and smile.

"I do, and I can see a connection between you two," I say simply, and he nods as he continues to pet the dog.

"Oh, I see you have met Rider!" Joy says as she approaches us. "You two really look like you have made a bond that partners do. So is Rider the one for you Reece?" Joy asks with a hopeful look.

I look at Reece and Rider and see how happy those two are. He better say yes.

"Rider?" Reece says softly to himself, and Rider licks him. "Yeah, he's the one for me," Reece says happily and wraps his arms around Rider to hug him, and Rider licks his face.

"Okay, we just have to do the paperwork which Carter told me he'll handle while you and Reece go through a training class," Joy says, and Reece nods with a big smile while they bond. I am so happy for Reece! This is a whole new step for him, and I could not be prouder!

Chapter Twenty-Nine

Reece's POV

"Here, hold this," the Joy lady tells me as she places my hand onto some kind of handle.

Rider and I had this instant connection. I just felt so much safer and not as worried as I have been. Since the shooting, I have had this feeling of fear of what is around me. It's really scary not knowing what you are surrounded by. Rider and I were an instant connection, and I could feel that I would be safe in his present. Joy brought Rider and I back here to teach me mainly how to work on everything. Carter came to watch while Payton chose to play with the puppies. From what I can tell, this is an open room used for this stuff.

Joy teaches Rider and me how to work together. She also trains him for cues about me and my safety. As Joy like to put it, "Rider is my eyes now."

We practice and work together for what feels like two hours and finally, we are working as a team. I am actually getting this down, and it's so awesome! If I am walking towards a danger zone, Rider bumps my legs in front of me to stop me. I can now get around and even release him from his harness. This is so exciting, and I cannot wait to get home and try this out. Joy says that they can even sell us all the things we need for him here. He also told me we would have to come back in once a week for the next few months for training.

Rider and I walk around, and he will bump my legs before I hit walls, which is a good thing. We worked on commands and things allowing myself to get the hang of it all. Finally, Joy says she thinks that we are ready and that she'll go pull up the paperwork. I hear Carter's footsteps go behind Joy, but I need to talk to him really quick while we are alone!

"Carter!" I yell, hoping to get his attention while Rider and I walk forward.

"Yeah," he says, and his footsteps freeze. I hear a door lightly shut and can hear Carter's breathes in front of me. About the same time, Rider bumps my legs, and I stop.

"Sit," I command to him and feel his body shift beside me. I use my other hand to reach over and pet his head quickly. "I need to talk to you real quick," I say to Carter taking in a deep breath.

"Ah, let me guess. It's about the lovely Payton," he replies in a horrible British accent.

I cannot help but to chuckle and shake my head at his awful attempt. "Yeah, it's about her man. I don't know what to do. I want to ask her out and all, but I am afraid she doesn't like me because I am blind. And so when I ask her out, she'll get all weird and reject me, and it'll ruin our friendship. I just don't think she could like me," I say simply as I begin to ramble. When I think about asking her out, I get so nervous at the what ifs.

Carter bursts out laughing, and it vibrates the room. I am sure the look I am giving him is one of utter confusion. Did this dude get dropped on his head as a baby?

"I didn't know my problem was so funny," I state very unamused by this.

"No, no! It's just you clearly got it hard for this girl. And the fact that you think she doesn't like you is just so funny! I mean this girl would do anything for you. I know you cannot see the way she looks at you or you at her, but I tell you what, if that isn't love, then I don't know what is," Carter says with an amused tone.

Love? Whoever said anything about love! I don't love her. I mean I really like her, but I would not go as far as saying I love her. Not yet at least; maybe, one day I will. But it is official that Carter has some serious brain damage.

"Love? I never said anything about loving her. I just really like her," I say simply to him shaking my head.

"Boy, you are so blind… Crap, that word doesn't work. Sorry. I mean you are so dense. You love her, but I guess you don't see it yet. And she definitely loves you. For one, she puts up with your crap, and I know from what you've told me before, you are so not the easiest person to handle. Two, she always makes time to help you, tries her best to treat you normally, and allow you to do things on your own. Last but not least, she forgets you're blind meaning she doesn't care or pay attention to that. She sees you as another human being and does not judge. Her heart is one made of gold, and people like her do not come around every day. When they do, they are gifts to us. She was made for you. Call her your angel if you will. She came to you, and she fell for you, which anyone could tell within the first fifteen minutes of being in both of your presence. Even a blind man can see that! Well, apparently, not you. But technically, I am still blind because I cannot fully see, but I can even tell. So stop being arrogant, grow a pair and just ask her out already," Carter says in a long lecture, leaving me stunned. Is that all true? If so, wow. "So did that answer your question, Reece?"

I nod my head very slowly. "Yep, it did! Thank you so much. I needed that," I say with a smile slipping on my face.

"Good, now, let's get all this done and head back to your house so I can drop you off and you can grow a pair," Carter says with a laugh, and I sigh shaking my head.

"Okay, man."

"Let's go." I hear a door open slowly. I pull lightly on the harness and feel Rider stand up.

I begin walking with him, guiding me through the doorway, and Carter shuts the door behind me. I cannot wait to get home because it is official. I am going to ask Payton out! As crazy as it may seem, it's time, and I really like her.

Chapter Thirty

Payton's POV

On the way back to Reece's house, Rider and I ride in the back seat of the car. Ever since we left the Guide Dog place, Reece has been acting funny. I have no clue why he seems... nervous. I wonder why.

The car jerks to a stop, and I look out the window to see Reece's house in front of us. Rider leans over against me, panting heavily.

"Well, guys, I must go. See you later!" Carter says.

"Alright. Bye, man. Thanks," Reece says as he runs his hands along the door before grabbing the handle and opening it. He shuts the door behind him.

"Bye, Carter. It was nice meeting you," I tell him as I grab the door handle.

Carter turns and looks at me with a large smile. "Goodbye, Payton. It was great meeting you too," he says to me, and I smile back as I open the door.

I reach out and grab Rider's harness handle so he can jump out. I shut the door behind us and walk up to Reece's side. He is standing stiffly in front of the car. Once I get to his side, I reach out and take his right hand placing it lightly on the handle.

"Here," I say, smiling up at him as Reece smiles down at Rider, and then his face rises to look up in my direction. I stare into his blue eyes, but not for long or else I get lost.

"Thanks," he says, and I smile.

"No problem. Let's go." I smile and walk towards the front door trusting Rider to lead Reece.

I reach the door and turn around, looking behind me. I see Rider leading Reece up the pathway very well. It truly impresses me, and I smile. I stare at Reece's shining eyes, and a small smile pulls up on his lips. They reach the steps, and I take a deep breath holding it. I really want to call out and warn him, but I want to see how he and Rider do.

Rider stops him and then Reece takes a steady step forward, landing his foot on the step. It's like somehow Rider told him there were steps. Rider guides Reece slowly up the steps. Once Rider finally stands on the porch, he smiles brightly. Rider walks to me and sits down, and I smile down at him. It is so crazy how far Reece has come! He is truly amazing. I just wish he'd come back to school. I feel like that is his fear, and he is never going to be able to fully grip everything unless he returns and faces his fear.

It's official. My new goal is to get Reece back in school… whatever it takes! I have found myself really starting to develop a crush on him, and I cannot help it. It's like there is something pulling me to him. Half the time, I forget he's blind. I just want to help him and be there for him as a friend or more. So today, I am going to start my new mission. Mission: "Get Reece back in school!"

"I did it!" Reece says in a very happy tone. Gosh, he is so darn cute!

"I am so proud! Now, let's go inside and show off Rider," I say as I smile brightly and open the door walking inside. Rider stands up and leads Reece inside.

As I shut the door behind them, Reece shouts for everyone to come down. And as we walk into the sitting room, I hear footsteps rushing from all over the house. Hmm… I wonder how they will like the dog.

Georgia appears in the room with Rayne right on her heels dressed up like a Princess. Then, Juliet appears along with Conner. Juliet is styling some ripped skinny jeans and a blue-and-gray striped top with some high tops. One thing I have noticed about her, she really pulls off the bad girl look, which is crazy. Conner is sporting a navy blue *Young and Reckless* shirt with dark jeans and just some white socks. Last is Leonardo, and he is just wearing a gray T-shirt and jeans, simple but effective.

"Yes?" his mom asks with a very worried face as she walks near us, and I decide to just take a seat. These couches are pretty fancy but oh, well. So I sit carefully down and realize they aren't that comfy either.

"Doggy!" Rayne yells as she races over to Rider, who is resting on his butt beside Reece's legs.

"Dog?" Leonardo asks a little stunned.

"Reece, did you get a guide dog?" Georgia asks.

"Cool, congrats on the dog!" Conner says, approaching Reece and patting his back.

"Aww. He's pretty," Juliet says, smiling as she walks over to Rider and stroking his head. Reece slowly begins to move and feels around until he finds the couch and sits down with Rider at his feet.

"Son, don't you think maybe you should have asked us if you could get a dog?" his dad asks in an authoritative tone. Rayne pets Rider while Reece undoes the harness, removing it from him.

"Release," he says as he leans back on the couch and Rider stands up and shakes. Rayne laughs as she continues to pet him. Rider licks her up her cheek with his slobbery tongue. Reece takes a deep breath and runs his hand through his hair. "Honestly, dad, I did not think about it. I mean it's not as if I decided to go out and buy a pet dog. Rider is a guide dog to help me so I don't have to depend on you all so much. He is way better than the cane," Reece breathes out loudly.

Juliet scoots down in front of Rider with Rayne and pets his cream-colored fur. Rider licks her too. Man, that boy is a player. He is crazy and already has a lot of girlfriends.

"The point, though, son, is you should have still spoken with your mom and me about this first. You can't just go behind our backs," his dad says in a scolding tone.

"Besides the point? All I wanted was to no longer be treated as if I was five again. I wanted not to walk into walls anymore! I wanted to feel safe again! I may not be able to see, but this is the closest I will probably ever get. So what if I didn't ask you two first? I am eighteen! It's not even like Rider is a pet! He is a therapy dog! I am sorry I didn't ask you guys first! To be honest, I thought you'd be perfectly fine with this," Reece says, and he is breathing kind of hard. I feel really awkward like I am invading a family conversation sitting here. It's like he just let out everything he has been holding in since the shooting.

I look up to see Leonardo in shock but also a little angry, probably from how he spoke to him. Georgia, however, has tears clouding her blue eyes. Conner is now sitting in a chair and watching them like it's something crazy while the girls are still playing with Rider. Georgia bounds over to Reece and tackles him into a hug.

"Aww, baby!" she cries as she holds him. "I am so sorry! I did not know you felt that way! You should've told me," she says as she hugs him. He mumbles something to her, but I can't hear it. This is a beautiful sight and shows just how amazing these people are. It goes to show there are still good people out there in this world!

"I am sorry, son. Just don't do it again," his dad says with a sigh as Georgia sits behind Reece, wiping her tears.

"Yes, sir," Reece says with a small smile returning to his face.

"So tell us about the dog!" Georgia says happily, and Reece complies as he tells her all about Rider, how we got him and everything.

It's sweet and nice! Finally, the awkwardness is gone, and I don't feel out of place. I feel welcomed.

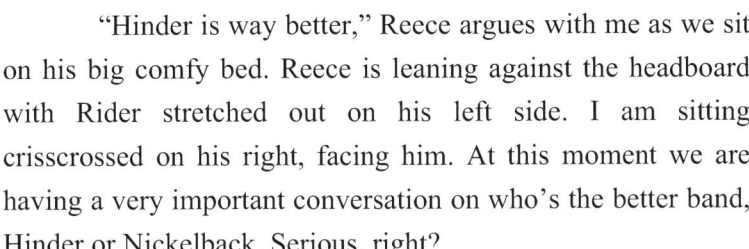

"Hinder is way better," Reece argues with me as we sit on his big comfy bed. Reece is leaning against the headboard with Rider stretched out on his left side. I am sitting crisscrossed on his right, facing him. At this moment we are having a very important conversation on who's the better band, Hinder or Nickelback. Serious, right?

"No way! Nickelback is the best. Hinder is so loud," I argue with a smile. I just can't help, but smile! Stupid Reece, he does this to me!

"That's the point!" Reece says as he tosses his hands up in exasperation and frustration.

"Oh, well, it's true!" I defend, and he laughs, shaking his head.

"That's your opinion, which in this case is wrong," he says with a smirk that causes my heart to race.

"That's your opinion, and as my momma says, we all have our own opinion like we all have assholes," I say bluntly, and Reece laughs.

"Did the innocent, sweet Payton Jennings just swear?" he asks in mock shock.

"Shut up, meanie," I joke back, and he smiles as he takes my hand. Our conversation dies down, and I suddenly feel nervous as I look at Reece's face.

"Can I ask you something?" Reece says really quietly and swallows hard, running a hand through his hair.

"You just did but go ahead."

"Um… will you…?" he stops for a moment and takes a deep breath. "Will you go out with me?" he asks me, and I sit there staring at him in shock.

"Me?" I ask in confusion. "Like on a date?" I ask again. I bet my eyes are huge.

"Um… well… yeah," he says as he makes a nervous face and rubs the back his neck. His grip on my hand loosens some.

Reece *freaking* Collins wants to go on a *date* with *me*! Holy cow! This is a dream! It has to be! This is impossible! I wonder how bad he wants this! And then a wicked plan hatches in my head.

"Of course, on one condition," I say with a smile as big as Texas on my face.

"Great anything!" he says with happy blue eyes and the most perfect smile.

"You come back to school," I state with a smile on my face. I really hope he agrees. I mean I'd go on a date with him anyways, but this will help him a lot even if he doesn't see it!

He is quiet for just a few seconds before responding. "Okay! It's a date," he states, shifting uncomfortably and then brings my hand to his perfect lips and kisses it.

Oh, my gosh! I am going on a date with Reece Collins! Ah! I have no clue why he asked me, and I don't know what he saw in someone like me. But I don't care. At this moment, I am one of the happiest girls on this planet we call earth. I also cannot believe Reece is going back to school! This is good for him! He needs to face this fear or else it is going hold him back for the rest of his life! I will help him every step of the way, but I know he can do it! He's strong, so he will make it.

Chapter Thirty-One

Reece's POV

What did I agree to? All I know is I would do anything for her to go on a date with me. So when she stated the condition, I didn't really think about it. Instead, I just answered. Now, I have to go back to school, and an aching fear creeps up on me. The thought of returning to school and walking the halls again makes me sick with fear. Within a month, my life has changed dramatically. I went from being someone who was going places, and anything was possible to being the blind kid who was going nowhere and everyone tiptoes around me. So do I really want to return to school and have everyone stare at me and treat me like a freak? Of course, I don't! The thought of those who use to admire me shunning me and treating me like a freak or like I am special kills me! Being blind changes everything and changes how everyone looks at me even my family.

Believe it or not, my family is not usually this happy and perfect! Before the accident, my family loved each other, but we fought. We would yell at each other, call names and break a rule or disobey our parents. I would be grounded and in a lot of trouble. If I spoke to my parents like I did today, I would have been grounded until I am married and would have so many chores to do that a maid would feel bad for me. My parents were very cool, happy, and loving people and they only want respect, honesty, and responsibility from their children. This meant if we break any the rules which weren't even that many, we would get a lecture and punishment.

My parents even had their own "Good cop, Bad cop" routine. My mom was the one who would supply endless love and cause you to feel bad for hurting her. My father, on the other hand, was the iron fist. He laid down the law and punishment and would not budge an inch. Don't get me wrong, my dad was a wonderful, loving dude. He enjoyed doing things with his sons, and his daughters were daddy's girls. He is the one who taught me football, play baseball. Conner, Dad and I used to gather in the den on game nights and watch football games.

I was the good son, compared to Conner. He was the wild child party boy, always getting into trouble. I, on the other hand, was calmer and the good kid. Granted, I got my fair share of trouble just like anyone else, but I learned from my mistakes.

Now, we don't fight, and it's like living in rainbow land, 24/7, which fucking sucks! It's all happy voices and laughter with saying things like 'It's okay.' I want to shout at them to stop! I want my real family back. Yeah, we argued, but it didn't seem so fake! I feel like no one is saying what they want because they are afraid of offending me or something. They are treating me like that precious plate your grandma has that was passed down from generation to generation. Maybe they think if they're happy, I will be. In all honesty, it's backfiring! I just want to forget I am blind and pretend it never happened!

I want to open my eyes one morning and see the shining light of the sun peeking through my window. I just want to stare into Payton's eyes and kiss her. I want to watch Rayne grow up, and I want to see Juliet go to prom! I want to see! I need to! How will I get a job? How will I live on my own? Who will marry me? All of these questions haunt me at night as I shut my eyes just like tonight.

"No! Don't shoot!" I shout, kicking my legs and then I sit up, blinking my eyes only to be met by darkness. Just another nightmare, you think I would get used to them by now, but I'm not.

I feel some weight lay on my lap. I move my hand to it and feel the softness of Rider's fur. A heavy, rough paw lies on my leg, and I pet Rider, allowing myself to calm down. It is like he is drawing my bad energy from me.

"What time is it?" I ask my phone as I reach over feeling for it on the stand.

"9:30 AM," the automatic voice says, and I groan. I guess I need to talk to my mom about returning to school. So I pet Rider and move off my bed and drape my legs over the edge. I feel the weight of Rider on the bed disappear and then a *thump*. His footsteps make their way to my feet. I stretch and crack my back. God, I miss my sight! Standing up, I walk to my closet with Rider beside me to keep me from hitting things. It's like he can sense my need for his help.

I open it and feel around the hanging clothes for some sweatpants. Finally, I find some and feel the tag and uses that to tell me the front from back. I slowly return to my bed and reach down to where Juliet placed Rider's harness last night somewhere on the floor. "Sit," I say to Rider, who is standing beside me, and I can hear him body shift to sitting. My fingers finally find the harness, and I slip it on Rider and stand up, taking a hold of it.

My mom is probably in her office working. Yes, my mom works. She came from a tough childhood and loved making clothes. She became a designer and opened her own store that sells high-quality clothes for lower prices. One store became two, and now, they are beginning to pop up all over the country. Now, Georgia Collins Designs is becoming a household name. I shut my eyes, trying to picture the house from my memory. I use that to guide me on directions and Rider to keep me from hitting things or falling.

Once I reach where the door to her office should be if I followed the directions correctly, I hear my mom's hum coming through the door. "Mom?" I call her and hope she'll open the door.

I hear the creaking sound of the door opening, and the humming has ceased. "Reece, dear, what is it?" my mom's voice asks me.

"I need to talk to you," I say simply with a smile.

"Come on in then and have a seat," my mom insists as she grabs my left hand and pulls Rider and me inside. She puts my hand on the back of the chair, and I sit down as fill around. I hear my mom sit down in front of me, and Rider sits at my feet.

"So what is it honey?" my mom asks her voice beginning to sound worried.

"I want to go back to school," I state simply, giving her the most confident look I could muster.

"Oh, sweetie! Are you sure about that? Do you think you are ready?" my mom asks me in a worry-filled voice.

Honestly, I don't feel even close to being ready! I can't tell my mom that, and I have to do this for Payton, my angel. "Yeah, I am sure," I say and give her the best smile I can even though I am so scared.

"Alright, sweetie. I will call and talk to your school tomorrow. I see no reason why you won't be able to," my mom insists, and I can hear the smile in her voice.

"Okay, good," I say with a real smile because that means I can start planning my date with Payton! I am going to make it one that she will never forget. It has to be something perfect and romantic because she deserves the best, she is my angel.

"Anything else?" she asks with her motherly voice, and I suddenly remember something I have been meaning to ask her.

"Well, I have something I have been wanting to ask you. Can I get eye surgery like what Carter got?" I ask with a hopeful face.

My mom is silent, and she sighs. "Your dad and I will look into it. But honey, there is no promises you will qualify or that it would work. I just don't want you to get your hopes up and be disappointed," she says with her soft, warming, motherly tone.

"It is okay, mom. I understand. I just want to be able to see again," I say softly, and I hear her cry a little.

"Oh, sweetie, I know!" she says, and I hear her get up and hug me.

She says she knows, but she really doesn't. She doesn't know my reasons for it! She never could! She is part of the reason! I love her, and I love my dad and siblings. I just want my life to return to normal but with Payton. Payton is the only good thing that has come from all of this. She's the only one who treats me normally. Well, Carter does, but it's different. Everything I do now is for her. I do everything for my angel. When I feel like I cannot just keep going on, she's there, and I think of her. This girl has gone through a lot with her sister, and compared to that, I have no reason to complain. At least, I am healthy; I wish I could say the same for Lila. Hell, I wish I could just make Payton happy. Then a light bulb goes off over my head, and the perfect idea for the date hits me.

I am going to make this a date that would take her mind off of everything and makes her the happiest girl ever. This is going to be awesome! I cannot wait! What is this girl doing to me?

Chapter Thirty-Two

Payton's POV

Reece's laughter fills my ears as we sit in the sand on the beach. Reece's arms are tightly wrapped around my waist as I sit in between his legs. I rest my head back on his bare, muscled chest. I glance up at his perfect face with a pair of black shades covering his blue eyes. I smile up at him.

"This is wonderful Reece," I say as I smile out at the water.

"You're wonderful," he says as he squeezes me tightly to his chest.

"You are so sweet," I say as I grab one of his hands from my waist and intertwine my fingers with his, playing with them.

"I would not want to have anyone else in my arms." He kisses the top of my head.

I twist my head around to stare through the black lenses of his sunglasses and bring my lips to his. His lips are gentle and amazing as they move with mine. It is like fireworks were lighting the sky on the Fourth of July. Our lips are two puzzle pieces perfectly fit together, and I smile into the kiss. We pull away, and I rest my forehead on the right side of his face.

"Payton," he says softly. "I lo—"

"Payton! Payton! Wake up, Pay!" a voice says, waking me from my wonderful dream. The first good one I have had since I was little.

I force my eyes open to my mom's smiling face. So, she is the one who ruined my dream! Thank you so much... not! Once I see her smiling face, I re-close my eyes and hope to pull the dream back. No such luck and I feel my mom shake me once more.

"Payton, wake up! It's time to spend the day together," she says as she shakes me, and I release a groan. I just want to sleep and resume my dream! Is it too much to ask to just go back to sleep?

"Payton! If you don't get up, I will go get cold water and pour all over you," my mom threatens as I pull my blanket higher up cover my face.

"No, you won't," I mumble, trying to stay asleep.

"Oh, but I will." I feel the bed move, and she walks away. Wait! Is she leaving? Oh no! My eyes fly open, and I sit up straight.

"I am up!" I yell, and I see my mom standing at my bedroom door laughing.

"Good. Now, go downstairs. I made breakfast," she says and leaves the room. She made breakfast? Where'd the food come from?

Throwing my blanket off the top of me and standing up, a wave of pain shoots through my back. Slowly bending down, I grab a pair of shorts off the ground and slip them on under my large shirt.

Yawning, I exit my room and head to the kitchen where the smell of bacon enters my nose.

"Mom, where did the food come from?" I ask as she sits a plate down on the table. I walk over and sit down as she carries over her own plate.

"The store, of course." she chuckles. I roll my eyes; she knows that's not what I meant.

"I meant where did you get the money?" I ask her as I take a bite of the bacon.

"I got paid yesterday," she says simply, and I sigh, knowing she hates talking about money with me. She still worries about the hospital bills and has to pay some of them, but there is also a very kind person who gives money anonymously. The donor is me, but my mom doesn't know. Confused on where I get the money? A year before Lila got sick my grandpa passed away, and he had quite a lot of money, which all was left to me when he was gone, and it was for college. When the bills first started piling up, I offered the money to my mom. But she refused to take my money, saying it was for college. It started getting really bad, and we barely had anything so I decided to start donating it secretly and paying off the bills. That's why I work my butt off in school, and the funds are getting smaller so I don't know how much longer I can keep it up.

"Okay, this is really good, Mom," I say to her as I continue to eat.

"Thank you."

After we eat, we get ready for our day together. We spent most of our time at the hospital with Lila and then we even visited Ms. Rose. It was a wonderful day with my mom, and now, I left lying in bed with my heavy eyes.

Quack, quack

I reach over and grab my phone, answering it and pressing it to my ear. "Hello?" I say in a groggy voice.

"Hey, Payton. Did I wake you?" Reece's amazing voice says with worry. Just the sound of his beautiful voice cause butterflies to erupt in my tummy.

"Hey, Reece. No, you didn't," I say with a smile peeling on my face, and I stifle a yawn.

"Good," he says with a smile in his voice which also makes me smile like a crazy, little kid.

"Is everything okay?" I ask him because I was wondering why he called.

"Yeah, I just wanted to hear your voice," he says softly, and blood pumps to my face. My heart thumps against my chest, and my stomach twists in a knot. A wave of nerves washes over me.

"Why?"

"Because I didn't get see you all day. And I missed you,"

"I missed you too," I whisper lightly, but I know he heard me. Smiling very brightly I cuddle into my blanket with the phone resting to my ear.

"So what are you doing tomorrow night," he asks me, and I bite my lip thinking. The only thing I ever do is go to the hospital.

"Probably the hospital, why?"

"Didn't know, you want to go on our date?" he asks me, and I can hear the hope in his voice.

"It's a school night."

"I know it," he replies with a smile playing in his voice.

"Fine, we can tomorrow night. When are you coming back to school?" I ask with a big smile. I am so happy yet so nervous about tomorrow night!

"Mom is going to talk to the school tomorrow so maybe on Tuesday," he says and doesn't seem happy about it.

"Are you okay?" I ask him and hoping he is.

"I guess," he says, and I sigh.

"Reece, I will be by you the whole time."

"Promise?"

"Promise." Then, I yawned, rubbing my eyes.

"Are you tired? I don't want to keep you from sleeping," he says in a worry-filled voice.

"I'm alright. I don't want to get off the phone," I say simply, and I curl deeper into my pillow and blanket.

"Alright. I am going stay on the phone until you go to sleep, angel," he says, but I don't think I heard him correctly; it sounded like he called me, "Angel." No! Why would he do that? I definitely misheard him.

"Okay, Reece," I say, smiling as I listen to his steady breathing. Reece begins chattering about random stuff in a soft voice.

"Reece?" I say as I begin to drift off into sleep.

"Yes?" he asks in such a sweet voice.

"Thank you for being so amazing," I whisper as I fall asleep.

A shining bright light cause me to pull my eyes open and sit up on my uncomfortable bed and stretching. Groaning, I get out of bed to get ready since it's the dreaded Monday morning. *Why do Monday mornings suck so bad?* I ponder as I grab a gray, fuzzy sweater and some jeans. I head to the bathroom where I get dressed. After I ready, I go to the kitchen and grab an apple. Yes, I have apples again! I then head to school.

My morning at school goes just as boring and dull as always, and the lunch bell rings so I head to my locker. As I stand in my locker, I hear the idle gossip from a crowd of the popular girls.

"Did you hear?" one of them asks the other.

"That Reece is coming back?" another one asks, and the first girl nods. These just so happen to be his "friends" and they were the snobby stuck-up, blonde, cheerleader girls.

"Yeah! I heard his mom talked to the principal! It's going be so weird!"

I groan as I shut my locker. Stupid people have no clue what they are talking about. Just as I turn to go the library, I see the counselor's door open, and a girl steps out with dark blue skinny jeans with a pair of knee-high, black, high heel boots. She's wearing a white, glittery top with a brown leather jacket over it. Her long, blonde hair has its sides pulled back, and her face looks so pretty but hauntingly familiar. The counselor steps out with her, and the gossiping girls stop to look at her.

"Welcome back to Washington High, Clair," the counselor says, and I try to think of who she is. Clair. Clair. Clair. Oh, crap! Clair!

Once I remember who Clair is exactly, I make my way quickly to the library and to my usual table, dropping my head onto the desk. Why is she back? Clair is Reece's ex. They dated freshman and sophomore year and broke up the summer before the junior year when she moved. That was almost *two* years ago! Why is she back?!

I cannot compete with her! Reece will go right back to her and forget all about me! This is just an awful day!

"I thought I would find you here," an annoying voice says.

I groan. "Great! Today keeps getting worse," I say, and he chuckles. I lift my head and look up at Jace.

"I am hurt." He jokingly grips his heart.

"Oh, well," I state, dropping my head back down.

"What's got you all down?"

"Nothing so stop bothering," I say simply, sitting up and crossing my arms.

"You aren't good at making friends are you?" he asks, and I groan.

"I don't want to be friends with someone who ditches their best friend because of something he can't control!" I say loudly at him as I stand up, grab my stuff, and storm off!

I just want to see Reece already! My day is just going sucky! I want our date to be here! Then my day will turn around, just like it always does when I am with him. What can I say? I think I may be falling for him. He just makes me happy no matter how bad my life is going.

Chapter Thirty-Three

Reece's POV

"So what do you need our help for?" Conner's voice asks me as we sit in the den. I can hear Rider on the floor chewing on what sounds to be his bone.

"I need you guys to help me get ready for my date," I state simply as I lean back into the couch.

"With Payton," Carter sings jokingly.

"Shut up," I mumble, wishing I could chuck something at him right about now.

"Oh! Bro, you finally asked her out?" Conner says; his voice full of excitement.

I groan and run my hand through my hair. "Thanks, Carter. Now, he'll never shut up," I say as I lean my head back shutting my eyes.

Conner laughs and then I can hear Carter laugh too. "Sorry, man."

"Whatever. So little brother what do you need use to do?" Conner says faking hurt.

"Well, Conner I need you to pick her up. And Carter can you help me get everything sat up?" I ask as I sit up straight and running my hands down my face.

"No problem, Reece. You just tell us what to do, and we'll do it," Carter says with his normal happy voice. I smile and begin telling them my plan for tonight. The date may not be normal or successful, but I want it to be different.

"Reece, dear! I am headed to talk to your school! Will you be okay here?" my mom's voice calls as she enters the room. I am currently stretched out on the couch with Rider, lying on my legs.

I pull my eyes open and yawn. "Yeah, I am good, mom."

"Alright, dear! I love you."

"I love you too," I reply as I shut my eyes again.

I listen to my mom's heels clicking against the hardwood floor as she leaves the room. My heart rate picks up as thoughts of returning to school skates through my brain.

My body slams into the hard metal that I can automatically recognize as lockers.

"Freak!" A strong male voice calls, and then laughter fills the halls. I feel different sets of hands shove me repeatedly as footsteps pass.

"SPED," another calls as footstep pass. Pain shoots through my side, and I grip it with my hands and wish the ache would stop.

"Go back home," another dude's voice says, and I groan.

God, why did I come back? I ask myself as I try to stand straight again. As I straighten up and hold my side, I remember why I came back. I came back for a girl. Not just any girl, I came back for Payton. Where is Payton when I need her? I don't know, but she's not by my side. I am left here alone in the dark with my fear. A fear that refuses to go away and eats my insides up, and it is awful.

"Reece!" Payton's angelic voice says as I hear her near me.

"Payton!" I say my voice so happy.

"Reece, I'm sorry I just can't handle you being blind. I can't do this anymore. I'm sorry. Goodbye, Reece," she says and with each word, my heart breaks and shatters into a million pieces, killing me. The sound of her feet walking away is a sound I will never be able to forget. With that sound, my earth collapses beneath my feet.

I sit up straight, wiping the sweat that I feel beating down my head. That was awful! Nightmares like that keep me from wanting to return to school!

Swinging my legs over to touch the floor, I feel Rider fur beside my feet. "Rider, ready to put your harness on?" I ask him as I feel around for his harness before putting it on him.

Then I stand up, grip the handle, and use him to help me guide myself back to my room. I also have my bedroom and bathroom's layout down to a T; any other room and I will probably end up lost.

I release Rider from the harness once I enter my room and grab my cane. Using the cane and tapping it ahead of me, I lead myself to my closet. Reaching out my hand, I run down the wooden door before it lands on the metal handle. I run my hands along the shirt, and they land on the silky feeling of one. Pulling it out and feel my hands down the front of it to find the buttons. I smile. This seems good enough. Turning around, I find a jean material and slip it off the hanger, carrying both in one hand and leaving my cane in the other as I try to find my way to the dresser. Once I do, I feel the top drawer and pull out some cotton boxers. Finally, I have all I need and use my cane to get to my bathroom where I strip off my clothes and feel around.

Thankfully, my mom has labeled all of my shampoos and body washes. Once I am showered, it's time to face the challenge of getting ready. I carefully step out of the shower and use the towel to dry off. Then I proceed to get dressed which takes a while, but I get it done.

"Reece!" Carter's voice yells from what sounds like my room. Picking up my cane, I find my way back out of the bathroom successfully, causing a smile to erupt on my face.

"Yeah, Carter?" I say as I make my way to where his voice is coming from.

"You look good, bro! It's time for the date!" he tells me, and I am so happy.

"Thanks." An excited yet nervous smile reaches across my face.

This is going to be great... I hope. I am going to ask her to be mine! What if she says "no"? Wait! Don't think about the what ifs think about the what is. I can do this.

"Alright, I am ready," I say with a smile trying to block out the nerves.

Chapter Thirty-Four

Payton's POV

Sitting my book bag down on the messy floor of my room, I walk happily over to the closet and search for some clothes to wear on my date! After school today, I swung by the hospital for an hour talking to Ms. Rose and see Lila. Once I was done, I rushed home to get ready for my date.

I search through my very messy closet. Note to self: Clean room! This is so hard! I don't have anything to wear. I guess it really doesn't matter I just want to wear something nice to make myself feel better. I release a sigh as I grab my best pair of blue jeans and then the nicest top I have, which is a pretty white dress top that is off the shoulder on one side and on the other, it joins together. It is very flattering. I just never have a reason to wear it. Carry the two articles of clothing in my arms I walk over to the dresser where I fish out the best underwear I own, hoping it'll give me a confident boast.

I carry the clothes into the bathroom. My hand shakes a little as my nerves begin to fuel up. Once I lay my clothes down on the back of the toilet, I strip out of my clothes and turn on the warm water trying to get it right. My hands are already beginning to sweat a lot as my nerves get worse. Stepping inside, I try to let the warm water soothe my nerves and clear my mind from all the bad what ifs that are floating around it.

I am still shaky though I'll live with it. I am so excited for the date. I don't care where he takes me or what we do. We could sit in his den for all I care; I just want to be with him. Once I am clean, I shut off the water and step out of the shower, wrapping a towel around me. Using the other towel to wring out my brown curls and then toss the towel aside. I pick up my hairbrush and pull it through my brown hair over and over again, removing the tangles. The curls become looser. It actually doesn't look that bad, kind of pretty. With the towel wrapped around me, I dry myself off and then pull on my underwear.

I quickly brush my teeth and then tug my jean on, and then I pull my top. I smile brightly as I look into the mirror! Damn, I am impressed! I have never been able to make myself look so good! Turning on my bare feet, I head back to my bedroom. I sit on my bed as I pull on some socks and my worn shoes.

Knock, knock.

I hear the front door, so I quickly grab my purse and phone, rushing to my bedroom door and turning the lights off with a shaky hand. I rush to the front door not really knowing whom to expect and with my sweaty, shaky hand, I twist the knob and open it. Conner is standing there with his hands stuffed into his pockets. He also has one of those black drivers' hats, causing me to smile.

"Hey, Conner!" I say as I step outside and shut the door behind me. My mom is at work and knows where I am going so I don't need to worry about that.

"Hello, Miss Jennings. Your carriage awaits," Conner says with a goofy accent and bows extending his hand to Reece's car.

"Why thank you, kind sir. May I say, you are a tad bit weird," I reply as I walk towards the car with him beside me.

"Me? Weird, madam? I am insulted that you say I am this weird you speak of," he jokes, totally switching accents back and forth.

"I am sorry I insulted you," I say with a smile. Conner being silly is keeping me distracted from my awful nerves.

Once I reach the car, Conner pulls the door open for me, and I slip inside. "Where is Reece having you take me?" I ask him before he shuts the door.

"That my young Payton is for me to know and you to discover," he answers with a smirk as he withdraws a black piece of cloth from his pocket.

"Conner, what is that?" I ask as he bends down towards me with it in his hands.

"A blindfold," he says simply as he nears it to my face.

"Why are you giving me that?" I ask as he continues to get closer.

"To put it on you," he says with a duh tone and rolls his eyes. What? Put it on me! Is he crazy? I swear this boy is nuts! Why is he putting a blindfold on me? Oh, my gosh! Is he a secret killer? I am going to die! Oh no! Oh, mom, I love you!

Lila, I love you and hope you wake up! Reece, I lov—! Wow, I will never get to tell him that! No, I can't die! I begin to think while my nerves and anxiety kick up again.

Yo, woman, put a can in it, you dummy! It's Conner. The likelihood of the big goofball killing you is one in a billion! The boy couldn't hurt a fly. Calm down! Just ask him why you have to wear a blindfold, my voice inside my head reasons.

"Why are you putting it on me?" I ask him, raising my eyebrow as my hands begin to tremble again.

"Why do you ask so many questions?" he asks me with a sigh and rolls his eyes again.

"Because I want to know why you are putting a blindfold me. So now, I repeat, 'Conner why are you putting a blindfold on me?'"

"Jeez, you're stubborn! I must place this blindfold on you for your date."

Hmm, that seems like a good enough reason. "Okay," I say as I bob my head up and down. In my lap, I twist my hands nervously together. Conner leans forward and ties the blindfold tightly around my head, covering my eyes and sending me into the blackness.

"We are here. Watch your step," Conner says as I hear the front door open.

"Thank you for bringing her, Conner," Reece's voice says out of nowhere, and I feel Conner's hand, which was guiding me, disappear. A few seconds later, though, they were replaced by a touch that always sends tingles through me and could only belong to one man — Reece.

"Hey, Payton," Reece's sweet voice says from in front of me, and he takes my right hand into his and leads me somewhere. He must be using the cane because I can hear it tapping against what sounds like wood.

"What are we doing?" I ask him as he led me somewhere. I have no clue what is happening around me. Is that what his life is like now? I honestly do not know how he does it.

"We are going to eat," he says, and I can hear a smile in his voice. He places my hand on a chair like I've done for him many times before, and I do what I have seen him do to sit down. I feel him still standing behind me and then his hands begin searching for the blindfold which he slowly removes. I shut my eyes bracing them for light but as they flutter open, all I am met with is more darkness, but I know the blindfold is off because I feel it gone.

"Why is it dark?" I ask him as I hear his movement away from me and then hear him sit down. It is dark, and I am not sure if I like it.

"It's called dining in the dark, and it is supposed to make the food taste so much better because it temporarily heightens your others senses," Reece tells me. That actually sounds pretty cool! The more I think about this, it is pretty awesome! I mean, this is what Reece everyday life is like, and this situation is supposed to make everything better. I am open to this as long as I am with Reece!

"This is really cool and very creative, Reece," I say with a big ole smile plastered on my face and nod my head.

"Thank you. I just wanted to do something great for you," he says, and that is so sweet! Reece is so amazing. I just can't get over it.

"So what are we having?" I ask him as I feel around blindly on the table.

"We are having some French food," Reece's voice says simply, and I smile. I have never had French food before except for French Fries, which apparently aren't even French. Crazy, right?

"Yum," I say with a smile, and he chuckles.

"It's already on the plate which is on the table in front of you," Reece informs me, and I smile.

"I really hope you enjoy this date! I want it to be the best you ever had," he says with a smile in his voice.

"Not a problem."

"Why's that not a problem?" he asks me, and I swear in my head. Dang him and his amazing hearing.

"Because this is my first date," I say to him with a blush rising to my cheeks.

"Well, then I will make this the best one ever because you deserve nothing but the best," he says, melting my heart, and I smile like a fool. This guy is just so sweet and kind of cheesy, yet he is so amazing!

Chapter Thirty-Five

Reece's POV

"Is this what it is like for you normally?" Payton's sweet voice asks me as I help her find her fork by guiding her hand around like I do with mine.

"Yes, pretty much," I say once she gets the feel of the plate and fork and starts eating.

"I don't see how you do it," she whispers lightly, and my ears pick it up crystal clear.

"It is definitely not without challenges, but I have learned to take it one step at a time," I say simply with a sad smile slipping onto my face as I pick up my fork and take a bite of the food.

"Reece, you are absolutely amazing," she says with a strong, clear voice, and I smile.

"You are too."

The room is silent except for some breathing and chewing of food which is quite soothing. Occasionally, I hear Payton mumble a few swear words as I guess she has trouble eating. There is also times when she lets out a small moan as she enjoys the food which I can tell because I can listen to her chewing.

"Reece?" her voice breaks the silence a few minutes later.

"Yes?" I reply to her as I take another bite.

"I noticed something about your parents," she states bluntly, and I hear the sound of her chewing again. What has she noticed?

"What would that happen to be?" I ask her calmly. I wonder what it is. Maybe it's the fact that my parents are totally 24/7 happy.

"It's just that your parents are always happy. They never seem to get angry. No offense, but it just isn't normal," she says, and I sigh. Of course! I knew it was going come up sooner or later. I don't blame her for finding this weird. I would too if it weren't my family. Heck, whom am I kidding? I find this weird.

"They weren't always like this. Believe it or not. They only have been this way since the accident. Before we were the normal family, we fought. I get in trouble like normal. It's different now and honestly, kind of sucks. Everyone is walking on ice around me, and it is an awful feeling," I tell her honestly, and it does feel amazing to get that off my chest. It has been driving me insane thinking about it. I take one last bite of my food, feeling full.

"That sucks, Reece. I have no clue what that would be like," she says to me, and I feel her warm hand slip into mine.

"It's okay. Are you done eating?" I ask her as I squeeze her hand.

"Yeah," she says, and I smile.

"Rider!" I call, and I hear his paws race against the floor as he nears me. His panting is at my side, and I stand up, grabbing the handle of his harness. *Thank you, Carter, for getting him set up.* I say mentally as I run my left hand over the tablecloth to Payton's hand. "Come on; onto the part two," I say with a smile.

"Ok," she says happily. She stands up, and I walk to where I know the back door to our guest house is located, leading us into what should be the backyard. Luckily, Rider gets us there safely, and I am glad tonight is a fairly warm night for this time of the year. It's almost sixty out, and Carter told me the stars were supposed to be out so I thought this was perfect.

I continue to walk forward and then stop, releasing Payton's hand as I slowly sit on the cool grass and unharnessed Rider, and I feel him shift. I run my hand down him and feel that he is lying down. I smile as I pet him and lay back onto my back, looking straight up trying to imagine the stars. I feel someone sits down beside me, and the warmth of her side against mine. My heart skips a beat. How did I manage to get her?

Payton's POV

My eyes adjust slowly to the light that the stars are giving off as I watch Reece lay onto the green grass. For the first time tonight, I can drink in his appearance. He is wearing a pair of nice fitting jeans and a dark blue button-down shirt. He is staring at the sky with a slight smile. His beautiful, blue eyes stare up at the sky, and I smile. It feels kind of nice outside, so slowly, I lay down beside him and our sides lightly touching. Looking up at the night sky, I stare at the twinkling stars.

"I wish you could see the stars too." My hand finds Reece, and he intertwines them.

With a light squeeze of my hand, he speaks, "I don't need to see the stars. All I care about is being here with you. I don't care where I am as long as I am with you that is where I want to be."

Tears form in my eyes as he says that, and it is honestly the nicest thing anyone has ever said to me. Why would he feel that way about me? Is he crazy?

"Why?" I choke; fighting back the tears as my heart melt.

"Why? Payton, why wouldn't I? You are the nicest, sweetest, most caring, and kind person I have ever met; not to mention, you are beautiful. When I am with you, I am not blind. I am normal. You make me feel like I am just like everyone else. When I am with you, I am happy and feel whole. I never felt this before. You give me hope and strength. When I am with you, I am comfortable. It's as if we are two pieces that just go together. Payton…" Reece says and pauses. I turn my head towards him and stare into his amazing blue eyes. The tears are streaming freely down my cheek as he says those things that cause my insides to melt and butterflies to take off.

"Yes?" I say in a thick, teary voice.

"I am falling in love with you," he says simply as he blinks and continues to look towards where I am. Uh… Did he just say he loves me? OH, MY GOSH! I have to be dreaming! Reece Collins loves me! No way! That is impossible, yet as he stares at me, I know it's true. But how do I feel about Reece? He is amazing, sweet, gorgeous, kind, and caring. When I am with him, the haunting pain I live with becomes dull.

"I am falling in love with you too, Reece," I say to him softly. He tightens his grip on my hand.

"Will you be my girlfriend?" he asks me, and my heart swells. He wants me to be his girlfriend? This is a dream.

"Yes, of course," I say softly, and I feel his hand slip from mine and slip up slowly to my chin, leaving a trail of tingles.

He leans up stroking my bottom lip with his thumb, and I stare into his eyes as he leans down and replaces his thumb with his perfect lips. This kiss is different. It is happier and more passionate as if we haven't seen each other in months.

His hand slowly slides to my cheek, and I roll over on top of him, straddling him as our lips move in sync. His hand that is not on my cheek rises up and is placed on my waist. I have my hand in his hair and the other on his neck.

Reece pulls lightly on my lip, and I open it allowing him inside. As we kiss, I begin to smile, and the happy tears end. We pull apart, and I rest my forehead on his, biting my lip as I breathe hard.

"I love you," he says to me. I smile as I roll off of him, and he keeps an arm around me.

"I love you too," I say as he holds me, and I stare at the stars. That was the greatest moment ever!

After about fifteen minutes, Reece speaks. "I return to school tomorrow," he says, and I can hear the fear in his voice. I will not leave his side. I mean, I do love him! Whatever happens, I am sure we can make it I think.

Chapter Thirty-Six

Payton's POV

My alarm clock wakes me, and I sit up on my uncomfortable bed to stretch and pop my sore back. A huge smile stretches across my face as I think back to last night. Reece and I had the most fun. He is truly amazing. I really do love him and being around him warms my heart. Today, he is coming back to school which I am really nervous about. I don't know if he's going to use Rider or his cane; he hasn't told me. Actually, he doesn't really want to talk about it. I understand, this is going be hard on him in so many ways. He has to face those who once fell to his feet and most importantly, go back to the place that changed his life forever. I can honestly not imagine what it will be like for him or what will be going through his head since Reece isn't exactly the sharing type. Reece doesn't share everything and neither do I. That is one the reason's I love him so much because we understand each other on another level. I am just happy Reece agreed to let me take him to school. I am not going leave his side for a single second.

Getting out of bed, I hurry to my closet and find a tank top and Reece's hoodie along with a pair of jeans. Carrying them to the bathroom, I take a quick shower and get ready. My smile is still stuck on my face, and I can't help it! I look okay, not pretty; just okay and normal. Plain and simple— two things I will always be.

Hey, but this plain and simple girl is dating Reece Collins, the greatest guy ever! "Reece! Crap, I need hurry up!"

I mumble to myself as I rush back to my room, yanking on my shoes and grabbing my backpack. Rushing to the kitchen, I grab an apple real quick and head for the door. I bite the green apple as I pull open the heavy door and leave, shutting it tightly behind me. My mom has already left for work. I feel so bad for my mom! She is always working!

As I get onto the road, I head towards Reece's home and eat my apple along the way. When I am almost there, I check the time. We have like twenty minutes until school starts so that boy better be ready. As I pull into his driveway, I throw the car in park and step out of it. Walking up the long pathway, a breeze wipes through the cool air and sends some of the small pieces of hair left out flying across my face. I tug the leaves down in my hand and fold my arms gently over

Once I reach the large door, I reach out and lightly tap my hand on it, waiting for an answer. When I stay there and wait for someone to answer, I begin to bounce up and down waiting.

"Ugh, hurry up!" I mutter as I continue to bounce. I don't get this freaking weather! It goes from being like fifty almost sixty degrees to thirty! I swear I am starting to think the Mother Nature is bi-polar.

Finally, the door swings open revealing Conner in a pair of plaid pajama pants and a white beater, his blond hair is a mess atop his head.

"Reece, your girlfriends here!" he yells super loudly, causing me to flinch. *Girlfriend?* Aww, the sound of that makes my heart thump very quickly, and butterflies burst to lose in my stomach. "Finally, you are here! Reece woke me up whining because he needed help picking out clothes! He wanted to look good for you! But now, the kid won't leave his room because he doesn't trust me! I swear I do not get him! He's all yours now. Have fun," Conner rants as he steps inside the house, allowing me to pass him.

"Okay," I say simply and decide to head for Reece's room.

"If you need anything today, let me know!" he adds before yawning and disappearing up the staircase. Conner is so silly. I am sure Reece is acting just fine and dandy.

Continuing down the hall, I can hear cursing coming from Reece's room so as I get closer, I slowly grab the doorknob and step inside. Once I get inside Reece's room, I see my hot boyfriend standing in the middle of the room in a pair of faded blue jeans, some kind of white tennis shoes, and a gray slight V-neck shirt with a blue plaid shirt over it left unbuttoned. His brown hair is neatly styled, and a pair of black shades rests on his face covering his eyes. Reece is facing the ceiling! He has his hands folded behind his head and is venting groans of frustration.

"Reece," I say softly as I walk towards him drinking in his appearance. Man, he looks amazing! I cannot believe that he is my boyfriend! He is mine! I would have never seen this coming. He loves me.

"Payton." He looks in my direction and smiles brightly. Even if I cannot see his eyes because of his glasses, I know his blue eyes are sparkling.

"Hi," I say shyly as I think of him as my boyfriend.

"Why the sudden shyness?" he asks me as he uses his stick to guide himself forward towards me.

"Nothing."

"Really? Payton, you can tell me anything. I love you."
My cheeks heat up. Quickly, I step forward and through my arms around his neck. He is shocked at first but then quickly recovers and wraps his arms around my waist.

"I love you too," I say as I hold him. His enriching scent fills my nose causing me to smile. He pulls away holding my arms at my elbow while my hands rest on his shoulders.

"So Payton, how do I look?" Reece asks me as I stare up at his face really wish I could see his amazing eyes.

"You look gorgeous as always, Reece," I say to him as I slide my hands up to his neck, holding it.

Reece gently and slowly moves his fingers up my arms and find my cheeks where he strokes them gently. "I am glad you think so. I'm sure you look beautiful too," he says as his face grows closer to mine, and his soft lips brush against my own, setting off the eruption of fireworks. Our lips move perfectly in sync as we kiss, and I am in total bliss.

I pull away from him, rest my forehead against his forehead, and try to see his eyes through his sunglasses.

"Whatever you say," I say softly. How would Reece know if I am beautiful? Reece has never seen me! So he cannot say that I am beautiful!

"Payton, I really love you," he whispers causing me to smile.

"I love you too, but we really need to be going!" I say knowing that we have been here for too long.

"I don't know if I can," he mumbles, and I shut my eyes, breathing.

"You can. I will be there the whole time and support you every second," I tell as I pull away and bend over picking up his walking stick that he dropped.

"Promise?" he asks me as he takes a deep breath. I look at my boyfriend and wonder why he wouldn't think so.

"I'll promise you a million times if that's what it takes, Reece. I am not going to leave your side, no matter what goes down. I am with you for as long as you want me." I refuse to use the word forever because if I say that, it will backfire. Also, I don't think he will love me that long.

"Thank you and I will want you forever," he tells me as I place the handle of the stick back into his hand.

"Give it time. I mean forever is a very long time. Now let's go," I say as I slip my hand into his left hand. I tug him along with me as I leave his room, down the hall and to the car. Once we reach it, I get the door handle for him so he is able to get in. Once all of his limbs are inside the car, I shut the door, walking around the front of the car and to the driver's side. I start the car and reach over to my wonderful boyfriend, who is sitting very stiffly beside me, and take his hand into mine.

"We're here!" I say as I shift the car into park and shut it off. I release a groan as I look around, noticing a lot of people standing around the school still.

"I meant to tell you earlier, my mom had all my classes change to the same as yours," he says as he feels around his left side for his seatbelt.

"Okay, that is awesome. So are you ready, Reece? I will be by your side and hold your hand the whole time."

He is silent for a second and has his head slightly bent down. I watch as his chest rises and falls over and over again in even movements. Finally, he takes a deep breath and looks straight up. "I'm ready."

I smile light at him as I grab my things and get out of the car. As I shut the door behind me, I see Reece's head appear on the other side. I begin to walk around to the front of the car. He carefully navigates his way forward before I walk beside him and slip my hand casually into my boyfriend's. I'm sorry. I can't help saying it!

The moment Reece and I begin our way across the parking lot, hand in hand, a walking stick in his other and glasses on his face, all eyes fall on us. There are just so many stares. Some are proud, honorable stares because they know what he did and that he could've saved lives. However, they were other with a look of terror, disgust, and mostly shock. Their stares are unnerving and almost plain out irritating.

"Everyone is staring," I whisper to Reece.

"It's because I'm a freak now," he mutters, and I look at him in shock that he said that. His face drains of color, and I watch his Adams apple bob up and down. "Um... did I say that out loud?" he asks me as he clears his throat.

"Yes, but Reece, you are not a freak! They are not staring because of that! They are staring because a guy like you is with a girl like me," I mumble as we enter the hall and people continue to share.

I lead him towards my locker to switch out my things and then to our classroom. I am going to do my best not to screw this up. For me, it feels like nothing I do is just ever enough. I am ready for this, and I can do it. I will be by his side the whole time, and I can try to help.

Chapter Thirty-Seven

Reece's POV

Payton holds my hand as she leads me into our first class of the day. The room is silent apart from the clicking of keyboards. She tugs me along further with her, and my pulse begins to race as my nerves grow. I have never been the nervous type, but I sure am today! Even though Payton is leading me, I still tap my cane to help and feel like I am doing something.

"Reece?" a surprised voice says, and my body tenses.

"It's just Mrs. Reed," Payton whispers to me, and I relax some.

"Hi," I say lowly and a little uncomfortable.

"Mrs. Reed, can I sit beside Reece and help him notes, work, and everything?" I hear Payton ask from beside me. I groan lightly because I do not want special treatment. I just want to be normal again!

"Yes, of course, dear. That is a splendid idea," the teacher says, and I smile.

"Come on, Reece, let's sit down," Payton says to me as she tugs my hand lightly and takes me to where I am able to sit down. She places one of my hands on cold, thick plastic chair. I slowly and carefully use my hands to feel my way to the desk. "I am right here beside you."

I suddenly hear the sound of a squeaking chair and then heels clicking against the floor as they near me.

"Reece," Mrs. Reed's voice says as the heels stop. She sounds very much closer, and her voice is softer and kinder. "I wanted to tell you that I admire what you did, and I am truly proud of you. You are a true hero and if it wasn't for you trying to calm him down and take longer time, then who knows how many people would not be here today. What you did was amazing and something to be proud of, and the fact that you're dealing with being blind is amazing. I truly admire your ability to come back to school. You are a strong boy, and I don't want anything to make you think otherwise. There is going to be people who do not realize what you've done for them. I wanted to thank you for being a hero and tell you how proud I am. Don't let anything stop you, Reece. I am also shocked yet very happy that you have found Payton," Mrs. Reed says, and I feel so special. When I did what I did, I never thought that people would be thinking of me like this. To be honest, I never thought I'd ever live again.

When that gun was pointed in my direction, I thought I was dead, and I am happy that I am not. I am glad I will still be there for all the important events even if I cannot see them. It makes me happy to know that not everyone hates me. I smile up to where I am guessing she is standing. "Thank you, ma'am," I say with the respect that I've always shown to my teachers.

"You've always been a good kid," she says, and then I hear her heels click to leave.

"Oh, Payton, congratulations on Valedictorian," Mrs. Reed says to Payton, and I smile. I am so proud of Payton for accomplishing this; she is amazing being able to keep up great grades while dealing with everything that she is.

"Thank you, Mrs. Reed," Payton's sweet, innocent voice says, and I smile brightly. The loud sound of the bell ringing fills my ears, and it is ten times louder than it was before. The sound of loud voice and footsteps enter the room quickly. I release a sigh. *Here goes nothing*; I think as gently rest my elbow on the table and then my head in my hand.

The talking is so loud in my ears, and I can catch pieces of conversations here and there, I never thought this would be so distracting. I find it hard to really concentrate on what Mrs. Reed is saying. This is the first time being in a room with so many people. I reach up, running my hand through my hair tugging lightly.

This is how my next three classes play out also, and my head is seriously beginning to hurt. I just want to return home and curl into my bedroom and hide. Whom was I kidding? I am not ready for this. This is a stupid idea. The other reason I am struggling with this is because I can hear the other kids. The kids who use to kiss the ground I walk on are now mocking me. They think I cannot hear the awful and cruel words that they spit out — the horrible comments they make about my blindness. Many are calling me *Special Ed* because I am blind.

Some even think it's like a sickness. There are others who seem so wrapped up in their own world they see my blindness as some major differing flaw. There are so much judgment and criticism, and to make matters worse, not one of my old friends have spoken to me. I have been counting the loud bells so when the next one rings; I know it is the lunch one.

"Ready for lunch, Reece?" Payton's angelic voice asks me, and I nod my head.

"Yeah," I say. I push myself up from the desk and grab my cane. The feeling of a warm hand reaches mine and intertwines with my own hand. I feel the sparks that are only ever caused by Payton, my angel. She pulls me along with her into the loud hall.

"We can grab our lunch and go anywhere you want." I sigh. I really don't want to go to the cafeteria because my head hurts so much. Everyone does not only hate my blindness, but also my relationship with Payton. Some comments are really mean towards me while there are others that are horrible and just cruel about Payton. A few times, I found myself really wanting to beat some people's butts!

"Payton, all this noise has given me a bad headache. Can you just help me get to the football field and then come back to get the food and come join me?" I ask seriously, hoping she will agree with me.

"Sure, Reece. I totally understand," she says as she begins leading me towards the football field I guess, and I use my cane to feel my way.

A few minutes later, the texture I am walking on changes, and Payton stops me. It's very quiet, apart from the sound of the breeze whipping through. "Do you want to sit on the field or the bleachers?" my angel asks me with her sweet voice, and I smile.

"There's no one here?" I ask her, not answering her question yet.

"No, there is no one," she replies simply squeezing my hand.

"Okay, can we sit on the field?" I ask her with my kind smile.

"Sure, of course," she says, leading me a few steps forward. "Sit here. I'll be back," she adds, and I nod. Her hand begins to slip from mine.

"Wait," I call to her, hoping to stop her.

"Yes, dear?" she asks, and I can hear the smile in her voice.

"Don't I get a kiss?" I smirk, and her musical laughter fills the air. I feel her body step closer to me, and my heart rate picks up as she places one hand onto my check. I feel her amazing lips press against mine, and they move together. She pulls away from me too soon, causing me to groan.

"There's your kiss. I will be back. I love you," she says to me, and I smile, shaking my head. This girl sure is something else.

"I love you too," I reply and gently sit myself down as I listen to her footsteps leave me on the turf. As I sit on the field where I once played on many times, I touch the turf and remember the many times that I have played on it. This field has seen me grow and change; it has helped me become a leader. This field made things possible, and I felt alive every Friday night that I stepped onto the green turf, and the big bright lights shone onto the field. Then there is every Saturday when I would step out onto the track to start running. Everything was different and will never be the same again.

I hear heavy footsteps near my sprawled out position, and I stiffen sitting up straight. The steps stop in front of me, and I hear the movement and sound of someone sitting down in front of me. There is a deep breath, and then finally, the unknown person speaks. "Hey," the deep male voice says, and I instantly recognize it from the years that we shared together.

I relax some, knowing that it was not a stranger in front of me. "Hi," I state simply still holding a slight grudge against Jace. He was supposed to be my best friend, but as soon as I got shot, it was so long sucker! What kind of best friend does that? I'll tell you not a good one! So I will admit. I do hold a slight anger towards him.

"How are you?" he asks, and I can hear a hint of nerves in his voice. He must be crazy to think that I am fine! Why ask that? It's a retarded question.

"Fine," I grumble, trying to keep my face emotionless. I reach up and rub the back of my neck in annoyance.

"So you are with Payton? How did that happen?" he asks me. Why the hell does he finally give a shit about how I am? Did he wake up this morning and think, "Oh, hey, I am an ass for ditching my best friend?" I doubt it. So what is his stupid ass motive now? I don't need his charity or pity, and when I needed a friend, he was nowhere in sight, so I don't think I am too rude.

"Jace just tell me what the hell you want?" I demand, rolling my eyes and trying to contain my anger.

"I want my best friend back," he says so very softly, and I laugh. That's right I laugh. Head falling back, stomach holding laughter at how stupid he is.

"Well, I wanted a friend when I was in the hospital and where were you?" I ask him my anger coming out in my voice.

"Reece, it wasn't that simple! Just let me explain before you throw our whole life worth of friendship down the fucking toilet," he argues, and I can sense the frustration in his voice.

To give him the chance to explain or not? I need this closure, and it makes me a bigger person than he was. "You get one shot to explain so it better be a hell of one," I state simply to him as I fold my strong arms over my chest.

He releases a huge sigh of relief. "Reece, we have been friends since diapers and have always done everything together. We joined little league together, we started playing football together, and we even ran together. We throw parties, and with our birthdays being two days apart, we even celebrated that together. We hung out every evening, played video games; hell, you even made me volunteer at the soup kitchen and homeless shelter. Even though after my first experience there and not wanting to go back, I still went with you every Christmas to help. I was there the day Rayne came into the world, and I was there to help you torture Juliet. You and I used to follow around Conner because we wanted to be like him.

"The truth is my whole life I wanted to be like you. My mom always saw you like her own son and sometimes, I think she liked you more than me. She would tell me I should be more like you, and I listened because I want to be. You were my hero and best friend. I remember the times when you and I would pitch a tent in your backyard and pretend to be camping. We did it all together.

"You have also saved my ass more than anyone. That time I stole the ten dollars from my mom's purse even just because I wanted some candy. Then my mom saw the money was gone and was going to kill me, but you stepped up saying that you took it and gave her your ten dollars. You covered for me then, just like when I ran through your house and accidentally broke your mom's favorite vase. Instead of letting me go down for it, you stepped up again.

"You were always the perfect one, and I was the screw-up. You always took up for me. That day I should have been there. My class may have been on the other side of campus, but I was still going swing by your locker. That was until the teacher stopped me. Reece, I should've been there for you! I should have been there to save you like the many times you saved me. I would've pushed you out the way or tackled the kid. If I were there, you wouldn't be blind. You wouldn't have almost died. Reece, I beat myself up over this, and I could not face you, knowing that I should've been there like you always were for me. So I did what I do best and screw up by staying away, afraid you'd hate me. I felt like I lost you.

"I know I have been stupid, but I just couldn't face you and see you in the hospital or struggling after everything we've been through. It was too much, and I am so sorry. I haven't been myself. It's like I am missing part of me and our friendship. I just need my best friend back," he says. Damn, Jace has never been so emotional, he sure is messed up from all this.

Should I be his friend? I mean, yeah, Carter is a great friend, Payton is the perfect girlfriend whom I love, and my family is there. But I feel as if a small piece is missing, and I always assumed it was sports. But what if it's my best friend? I never knew he felt that way. I never meant for him to see me as better than him. We were the total opposite and yet friends. I miss it, but I don't know if we can ever go back. If I did, he would have to accept Payton, or I'd be done with him. So now the question remains. What should I do?

Chapter Thirty-Eight

Payton's POV

Silence. That's all I hear. The awkward, uncomfortable silence, when I enter the cafeteria. Every set of eyes seems to be glued on me as I walk into the overly crowded room. I take my place in the shrinking lunch line, keeping my head down. I hate attention, always have and always will. So all these eyes on me are seriously causing me discomfort. Hugging my arms to my chest tightly, I just want to disappear as I try to ignore all the stares and slight whispers filling the air. Looking down, I watch as the feet in front of me move along the line, and I follow.

Keeping to myself in high school was great because I never got bullied. No one knew me, and I was left unbothered. Now, it's gone, just like many other things. I am no longer invisible. Instead, it's as if there is a spotlight on me, and I am wearing a flashing shirt. How can dating one guy make such a big difference?

Dumb question because the answer is simple. The guy is Reece Collins, or as rude, insensitive people around here like to call him when they think we can't hear, "blind boy." I swear people are so cruel to treat him that way. He is a freaking hero. Taking a step forward, I finally reach the lunch window.

I look up facing the lunch lady behind the counter. A scowl looks to be engraved on her face, which is not fitting. "What would you like?" the lady says in a monotone, uncaring voice.

"Two bags," I say simply, and the lady looks at me lazily and places two brown paper bags atop the counter. I grab them, walking to the ID card scanner that pays for our food.

I turn around to head back to the football field when my eyes land on someone I am really trying to avoid seeing. In this dead silent room, I watch as her blue-gray eyes lock with mine, and I quickly look away. The beautiful blonde is wearing a sparkly turquoise top with white skinny jeans and a high, black leather boots. A smile appears on Clair's face, revealing her shining white teeth as she nears me.

Oh, crap! I have to get out of here! There will be no good coming from her nearing me. So I will my feet to move quicker as I reach the door and go as fast as my feet will carry me out the side door of the building. Stealing a glance behind me, I see no one is there, so I slow down and steady my breath. The big tall bleachers come into my view. I walk closer to it and reach the chain-link fence ahead of me that surrounds the bright green turf. Reece is perched in the center of the field where I left him, and I spot a broad back and short black hair that belongs to none other than Jace.

What is that boy up to? I cannot believe he is actually talking to Reece. I walk through the opening and head very slowly to where they are seated. When I get into the hearing distance, I hear Reece say *yes* to Jace. Continuing towards them, I finally stop beside Reece and sit down on the turf beside him, folding my legs over each other.

"Here," I say as I drop a brown bag onto Reece lap. I am not sure how Reece wants to do this so I sit there and open my own bag.

"Hi there, Payton!" Jace says to me with a big smile, and I roll my eyes. He is wearing a gray football T-shirt with a blue baseball jacket on top and a pair of blue jeans and *Nike*. He looks ok, nothing compared to Reece.

"Jace," I groan as I pull some foot from my bag sitting it on the ground, don't worry it's in containers, and then I pull out a gleaming apple and smile taking a bite from it. I watch as Reece feels around his bag finally making it to the top of it and opening it. Sticking his hand within the brown paper, he retrieves the food and carefully brings it to the ground. I glance up at Jace's impressed face.

"So Payton, this has been what's different. I had my suspicions about you two, but could not figure out how it came to be," he says smugly as he reclines back on the grass place his hands behind him.

"What are you doing here anyways?" I ask the as I take another bite of my delicious apple and rest my head on my boyfriend's shoulder.

"Hanging out with my best friend," Jace says with that annoying smile, and I roll my eyes as I rest my head on Reece's shoulder, munching on my apple. Reece seems to have found his and takes a cautious bite.

"Reece, you're friends with him again?" I ask in slight disbelief.

"I am, angel. Someone has to keep him out of trouble, and that's always been my job so I can't quit. Plus, he's my best friend," Reece says softly to me as I peek up at him. From the angle I am laying, I can see beneath his glasses to the thick eyelashes and blue eyes.

Wait! Hold up! Freeze! Did he just call me an angel to my face? So I am not dreaming? He really calls me "Angel!" My heart rate picks up as it slams against my chest, and I can hear the pounding in my ears.

"He wasn't there for you, though, and did you just call me, 'Angel'?" I ask. I know he did so I don't know why I asked him.

"Yes, I did because you are my angel, and you know everyone makes mistakes, so I can't punish him for his one he made," Reece says to me, biting his apple.

Aww! That's sweet, man. I am so in love with this boy. I lean my head up and lightly kiss his cheek. "I love you," I say to Reece before turning my head to look at Jace. "You still annoy me, though," he laughs.

"You know you love me," he jokes with a smirk, and I crunch my face up in distaste.

"Only in your dreams," I say as I shake my head and finish my apple, placing the core back within the bag.

"Reece, buddy you got yourself a good one. I approve," Jace says smiling at me happily, and I shake my head.

"Reece, can we share Carter and you keep this one to yourself?" I ask jokingly as I take his left hand into mine and tangle our fingers together. They fit perfectly, and his thumb rubs circles on my hand.

Reece laughs, leans his head back and smiles. "He's not that bad, but that's good enough," he tells me as he looks in front of him again. I glance at Jace, who is sitting there with a look of confusion.

"I don't understand," Jace says, scratching his head, and I laugh and so does Reece, causing his chest to vibrate.

"Wha—?" Jace begins to complain but is cut off by the lunch bell. He groans. "This isn't over," he grumbles as he jumps up and scurries off. I laugh as I stand up, and Reece takes a couple seconds, but finally get himself up off the ground. I bend down to gather the trash and then taking his cane, placing it inside his hand. Slipping my hand back in his, I lead him off the field and toss the bags into the trash as I pass. We head to class.

The rest of the day goes by with a few bumps which were caused by rude, idiotic people. Finally, Reece and I are lying in his bed. I'm curled up in his arms, and we are both worn out from today. I know it's sad to say, but I am too tired to attend the hospital.

"Reece," I whisper softly as I draw circles on his chest over the top of his shirt.

"Yeah?" he says back just as softly. His sweet voice causes me to smile.

"Everything that Mrs. Reed said today was true. You are a hero. You don't know this, but you saved me," I say softly as I snuggle closer to him and breathe in his amazing scent.

"How did I do that?" he asks me in complete confusion.

"I was there. I saw it. I saw you. I thought you were dead. If you hadn't talked to him, trying to calm him down, and help him, I thought I wouldn't be here as well. You stalled him. Because of you, the police had time to get there, and when he shot you, he then shot himself because they showed up. If you hadn't done that, he would've shot you sooner and then shot others, maybe even me. So because of you, I am alive, and to me, that means a lot. It's not just me but many others. You are amazing, and I love you." Soft tears roll down my cheeks.

I look up at him and see a few tears stream down his face, and I reach up wiping them from his water blue eyes. "You are the most amazing girl I have ever met, and you are my angel. I seriously thank God gave me you. You are like an angel he sent down for me, and I love you," he says, and I smile through the tears and lean, pressing my lips against his. The kiss tastes a little salty from the tears but is otherwise perfect. I pull away and press my forehead against his smiling.

"Can I ask you a question?" he asks me, and his warm breath fanning my face.

"Sure," I reply, returning my head to his chest.

"Why don't you speak of a father?" he asks me, and my

Chapter Thirty-Nine

Reece's POV

Payton's body stiffens in my arms, and I bite the inside of my lip, regretting of asking her such a dumb question. She is probably not going to answer it and in all honesty, I do not blame her. I was totally stupid for asking her that.

"He left; it was when I was younger. He was a very bad man, and I don't consider him my father. I call him a sperm donor. He is the meanest men I know, and he is a major jackass. He cheated on my mom all the time but had her so brainwashed that she would not leave him. I remember Lila was still so healthy, and I would always protect her. He would lay down beating us, mainly me because I stood between him and Lila. I thought she was too young to see the horror of this man who was supposed to be our father. He would hit me repeatedly until I was knocked unconscious. Most the time, he would continue to hit me causing me to release cries of pain and then the beating got worse from me being a 'cry-baby.' The pain was awful. That pain, however, could nowhere near match up the emotional and mental pain I suffered. As he beat me, he barked out horrible comments to me like that I am ugly, fat, worthless, stupid, nothing, waste of space, a mistake, and much more," Payton breaks off from what she is saying as I hear her voice thickens, and her body begin to shake. I hear a few sobs escape her, and my anger within me begins boiling to a peak.

"After so long, hearing all those things I began to believe them and look at myself in those ways. And to tell you the truth, I have never ever spoken to anyone about this ever," Payton begins to cry even more, and I bring her closer to my chest, clinging to her and not wanting to let go.

How can any man treat a child that way? Guys like that belong on the electric chair. He is an awful man, and I hope I never met the man because I may not be able to see but my fists still work fine.

"Payton, never ever think of yourself that way! None of that is true! You are beautiful and sweet. You are kind, skinny, and a genius. You are nowhere near worthless because to me, you are worth everything. Without you, I don't know where I'd be right now, and when my accident happened, I never thought I would fall in love or meet the one in my life. Then you appeared like a gift from heaven, my very own Angel. Everything about you is amazing. I have fallen in love with you, and I love you so much! You mean a lot to me! I love you, and you are my world, my whole wide world," I tell her as I hold her and her nails bury through my shirt and into my skin.

I feel shifting in my arms as Payton moves around and then I feel a set of wet, salty and soft lips touch mine and tingles shot throughout my whole body. Slowly, I raise my hand and rest it on her cheek while the other on her back. Our lips move in sync like two things on the same wavelength. The perfect kiss full of love soon grows passion as I use my thumb to wipe away her cool tears. Gently, I nibble on her bottom lip, but her lips remain sealed very tightly together. Groaning, I continue to kiss her. Kissing her is the most amazing experience I've ever had. I have had my fair share of kisses, but this is nothing like I felt with any other person ever. Finally, she caves in and parts her perfect lips, allowing my tongue to slip into her sweet mouth which tastes like green apples and is delicious.

Allowing my tongue to explore her mouth, I feel her thin fingers twist in my hair. She takes my lead on the kiss and does what I do, and finally, I force myself to pull away from the perfect kiss and peck her lips again before pulling her into my arms.

"I love you so much, Reece. You are truly the best thing that has happened to me, ever," she says softly, and a smile finds its way to my probably swollen lips.

"I love you too, and you are definitely the best thing to happen to me," I say to her as I squeeze her. I shut my eyes and concentrate on her breathing.

It begins to even out, and I know she is beginning to fall into a nice sleep which she deserves. This girl deserves the world, and I will give it to her if I could. It's crazy to think that you could know someone so well and yet not know the hell what they have been through. You can't see all the pain and suffering that someone goes through. Just because someone seems like they have it together and their life is perfect, doesn't mean you fully know them. That could all be an act; they could be hiding things like Payton did. You can know someone forever and not realize who they are or their past. People take things for granted. Payton, who have been going through hell, still manages to smile, help people, do things for others, and become valedictorian. That is just a sign of an amazing person. An amazing person that is all mine and I love her.

———————◆———————

Payton's POV

"I should have pushed you downstairs or something when I found out you were pregnant!" his voice booms and echoes through the hall. *"That way, that mistake would've never been born!"* his voice matches with the thunder as I sit in a shaking ball beside my door. The flash of lighting lights the black room with a scary glow.

"Don't ever say that about our daughter again!" my mom's voice shrieks at him, and I wrap my arms tighter around my knees and bury my face into my small legs. A soft whimper escapes as I listen, praying silently that tonight he doesn't come inside and hurt me. Why does he hurt me? What did I ever do for him not to like me? Was I not good enough? What could I have done to make me love him? Why God, are you not listening to my prayers?

"Our daughter?" His horrid laughter feels my ears and causes me to shake and whimper. "There is no way something that ugly and stupid like that child is mine. It is all yours. She's yours, not mine, so don't offend me by saying that I had that thing as my child," he roars, and I hear the sound of a struggle. My tears find their way from my eyelids and skate down my cheeks as my body begin to shake with fear.

"Please, don't let anything happen to my mommy! I don't want to be left alone with him. No! Please, please don't let anything happen to my mommy!" I say to myself as I cry into my knees.

I hear the sound of a baby crying and stand up, wiping the tears from my chubby face as I stand up stumbling, clumsy over my own feet. Gripping the edge of her crib, I see her crying. "Shhh..." I soothe her, trying to get her quiet so he doesn't become angrier.

Taking a deep breath, I push all my fears aside as I scoop my baby sister within my arms and hold her, gently rocking her.

"Shhh... Lila, I'm here," I whisper to her as I make my way to my closet. With one hand, I open it, push apart my clothes, and push a brown box over to reveal a secret door. I climb inside before pulling the box back along to block the door and then shut the small door. The room is small, but safe and is lowly. Lila is still a little fussy, so I gently rock her back and forth.

"Hush, little baby. Don't say a word. Momma's going by you a mockingbird. If that mockingbird..." I sing softly to her as I rock my barely a few months old baby sister.

I hear the sound of a door flying open and feet stomping around. "Come out where ever you are, and I won't hurt you too bad!"

I shake as I hear the closet door open. I hold my breath and rock Lila to keep her asleep.

"They're gone! Where are they?" he yells at my mom, and I bite my little lip.

"Like I'd tell you if I knew!" she says, sounding angry. I hear screaming of both of them and then my mom slapping him.

"Ah!" I scream as I still up, running my hand through my hair. Where am I? I ask myself as I look around. I feel the warmth and movement below me causing me to move. My eyes land on Reece who now is moving his arms to find their way around me.

"Are you okay, Angel?" he asks me, and I sigh. "Did you have a nightmare?" he adds.

"I'm fine, and it wasn't a nightmare, Reece. It was a memory," I state before flipping my arms around his shoulders and holding him.

Chapter Forty

Reece's POV

"Juliet!" I call as I stand by my closet, and Rider is panting by my side. I would holler for Conner, but he had a morning class and is already gone, leaving Juliet or my mom to help me. I will go with Juliet.

Running my hand through my hair that is beginning to get longer, too long for me, I'm starting to feel like I have *JB*-hair. I can hear footsteps near my room and then finally enter it.

"What can I do for you, my dear brother?" he asks her voice seems tired.

"Can you please help me pick out some clothes?" I ask, and my nose begins to pick up on a strong smell. Scratch that. Two strong smells— one is a strong perfume that tries to cover up the other odor. *What is that smell?* I ask myself as I hear her footsteps near my side, and the smell grows closer, and the bitter, smoky smell grows stronger as well. The clinking of the clothes hanger as she goes through my closet distracts me for a second before I return to think.

"Here is a white shirt, black jacket, and dark jeans so go get dressed," she says as I groan. Juliet drapes the clothes onto my arm not holding Rider's harness. Making my way carefully to the bathroom, I do my normal way of getting ready and the step back into my room.

"How do I look?" I ask her.

"Let me do your hair," she says as she nears me and finally, she is right in front of me. And I can smell her very well now.

"Sure," I reply and feel her begin to mess with my hair. Finally all of a sudden, like a train, I recognize the smell.

"Juliet, have you been smoking?" I ask her. My voice is slightly laced in confusion. Why would my sweet, little baby sister smoke?

"What? Reece, are you crazy?" she asks me in shock, and I feel her hands in my hair and then finally, she retrieves them. "Done." She mumbles.

"I'm not crazy, Juliet. You smell like cigarettes," I argue back, and then the doorbell rings.

"I'll get that," Juliet says, and I can hear her feet start to move.

"This is not over," I call to her, crossing my arms over my chest.

Groaning, I reach down, grab the harness walk over to my bed, and sit down. Please, don't let my sister smoke! I don't understand why she would? Did I do something? Is she okay? I am so confused. I feel like this is all my fault, and I cannot help but blame myself. I rub my face in my hands and release a groan. I am an awful big brother.

"Morning, Reece," the sweet angel-like voice says as I hear footsteps come into the room.

"Morning, Angel," I say to her as I bend down, feeling the ground for my shoes I wore yesterday. My fingers finally stumble over what feels to be them, and I take one into each of my hands and sit them down.

"How are you?" Payton asks me, and I sigh. I turn the shoe to where I can run my hand down the sides to figure out where the curve is to know which foot is which. Once I figure it out, I put them on my feet, which has taken a lot of practice to get down.

"I'm okay. Really don't want to go to school, but that's all," I lie a little bit, not admitting the worries I have about Juliet or the pitiful feeling I have inside of me today. "How are you?" I ask her while I undo Rider's harness and release him with command. Then, I stand up and take a deep breath.

"I'm alright, but I have to talk to the counselor when we get to school." She gets closer to me, which I can tell by her voice being louder and her feet moving. "Will you be alright?" she asks me, and I sigh. Honestly, I will have to find my way around on my own, which will be next to impossible so I will not be all right. Payton cannot baby me all the time, and she has a life so she cannot always be with me. So I say the less selfish answer.

"I'll be fine. Do what you need too," I tell her, and I feel her hand touch mine which causes the usual explosion of sparks.

"Are you sure? I feel bad for leaving you," she says softly as she steps close to me, wrapping her arms around my neck. Reaching out, I place my left hand gently onto her waist. I use my right hand and slide it up her arm over her thin shoulder and then against her neck. Then, moving it to her cheek where I run my thumb gently over the edge of her mouth.

Leaning forwards and moving my lips closer to hers, I say, "I am sure." Then, with that being said, I lean forward and meet my lips with hers, and it creates sparks of fireworks.

As our lips move together in a perfect sync, I think back to last night. Last night after we woke from our nap, we ate dinner. The thought of her past was haunting every thought I had. I couldn't and still cannot grasp what kind of man, *no*, what kind of human could do that! After dinner, Payton left for home, and I would be lying if I said I didn't wish she'd stay with me.

Valentine's Day is getting close, only a few days away, so I am on a mission to come up with the perfect thing for her. She deserves it. She deserves the whole world. I pull Payton's perfect body closer to my body as I hold her close. To be honest, I am getting a little excited if you know. What I mean is as our once innocent kiss becomes more serious as our tongues search each other's mouth.

Deciding we are getting a little carried away, I tug my lips away from hers. "We better head out," I say with an unsteady breath. Her breathing is ragged too.

"Yeah, we should," she says, and I smile.

"I love you, Angel," I say to her.

"I love you too," she replies and then slips away from me her footsteps heading somewhere.

"Here," she says to me as she returns and slips my cane into my hand. I wish I could bring Rider with me. But I can't, at least not yet.

"Let's go then," I say to her as she takes my left hand into hers and intertwines our fingers.

As she leads me to the car, I still hold the feeling that something bad is going happen today. I don't know what it will be, but I can feel it. And it is not good.

"Are you going to the hospital after school?" I ask Payton as I play with her fingers.

"Yeah, more than likely. Do you want to come with me?" she asks me with a happy voice.

"Sure, can we swing by and pick up Rider, though?" I reply, I think Rider will want to get out of the house and to be honest, I miss having his help and the safety he provides me.

"Of course, we can, Reece," she answers. I smile brightly even though there is something biting inside of me and telling me something's going to change today. I just am not sure what.

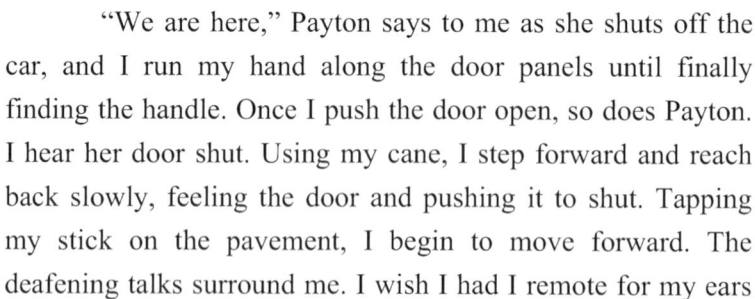

"We are here," Payton says to me as she shuts off the car, and I run my hand along the door panels until finally finding the handle. Once I push the door open, so does Payton. I hear her door shut. Using my cane, I step forward and reach back slowly, feeling the door and pushing it to shut. Tapping my stick on the pavement, I begin to move forward. The deafening talks surround me. I wish I had I remote for my ears so I could turn down the volume or just hit mute. There is just so much going on, and I cannot focus.

I feel a hand grab mine and from the sparks, I automatically know that it is Payton. I smile slightly as we walk hand in hand to the school's front door. The air changes and I hear a door shut behind me.

"Reece!" deep male voice calls, and I immediately recognize it as Jace.

His quick heavy footsteps near us, and I hear Paton groan by my side, causing me to chuckle lightly. "Hey, guys," he says once his footsteps stop, and I hear his voice close to me.

"I'm going to go see the counselor now," Payton says to me, and I feel her hand slip from mine. Then her lips brush mine for a second, just long enough for me to taste the sweetness of her lips and she pulls away. I reach up to fix my sunglasses that are turned a little.

"I love you," I say to her with a cheerful smile.

"I love you too," she replies, and I can hear the smile in her voice. Then, her feet carry her away from me.

"Does she not like me?" Jace says with a confused tone, and I laugh lightly. Honestly, I think she finds him annoying, but deep down I think she will like him.

"She likes you," I say, shaking my head. It could've been a lie. It also could have been true.

"But she runs off when I'm around," he states, and I bit down on my lip to refrain from any laughter that is threatening to break free from my lips.

"She'll come around. But are you sure you really want to be seen around me? You may get hate," I warn as I take a step forward.

Heavy arm slings over my shoulder, causing me to release a groan. "You are my best friend, and I just got you back. Of course, I want to be seen with you! Who gives a fuck what people say or think? I haven't been friends with them since I was in my diapers. You, my friend, are stuck with me. We are like two opposites which when put together equals perfection and pure awesomeness. You're the good kid, and I'm the bad one. So you see, Reece, I have to be around you. Your goodness levels out my badness. If people want to say shit, I say fuck them!" Jace completes his speech leaving me shaking my head.

"You are truly something else, Jace," I say simply, and he chuckles.

"Thank you! Now, let's start our way to your first period since you girlfriend scurried off." We walk down the hall, his arm still tight around my neck and my stick tapping the ground ahead of me.

We continue our walk for a few minutes and Jace yapping my ear off about all kinds of things because he loves to talk, which is okay with me because I've always been the quieter one. Suddenly, he stops me and falls silent.

"What is i—?" I begin to ask but cut off but a familiar voice that I haven't heard in years.

"Reece!" her female voice says, and I freeze. Every inch of my body stiffens as I hear the voice of the girl I once thought I loved.

"Clair?" I ask speechless and not believing what I am hearing. This is not possible.

Chapter Forty-One

Payton's POV

Leaving the counselor's office, I stuff my hand into my pockets and walk down the hall to English, where hopefully Jace was kind enough to take Reece to. As I twist the cool metal handle to the door, I pull it open and walk inside the room. Inside, my eyes scan over the class since the bell rang about fifteen minutes ago and it took longer than I expected with the counselor. Looking at all of the faces, I drop my note onto Mrs. Reed's desk and proceed to my seat. Reece's desk is empty. Where is Reece? I think as I scrunch up my face in confusion. Sitting down at my desk, I remove my English book from within my bag.

"Payton, we are reading page 598," Mrs. Reed informs me with a kind smile, and I nod my head.

I tap my fingers nervously as I attempt to read what is on the paper in front of me. Instead of actually being able to read it, I wind up reading the same sentence a billion times over.

Where is Reece? Why is he not here? Is he okay? I ask myself worriedly. Deciding to take away some worry, I pull out my cell phone from my pocket and sneakily hide my phone in my lap and pull up a new message to *"Reece<3."*

Me: Reece, are you okay? Where are you?

I hit send and then slip my phone back into my jean pocket. Please let him be okay! I seriously hope Jace isn't dumb enough to leave his best friend, who's blind, to find his own way to class. If he did, I would kill that boy! I attempt to read again, and it turns a failure.

Reece<3: Angel, I am fine. Don't worry about me. I am just talking to someone, Payton. It is all okay; I will be in next period. I love you.

I smile brightly at the cute message and type back a quick "I love you too" and then put my phone away. I am glad he is okay. But whom could he possibly be speaking to? I groan, unable to read as I have a new thing to worry about now.

The ringing of the bell dismisses me from class. I shut my book a little hard, stand up, and stuff my things into my book bag. As I toss my bag over my shoulder and head for the door, I walk quickly to me next class, wanting to see Reece so that I know for sure he is okay. Reaching my next classroom, I walk inside and slip into one of the desks. I look around for Reece.

Finally, however, I do catch him. He is smiling and nods his head to someone that has blonde hair as it bounces away. I clench my fist and bit my lip, withholding my anger that is threatening to spill over.

His cane taps the floor as he walks into the room and to his desk. I look up at his smiling face and roll the tears that are threatening to spill out of. I know it was Clair, but why? Does he still have feelings for her? What did they talk about? I feel my stomach churn, and I don't feel that well.

I can feel Reece's eyes burning through his glasses and into the side of my face. To be honest, I am a little ticked off at him for just not telling me it was Clair he was talking to. No, instead I get totally blindsided by the fact. Tapping my foot, I cannot seem to concentrate on what the teacher is yapping about.

The bell rings after a long period, and I stand up grabbing my things and waiting at the end of the aisle for Reece. I may be pissed at him, but I will not just leave him on his own. Once he makes it to my side, I grab his wrist.

"Come on," I mumble and he walks along with me.

"Angel, are you mad at me?" his voice asks me softly, and I groan.

"No," I mumble again, taking a deep breath.

"Payton, tell me if you are mad at me. I deserve to know!"

"I'm not! Drop it," I say lowly as we enter the next class, and I sit down.

This class goes the same as the last and so does the next class. Luckily, the class now is with Jace, so I am just going leave when the bell rings. I need some space, and I have the right to be angry so I will be.

Once the bell rings, I grab my things and jump up, leaving the room and walking quickly down the hall and around curves. I make it to the library and slump into one of the hard wooden stairs. I lay my head on the table and allow the tears to begin down my cheeks.

Reece's POV

"Can we talk?" Clair's haunting voice asks me, and I swallow the dry lump forming in my throat.

"Sure," I say to her, my voice coming out a little deeper than normal.

"Well, I will just leave you two alone. Bye," Jace says in an awkward voice.

"Bye. Shall we go somewhere to talk?" I ask the girl from my past as I stretch out my arm to her.

"We shall. Are the bleachers fine?" she asks me her voice is sweet and light just how I remember it.

"They're fine," I reply to her and feel her arms slip through mine as she begins to lead me off.

Hearing doors open and cool air brushing my face tells me that we are outside. Then, we begin to walk in silence until I feel my cane tap something.

"We are at the bleachers now," Clair says to me kindly, and I am able to walk up the metal bleachers, and she helps me sit down.

"So Clair, what are you doing back in town?" I ask her as I lay my cane beside me and place my arms in my lap.

"Would you believe me if I said I came back for you?" she asks me, and her voice is light and joking.

"Well, if I haven't known you for as long as I have, then yes. But since I do, I say no. So what's your real reason?" I ask her with a smile. To be honest, I never realized how much I have missed Clair. Talking to her is as easy as eating.

She laughs, and I smile wider. I did miss her laugh because it was one of those silly ones that could make everyone around you burst into laughter too. "Good point, I moved back because my parents' jobs moved them back here, so here I am," she says in her cheerful tone, which she always has. I mean, this girl is always happy. And back when my life was great, I loved that about her. Now, I find it very annoying. I mean I keep comparing little things already about her with Payton.

"That's great that you are back," I say to her, smiling.

"Yeah, so how are you?" she asks me casually, and I shrug even though she is smiling.

"I am okay, doing better. It's all thanks to Payton," I say with a big smile as I say her name.

"Oh, the new girlfriend?" Clair says with a joking voice, and I laugh lightly.

"Yeah, my girlfriend," I say proudly as I think of her. Every time I think of her, everything becomes better. I know that seems crazy, but it's true. I may have once loved Clair, and I still do. I love Clair like a friend; I love Payton like a soul mate. She is the one for me, and I know it. I just hope she feels the same.

Chapter Forty-Two

Reece's POV

My phone vibrates against me, and I pull it out. "New Text Message from *My Angel*," my phone says.

"Open message," I instruct to it, completely aware of Clair still sitting by my side.

"Angel. That's cute," Clair says in her usual chipper voice.

"Reece, are you okay? Where are you?" The phone says, reading my message. Why is Payton so worried?

"Clair, what time is it?" I ask as I scrunch up my face in confusion.

"Crap. I'm sorry, Reece. It is half way through first," she replies. Her voice sounds sad, and I sigh.

"It's fine, not your fault," I tell her and offer a smile to her. "Reply to message," I tell my phone.

A few minutes later, it vibrates again. She replies with an "I love you too," and I return my phone back to my pocket.

"That is really sweet. You seem really happy, Reece," Clair states with a still chipper voice, and I nod my head smiling.

"Thank you, Clair. You don't sound like you've changed too much. What have I missed with you? Do you have someone now?" I ask her, raising an eyebrow with a smile.

"Well, thanks, Reece," she says sarcastically and giggles as she lightly punches my shoulder in what seems to be a playful manner.

"I didn't mean that in a bad way," I chuckle, shaking my head. I am really enjoying being around her again. It kind of reminds me of the past. I am really shocked at how okay and normal she seems around me, but she was always the kind of girl who don't dwell on little things.

"I know, but to respond to your question you've missed a lot. I am now super ugly and just the total opposite of what I was," she says in a joking tone, and I chuckle. "No seriously, though, I haven't changed that much at all besides growing up. Other than that, I am still me. As for you other question, I did have a few boyfriends after you, none stuck except for the last one, up until I found him in bed with my friend the day before I moved so that went down the toilet," she says in a slightly less happy voice almost coming off forced.

"I am so very sorry, Clair. That is awful. You want me to go beat him up for you?" I offer with a cheeky smile, and she laughs. I don't blame her I can be pretty darn funny.

"No, no, that's okay, Reece." I feel her pat my leg, and I smile to where her voice is.

"Alright, I guess I will spare him," I joke with her, and she laughs. "So why did you decide to talk to me?" I ask her curiosity getting to me.

"Because I want to be your friend. I also want to be Payton's friend," she replies, and I smile.

"Well, there is a long line to be my friend," I inform her with a smile.

"Oh really, there is?" she plays along, and I try to control my smile.

"Yeah, but seeing as we used to be close, I guess I can bump you up to the front," I say with a sigh and charming smile.

"Oh really, yay!" she says faking excitement, and I chuckle. "So friends?" she asks me once the laughter dies down.

"Friends," I reply with a happy smile and the bell rings.

"Let's go," she says as she takes my hand, helping me stand up and taking me along with her.

She drops me by my classroom, and I find my way to my seat. I know that Payton is beside me because I can feel her presence. I need her to talk to me. I need to hear her voice and talk to her. When class ends, she waits for me, and I can feel the tension as it hangs in the air needing a knife to cut it. It's too much. I cannot take it! I have no clue what I have done.

"Come on," she mumbles to me and pulls me along.

"Angel, are you mad at me?" I ask her softly, needing to know what I did.

She releases a groan of frustration. "No," she mumbles once again and then takes in a deep breath.

"Payton, tell me if you are mad at me. I deserve to know!" I say as my anger begins to rise. This is unfair! I did nothing to deserve this! Why are we going through this?

"I'm not! Drop it," she says to me softly as I hear the surroundings die down and this means I know we have entered the classroom, and though she may be angry with me, she still helps, which just shows how amazing she is.

The class goes the same as it did the last time and so did the changing. I tried and tried to ask her what's wrong, trying to figure out what I could have possibly done.

Once the bell rings, I can hear her jump up and run off, leaving me with Jace, I guess.

"Man, you have seriously pissed Payton off," Jace says as he comes to my side and helps me get out of the classroom.

"Damn, that oblivious?" I groan and run my hand through my hair.

"Man, even a blind person could see... will scratch that. I guess not," he says, pausing and sounding like he just screwed up.

"I could feel it, but she wouldn't tell me why," I complain to him as we carry on, and the halls begin to quiet down.

"Damn, that sucks."

"Damn, that sucks? Really, you have no advice or help?" I groan and shake my head. My best friend is so much help.

"Fine, well, did you tell her you were with Clair?" Jace gives up and asks, attempting to be helpful meaning he used a smart tone.

"Well, I told her I was talking to someone. I may have left Clair out of it," I say casually, not seeing the big deal.

"May have means you did. Now, what if she found out it was Clair? That may be the reason she is upset," Jace says in a wise tone.

"Why in the world would that upset her?" I ask scrunching my face up in complete confusion.

"Have you honestly not met Payton? She is insecure, and I am pretty sure when she sees Clair, she sees the past you share. Now, since you lied to her, and that lie involved Clair, you can hopefully understand where I headed," Jace says in his smart tone once again, which I think he may be enjoying since I am sure he hardly gets to use it. Oops, that was kind of mean of me to say.

Is what he was saying true? If so, shit. I am in a heap of trouble. "Do you think that Payton thinks I will leave her for Clair?" I ask Jace, raising my eyebrows.

"Well, duh," he replies in a tired tone.

Shit, shit, shit, I am in so much trouble. Crap, I need to find Payton and fix this. "Help me find Payton."

"Alright, alright, she's probably in the library. Let's go," he says, releasing a breath and tossing his arm around my shoulders.

Jace leads me down a hall that grows quieter and quieter until I finally hear the sound of doors being opened. We have entered a room.

"Follow the sobbing. She's at the table straight in front of you," Jace whispers into my ear before he releases my shoulder and disappears.

Taking a deep breath, I walk forward and tap my cane ahead of me. Finally, I tap something hard and slow step forward feeling for a chair as the sobs grow louder. As I pull out my chair and sit down, the sobs quit and sniffling fill my ears.

"What are you doing here?" Payton's crackly voice asks me, and I can feel a piece of my heart break. I am an ass! I made her cry! Now, I feel like crap.

"Do you honestly think I would leave you for Clair?" I ask and turn my head towards where I guess she is. I answer her question with a question, not caring to be blunt.

"Of course, I do! She is perfect, and you two used to be together. I'm nothing compared to her. So yes, I do!" she replies to me in a feisty tone. This girl is crazy to think any of that!

"She was perfect for the guy I *was*! Payton, I am not that guy anymore! The guy I am now, that is who I will always be, and you are the girl I was meant to be with! So stop thinking that way. You are perfect," I say to her, meaning every word. I even reach up and lower my sunglasses down to show her my eyes.

"If that is true, why not tell me?" she demands, and I can hear the anger in her tone.

"It didn't seem important," I argue, and it hits me. We have never fought before. This is our first fight, and it's about Clair. Great!

"Not important! Yeah, right! Your *ex* wanting you back is so not important," Payton hisses back, and I am feeling a whole new level to her.

"For one, she doesn't want me back! She wants to be both our friends! And two, it doesn't matter if she wants me. I don't want her. I want you," I reply with a voice full of desperation.

"I don't trust her," she mumbles to me, and I shake my head.

"You don't need to trust her. Trust me. That's all that matters," I reply as I reach out, trying to find her hand and once I do, I pull it in mine and am met by the sparks.

"I trust you," she whispers, and I smile as I lean forward, and soon, our lips met in the perfect kiss.

I love her. I love her so much. I love a lot of things, but never this strong. She is the one— the one for me.

Chapter Forty-Three

Payton's POV

I lay in Reece's arms on the couch. His arms are around my waist, and my hands are intertwined with his. I gently play with his fingers as we lay on the couch.

"Payton," Reece says in a soft voice, pulling my attention to his face. Looking through my eyelashes, I smile up at him. How can anyone be so perfect?

"Reece," I reply with a smile and watch as the corner of his perfect lips pull up into a smile. His blue eyes are shining so bright, and my heart is slamming against my chest.

"You know, I have been thinking. I think that God did this for me on purpose. God took away my sight for a bigger reason. He led me to you. I mean there is a lot of bad things that have come from this. I will never see my sisters grow up, or my brother settle down. I will never be able to play sports or run track again. I will never be able to drive a car again or be normal. All the things are bad, and they hurt. But with you by my side, I can face it all. You are better than all the worst. You are the best thing to happen to me. I'm sure if this hadn't happened, I would find another way to you. But I am happy I got you this soon. God work in mysterious ways, and this was our way of supposed to be coming together. I love you," Reece says to me as he continues to play with my fingers.

"Reece, that is so sweet. But can I ask you a question?" I ask and look away from his face in fear. I know the question. It has haunted me for a very long time.

"You just did, but of course, you can ask more," he replies as I sense calmness in his voice, and his hands continue to play with mine.

"If you were to get your sight back today, would you still love me?" I ask. I know it may seem like a very stupid question, but I cannot help to ask. I am curious. Would he or would he ditch me?

Reece's heart rate begins to pick up, and I can feel his body tense. "Why would you ask that?" he asks me, shifting upward so that I am now right by his head. That really helps my fear, I think sarcastically.

"I asked because I am afraid of what would happen," I whisper softly, knowing he could hear me.

He releases a sigh and tightens his grip on me. "Payton, if I were to see again, nothing would change. I would love you just as much as I love you now, maybe more. I love you, and nothing will change. I hate to break it to you, but you are stuck with me forever. Never getting rid of me. Stop worrying. I have never felt this before, and it's real, so don't doubt it. I love you no matter what." I smile brightly, feeling my heart melt.

"I love you too," I reply simply, leaning up and kissing him. He kisses me back, and the kiss quickly turns passionate as he runs his tongue over my lip and I part my lips to allow his tongue into my mouth. Our bodies are pushed up against each other, and the kiss gets steamy.

As bad as this may sound, all I can think about right now is what it would be like to rub his abs and go farther with this. I know sex is not something I want right now, but honestly, my brain is not working. All I am thinking about is how much I love him and want him.

I feel him pull away and stop kissing. Without meaning to, I frown at the loss of contact. Why did he stop? Shouldn't I be the one stopping him? Do I disgust him? These thoughts cloud my mind as I roll off him and look down at my body. My brown hair is frizzy over my shoulder. My body is nothing special. I mean I could understand why, but he cannot see me so I am a little more confused.

"I'm sorry," Reece says softly as he runs his hand through his brown hair. My eyes blur as I feel like crap. He doesn't want me.

"I am sorry too... that you don't want me." I mumble the last half under my breath, not thinking.

"Do you honestly think I don't want you?" he asks me his voice sounds shocked. Damn, him and his super hearing! He sits up on the couch and puts his face into his hands.

"Maybe," I mumble, sitting up to feeling ridiculous about all of this.

"Oh gosh, you could not be any more wrong. I want you very much. For many reasons, one, I am a teenage boy, and you are a beautiful girl. The second is that I love you so much.

And for the third, the sparks and things that happen to me when we kiss are so amazing. I have no clue how I could possibly not want you. I had to make myself stop. I stopped because I know you, and you are not ready. I love you, which means I respect that and am not going push you. So please don't be mad or upset. I did it for you," he says to me with a very sad, regret-filled face.

My heart melts, and a tear slides down my cheek as I crawl over to Reece and throw my arms around him to hug him. I love him so much. He holds me tight, and I smile into his shoulder.

"Thank you," I mumble into his shirt.

Reece wants to be able to do something again. So what if he could do a few things that he used to? Football is out because he needs his eyes for that and the same with baseball. I sit in Reece's lap at the hospital in Lila's room.

I look at Lila's limp body, her eyes are shut, and she looks paler than normal. She is really frail, and it eats away at my heart seeing her this way. Reece's arms tighten around me as if he caught on to my sudden change in mood.

What is something Reece doesn't need his eyes for? I continue to think as I look down, seeing Rider lying on the floor beside our chair looking very content; his head is on his paws. Then it hits me, Reece can run! He doesn't need his eyes, and Rider could even help. All he has to learn is the feel of the track, and he is good.

I sit up straighter as I take in Reece's blue eyes and smile. "Hey," I whisper softly to him, wondering if he had fallen asleep.

"Hmm?" he mumbles, peeling his eyes open to face me. I smile as I stare into his amazing blue eyes.

"I know something you can still do," I say with a bright smile as I glance at Lila on the bed. She's the reason I stay strong. Reece deserves a reason too.

"You do?" he asks me, sounding somewhat shocked not that I blame him. His girlfriend just tells him she knows something he can still do, a little crazy. Now that I think about that again, it could have been kind of pervy. *Whoops.*

"I do," I confirm with a smile as I look into his eyes. His lips twitch upwards a little, and I smile.

"Are you going to share what it is with me?" he asks as he raises his eyebrow, making me smile at how perfect he is.

"Maybe…" I bite my lip as I suppress a smile that is threatening to make its way onto my lips.

"Why maybe? Just tell me," he says as his hands hold tightly to my sides as if he will try to squeeze it out of me.

"Fine," I say as I cave in and decide to tell him. Plus, teases him is starting to be less fun.

"So what is it?" he asks me, and I smile again as I take in his face and see how curious he is now.

"You could run track," I say proudly with a bright smile. *Oh yeah, a great idea brought to you by my mind. I could just high five myself.* I think in my mind not paying attention to the sudden change in Reece's face.

"No, I hate to break it to you, but I can't. Thanks for trying, though," he says with a sad face. He just totally shot that down without thinking. I shift in his lap so I am able to face him more fully.

"Um, why the heck not?" I ask him stunned by him saying that. How would he even know?

"Because I am blind and won't be able to see," he says bluntly to me in a *duh* tone.

"Uh, I'm pretty sure if a blind girl is able to figure-skate than you can run track. I mean, all you have to do is know the track and imagine it. Besides, you could even have Rider help you," I say, informing him of the possibilities and at the mention of his name, I see Rider head pop up and his ears perk.

"Do you know how much work I would have to put up just to be half as good?" he asks me and raise his eyebrows.

"It would be worth it, and I am going help you the whole time. You have Rider and me and a whole family who will help you and support you and Carter and Jace," I tell him reaching up and stroking his cheek. His eyes flutter shut.

"Do you really think I can do this?" he asks me. His voice is a little weaker this time.

"Yes, I do Reece, I believe you can do absolutely anything that you set your mind to," I say as I take his face into my hands.

"Really?" he asks me, opening his light blue eyes.

"Really," I confirm and smile.

"I love you, you know that?"

"I think I have been told that for a time or two."

"Well, it's true. I love you so much," he says as he holds me close to his chest.

"I love you too, Reece," I reply as I lean down and press my lips against his sweet ones, and he pulls me even closer if that is possible.

I pull back for a second. "So are you going to do it?" I ask with a hopeful smile.

"Yeah, as long as you help me the whole time," he answers, and my smile grows.

"I will be by your side every step of the way," I say as I hug him tightly and kiss him again. I love him so much. I haven't been this happy my whole life. The only way it could get better is if Lila would wake up or Ms. Rose got out the hospital.

Chapter Forty-Four

Reece POV's

"Conner!" I call as I lean against the bottom of the stairs with Rider sitting on his hind legs.

"I'm coming. I'm coming. Don't get your panties in a knot," Conner calls as I hear his feet thundering down the stairs.

"I don't wear panties," I call back as I run my hand through my messy brown hair. Then, I stuff my hand into the front pocket of my hoodie as I wait for him.

Payton had the most amazing idea to run track again. I mean I will admit I was a little skeptic at first. The more I began to think about it, I became more aware of the possibilities, and Payton was right. If someone can ice-skate blind, then I can run. Life is full of challenges; it's all just about what you make of them.

"Fine, fine, boxer's in a knot," Conner laughs as he reaches beside my side. "Let's go, buddy," he adds as he grabs one my arms. I grab Rider's harness, having him come with. "Reece, why didn't you ask anyone else to come with?" he asks me as he leads me outside. Payton went home awhile ago to see her mom, which is fine with me.

"Because I am scared to see how it turns out with me running again. I haven't tried and don't want to make a fool of myself in front of more people other than you," I explain as Conner stops us, and I hear the sound of a car door opening. Then, he helps me get inside.

"What about your girlfriend?" Conner asks in a teasing tone. Then, I hear the sound of the truck starting.

"I want to be able to impress her the first time because I'm not sure if I'll be able too," I explain, leaning my head back onto the headrest.

"Well, I am here for you brother," Conner says with a happy voice, and I sigh smiling. Conner may be crazy, but he is always there when I need him. He is always there for me no matter how bad things may get he is there.

"Thanks," I mumble as I sit down, leaning my head against the rest.

"So, just walk a lap around the track to get a feel for it again?" I ask Conner, raising an eyebrow in confusion. I turn my head around as I listen to the quietness around here. There is definitely no one around here.

"Yep," Conner says, and I sigh as I take a hold of Rider's harness.

"Why is no one here?" I ask before I begin my walk. I am honestly not sure what time it is outside. I mean I want to come after everyone's gone, but I'm a little worried if it's dark.

"It's seven, and there are no practices," Conner says casually. "Now, get to walking!" he adds laughing, and I groan taking a step forward. Why did I make him my coach again?

It was because he is the one who originally helped me learn how these things do, and he was always really good at this stuff. I can feel the differences between the track and the turf. So feeling the difference beneath my feet I know where to stay.

"Okay, you made it! I am very impressed. Nice job," Conner praises me as Rider and I come to a stop. He claps his hand one to my shoulder in a proud way. "Now, I would like you to do it again but this time jogging," he instructs, and my heart beats faster. I don't know if I can do this.

Hesitantly, I take steps forward and try to get my legs to move. Squeezing my eyes shut, I take in a deep breath and then force my legs to move. Slowly, I begin to speed up my walk into a jog. As I jug, I keep one hand securely on Rider's harness.

At first, I stumble a little and mess up my feet. But after two minutes, my legs decide to work, and I jog. All too quickly, my breath becomes short, and I realize just how out of shape I am. Forcing myself to continue, I feel the burning spread through my legs as I force them to go quicker.

Slowly, my breath comes out as pants, and I slow down a little as I continue to push myself farther. "Done," Conner's voice calls to me.

Coming to a stop, I lean down and press one hand to my knee as I bend over and breathe hard. Rider is panting lightly by my side. Dang, I didn't realize I was so out of shape.

"Well, you did well. You need to work out more push harder to be able to get yourself back into shape." As I breathe heavily, I nod my head.

"I can do that," I say between breaths. I am glad it did go to bad. Running again was amazing. Words cannot describe how great it was to run again. I feel like a part of myself has returned. I cannot wait for Payton to come see. I am bringing her with next time. It feels so great to push through my blindness and find a way to have something I use to be able to do again. I love running, and it feels great to have hoped I may be able to again.

Chapter Forty-Five

Payton's POV

Curling into a tight ball in my bed, I cry. The yelling echoes throughout my house. I can hear things being thrown, slamming against walls, and screaming. It does not help my fear knowing that my mother and father are alone down there. The tears stream down my face quickly, one after the next. This is my entirely fault! If it weren't for me, none of this would be happening. If I weren't born, then, my mom wouldn't have to go through this. If I weren't so ugly and worthless, then he wouldn't beat me.

I cry harder. My whole body shakes as the tears stream down my cheeks. When I cry so hard, I begin to have an asthma attack. My chest tightens and I cannot breathe. With shaky hands, I reach over my nightstand and move my hand around, trying to find something. Finally, I find my inhaler and bring it to my lips inhaling the medicine. I put it back in its place as I try to calm down.

My bedroom door bursts open, bouncing off the wall behind it. The large male figure nears me as I attempt to shrink away and become invisible. It does not work, though. His steps slam against the ground as he inches towards me. "Pl-please, n-no," I beg as I continue to shake.

"Shut up," he spits out at me, and I begin to cry again cover my face with my small arms. "Stop crying, you stupid baby," he snarls as he reaches my bed and grips onto my shirt. He drags me up from the bed by my shirt.

Drawing back a fist, he begins hitting me, and I cannot help but cry. I squeeze my eyes shut and pray for him to stop. But he keeps hitting until the world turns black.

I sit up straight in my bed, breathing very heavily. Sweat streams down my face, and my hair is drenched with it. I reach up and use my hand to knock the hair out of my face. I attempt to slow down my heartbeat as I kick off the blanket from my legs and turn, sitting my legs off the bed. Looking at the time, I see that it is five in the morning. I might as well go ahead and take a shower. I decide as I stand up stretching.

Dragging myself out of my room and down the hall to my bathroom, I strip out of my sweaty clothes and turn on the shower, making it nice and hot. Hot showers have always relaxed me, especially after my terrible nightmares. Stepping into the steam shower, I allow it to fall down me and relax. I massage the shampoo deeply into my scalp, wishing I could scrub away the haunting memories.

Once back inside my very messy room, I make my way to my dresser where I retrieve a pair of black panties and a black bra. Dropping my towel onto the ground, I pull on my underwear and walk to my closet. Thank God, It's Friday! The last couple of days has been odd. Reece has been busy a lot in the evenings so I spend my time at the hospital with Lila and Ms. Rose, who I have been talking with about Reece.

Valentine's Day is also tomorrow. I don't think Reece and I have any special plans. I decide on my dark blue t-shirt and a pair of blue jeans, along with a jacket. I slip on my shoes and look at the time. Six in the morning. Great, I guess I could always leave for Reece's early. Tonight is movie night anyways so I can drop off my stuff.

Grabbing my bag and a little overnight bag, I walk down the steps. I realize my mom must be asleep, so I try to be extra quiet. She deserves to rest any time she would like to. I grab a green apple from the counter and take a bite. I finish my apple and toss it into the trash can. Then, I leave and head to Reece's house.

"Come on, Reece," I say as I lead my wonderful boyfriend out to the football field for lunch, which has become our usual eating spot. As we walk across the field, I can already spot Jace sprawled out on the turf and smiling as he pops purple grapes into his mouth.

I smile, shaking my head as Reece and I make our way towards him. Once we are near, he looks up with his happy smile and waves to us.

"Hey, Reece!" Jace says happily, and I smile, sitting down. Reece sits down too, and I drop his bag lunch down into his lap.

We are sitting so close. Our sides are touching, and it feels great.

"Hey, Jace," Reece says smiling, and I can imagine his blue eyes shining behind his black sunglasses.

"Tonight is going to be awesome!" Jace says flinging one of his fists into the air smiling.

Did I mention that Reece invited Jace to our movie night? Well, he did, and I'm kind of thinking, he did this to bug me because Jace truly gets on my nerves. Also, he may be doing this because Jace is actually his best friend. On the bright side, he invited Carter too! I love Carter. He is a great guy so at least I will have someone I get along with. Tonight may actually be pretty awesome. It is going to be Reece's whole family, Reece, Jace, Carter, and me. I honestly can't wait and can already imagine all the fun it will be.

As I lean back on the turf, I look around, tuning out of Reece and Jace's silly conversation. I just look around and then my eyes fall on my less favorite person there is, or at least one of them. She is wearing a pair of red skinny jeans and black high heels along with a white top and black jacket. Her blonde hair is in a bun that has a few pieces hanging around her face. I groan as she gets closer and closer, finally reaching us.

"Hi, Reece. Can I sit with you guys?" she asks my boyfriend who shrugs his shoulder.

"I don't see why not," he replies, and Jace just nods his head like crazy.

I groan, hoping she does not hear. I don't think she does, but Reece shoots me a curious look. I choose to ignore it. "Oh, I don't think we have met. I am Clair!" the overly bubbly blonde says before me, and I keep in my disgust as I return her smile.

"I'm Payton," I say simply, and she smiles bigger.

"The new girlfriend, I know! It is so great to meet you," she says to me, giving me what appears to be a happy smile when I feel there is way more to it.

"Likewise," I say forcefully, trying to seem nice, which usually isn't that hard for me. I mean, normally, I am really nice, but for some reason, this girl rubs me the wrong way. She may try to be all happy-go-lucky and smiles, but she is up to something. I can feel it. No, this is not my jealousy or insecurity. It's my ability to read people, and she is no good.

There is definitely something very fishy about this girl. I cannot seem to put my finger on it, but I will sooner or later. I hope she realizes that I don't want a fight, and I believe Reece every time he tells me he loves me.

Reece's hand travels up my back until it rests on my shoulder so that his arm is around me. I smile as I snuggle up to his side.

"I love you," he whispers softly into my ear. His breath fans over my ear, giving me chills.

"I love you too," I reply with a smile.

I smile up at Reece, whose brown hair is really hanging in his face but is still very attractive. I cannot imagine anything without him. I just love him that much. I have never really been that sure about love, but being with Reece is really opening my eyes. Life with him is perfect. I know there is a rough stop, but

I don't care. We are strong and make it through. We can make it through anything, I hope.

I just cannot wait until movie tonight. It's going to be fun.

Chapter Forty- Six

Reece's POV

"What are we going to watch?" Jace whines, being himself.

It is Friday movie night. I invited Jace, partly to annoy my lovely girlfriend but mainly because he is my best friend and is fun. Then I invited Carter to make sure that Payton doesn't get too mad at me. On top of that, there is my mom, dad, and sister; of course, you cannot forget my angel. Right now, we are all in the den and grabbing seats. Or at least that's what it sounds like they are all doing. I am already seated on the couch, stretched out and ready to attempt to listen. I mean, to me, it doesn't matter what we watch. All I care about is being able to hold my girl in my arms.

"*Transformers*?" Carter pipes up, saying. I hear Jace make a sound like one of acceptance of the choice. Having Jace and Carter in the same room together has open my eyes. I now realize how different they are. Different does not even describe them. They are opposites. Like cold and hot, north and south, and up and freaking down. The weirdest part is that they seem to get along just well.

Jace is the playboy, and some could even say bad boy, but he's fun and an amazing friend. He acts like a little kid and is silly; I can admit he can be aggravating. Then, you have Carter, who is extremely mature and is serious and helpful. He has been through a lot and relates with me. He also is really nice and kind-hearted. He is a great guy, and I guess that's why he's one of my best friends now. That and the fact that he inspires me and makes me feel as if anything is possible.

The couch beside me sinks and as a leg push up against the side of mine and the instant sparks automatically inform me that it is Payton. A smile sneaks onto my face as I reach my hand over for her hand. I feel her soft hand intertwines with mine. Gosh, this girl makes me feel so girly. I can't help it, just as I cannot wait for tomorrow.

Valentine's Day is tomorrow, and I cannot wait to see Payton's face when she sees what I have planned. I just have a really great feeling about tomorrow.

"Does it matter to you what we watch?" Payton whispers to me, her warm breath fanning against my ear.

"No, all that I care about is having you here in my arms," I say to her as I take my hand from hers, sliding it up her arm until I wrap my arm around her neck.

Her heart rate picks up rapidly, and all the noises of the people around me disappear while all I can focus on is her quick beating heart that causes me to smile. I love this girl so much.

"I love you," I whisper to her quietly and feel her curl up into my side. My arm tightens around her, and I wish there is a way she could be closer to me.

"I love you too," she whispers back, and I smile as I take in a breath and smell her fruity smelling hair.

"Hush, everyone! Movie time!" The loud room falls silent, and I feel something jump up beside me and what feels like a head rests on my knee. I automatically knew that it was Rider. With the hand that is not around my angel, I reach down to where I feel Rider's head and begin petting his fur.

The movie actually goes really normal, and I know what's happening because I use to watch this all the time. Half the time, this time, I spent concentrating on the angel in my arms. Finally, in the end, I hear Prime doing his end speech as I smile.

"I better be heading out!" Jace says as I hear the TV turn off.

"Me too!" Conner agrees as I hear more movement in the room.

Payton's body disappears from my side, and I can sense her standing up. Even Rider moves and I can hear his panting.

"Reece I'm tired," I hear her whisper, and I stand up smiling lightly.

"Then let's go to bed," I say to her.

"Bye, Reece!" Conner and Jace call at the same time, and I smile, raising my hand to wave in the direction I heard their voice come from. Juliet's voice fills my ears as it sounds like she is leading them out. A warm hand slips into mine, causing fireworks to explode up my arm and finding their way to my heart to warm it.

"Ready?" she asks me, and I smile and nod my head.

"Come on, Rider," I say as Payton begins to pull me with her, leading me to my room.

Once we walk the course, which I have come to know as the one to my room and when I feel the door shut behind us, "Can I borrow a shirt?" Payton's sweet voice asks me in a very soft tone, and I smile as I nod my head.

"Of course, Angel." I find my way over to my bed with some difficult. Once my stick taps the bed, I know I am there. So then I begin to feel for the bed and sit down on its softness. The bed shakes and moves as something jump on it, and the panting and clicking sound of a dog collar gives it away. I automatically now that it is Rider. The moving stops and I hear what sounds like a sigh, so I am guessing he is lying down. Time like this, it really sucks being blind. I hate it!

I pull my shirt off my body and over my head, lazily tossing it onto the ground and then I fumble around the front of my jeans until I am able to unhook the button and rise up, allowing them to fall off my hips.

Running my hand over the top of the big comforter, I look for the top of it. Once I find it, I pull the fluffy comforter down. I slip inside and scoot over. I feel a lump on my side. Reaching out to see what the lump is, I feel a furry creator and smile know that it is Rider.

After what seem like ten minutes, I feel the bed sway and Payton crawl under the covers. Stretching out my arm, I find her waist and can fill the cotton of the shirt of mine that she is wearing. A large smile spreads across my face as I think of how great she must look in my shirt. I pull her tightly against me, and I feel her soft breath hit my face which tells me that she is facing me, and I smile. I take a hand up to her head and gently sweep my hand across her soft hair.

"I love you so much, angel," I whisper lightly to her.

"I love you too," she whispers back to me, and all of a sudden, I feel her lips crash onto mine. Our lips move together in sync in a kiss not full of lust and passion, but love and happiness. Payton's hands tangle in my hair as we kiss, and my tongue enters her sweet-tasting mouth and explores it. I place my right hand onto her left cheek, and then allow my left hand to slide down her body, feeling every little curve, and painting a picture within my brain of it. She is so beautiful! I think she is the most beautiful girl in the world, at least to me, she is.

Our lips continue to move together, and I feel like I am in total bliss. I slowly move my lips from hers so we can regain our breaths, and I kiss lightly over her cheeks and to her neck. I began to kiss her lightly, moving my lips softly on her skin. She is so sweet-tasting, and I love it. She brings my lips back to hers and kisses me. As we kiss this time, simple and perfect, she pulls away, and her warm breath brushes my face causing me to smile.

"I love you so much," I say as I release my breath.

"I love you too," I smile as I pull her into my chest and wrap my arms around her thin waist. She snuggles into my chest making me smile.

Shifting slightly, my body wakes up on its own, and I smile as I feel the warm body in my arms. I love this feeling and waking up with her in my arms. Honestly, I didn't know what love really is until I was with her. Since I met Payton, I just knew which is super cheese yet true.

Suddenly, I feel something poke my arm. Poke? Huh? What? I think I am going crazy! "Pst, Reece, I need you to come with me!" a voice whispers, and in my foggy head, I realize it is Juliet. What does she want so early? Wait, it's Valentine's Day! Oh, yes! Time for my big surprise for Payton!

Gently, I release Payton. As bad as I do not want to, I had to. Slowly, I get out of the bed, stand up, and feel around for the cane. "Here," Juliet says softly, shoving something that feels like cotton into my hands. As I run my fingers over it, I realize that it is a shirt. "Put it on." I pull on the shirt and then stretch my hand to her, gesturing for my cane. I feel it being placed into my hand, and then another hand grab mine and lead me somewhere with the shutting of a door.

"Okay, today's the day!" Juliet says, referring to the big date I have planned for Payton and me.

"I know! I cannot wait! Is the plan a go?" I ask my sister as I smile so happily. The first part of the plan is for Juliet to take Payton out to go shop for clothes, which I will pay for. Then, on to our date!

"Yeah! Just one little thing, when I get Payton out without seeing you, you can go see mom. She wants to see you, anyways. So hurry and go now, she is in her office, and I will wake Payton," Juliet says, and I nod my head. I wonder what is so important for my mom to want to see me at this time. Sighing, I nod and begin to try to find my way as I shut my eyes and remember the path to her office using the cane to make sure I didn't knock into something.

"Oh, good. There you are, Reece!" my mom's voice says in what sounds like a happy tone.

"Yeah, mom?" I ask as I feel her hand grab mine and tug me into I guess her office and the sound of a door shuts tells me we are inside a room.

"I had my door open, waiting," she states, and I nod my head; that makes sense.

"So what did you need, mommy dearest?" I ask her giving her a big fake smile because I miss being in bed with my angel in my arms.

"I have a question first," she says with a timid sound in her voice.

"Okay ask," I tell her, shrugging my shoulders. I am a little afraid of where she is going with this.

"Do you want your sight back?" she asks me, and my nonworking eyes widen, as I am shocked from what she just asked me.

That is a dumb question! Of course, I do! So much has changed, but this is way worse than anything that'd appear in my nightmares, and you cannot wake up from this. As I've said a million times, Payton is the only good thing to come from all of this. I honestly believe, however, that this is all apart God's plan to bring me to Payton. If it were possible, I'd get my sight back because nothing will change the way I feel for Payton.

"Yes," I say, nodding my head.

"Well, I contacted the doctor who did Carter's surgery, and he said you can come into the hospital tomorrow. He will run some tests and see if you are able to have the surgery done." Her voice goes up a couple notches in happiness.

My face lights up. "I may be able to see again?" I ask in disbelief. I always fake hope and cannot believe that something good like this may happen.

"It's not for sure, but maybe," she says, trying to keep me from getting too excited. I cannot help it, though! I get to go the doctor who may restore my sight! I may be able to see again! I may see Payton's beautiful face! I really hope it does work!

Today is a great day so far and can only get better!

Chapter Forty-Seven

Payton's POV

"Wake up, sleepy head!" a girl's voice sings, and I peek open my heavy eyes to see a smiling Juliet standing over me.

"W-what are you doing here?" I ask as I sit up, rubbing my eyes. I look around Reece's room and taking notice of his absent which makes confusion fill my head.

"I live here," she laughs as she rolls her blue eyes that remind me slightly of Reece's. I smile lightly at her, shaking my head and then groaning when I realize my hair is a big, frizzy ball. It is a great thing Reece cannot see at times like this. I mean my hair is always so bad in the morning, and I always look so pale.

"I know that, silly. I meant why are you waking me up and where is Reece?" I ask her as I stretch, and a big smile appears on her face.

"I am waking you up, dear Payton because we are going shopping! And Reece is talking to my mom," she says, and my eyes widen. I don't go shopping mainly because I don't have money, and the other reason is no one to go with. My life is so pitiful, I know.

"I don't have any money," I say ashamed, especially I am around her or just in this big ole house. Sometimes, I feel out of place around all this money and even angry because I am poor. But in the end, all I have to do is take one look at Reece or even his family, and I feel at home and not so bad about it. Juliet smiles and shakes her head.

"Oh, Payton! It's fine! It is all on Reece! It's a Valentine's Day present or well presents," she says with a smile. I cannot accept this. This is too much and way too kind! I haven't gotten him anything either! Dang it!

"I can't spend his money, and I didn't get him anything," I say, shaking my head and yank my hand through my hair.

"Oh yes, you can, and you don't need to get him anything because honestly, you are the best thing he could get. So come on, we are going my room to get ready, and I'm lending you clothes," she says and pulls the covers off me, and I climb out the bed. Suddenly, Juliet begins to laugh. I raise an eyebrow in confusion. "No! Don't tell me you two did it!" Juliet cries and I sit there in confusion.

Then, I look down at what I am wearing, and a blush rises on my face as I stand there in Reece's shirt with my panties underneath. "W-we didn't! I swear!" I say quickly and hold my hands up in surrender. Oh my gosh, how could she think that? Wait, I will admit this probably did not look too good so I can understand.

Juliet throws her head back laughing. "I was just kidding with you!" she says smiling. "Now, come one," she adds and gestures for me to follow her. Sighing, I follow her out of the door, up the staircase, and into her room.

She walks to her closet, and I realize that she is already dressed. I see that she is wearing a pair of white skinny jeans, which not a lot of people can pull off but she can perfectly, and a she is wearing a black jacket on top of a blue silky shirt that. She pulls some clothes out from the closet and turns around walk over to me.

"Here, put this on so that I can work on your hair and add some makeup to your pretty yet bare face," Juliet instructs me smiling.

I release a sigh as I take the clothes from her hands and disappear into her attached room. Once in the bathroom, I strip out of my clothes and pull on the black tights she handed me followed by a royal blue sweater dress over my head. I smile in the mirror as I see that the dress fits my body perfectly.

I leave the bathroom and see Juliet smile again at me as she stands behind her vanity chair. "Sit," she instructs, and I listen, taking a seat where she is pointing. I sit down, and she smiles, taking her brush and moving it to my head. Finally, she drags a brush through my hair, and it slides through with ease. It only took her an hour. She takes a step back placing her hands on her hips as she looks at me. A smile lifts on her face as she grabs some things from the top of her vanity and begins to put makeup on my face. She runs a brush over eyelids and all that other stuff that I don't even know what's called.

"Voila!" she steps back and raises her hands up, smiling. I sigh as I stand up and look into her floor-length mirror. My brown hair is now spilling over my shoulders straight, and my brown eyes pop with the blue eye shadow. The dress actually looks nice on me, which is shocking.

"Wow, I look pretty," I say softly, not meaning for Juliet to hear.

"Yes, you do! Now, put on these flip flops and let's go," she says pointing over to a pair of black and white flip flops.

"This good?" I ask as I stand there and force a smile on my face.

"Perfection!" she says smiling. "Now, let's go! Busy day ahead!" she adds as she quickly grabs my hand and tugs me with her, and we are off to a day of shopping.

"I am so happy! You are finally ready for the next step in your day! And trust me, it's the best part!" Juliet says happily as she claps her hands together.

"Um… what is it, Juliet?" I ask nervously, seeing she has already forced me to buy ten outfits, four pairs of shoes, make-up, and then drags me to get a haircut!

So now, as we reach her car, I have five bags of clothing, one *Victoria's Secret* bag she forced me to buy *sexier* underwear, a bag full of make-up and hair supplies, and lastly, four boxes of shoes. I dump them all into the trunk of her car. I then touch my hair which feels so much lighter. Juliet had me cut about two inches and get layers put in it. I can tell it has lost a lot of weight!

"If I told you, I'd get killed," she says in a sing-song voice as she dumps some bags in the trunk too and then walks to the driver's door.

Sighing, I shut the trunk and walk around to the passenger door and slide inside. "Does this have to do with Reece?" I raise my eyebrows in suspicion, and she laughs lightly.

"Of course, it does," she says simply with a smile. At this new information, a smile spreads across my face. I stare out the window as we drive down the road and watch as trees pass and then some houses. What does Reece have up his sleeve?

We ride in a relaxing silence as I think, and she listens to the radio. Finally, the car pulls to a stop, and I look out of my window to see the large sign that reads Washington High School.

"Why are we here?" I ask her, and all she does is smile.

"This is where we part ways. Go to the football field, and I will take all this stuff back to the house," she instructs, and I raise my eyebrows at her in confusion, begging for her to tell me what was going on. But instead, she shakes her head and raises her hand, gesturing me to go outside.

"Fine," I groan as I push open the door.

"Have a great time!" she calls, and I shut the door, groaning. If you cannot tell, I am definitely not one for surprises. So I sort of stomp my way over to the field annoyed by the fact that I have no clue what is going on.

Once I see the field, I find Reece and Rider standing on the track. Reece has one hand in his pocket and the other on Rider's harness. Reece is wearing a gray V-neck shirt showing off his chest muscles underneath, and a pair of fitted blue jeans hung off his hips along with a pair of white shoes.

"Reece," I say as I walk towards him smiling, and Rider stands up panting happily.

"Hey, Angel," he says as I stop in front of him, and he takes the hand from his pocket and places it onto my waist. He pulls me in closely with his strong arm. I grab onto him, holding him tightly. Gosh, my whole body gets tingly, and all I can do is smile. He makes me feel so safe and protected; something I haven't felt before apart from my mom.

"You do know I hate surprises."

"Oh well," is his great response. "I have something to show you," he says and then kisses the top of my head causing me to smile and roll my eyes. I step back and look at him. He looks so happy and cheerful. So much like a child!

"What is that?" I ask, staring into his beautiful eyes.

"I will show you," he says with his bright, perfect smile. "Keep in mind I am wearing jeans," he says, and I look at him not understanding how his choice of clothing is important.

"Um… okay," I say as I reach up scratching my head.

He begins to walk away from me around the track. Suddenly, the walking changes to jogging as he rounds the first turn. As his feet hit the straight stretch, he runs faster, and I watch as Rider guides him. My eyes widen in astonishment.

As he nears me, I see that his running may not be perfect like it once was, but it is so amazing. He may not have gone that fast but knowing him and the struggles he is facing, it seemed like he was speeding.

He slows down to a walk as he finishes the last turn coming towards me. "Wow, Reece that was amazing," I say. My voice cracks, and I reach up wiping the tear away from my eye. Yes, I am crying! It's just, that was so beautiful, and I am so proud.

"Thank you. It is all thanks to you! You made me see that just because I can't see doesn't mean I can't do anything," he says, and I smile through my tears, walking over to him and flinging my arms around his neck kissing him!

"I love you," I say to him breathlessly as I pull away.

"I love you too, Angel. Now on to part two," he says and pulls away. His hand finds mine, taking it into his as he leads us away. As we make our way to the parking lot, which he must have the path memorized, I spot Carter resting against the side of a black Escalade.

"Aww, the beautiful couple," he says as he opens the door to the back seat.

"Carter, what are you doing here?" I ask as Reece let's go of my hand, and Carter put Rider into the car. He then helps Reece in. I climb in the backseat last. I am not going to bother asking what's going on so I am just going rest my head here on Reece's shoulder.

"Where are we going?" I ask as Reece and Rider lead me into an elevator at our town's large hotel.

"You'll see," he says as he runs his hand gently over the buttons and finally clicks on one at the bottom which I do not know what it stands for. The elevator starts to rise, and I reach out, holding onto Reece's arm for no reason.

"I really do hate surprises," I state, and he just chuckles. The doors slide open, revealing an open roof and one of my hands slip into his as we walk together out onto the roof with, of course, Rider by our side.

I stare out ahead of me and see the sun setting over our town. This boy has pretty great timing. I look around and see a table set up like a picnic and two candles burning in the center. Rose petals are scattered in a line leading to the table which it surrounds completely. Honestly, I am not that hungry, but this does look amazing.

"Come on," Reece says as my mouth hangs open, and we walk over to the table. I place his hand on the chair, and he sits down with Rider beside him. I take a seat, and he manages to as well.

A plate is sitting in front of us with what looks like *Chicken Alfaro* on the plate. "This looks good," I say, and he smiles.

"Let's eat," he smiles as he picks up his fork and begins to eat slowly as it is still kind of hard for him. I begin to eat too.

Our eating is silent but not awkward. It's peaceful. Life is peaceful when I am with him. I feel normal. I am not that nobody, I am not that abused girl, and I am not the girl with the sister who is never waking up. When I am with him, I am me. I am Payton Jennings. The girl who fell in love with the jock. The girl who fell in love with the blind boy. The girl who fell in love with Reece Collins. The craziest part, I am the girl he fell in love with too.

I rest my fork on my plate as I finish eating and grab the glass of water taking a sip. Reece finishes after me and takes a drink.

"Do you still hate surprises?" he asks me as his smirk sneaks onto his face.

"Yeah." I think I may be starting to like them. This is so sweet.

"Well, I have one more left," he says trailing off.

"What's that?" I ask him, wondering what he has up his sleeve now.

He reaches across the table and takes my hand into his own. "Payton, you are my angel. I swear God sent you down just for me. If it wasn't for you, I know I would never have made it. You are the best thing to happen to me and as crazy as this may sound, no matter how bad I hate the accident I am thankful for it. It brought us together. Loving you has helped me become who I am now. You have taught me strength, courage, will, and love. I love you. I will always love you. So this is my promise to you that I will love you forever and always. One day, I want to marry you," he says and reaching into his jean pockets and opens a box in my direction. It is an infinity sign in diamonds with a large diamond in the center.

Gasping as I hold my hands over my mouth, I cannot believe it, and he runs his hand over my finger, finding the ring finger on my right hand and places the stunning ring on it.

"I love it! I love you!" I cry as I get up and walk over to where he is sitting and wrap him in my arms.

"Still, hate surprises?" he asks me, and I smile.

"I am starting to like them," I say as I move to brush my lips on his when I am stopped by the ringing of my phone. I look at it, and my heart stops. "I have to take this," I say simply, standing straight up.

"Hello?" I say into my phone as my heart beats so quickly.

"Is this Payton Jennings?" a female voice asks.

"Yes," I say quickly in fear of what's going on.

"You need to get to the hospital as soon as possible," she says in what seems like a fake calm voice. My panic begins to boil over.

"What? Why?" I say quickly, feeling my chest ache.

"It's your sister… she is awake."

Chapter Forty-Eight

Payton's POV

The phone slips from my hand and crashes onto the roof. My heart stops, and I cannot think. I cannot move. I cannot function at all. My body is frozen in place. I feel like everything thing has changed. Hope burns bright inside of me, and I cannot believe it. I have waited for so long, and to be honest, I am starting to lose hope in her waking. But she did! She is! Why am I just standing here? I ask myself.

"Payton, what's wrong?" Reece's panic-filled voice says, and I look up at his moving figure through my tear-clouded eyes.

"It's Lila," I say with a smile, allowing a few tears to skate down my cheeks. I am so happy that I cannot believe it.

"Is she okay? Please tell me she's okay?" Reece says, seeming worried. "She's awake," I say still in surprise because I was honestly not expecting this.

"What? That's great, Payton! What are we still doing here?" he says really in an upbeat tone, and I watch as he gets closer to me.

"How will we get there?" I ask in confusion as my brain finally starts working. Rider brings him to me, and he reaches out finding my hand.

"I had Conner drop my car off here so Carter didn't have to stay. I thought you could drive it. So let's go," he says in his caring tone, and I nod.

"Thank you so much!" I say happily as I take his hand not on Rider's harness and lead him out. My shocked being quickly turns into excitement. I am so excited and nervous that I cannot sit still. We make our way out to his sports car and all cram inside. I start the car revving the engine.

My entire mind thinks about as I speed down the road on my way to the hospital, for sure breaking tons of speeding laws, is Lila. I want to get there in time! Finally, I will get to see her sparkling eyes shine up at me. I get to see life return to her lifeless body! With that thought, I speed up. It's a good thing that Reece can't see. He may have been flipping out if he saw how fast I am driving his car. At this moment, however, I can care less.

Before I know it, I am at the hospital, dragging Reece and Rider inside with me. May looks up from her spot behind the desk and is stunned for a moment and quickly recovers. I really am not paying attention to anything as I make it to the doors beside the desk. She appears in front of me and the door and gives me a light happy smile.

"Come on, Payton," she says and leads me through the doors. Reece and Rider come with mainly because I refuse to release his hand. His hand is the only thing keeping me from floating away in excitement and joy.

She leads us through the halls and Lila's room. "She's inside. Your mom is on her way. You can go ahead," May tells me as she places her hand lightly on my shoulder.

"May," I choke out and hold back my tears of joy. She raises an eyebrow at me as if to ask what. "How did she wake up?" I ask wanting, *no*, needing to know the answer.

"Sometimes, Payton, people just wake up. Sometimes, it is after years, others days. Something in their brain and body just changes and switches on. These are the miracles of life. She is extremely weak, and there are no promises of the future if she survives, but right now, she has woken up and seems okay besides worn out," May says to me with a gentle voice, and Reece squeezes my hand.

"Thank you, May." I open the door, push the door, and walk carefully into the room a little afraid to see her.

"It'll be okay," Reece whispers to me, comforting.

We walk completely inside, and I look to the bed and see the frail body of my baby sister laying there. My heart drops as I see her eyes shut. *Please don't let her be gone again*, I beg as I lead Reece to the couch and place his hand on it.

"Have a seat," I say to him softly and look back over to the bed.

Suddenly, her eyes pop open, and her brown-blue eyes shine brightly as she slowly moves her head to look at me.

"Pay?" her voice asks weak and soft, but I know it's hers.

"Lila!" I say in a voice full of shock. I fight back the tears that threaten to break the barrier of my eyes. Walking to her, I wrap my arms gently around her and hold her tight. "I am so glad you're awake. I missed you so much! I was so worried! I love you, Lila," I say to her as I feel her small hands hold onto my waist.

"I love you too, Pay," she says using her nickname for me causing me to smile. It means so much to hear her say that.

I pull away and sit on the edge of the bed with my hand in hers, and I cannot fight the large smile that is planted onto my face. My sister is awake, and Reece promised to spend forever by my side. At the thought of Reece, I look up to find him and Rider on the couch. It was so cute. Reece's head was bent down, and his long hair fell lightly into his face. Rider has his front paws and head on Reece's legs, and Reece is casually stroking Rider's head. All in all, they looked so adorable together. A cute smile is resting upon Reece's face and it's one of my favorite smiles. It's a rare one, just a causal permanent cute, happy smile.

"Who's he?" Lila's weak little voice asks, and it breaks me from my glaze on Reece.

I look down at her thin face, and her eyes are so alive and shining. She may still be weak, but I can still see it in her eyes. The fire inside her is burning strong with the desire to live. The thought of that makes me happy.

"That's my boyfriend, Reece Collins," I say to her as I look down at her and give her a smile.

"Boyfriend? I really have been out for a while," she says slowly in her weak voice, and I smile at her, shaking my head.

"Yeah, boyfriend and you have. Please don't do that again," I beg her even though I know she cannot control it.

"The doctor told me how long I was out and all," she says simply. "I'll try my best to not do it again," she tells me with a small smile. I shake my head.

"Thank you," I tell her and I lean down, gently kiss her pale forehead right below where they have a pink bandana tied over her little bald head.

"Can I meet him?" she asks me with her same weak voice. I glance over at Reece, who is still sitting with his head down as he strokes Rider's head.

"Sure," I say as I stand up slowly and release my hold on my baby sister's hand. Walking to Reece, he lifts his head up, and I stare down into his sparkling blue shining orbs. "Care to meet her?" I ask nervously as I fidget in front of him. I'm not really sure how he'll handle meeting her.

"Sure," he says with his sweet, cheeky smile. Gently, he moves Rider and rises up. I smile as he runs his hand through his hair, and I catch it as he places it back to his side.

Tightly squeezing the hand of my wonderful boyfriend, I lead over to my little ten-year-old sister who is lying weak and broken in her bed. As we reach her bedside, her bright eyes stare up at Reece in amazement. "Reece, this is my little sister, Delilah and Lila this is my boyfriend Reece," I introduce them, and Lila's eyes seem to shimmer like she is impressed.

"Hi there," Lila says weakly, and I smile at her as Reece looks down at where her voice is coming from.

"Hi cutie," Reece says with his friendly smile, and I smile at how he called her "cutie" in an older brother kind of way. I know for a fact that that probably made Lila's life since she has had such low self-esteem since her hair fell out, and she lost a whole lot of weight. I know Reece knows about her dramatic change in appearance and could probably guess that she would have low self-esteem seeing as he does have two little sisters.

"You have really pretty eyes," Lila says as she stares into his trapping blue eyes.

"Thank you," he says to her kindly, still with that award winning a smile.

"How'd you get a dog in here?" she asks him or us, I guess, as she points towards Rider sitting at Reece's feet.

I watch as Reece's body stiffens at her question so I squeeze onto his hand, and he visually relaxes. "I'm blind," he says simply, fighting to keep a smile upon his face.

"Oh," she says slowly and looks at me questioning. I shake my head at her signaling not now. "That's cool," she says, smiling happily, and I can tell that she is seriously finding it cool. Maybe because she feels he may understand her, or it's her just being her.

"Cool?" Reece asks shock as if he cannot believe that those words just left her mouth.

"Yeah, cool," she confirms with a smile, and I shake my head at her.

Reece goes to reply but is cut off by the sound of the door opening and a set of feet rushing inside. I look up and am greeted by my mom, her eyes teary and full of excitement. "Lila!" she calls as she rushes to my sister's side and I tug Reece back.

"Mom," Lila says with a smile.

I know right now, they needed to bond. And mom doesn't need to meet Reece at this second. She is busy. So I tug Reece to the door, "Come on," I say as I pull him with me. "We are going to see Ms. Rose," I call over my shoulder and walk out, leading Reece and Rider along with me as we make our way to the one person outside of my family and the Collins family who is like my best friend. As I sit her, I refuse to revile anything to anyone. We make our way to Ms. Rosa's room, and as soon as I reach the door, Reece stops me and gives me a slow, perfect kiss.

"I'm ready," he says nodding his head smiling and kisses my forehead quickly.

Chapter Forty-Nine

Reece's POV

Ms. Rose is a kind, very funny woman who is so helpful and nice. While she and Payton chats, I can feel the change in how Payton was talking. She seemed happy like she is when she talks to her mom and sister. I have decided not to tell Payton about the doctor appointment until I know for sure. I don't want to get her hopes up only for them to be crushed. I am feeling the same way, I wish someone wouldn't have told me until after I knew for sure, but that's impossible.

Payton snuggles deeper into my arms as we sit on the couch in her sister's room while Riders lies at my side. I hold her tightly to me loving the feel of having her in my arms. Her mom, who I have yet to meet officially, had to go home and pick up some things. It's been a little hectic. I know it's near six in the morning, and I can hear the rhythmic breathing of Lila, with the slight shallowness here and there.

Now, I'm not running on zero hours of sleep, I was able to sneak a quick nap here and there. Payton, on the other hand, has been wide awake. Right now, as she snuggles into my arms with her sweet head on my chest, I can feel the way her body is breathing that she is still awake. I am kind of starting to feel like maybe she thinks if she closes her eyes and goes to sleep, she will wake up and Lila's gone, or it was all a dream.

"Angel, why don't you rest those eyes of yours?" I whisper to her, breathing in the fruity smell of her hair. She shifts in my arms, and I hear a sigh escape her lips.

"I can't if I do, who knows what'll happen." I know she is worried, but I wouldn't let anything happen.

"Nothing will happen, angel," I whisper in an attempt to soothe her fears. I gently rub her arm with my hand as I hold her.

"I can't, Reece. I'll wait until my mom gets back and then we can go. I want to talk to your mom about something, anyways," she replies to me. I release a sigh. It doesn't look like I am going to win this battle. Why does she want to talk to my mom?

"Alright," I say simply, not bothering to ask why. I just figure it's personal and if she wants me to know, she will tell me.

"You can take another nap if you would like too," she says as I feel her draw light circles on my chest, leaving a trail of tingles.

"Are you sure, angel?" I ask and lean my head back with a light smile on my face.

"I'm sure," she confirms as she continues drawing light circles on my chest.

"I love you," I say in a sleepy voice.

"I love you too, Reece," she replies, and I smile as I tighten my grip on her and shut my eyes, turning off my brain.

"He's really good looking," a voice says, and I keep my eyes shut tightly, thinking that I just hear voices.

"I know, mom," Payton's sweet voice says in a whisper.

Her mom? Am I losing it?

"I can't believe I wake up and find you with a guy like him," a weak voice says, and my brain is suddenly working. I choose to keep my eyes closed because for one, I am curious to hear what they are saying.

"Yeah, he has helped me get through so much. I love him to death," Payton's sweet voice says shyly.

I feel the couch deep beside me, and warmth returns into my arms as Payton returns. And I know it's her because she is the only one who can affect me this way.

"You two are so darn cute together," her mom says in a happy voice.

"Thanks," my angel mumbles into my chest.

"You're awake," she whispers to me.

"No, I'm not," I reply without thinking and suddenly feel very stupid. Now, she knows I am because I responded. What can I say? Not my best moment.

"So you talk in your sleep?" she asks me with a humorous tone.

To reply or to not reply... that is the question. "Exactly," I state with my sleepy voice.

"I know how to wake you up then," she states, and as I go say something, I feel a warm, soft lips press upon mine. My eyes instantly open and then shut again as I kiss her back. She pulls away, and I know she is probably smiling at me.

"So this is Reece," her mother says, and I feel Payton slip her hand into mine and pull me up onto my feet.

"Yes, ma'am. I'm Reece Collins. It's nice to meet you, Ms. Jennings," I say as I outstretch my hand to where I heard her voice come from. I feel a warm hand slide into mine, and I know that it is her mom.

"It's great to finally meet you too, Reece and please call me June," she says in a sweet, kind tone, one that reminds me so much of Payton's.

"Alright, June," I say with a smile as she releases my hand. I feel Payton's hand intertwine with mine at my side and smile at how our hands fit together just right.

"Good morning, Reece," the sweet, weak voice of Lila says, and I smile.

"Good morning, cutie!" I reply smiling at her. As I stand here among the Jennings women, I learn that there is more to them than you'd think, and they love each other more than anything.

An incoming call from your mom. An incoming call from your mom.

My phone rings repeatedly. I pull it from my pocket and release Payton's hand. "Excuse me," I say as I begin to walk. I feel Rider brush my legs, and I reach down grabbing a hold of his harness.

Luckily, I am able to find my way to the door and into the hall. Maybe not so much as luck as it is practice, a lot of practice.

"Answer," I say and raise my phone up to my ear. "Hello."

"Hey, Reece. Honey, where are you?" my mom's voice asks me, sounding kind of worried.

"At the hospital. Payton's sister woke up," I say simply like it explains everything. It probably would have to if, you know, my mom knew about her sister.

"I would ask for you to elaborate on what you are talking about because I don't know why her sister would have not been awake. But if Payton wanted me to know, she'd tell me and I respect that. Is she at least dealing with what is going on well?" my mom asks being her usual caring self. My mom was blessed with a heart, but it's understandable she comes from a bad past so I understand. It actually makes me happy that she cares so much about Payton.

"She's fine, mom. She's really happy. But she is also tired so we are going leave soon, so she can take a nap before returning to the hospital," I inform her as I lean against a wall with Rider by my side.

"That's so good! Are you guys coming back here" she asks me as I rest my head against the wall, shutting my eyes and trying to keep the thoughts of missing my sight at bay.

"Yeah, I think so. Is there any certain reason you called?" I ask her, trying my best to not sound rude. I mean I don't want to sound rude. It's just sometimes, the thoughts of the everlasting darkness I am faced with causes me to be depressed, and I don't want to take it out on anyone. I don't want to think about it. I feel like it's not fair for me to get so upset about it when there are people who have it worse. Payton taught me this.

"Oh, yes, yes there is! I talked to the eyesight doctor today," she says with a happy voice, and I perk up at hearing this. What did he say? Is this good news? Can I see again?

"You did? And?" I ask, prodding her to continue because patience is not something I was gifted with.

"You have an appointment there bright and early tomorrow morning," she informs me happily.

"Really?" I ask in shock, and I am suddenly overcome with excitement.

"Yes, so you will have to miss a day of school," she tells me, and suddenly, my excitement is replaced with worry. I am going to have to miss school? Payton is going to know! I am still not planning to tell her yet because I feel like I can't, and I don't know why. How am I going to get out of this one? I guess I have to wing it.

"Oh, alright. Thanks for letting me know," I say a little bit in a spacey tone.

"You're welcome son! I'll see you soon."

"Yeah, see you soon," I reply, shutting my eyes tightly.

"I love you," she says in her usual upbeat tone.

"I love you too, mom," I reply and hit a button on the side of the phone to hang up.

I rest my head on the wall as I think, think about everything— life, Payton, seeing again, not seeing, running, and how my life got this way. A million thoughts crash into my brain at once.

"Are you okay?" Payton's sweet voice asks me, and I sigh.

"I'm fine," I say as I take a deep breath, pushing away all my thoughts.

"Let's go," she says, and I raise an eyebrow.

"I need to say goodbye to your family," I say, slowly turning.

"No! It's fine. You'll see them later," she says as she slips her hand into mine.

"Alright, let's go," I say somewhat confused. It's okay, though. With Payton by my side, I can face anything. She makes me strong and brave.

Chapter Fifty

Payton's POV

"I'm going to go take a shower while you talk to my mom," Reece informs me.

"Alright," I say as I smile at him. His brown hair is a mess atop his head, the bottom of his blue eyes is lined with circles, and his clothes are wrinkled. He looks so tired, and I feel so bad because it is my fault that he is tired.

"See you soon." He drops my hand, and with Rider, he disappears down the hallway.

I sigh as I glance around the hallway before walking to the sitting room to see if Georgia is in there. I rub my eyes as I yawn. I am beginning to feel just how tired my body is. I have been too afraid to sleep in the fear that I will wake up, and it'll all be a dream and that Lila will disappear again. As I enter the room, I find that it is empty of life except for the figure seated on top of the brown leather couch by a warm, dancing fireplace.

As I near the figure, I take in everything. On the nice wooden coffee table sits a cup that says, *World's Greatest Mom*, and its contents either coffee or hot chocolate. I can tell it's Georgia by the calming feel in the air. Her blonde hair is falling loosely around her shoulders. She is wearing a blue sweater and some pajama bottoms. Her knees are bent under her, and she has a book in her lap. She is so pretty and kind, so I can do this.

"Hey," I mumble meekly as I walk to the other end of the couch to sit down.

She looks up from her book, and her eyes glue onto me. "Hi there, Payton," she says with total ease and kindness.

"Hey," I say a tad bit stronger with a smile. By the sounds of the house, no one else is home, which is somewhat understandable since it is morning, and Reece and I have been at the hospital all night long.

Throughout the night, I stayed awake because I did not feel comfortable enough to sleep. Lila slept most of the night, but she would wake up a few times mainly when the nurse would come in to do a checkup. Every time her eyes would open, I would be right there by her side, greeting her with a smile. Words cannot explain just how happy I am to have my little sister awake.

"Where is everyone?" I ask her as I pull my knees up to my chest and turn facing her with my back against the arm rest.

"Leo took Rayne to go and have a father-daughter day; I think they may have head to an amusement park or something. Juliet spent the night with one of her friends, and as for Conner, I think he is doing something college-related. I'm guessing Reece is here, though," she says with a smile and raises an eyebrow.

I laugh lightly at her and nod my head. "Yeah, he's showering," I say, nodding my head.

"So what brings you here? Want to have some girl talk? Complain to me about my son? He may be my son, but if he did anything to you, I would have to hurt him," she says with a serious look on her face. I burst into laughter, and a smile rises on her face.

"No, no!" I say waving my arms. "He didn't do anything," I say, allowing my laughter to die down. "I just needed to talk to you about some stuff," I say all serious now.

"Okay, sweetie. We can talk about whatever it is," she says as she folds the tip of her book page down, and shuts it, placing it on the table and giving me her full attention.

I rub the back of my neck, not sure how to start this. I really need to get my emotions off my chest, and there have been a few questions haunting me for quite some time.

"Can I ask you a question?" I say, deciding to start with a question that has been on my mind since the day we met.

"Sure, sweetie, ask away," she says gesturing with one hand, and I take in a deep breath before releasing it in a deep sigh.

"Why are you so nice to me? I mean not just me but everyone. From the first moment we met, you have been so sweet and kind to me. You didn't even know me that well and gave me your car to use. Nobody I know is as happy and kind as you," I say with a face of confusion, and my heart weakens as I think of how kind this woman has been to me, a kindness I've never known before. Sure, my mom is kind, but not this kind she has too much damage and hurt too much to show too many emotions.

Georgia seems to be a little taken back at first by my question, but soon recovers with ease. "Has Reece told you anything about my past?" she asks me with a sigh and runs her hand through her hair.

"No, not really," I say as I shake my head.

She nods her head inhales a deep breath. "When I was five, my mother died from breast cancer. After that, my father and I barely got by living in a trailer park. Over a short amount of time after her death, he changed and wouldn't even look at me. Then, he began to drink; he would drink so much until he passes out. He lost his job when I was six, and everything began to fall apart. I remember some nights I went to sleep hungry and had not eaten the whole day before. There was this really nice old lady next door who would see me all hungry and give me some soup or a sandwich. A lot of the times I thank her for my life. Eventually, one night, my father drank all his pain away. I found him on the couch, holding a picture of my mom. I tried to wake him because I was cold, but as I touched him to shake him, I realize how abnormal his temperature was. To this day, I still remember it all too well. When I was not able to wake him, I rushed out the trailer and to the one next down. With my little six-year-old hands, I banged on the old lady's door. Fear was seeping into every part of my body and tears were clouding my eyes. Finally, the door flew open and when she saw me she wrapped me in her arms asking what was wrong, I told her that daddy would not wake up. She rushed over to the trailer and then called 911. I was later told he died from alcohol poisoning. Never once did I ever blame him for anything that went wrong. He couldn't help it. He missed my mom." As she told me this, I could see her fight to keep her tears at bay. I, on the other hand, was tired of fighting them back so I allowed them to be free.

"I'm sorry," I murmur, and she just shrugs it off running her hand once again through her hair.

"It's alright. I got put in foster care and bounced from house to house. Most of the time the conditions were poor, and I never had a lot of money. When I turned sixteen, I was adopted along with a boy named Asher. The family was a nice middle-class family, who were unable to have children. They both knew that younger kids got adopted before older kids so they wanted to make a difference in the older kid's lives so they adopted me and Asher, who was seventeen. We didn't have a lot, but we had each other. My adoptive mom, Anne, often times made our clothes, and she let me help. That's how I discovered my love for fashion design. When we would buy clothes, they were cheap or hammy-downs. We lived and got by just fine," she tells me, wiping away the tears still falling down her face away.

"I am so sorry," I say softly. To be honest, I cannot believe that she has been through all of that.

"Yeah, it's okay. It all made me who I am today. I worked hard to get a scholarship for college, majored in fashion design, became a designer, and now, I make clothes for lower-income people and middle class. I design clothes that are in style, well made, and not too expensive. I met Leo at college. He was studying business. His family had money, but he wanted to make money separate from them. We fell in love, got married, and both of us became big and successful. Now, here we are," I smile, I am so happy she got a happy ending. She deserves it. Sometimes, I wish I will get a happy ending, and maybe, it will be with Reece.

"So dear, tell me your story," she says softly as she reaches out, grabs the mug from atop the table, and takes a sip.

I sigh, as I look up at the ceiling and think of where to begin. "My sister, Delilah, got sick with Leukemia when she was eight years old. It was one the hardest things we have been through. We were already struggling by. She was fine, and happy, dancing around all smiles, then she relapsed. Leukemia came back and this time, worse. She had to have surgery, something happened with the anesthesia, and she didn't come out of it for months. Last night, she woke up, and it felt like a weight had been lifted from my shoulders," I say as the tears blur my eyes, and I can see a very shocked-looking Georgia in front of me.

"What about your father during all of this?" she asks with motherly concern.

I shift uncomfortably at her question. To be honest, I have never really shared this part of my life with anyone before. Maybe I should, I trust her. She's easy to talk to, and I cannot talk to my mom about this. It is too hard on her to talk about it. I need to get it out, and I am terrified to share too much of this with Reece.

"Um, my father left when my sister was young. I have no clue where he is. Hopefully, he's in hell. My father was a very bad dude. He used to beat me, and my mother would come and defend me only to be beaten as well. I'd cry, and he saw it as a sign of weakness and beat me harder to make me 'tougher.' When I was silent, he thought he was not hitting hard enough. Nothing would stop him. He wasn't even a drunk either; he was just a jerk. I used to lock myself in a closet, hiding from him. As he beat me or when he saw me, he would call me names and constantly tell me how ugly I was, how stupid I was, how fat I was, and much more. When Delilah was born, I took more beatings, trying to protect her from the monster who was our father. Finally, he got up and left and without him, it was hard to pay the bills and everything, but we are managing. Life is better without him, and I can honestly say I don't miss him," I say as tears roll down my checks. I never told anyone that. It feels so good to get it out there. Georgia leans forwards and takes me into her arms, and I release all the tears I've ever held back.

"Shhh… I'm sorry, sweetie. It's okay. You can cry. Let it out," she whispers as she strokes my hair. My hands cling helplessly to the back of her sweater as the tears rush out of me. I cry and cry. I cry for a really long time.

Finally, the tears slow as I run out, and I calm down, just left with ragged breathing. "Honey, go, get some sleep so you can return to the hospital to see your sister," she tells me as she pulls away and dries my face.

"Thank you, Georgia," I say softly, with a cracked voice.

"You're welcome, sweetie. I am here anytime you need to talk. Talking helps, trust me," she says, and I nod as I stand up, forcing a tiny smile, and her sad looking face also turns up into a small, weak smile. I walk to Reece's room and hope he doesn't notice anything wrong. All I want to do is sleep. I am drained from energy from keeping my emotions bottled up and finally releasing them.

Chapter Fifty-One

Georgia's POV

"Mommy," Rayne says as she tugs on the bottom of my shirt. I stare down into her eyes as she smiles up at me.

"What is it, sweetie?" I ask her and stroke her soft brown hair that she has pulled back with a green ribbon. She is wearing a pair of jeans and matching green shirt. She looks so cute and sweet. I smile at her softly.

"It's daddy-and-me day!" she says very happily, and I smile at her stroking the side of her head.

"I know, sweetheart," I tell her as I shake my head lightly.

"Sweetie, are you ready to go?" Leo calls as he enters the room. He runs a hand through his hair while spinning the keys around his finger.

"Yeah, daddy," she says as she throws her arms around my waist. "I love you, mommy," she says, and I hug her back, smiling.

"I love you too, sweetie," I say as I kiss her forehead.

"Go, put on your shoes," Leo tells her, and she nods, scurrying off. Leo walks over to me and wraps his arms around my waist. "Sorry, we have to leave so early. It's a long drive," he says as he reaches up and strokes my cheek softly. I stare up into his amazing eyes that are still the same shade of green that they were years ago. I remember meeting Leo and falling in love. From the moment we met, it was sparking like on the fourth of July. I was this damaged, scared girl with trust issues, and even depression. Leo was my superhero. He is just so kind, sweet, warm-hearted and funny. He always knows how to cheer me up and bring a smile to my face.

I know people talk about love fading as they grow old, but our love is just as strong today as it was twenty-three years ago. He makes me feel young, and these past few months have been a struggle for us, but we push through it all. The struggles make our love stronger. The secret to lasting forever and true love is when times get tough and you struggle, your love only continues to grow. When we first got together life was hard, and I was something he wasn't used to. I was troubled, depressed, and quiet while he was outgoing and charming. No one ever dreamed we would be together, but we did. Every time I look in his eyes, I am taken back.

Leaning forward, I kiss him; his kisses can still manage to get to me after all of these years. "Have fun with Rayne, she needs a day that she doesn't have to think about Reece's problem," I say gently as I rest my head in his neck, and he rubs my back.

"Will you be okay, though?" Leo asks me, and I force a smile and sigh.

"I'll be fine," I whisper into his neck. The truth is I'm far from fine. Every time I watch any of them leave, I feel fear for the unexpected things that could happen, and it eats me from the inside. I still remember that day all too well. It flashes in my head like a nightmare on replay. Anytime I have to send my kids to school, all I can think about is that day. That phone call and that fear, a fear I would not wish on my own enemy. A pain so bad, thinking that you may have to bury your child. A child you raised, treated when he was sick, loved through it all, a mother's love for her child cannot be matched, so a mother's pain for losing one is worse. It's almost as bad as watching your child suffer and have problems he never did before.

The day he got shot did not only take away his sight, but it also affected this family greatly and hurt us all a lot. Our family has never been perfect, but now we are all walking around Reece carefully. We don't want him to suffer more than he already has. We all try to stay happy and upbeat because being sad won't change a thing, and being sad only makes life worse. I don't want Reece to see the pain I see when he suffers from this. How much I wish that I could easily give him his sight back again. I would love to see him racing around the track again and his smiling face when he crosses the finish line first. I wish I could see him on the baseball diamond, his face in concentration as he draws up his knee, and sends the ball flying to home plate and into the catcher's hand. I would give anything to see him on Friday night under the bright stadium lights as the clock ticks down, and it's all on him. He releases a perfect pass and scores a touchdown winning the game. I would give anything to see him this happens again, not because I am one of those parents who push their child but because I know how much it means to him. His face lights up very bright, and he was always so happy. That's a look I've haven't seen since the accident, except the times he is with Payton.

Payton coming into our lives was a miracle. I never thought we could be so lucky, but we are, very, very lucky to have her in my life. I believe that she was a gift to Reece from God because if it wasn't for her, I have no clue how he would have ever made it through this. I don't even know how our family would have survived without her. When Reece is with her nowadays, her face shows pure adoration.

"I love you, honey," Leo says as he presses his lips against my forehead.

"I love you too," I sigh, and he smiles at me before giving me a soft hug and walks away going to his Rayne.

A sigh escapes my lips as I slump against the counter. The house is silent, and I am home alone. Juliet went to a friend, Conner is doing something for college, and Reece is probably with Payton. I take a deep breath, attempting to keep myself calm.

The phone ringing breaks the long-lasting silence, and I quickly answer it.

"Hello, I'm calling regarding the request of an appointment with Doctor Martin. Is this Georgia Collins?" a lady's voice says through the phone.

"Hi, yes, this is Georgia Collins," I confirm as I stand up a little more alert.

"Hi, I wanted to inform we have an opening tomorrow morning, and if you would like, you can bring your son in. Doctor Martin will take a look at him run some tests and see what he can come up with. So will eight in the morning be okay with you?" she asks me, and I am astounded we can by now.

"Yes, yes that's fine! We will be there," I say to her very quickly! All I can think is how happy I am.

"Alright, we will see you then. Have a nice day," the lady says in a sweet tone.

"Thank you very much! You too!" I say quickly smiling as hope feels me.

As soon as I hang up, I dial Reece's number, waiting as it rings through. "Hello," his voice says as he answers my call.

"Hey, Reece. Honey, where are you?" I ask a little bit worried about where he is and why he's not home. I figured it was because he with Payton, but I am still a little worried.

"At the hospital. Payton's sister woke up," he says, and I scrunch my face in fear. Why is Payton's sister in the hospital? Since when does she have a sister? I am so confused.

"I would ask for you to elaborate on what you are talking about because I don't know why her sister would have not been awake. But if Payton wanted me to know she'd tell me and I respect that. Is she at least dealing with what is going on okay?" I say, understanding that she probably didn't tell me for a reason, and I respect that. I know I wouldn't want someone prying into my life.

"She's fine, mom. She's really happy. But she is also tired so we are going leave soon, so she can take a nap before returning to the hospital," Reece tells me. I am glad to hear she is okay, and I am sure she is worn out.

"That's so good! Are you guys coming back here?" I ask wondering when the silence in the house may dissipate.

"Yeah, I think so. Is there any certain reason you called?" He asks me.

"Oh, yes, yes there is! I talked to the eyesight doctor today," I tell him with a bright smile as I balance the phone between my ear and shoulder while I pour me a cup of coffee.

"You did? And?" he asks me with a slight excitement in his voice.

"You have an appointment there bright and early tomorrow morning," I let him know with a smile and take a sip of my coffee.

"Really?" he asks in a tone of shock as if he doesn't believe me.

"Yes, so you will have to miss a day of school," I add as I carry my coffee into the sitting room and placing it gently on the table by the fire.

"Oh, alright. Thanks for letting me know," he says, and I can tell by the change in his voice he is thinking.

"You're welcome, son! I'll see you soon," I reply and sit down on the couch.

"Yeah, see you soon," he answers me.

"I love you," I say with a smile because I never want him to forget I love him.

"I love you too, mom," he replies to me, and I smile as the line falls dead and I set the phone aside.

Chapter Fifty-Two

Reece's POV

I stroke her brown hair as I stare into her chocolate eyes and lean in, pressing my lips to her cute, perfect ones. The kiss is intense and full of love and passion. It's full of all the words I could never say. Her hands tangle in my brown locks while I move one hand to her waist to pull her closer to me and hold the back of her neck, keeping her to me as the kiss heats up. I run my tongue softly over her lip, begging her to grant me entrance.

She moans lightly, parting her lips and allowing my tongue inside so they can fight it out for control. I win, of course, and explore her mouth. She pulls away, leaning her neck back panting, and I smirk as I move my lips to her neck and give her neck love bites. She moans again, and I feel a stirring in my pants. This is not good, I think as I try not to think about my growing problem below. It's a good thing this heads to making love because honestly, I haven't had sex since Payton, and it is very painful for me since I'm used to it every week.

I pull my lips away from her warm neck and try to regain my breath, which suddenly hitches, and I feel the warm moist touch of her lips to my neck, sending my body into overtime.

Suddenly, everything disappears. The sight of Payton is gone, the kissing and lovemaking vanish. My eyes open and once again, I am met by the unwelcoming darkness. It had all just been a very good dream. Just then I realize, I could feel every inch of Payton's warm body against mine, and another thing I realize that she is going feel how happy I am this morning. Thanks to the dreams and the fact that I haven't had sex since before the accident. I can feel all of her body touching mine and sending shocks through me which causes my hormones to go crazy. *Crap! Stop thinking about it!* I yell at myself.

I love Payton more than anything and would love to make love to her, but I'm scared. I'm scared that I will not be able to see; that it may be extremely hard to do. I don't even know how I would. Payton is a virgin, so she never did this before. I don't know!

Think about wrinkly old women. I tell myself as I imagine old granny's in hope to make my problem disappear. Thankfully, my problem reduces, and I sigh in relief that she will not be feeling that. That would have made life extremely weird.

Shutting my eyes, I try to listen for any noises in the house, but I hear nothing except for the calming breathing of my angel. She probably wants to wake up since I'm sure she's been asleep, so she can go see her sis again.

Gently, I shake her and attempt to wake her. "Payton," I whisper as I shake her. I can hear her breathing change and feel her move in my arms.

"Hmmm," she mumbles sleepily, causing a grin to pull onto my face. "Yeah?" she says as she shifts some more.

"Wake up, don't you want to see your sister?" I ask her as I rub my hands over her arms.

"Oh shoot! Yeah, I do!" she says in a worried tone. I can feel her body pull away from my arms. I groan as I feel the warmth of her body disappears from the bed. "Do you want to come with me?" she asks in her usual sweet voice.

"No, you go ahead spend time with your sister. I will find something to get into," I tell her as I sit up in my comfy bed.

"Are you sure, Reece?" she asks me, and I smile brightly at where her voice is coming from and nod my head.

"I'm sure," I tell her. I know I want her to go by herself so that she and her sister have time to bond together.

"Okay then," she says, sounding very close to me, and I smile. Her warm breath blows gently against my face, and I can feel her leaning closer before giving me a quick kiss. "I love you," she says to me as she pulls away.

"I love you too, angel," I say to her and smile.

"I'll see you later," she says, and I just nod my head smiling.

"See ya, have fun and tell her I said 'Hi,'" I reply as I listen to her leave the room.

Swinging my legs over the edge the bed, I place my forehead in the palms of my hands while my elbows rest gently on my knees. I need some way to vent my frustration. I feel Rider's soft coat as he sits next to my leg. Then, the perfect idea comes to me on how to deal with my sexual frustration. Thinking about it, this hasn't really bothered me until my body needs some form of a release from this pent up energy and emotions that I am not exerting on sports. Reaching my hand out, I search for my nightstand, and once I find it, I look for my phone. Finally, my hand slips over the slick metal of my phone. I pick it up and decide who to call.

"Call Juliet," I instruct my phone as I slide a hand through my hair and tug lightly. The phone ringing noise begins, and I reach down to Rider and stroke his head.

"Hello there, darlin' brother of mine," Juliet says through the phone in a silly voice.

"Sister of mine, are you on your way home?" I tell her, attempting to cover my frustration with silliness.

"Yes, brother, I am actually home, why?" she asks casually. When did she get home? Must've been while I was asleep with my angel.

"Can you give me a ride to the high school?" I ask, secretly begging that she will. I don't want to bother Conner or Carter because they already did so much. That's why I decided to ask Juliet.

"Why?" she asks me, seeming very confused.

"Because I need to go to the high school," I state, a little bit annoyed with my little sister for asking questions, but that's what they are for.

"Reece, you do realize that there is no school today, right?" Juliet asks me slowly as if she is talking to a five-year-old.

"I'm blind, Juliet, not stupid. I know we don't have school today. I need to go there to do something," I say, starting to feel grumpy, as I'm a little on edge and all.

"Okay, okay. Geez, I'm sorry. I'll take you if you tell me what you need to do," she says in a happy, you know, '*got ya*' tone.

"I'll tell you in the car," I groan and stand up, reaching for my stick and using to make my way to my dresser where I search with my hands in drawers and look for some basketball shorts and a t-shirt.

"Be right to your room," she says and hangs up before I can object, making me even angrier.

"We are here, so you can finally tell me what's going on," Juliet says in an irritated tone as she shuts the car off, and I run my hand over the door in search of the handle. Eventually, my hand finally stumbles over the handle, and I open the door. I climb from the car and stand steadily on my feet.

"I'm going to run," I say simply to her as I hold onto the door. "Rider, come," I direct and can hear the sound of Rider climbing out of her car until he brushes my leg, sitting down. Reaching out, I take his handle; attach his harness to my right hand.

"You... run?" Juliet's voice asks me in a very shocked tone. I smile because, to me, her knowing I run is like her being able to see the person I was before I was shot.

"Yeah," I say proudly as I manage to step around to the back side of the door and shut it.

"How?" she asks as I decide to take a step forward before stopping, realizing I do not exactly know where Juliet is parked, so I am not sure what way to go.

"Conner has helped me, and Payton inspired me," I say simply as I shut my eyes looking around hoping something would tell me which way to go. Releasing a long sigh, I run my left hand through my hair. "Can you help me get to the track?" I ask her, hoping my tone shows her I am not pleased with having to ask for help, which always has come as a struggle for me.

"Of course," she says with kindness etched in her voice as I feel her arm slip through my left one that is now hanging by my side.

She leads me along with her, and I remain silent, not really wanting to talk. Today is one of those days that I hate being blind and cannot help but see it as the horrible thing that is killing me. I want to see. I want my old life back with the addition of Payton. I want my crazy, bickering family back. I want the ability to play again and make people proud of me. I wish this had never happened to me. Today, I am struggling to see the upside because the downsides are filling my head. I want to be able to have sex if I want to or at least, know it is possible to do that. I want to not have to ask for help. I want to be the one to take care of Payton and do everything for her, rather than weigh her down.

"You're on the track," Juliet says as she withdraws her arm from mine.

"Thank you," I say as I attempt to shut out my thoughts.

"You're welcome. I'm going to go sit on the bleachers," Juliet says, and I nod my head letting her know it is okay.

Listening to her leave, I begin to walk and slowly start to run. As me legs start moving faster, my mind begins to dance away from my thoughts. Tomorrow, I find out if I'll ever be able to see again. I hope so badly that I can. If the doctor gives me any chances to see again, I will probably take them. I will do just about anything to be able to see the life I'm living.

I push my legs harder as I hear the thumping of my heart be in my ears. If I can't see again, I don't know how I will make it through life. Eventually, Payton will get so sick and tired of having to take care of me and help me always and will leave. I can already think of the haunting thought of waking up one morning to an empty bed and a tape recording of Payton's voice telling me she fell out of love with me because being with me was too much work. I can see it happening, and I can see my life fall to part after that. Life without my angel would be a disaster.

I keep pushing my legs harder and harder, releasing my frustration. This is the fastest I have run since losing the ability to see, and I can feel like flying. Suddenly, I feel it all stop and instead, the force sending me to the ground and my head banging off of the track. The blackness shakes but remains black. A killer headache strikes through my skull causing me to groan. When I feel like I can finally move again, I lightly roll over to my back and feel a dog breathing on me.

"Oh my gosh! Reece, are you okay?" Juliet screams as I can hear her, racing over to me. I reach my arm out slowly to Rider and pet him because I can feel the change in his attitude. "Reece, Reece," Juliet demands now at my side, and I groan as my forehead stings.

"I-I-I'm f-fine," I stutter in pain, trying my best to open my eyes. I peel them open and meeting the blackness.

"No, you're not. Your head is bleeding," she says, and I groan, reaching up and touching my head. When I withdraw my hand, I can feel a wet substance on my fingers.

"Crap," I groan as I sit up, holding my head. I'm so freaking stupid. I tripped over my own feet. I tripped, over my own feet! Un-freaking-believable.

"We need to get you home and get you fixed up," Juliet says to me, and I groan, nodding my head. I feel the liquid slid down my forehead. Reaching down I pull, off my shirt and roll it up into a ball of some sort and press it onto my head. I hold pressure where it hurts, and I feel Juliet help me up. I take Rider's lead, and Juliet guides me back to the car with a hand on my back. The whole way, my head is throbbing, and I feeling burning from the scrapes that I must have gotten.

I get inside the car after Rider is in and hold my head as Juliet drives us home. My head hurts badly. It's a constant throbbing feeling. I shut my eyes and try to block out the pain.

"We're home," Juliet says softly, shutting off the car. Grabbing the handle, I get out and the wait for Rider to follow. When I feel him at my leg, I reach for the handle and then shut the door. By now, Juliet is by my side with a hand on my back, guiding me inside.

"I'm going to take you to your room and fix you there," she says as we enter the house, and she leads me through the silent house before opening a door to my room I guess. "Lay down on your bed," she instructs, and I can hear her rush off. Sighing, I remove the shirt from my head and undo Rider's harness, allowing him to jump onto the bed and lay down. I reach in my pocket, withdrawing my phone and placing it onto my nightstand. I sit down on my bed and kick off my shoes and lay down to rest my throbbing head on the pillow. Rider decides to lay at my side.

I hear Juliet re-enter the room and walk towards me. I can hear the sound of her, setting things down. "Hold out your hand," she instructs and places what feels like pills into my hand. "Take them," she says, and I pop them into my mouth and hold my hand out for water to chase them down. She hands me one, and I swallow.

I feel my head being touched with a warm rag, and I know she is probably cleaning off the crusty blood. After she cleans it, I feel an awful burning on it as she runs what feels like a cotton ball over it. Finally, she smoothens a cool jelly on it and places a band-aid. "Keep this there," she says as she places an ice on my head. Then she tends to my scrapes. Once I am all cleaned up, I can hear her throw things into what sounds like a plastic bag. "Now, just rest up and you will be as good as new," she tells me, and I sigh, holding the ice pack still firmly to my head.

"Thank you for helping me," I say softly suddenly very tired as my eyelids begin to drop, and my mind becomes cloudy.

"Anytime," she says, her voice soft as I hear her walk away and shut my eyes. I stroke Rider's head until sleep captures me.

Incoming call from my angel! My phone blares, causing me to sit up and rub my eyes. With one hand, I reach over and snatch the phone from the top of my nightstand where I had left it.

"Answer," I command and then yawn while stretching my other hand on Rider's fur. "Hey, Angel," I say as I answer it my voice still very full of sleep.

"Hey, honey, did I wake you?" she asks, sounding a little worried and somewhat tired.

"Yeah, but it's completely okay. What's up?" I ask as I run a hand through my hair.

"I was just leaving the hospital and was calling to let you know. I will swing by your house if you want me to," she says, and then I can hear her yawn on the other end. God, she is so cute. I just love her.

"No, Angel. It's okay. You sound tired. Go home, get some rest, and I will see you tomorrow," I say to her, still very tired. I could fall back to sleep at any moment, and my head is still aching.

"Okay, I will see you tomorrow then. I'm going to let you get back to sleep. I love you," her sweet voice says, and I smile.

"I love you too, Angel," I say with a smile, and my phone falls silent. I allow my sleepiness to take over and take the aching head away too. Hopefully, tomorrow, I'll find out if I can see again. Hopefully, I will see again. I want to see again. I want live again. If I can see again, life will be so wonderful.

The sound of The Fray's *How to Save a Life* blares in my ears as I shut my eyes, doing my best not to think about everything.

To make matters worse, I didn't tell Payton I wasn't at school today,

Chapter Fifty-Three

Reece's POV

I plug my headphone in my ears in an attempt to tune out the constant tapping of my mother's heel on the hard floor. We have been at the hospital filling out paperwork for a while. My nerves are on a slow rise and are soon to overflow.

What if he tells me the damage is irreparable? Will I ever be normal again? Will I ever see the sun? Will I ever see my angel? My mom? My sisters' weddings?

Thoughts like these are everywhere in my mind. It's like an annoying song on replay. I just want it to be over and know the answer. Will I see again or not? I feel something knock my arm, and I open my eyes but see nothing, and remove my headphones.

"What?" I ask my mom, who I guess is the person who bumped me.

"The nurse is ready to take you," my mom says, and I nod, standing up. I hear her also stand and the loop her arm through mine. We walk straight until my mom stops me.

"Hello, Reece. I'm Mary, your prepping nurse for the MRI," a kind-hearted female voice says, sounding to be a middle aged woman.

"Nice to meet you," I say, trying to be polite.

"You too. Now, come with me. You can come too," Nurse Mary says to my mom, and I feel my mom's body relax as she walks me.

"Once you change into this hospital gown, we can start the testing," the nurse tells me, and I hear us enter a room. "This will be your room, and you can change in here. Just have your mom fetch me once you are done," she adds, and I nod my head. My stomach is doing nervous somersaults. I listen and hear the door shut closed.

"Here, sweetie," my mom says as she releases me and places some kind of fabric into my hands. "The hospital gown," she explains. My face may have shown a little confusion.

"Oh, okay," I say, still very nervous. I pull off my t-shirt, revealing my bare chest, which I feel already needs some workout. Then, I undo my pants and take them off next, leaving me in just my boxers. "Can I at least wear them?" I ask my mom pointing down at my bottoms.

"I don't know why you couldn't, so I guess," she says, and I sigh out in relief. Feeling with my hands, I attempt to turn around the object within my hands. Finally, I am able to pull it onto my arms.

"Can you tie the back?" I ask my mom as I turn my back, hopefully to where she is.

"Of course," she says in her kind, motherly tone as her hands tie the back and her cool fingers brush my back.

"I'm ready, mom," I inform her, the nerves jumping around inside of me.

"I'll go get the nurse," my mom says, and I listen as she disappears and leaves the room.

I feel my heart pounding. If I can't see again, will I continue to run? More than likely, I will.

My thoughts are broken when the door reopens, and two pairs of footsteps enter the room now. My guess is they are my mother's and the nurse's.

"Ready? It's time to go. It's MRI time," Mary says, and I nod my head, tugging lightly at my hair. Finally, I am being led away to find out what the future hold for me.

Payton's POV

I arrive at school. This morning I received a much unexpected text from Reece saying he doesn't need a ride. I replied a simple, "Okay, why not?" But he didn't reply and still, hasn't. He isn't replying, and I have no freaking clue to why not? I pull the keys from the ignition and get out the car, grabbing my backpack and sling it over my shoulder.

My heart races as I walk towards the school, glancing every hallway in hopes of finding my boyfriend but have absolutely no luck. I head to my class early as normal and sit done, taking out my phone and hiding it behind a book. I try texting again but no response and is seriously starting to worry me. What if something awful happened?

The bell rings, breaking me from the never-ending fears. I search the room for him but of course, he is not here. All throughout this class, I cannot focus on what is being taught, and I tap my pencil. The bell rings dismissing the class, and we all rush off. Normally, I move slowly, but today, I am in a big hurry.

I make it to my next class and sneak a peek at my phone to check it. What do I see? Absolutely nothing! *Na-dah!*

My frustration and worries continue to rise at a very unhealthy rate, and I lose all ability to focus on the lecturing teacher at the head of the room. Before I can process what I am doing, my hand launches into the air, like a space shuttle.

"Yes, Miss Jennings?" My teacher as she notices my hand in the air. Oops, I didn't mean to raise my hand up.

"May I please use the restroom?" I ask and remember how they pounded into our heads in grade-school to say, "May I?" Every time I would say, "Can I?" I'd receive the smartass remark, "I don't know. Can you?"

"Yes, you may," she says, recovering from her shock and began teaching once again as I race for the restroom.

Once in the safety of the bathroom, I retrieve my phone from its spot inside my pocket. Quickly, I call Reece and wait intently.

"Hey there, you've reached Reece Collins. I am not able to get to my phone so leave me a message after the beep." The beep chimes, and I groan in frustration, hanging up the phone. After hitting redial a bunch out of worry, an idea hits me. I search in my contact for the name praying she answers.

"Payton, dear, are you alright?" is the first thing I hear after two rings. Georgia's caring voice is filled with concern.

"Yeah, I'm fine," I say, confused by why she is so concerned.

"But, aren't you at school?" she asks me, now, the one who sounds confused.

"Yeah, I am," I say not really sure what she wants me to say to that.

"Then why are you calling, dear?" she asks me her voice is mixed with confusion and concern.

"Is Reece okay?" I ask, letting worry slip into my voice.

"Why, yes, Payton. He's fine. Did he not tell you anything?" she asks me with a weird tone to her voice. Honestly, I was completely clueless to what she was talking about. Tell me what?

"No…" I say, hoping my answer did not make me come off as an awful girlfriend.

"Oh, he just had a doctor appointment, no biggy," she explains, and I release a large sigh mostly of relief.

"Thank you, Georgia," I say, feeling somewhat better aside from him not telling me the truth or about all this.

"No problem. I'll see you later, dear," she says, and I sense oddness in her voice.

"Okay," I agree with her and hang up the phone. I wonder what the appointment was for. I really hope he is okay. I wonder what he couldn't tell me. Does he not trust me? I love him so much and just want him to be okay.

Chapter Fifty-Four

Reece's POV

It feels like the time is moving in slow motion as I sit on this stupid hospital bed, waiting for this doctor to return from looking at my MRI and tell if I will ever be able to see again. My mom is right by my side, clinging to my hand. The doctors need to hurry up. I cannot stand the suspense.

"Reece," my mom's voice breaks me from my agonizing thoughts.

"Yeah?" I ask, knowing my hand is a little shaky and very sweaty. I am so freaking nervous, and I am also very anxious!

"Can you answer a question for your dear mom?" she asks me, and I can hear a little concern in her voice.

"Sure, mom," I reply, shrugging my shoulders.

"How come you didn't tell Payton about today?" she asks me after a few moments of silence.

"Because I didn't want to get her hopes up and all," I say and for some reason, a part of me feels like there is more to it, and I just don't know what. "How did you know I didn't tell her?" I ask shocked at how my mom knows this. She is my mom. I swear that she knows everything. Maybe she's a spy...

"It's simple. For one, if she had known, she would be here right by your side. Second is that she tried calling and texting you, worried out of her mind that you may be dead and calls me. I told her you were with the doctors. I don't think you should be lying to her," my mom says, seeming so sure of herself.

Suddenly, ending our conversation, I hear the door open, and footsteps enter the room. My mom's hand squeezes tightly onto mine.

"Hello, Reece and Mrs. Collins. I am Doctor Martin, a leading specialist and surgeon, dealing with the brain," he introduces himself, and I can feel the shift in my mom's body, so I guess, they shake hands.

"Hello, sir," I say politely.

"Can you tell the news?" my mom is to the point. I fear she may beg.

Doctor Martin clears his throat. "Reece," he begins with a gentle tone. "When you were shot, the bullet did damage to some of the optic arteries. After that, the bullet pretty much severely injured your occipital lobe.

There is a small chance we can fix it, or we may not be able to fix it. We won't know for sure until we get inside. If you chose this surgery, you need to be aware of what is going to be your odds. There is a forty percent chance that you will be able to survive it. There is a thirty percent chance you will get to see again. You may be able to see lights or shadows or anything like that," the doctor says to me, and his voice is dripping with sadness. "The choice is your Reece, and we will do the best we can to make sure you are in the lucky percent," the doctor finishes with a sigh.

I could die. I may not be able to see.

"Thank you, Doctor Martin," my mom says, but I am speechless. I don't know what to say.

"Think about it and let me know within the next couple days," the doctor finally says, and I hear him walk.

I just nod my head, not knowing what to say. I cannot help but think about *death*. I could die. I may not be able to see again.

"Honey, I am leaving this decision to you," my mom says simply as she helps me get up and leave the room while everything is mixing up inside my head.

What if I go through with it and can't see? What if I miss the chance of seeing again? What if I don't wake up? What if Payton leaves me? What if I can run track again? What if I can't? What do I do? What choice will I have?

I need some advice and don't want to go to Payton because I am scared. But I need to get rid of these what ifs. Finally, as I sit in the car, we head home. I know just who to call. One person who can help me and give me advice. This will help me with my choice.

Chapter Fifty-Five

Payton's POV

I stand up stroke the side of my sister's face. "I better head out," I say softly, and Lila smiles up at me.

"I really like Reece. He is really nice and handsome," Lila says as she musters up a smile.

"I do too, Payton. He is a good kid," my mom says from where she sits on the couch.

Blood rushes to my cheeks as they flush. "He is. I am glad you guys like him," I mumble with a little smile.

"We'll see you later," my mom says as she gives me a soft smile.

"Alright, I love you guys," I tell them and lean down pressing my lips against her Lila's forehead.

They reply with I love you's, and I leave, making my way to the car and then to the Collins so that I can see my amazing boyfriend. As I pull up, I see a car I do not recognize but I mean it could be anyone. I throw the car into park and climb out, slipping my keys into my pocket. I sigh, looking up at the large home and head up the path to the front door.

I reach out and knock on it, waiting for an answer. The large door swings open, revealing the always beautiful Georgia sporting a light blue know length dress.

"Oh, Payton!" Georgia exclaims and tosses her arms around my shoulder to hug me.

"Hey," I smile as I hug her back, and she pulls away with an almost sad like face.

"Reece is out back with a friend," Georgia tells me kindly, and I smile.

"Thanks," I nod my head, and she nods while I walk through the house and open the back door expecting to see Reece and Jace but who is with him is someone I was never expecting, and I can't believe my eyes.

Reece's POV

One Hour Ago

As I reach my room, my mind is haunted with all of these nightmarish thoughts. "Call Clair," I instruct my phone as I sit onto my bed.

"Hello," her happy, upbeat voice says happily.

"Hey, Clair. It's Reece," I inform her feeling sudden nerves wash over me.

"Reece! Is everything okay?" she asks me her voice seeming to be laced in concern.

"Can you come over? I need someone to talk to, and we used to be very close," I say hoping she will. I would love more than anything in the world for it to be Payton, but I feel like I would be weighing my decision on her, and I just don't know. I want to see what Clair says, and then I will talk to Payton about it. I am just so afraid. I love Payton so much and am trying my best to avoid losing her.

"Sure. I will be there in ten minutes," she replies, and the phone line falls dead. I knew she could be here soon because of how close she lives to me.

I run my hand through my hair while all that I can think about is Payton. I love her and would do anything to see her face. Anything to be able to be the one taking care of her and not always having to be waited on even if that thing is to risk my life. I know my real shot at happiness would be to see again, or at least, that is how I am feeling right now. I wish my life could just be simple. I wish that I could run again, play football and baseball, and stare into Payton's gorgeous eyes. I want the feeling of knowing I can do anything I want to because I no longer have that chance.

"Reece! Clair is here," my mom shouts so I grab my stick because I don't see the point in harnessing Rider at the moment and guide myself out to the hall and hopefully, to my mom and Clair.

"Hey, Reece," Clair's kind voice says stopping me, and I smile.

"Hey, let's go out back and talk," I say with a sigh.

"Alright," she says, and I feel her slip her arm through mine and guide me to the back yard. Unlike with Payton, touching Clair is like touching my sister. I feel nothing. No fireworks. No butterflies. No tingles. Nothing. I can hear a door open and then the sound of our feet on the back porch. I then hear Riders feet running off the porch too. Clair slowly guides me down the steps. Once I am off them, she leads me somewhere and pulls me to a stop.

"We are on the bench," she informs me, and I smile. I love this bench. It has always relaxed me. The bench always sat under an amazing dogwood tree.

I reach out and find my way sitting down. She sits beside me. "So Reece, what's wrong?" she asks me, and I release a very heavy sigh.

"I went to the doctor's today," I state as I slouch my shoulders.

"What for?" she responds.

"To see if it I can have the surgery that gives me my sight back," I reply, running my hand through my hair once more.

"Can you?" she asks hope seems to fill her voice.

"I can have the surgery but at my own risk. If I have the surgery on the scale of being able to see, I only have a thirty percent chance, and it's possible I may able to see bright lights or shapes and maybe even fully, but that is not a very high chance. They won't know for sure until they go inside," I explain.

"That doesn't sound too bad. At least, you gave it a shot," she says to me, and I feel her take my hand into hers.

"That not the bad part. On the survival scale, I only have a forty percent chance of actually living through the surgery," I say, shutting my eyes and leaning my head on my hands.

"Oh. Now, I understand," she says softly.

"Yeah. I just don't know what to do. I want to see again. I want to be myself again. I want to run. I want to see Payton's face. I want to be normal again," I tell her as I sit up straight and lean my head back. She takes my hand into hers again squeezing it.

"Maybe you could take a chance with the surgery," she suggests to me.

"I thought about that, and I've thought about opening my eyes and seeing my mom's face and my family's and Payton's. But also, I think of what may happen if I wake up and still cannot see. Honestly, I don't think I can handle the disappointment. And lastly, the worst fear I hold is what if I don't wake up? What if I die? I can only imagine how torn up Payton would be, not to mention my family. It would kill those around me, and they've been through plenty. Honestly, I hate that kid who shot me because I am not the same person I was, and I know I never will be again. At the same time, I kind of thank him because if he hadn't shot me, then I would have never met Payton, and I love her. She is the one for me. I just don't feel right that she always has to take care of me. That should be my job. I want to see again, but I am honestly afraid of not seeing or even dying, and I don't know what to do anymore," I say aloud everything that has been going on within my head. I refuse to cry over this no matter how bad I felt like it.

"Reece," Clair says, and I can feel her scoot closer to my side. "You deserve a chance to see again. Everything in life has risks, and anything could kill you. You just have to allow yourself to think of yourself and no one else," she tells me, and I sigh. She holds my hand tighter. Suddenly, I feel her soft lips press against the corner of my mouth, and I feel nothing at all. They linger too long there, making me feel awkward. Why in the hell would she kiss me?

BANG!

I hear what sounds like a door slamming shut.

Payton's POV

Well, this was not what I was expecting at all when I showed up to see my boyfriend. I feel my insides burning as the bitch Clair leans over and kisses Reece's cheek. Way to close to his lips and for way too long! It also does not help that she is practically on top of him and her hand in his! Is this why he's been so weird? Is he cheating? I guess exes always win!

I slam the door after Reece had pulled away confusion on his face. "Reece!" I say sternly as I get off the porch, glaring daggers at Clair stupid face. Reece leaps up tearing his hand from her.

"Clair, leave," I say with a very hateful tone.

"Um… you are not my boss," Clair says, flipping her hair over her shoulder, and I want to rip it out of her head.

"Clair, leave now," Reece says sternly. Clair's face drops, and she stomps past me and shoots an angry glare.

"Careful, I'd hate for your face to freeze like that," I say to her as she passes. What has gotten into me? Maybe, it's my anger.

"Payton, trust me when I say it's not what it looks like," he says, raising up his hand that is not on his walking stick up into the air as he walks up to me.

"So you weren't with your ex?" I ask in confusion and sarcasm.

"I was but only because I needed some advice," he shots back as his voice gets louder, and I get closer to him.

"What do you need advice about? Does this have to deal with the appointment you did not tell me about?" I yell angrily from how damn worried he had me.

"I didn't want to get your hopes up!" he yells back, and my anger pumps through me. Now, do not get me wrong. I never show my anger. I am the type who bottles it up. I guess, these are years of my anger coming out in one.

"My hopes for what!" I shout back at him still in confusion.

"That I can see again!" he screams at me.

"What the hell are you talking about?" I yell tears of anger filling my eyes.

"My appointment was to see if I could see again through surgery. They said the chance of being able to see after surgery is thirty percent, and there is only a forty percent chance I will survive it," he says. I stand there stunned. "That's why I needed advice!" he hollers through a hand angrily into the air.

Reece and I do not fight... *ever*. It's not us. We are not angry people. Why now? Why one big fight?

"You needed advice for that?" I ask him as if he is stupid. "Is it not simple? You could be blind and live *or* maybe, get your sight back but die! Die! Do you hear me, Reece? You debated this! Are you nuts? Death? I am pretty sure you have got to be dumb if you even need to think about it. Why do you need it anyway when you can be alive?" I yell back using more force to hold back the tears.

"To take care of you! To run again! To be normal!" he screams at me, breathing hard as his chest rises and falls.

"Normal is not worth dying because then, you will just be dead for nothing! If you have to think about this, then you are crazy! Call me when you come to your senses!" I yell at him as I release my tears down my cheeks and storm away. I cannot believe him or myself. I know I over reacted, but I am so mad. He had to think about it, really! It's just that people out there want the chance to live, and he's worried about his eyes. I just cannot listen to him complain about that!

Chapter Fifty-Six

Payton's POV

The tears skate down my face as I lay uncomfortably in the silence of the house. How could Reece even think about that surgery? Can he not just be happy that he actually has the chance to live? My sister had no choice with her surgery, and her survival rate was a lot higher! Yet, I almost lost her! And he is thinking about a surgery that he does *not* need that has a much lower survival rate. Why would he do that? I am not overreacting that much.

With that put to the side, there is another reason why I am so pissed at him. Why in the hell would he go to Clair for advice? If not me, why not Jace, Carter, or even Conner? I mean, really, why her? Does he not have any trust for me? It kills me to think that he does not trust me. I mean I want him to realize what he is actually sacrificing, then maybe he would reconsider.

I just want sleep to take me away so my mind is no longer clouded with all of these thoughts.

I watch Reece while we sit in English class. He is casually tapping his pencil against the desk making a loud tapping noise. His amazing blue eyes are focusing lazily on Ms. Jennings, who is in front of the room teaching. Now that his sight is back, he seems so happy and full of life. Reece no longer needs me to be by his side. Actually, everything had returned to how it was before everything happened with the addition of Clair being back and they are practically dating.

Me? I've return to being a nobody, watching Reece from afar. Ever since he woke up from his surgery, it's like I no longer exist to him. All I am left with is the aching in my heart as proof that it was all real. I miss everything that we used to be. I miss our late-night phone calls. I miss the "I love you." I miss his hand in mine and the kisses. I miss him. Without him, I am lost.

The bell rings, pulling me from my thoughts, and I shuffle my books into my backpack. I walk out into the hall as I am bumped into by multiple people just showing me that I am invisible and that no one cares anymore about me. I am back to being that nobody as I continue to my next classes, and finally, the bell rings for lunch. I wait till the hall crowd has died down before making my way to my locker. As I open my locker door, I see Jace whose eyes just made contact with mine, and he gives me a small, sad smile. In return, I just stare at him sadly as he stands there being a reminder of what use to be. A friendship we had that was kind of love/hate. Slamming my locker door shut, I begin my way down the hall and to the library.

Suddenly, something slams into me, forces me to look up and see the blue eyes which cause my voice to get stuck in my throat and tears to well in my eyes. "Payton," he says in a breathy tone, and I clench my eyes shut, loving the sound of his voice.

With a deep breath, I open my eyes to see his face full of pain and misery. "Sorry," I mutter out as I slip past him and force myself to bolt down the hall.

As I see the library in my far away and feel the aching pounds in my chest, I hear a ringing noise. Suddenly, everything begins to get fuzzy until it disappears.

I sit up straight in my bed and grab my phone without looking at it in tiredness and sadness. It was just a dream. I tell myself in relief.

A dream that could come true. My evil inner voice chuckles as it makes its appearance.

"Hello?" I say into my phone with a voice that sounds as if it belongs to a dead person.

"My brother is a freaking idiot," Juliet's voice shouts through my phone speaker, and slowly, I withdraw the phone from my ear to prevent hearing loss.

"I agree," I say with a monotone voice.

"My brother is a complete dipshit for calling that whore!" she continues to rant, and I sigh. Those were some harsh words, but I cannot say I haven't thought of worst.

"Agreed," I say as I fall back on to the stupid hard bed, releasing a sigh.

"Aargh! I just cannot believe his stupidity! He is supposed to be the smart one!" she continues, and I can imagine Juliet pulling at her blond hair.

"I know, but everyone can have a stupid moment," I tell her as I rub my face, attempting to keep my emotions at bay.

"Payton, are you okay?" she now asks me. Her voice is filled with concern.

"I'm alright," I lie because the truth is that I am far from all right.

"Payton, why the hell would he even consider a surgery that he can die from?" her voice now asks in sadness.

"I don't know, Juliet. I don't know," I whisper as I shut my eyes fighting back the tears. Surgeries even in your favor contain high risks, let alone when the odds are not in your favor.

"Please tell me he won't do it," Juliet sounds so sad, but then I put myself in her shoes and imagine my sister having her surgery knowing that there was a good chance she could die. It is an awful feeling. I'm sure of it.

"I wish I could Juliet, but I don't know. I truly hope he won't," I tell her wishing I could be there to hug her and hold her tight.

Reece's POV

Shit! I have truly fucked up this time! I honestly do not know what the hell I was thinking. Who knows what I will do? I called Clair because I have known her so long. I never thought that this would spiral so far. Payton will probably never forgive me. Was that her way of dumping me? Can I live without her? Who am I kidding? Without Payton, I have nothing. She is my everything and the only good thing, besides my family, that I have.

So now, here I am… lying here on my bed and wallowing in self-pity. Even though my decision should be clear, I am still debating it. If I could see, I'd be staring at the ceiling, but since I can't, I am staring into the deep abyss of darkness.

"You screwed up big time," a deep voice says causing me to shot up, and all my thoughts fall to the back of my mind as I try to process who it is.

"No, dip shit," I grumble as I figure out that it is Carter.

"Hey man, no need for the cruel words!" Carter says in a defensive tone. I can hear his footsteps as they make their way over to me. The bed dips and sway as Carter sits down.

"I apologize that I can't be Mister Cheerful right now; I'm a little miserable," I mumble, as I fold my arms on top of my chest.

"Maybe I can help you with your choice?" he suggests, and I roll my non-working eyes.

"How would you do that?" I ask him with a snort of laughter.

"If you get off your ass and come with me, I guess you will see," Carter says curtly as his weight disappears from beside me.

I can go with him, and it can make my choice easier, or I can go, and it can make the choice harder. "What the hell," I say as I stand up shrugging my shoulders and reach for my stick.

"I think you may want to take Rider," Carter says, and I sigh.

"Rider," I call, and in no time, I hear his paws beating against the floor as he runs to me. I feel him touch my leg, letting me know that he is there. I run my hands around in search of his harness. Putting it on him, I reach down and take the handle.

"We're ready," I say heaving out a long, loud sigh.

"Good! I promise you, Reece, this may actually help," Carter says to me as he places his hand on my shoulder to guide us to his car.

Carter places my hand on the cool metal of the car door and takes Rider from me, putting him into the car I guess. I feel my way around and make my way inside, sitting down, reaching for the seat belt, and fumbling to lock it.

"So where to, Carter?" I ask as I lean my head back and run a hand through my hair.

"Somewhere that will give you answers," he replies to me shortly with a smirk.

"God, tell me you are not taking me to a fortune teller," I plead with a groan, and Carter just bursts out laughing.

"No, dummy," Carter says while laughing at me.

Where could he possibly be taking me? This is killing me. Is this how girls feel when a dude takes them somewhere and doesn't tell them? If so, it freaking sucks! The car ride seems to be going on forever.

"We're here," Carter finally says as I suffer in my own thoughts and aching choices. There is just so much on my mind, and if you'd told me a few months ago this would happen, I would have laughed in your face.

"Where's here?" I ask him, unlatching my seat belt.

"The hospital," Carter states, and then, I hear a door open, and I sit in my seat confused. Why are we here? What is Carter up to? How will this help?

Chapter Fifty-Seven

Reece's POV

Carter leads me down the halls of the hospital, and I have no clue where I am being taken. I hear the sound of Carter opening a door, and I'm met by an overwhelming sound of little kids. Am I losing it? Is this really what I am hearing? I can hear little boys making train and truck sounds and little girls giggling, but I also hear the sound of kids who are older. All in all, it sounds as if everyone is having a good time. "Where are we?" I ask Carter as Rider, and I walk into the room along with him.

"We are in the game room of the children's part of the hospital," Carter explains.

Why did he bring me here to the children's part? How is this going to help me?

"Hi there, Carter," says a soft little voice.

"Hi, Madeline," Carter replies at my side with a kind tone. I can hear the little girl run away, and I turn my head to Carter's direction raising my eyebrow.

"What's wrong with these kids?" I ask him since I cannot see what it is.

"Diseases from cancer to polio to many different ones. Some have Down Syndrome, and some are disabled. There are even some who are blind, deaf or mute," Carter says as he rests a hand on my shoulder.

"So why are we here?" I ask him still not fully understanding the meaning in all of this. How is this going to help me?

"I want you to meet to people, and then you will see," he says to me and leads Rider and me somewhere. I can hear the sound of what seems to be a pencil scratching atop a piece of paper. "Reece, I would like you to meet Samuel," Carter says as he points me in the direction of where the noise is coming from.

"Hi! It's so awesome to finally meet you!" a young boy voice says. He sounds like he is anywhere from nine to eleven.

How does he even know me? I ask myself.

"Hey there, it's nice to meet you too," I say with what I hope to be a kind smile and polite tone.

"Samuel, why don't you tell Reece about yourself," Carter suggests to the boy. "Here, Reece, let's sit down," he adds as he helps me sit down in a plastic chair.

"Well, let me see. My name is Samuel, and I am 11 years old. That not so important, though. You see, when I was eight, I was my little league football team champion. I couldn't wait to get older and play high school football. My dream was to go all the way to the NFL. I wanted to play for the Colts. Things took a turn for the bad, however, when my mom, dad, and I were driving home after getting pizza after winning one my football games. A drunk driver appeared out of nowhere and was in our lane. My father swerved to miss him and ended flipping over the hillside, and the car wrapped around a tree. My father was killed instantly, and my mom was in a coma for three weeks until she finally woke up. The drunk driver walked away from the accident. As for me, the car's roof ended up severing my legs, and they were unable to save them. At first, I only lost my legs to about my knees. I was only ten years old, and then, I suffered an infection so they had to take more from one knee. Anyways, I suffered from really bad depression because I am unable to play football or walk. I also was talking about the loss of my father really hard because he was like my best friend, and I would give anything to have him back. The point of all of this is that I want to thank you. If it weren't for you, I would never have gotten my hope back. Carter here has been trying to help me for a while, but finally, he told me your story and your struggle, and he told me how you were trying to run again. You are my hero! You showed me that just because I am disabled doesn't mean my life is over, and I can't do anything. So thank you! I have begun to realize that I have a talent for drawing and art," Samuel tells me his story.

Have I really been able to help him? Is that even a possibility? How can I make a difference?

"I have helped you?" I asked the kid probably looking at him like he has grown a third head.

"Yeah, you inspired me, and you are my hero, just like I am sure you are many other people's heroes too," Samuel says, and I am amazed.

"Thank you, but I am no one's hero. I don't deserve it," I say not trying to be modest. I was just honest.

"You are, though. You haven't let your disability get in your way. You have the ability to inspire a lot of other people," Samuel tells me in a very serious tone.

"Reece, I want you to meet one more person," Carter says as I sit there still very stunned.

"It was really nice to meet you, Samuel. Thank you. I will be back to visit you. Don't give up on anything," I say, still trying process things. I have let my disability stop me from doing things. I am nowhere near as strong as he makes me seem.

"Thank you so much! I really hope to see you again," Samuel says, and I hear Carter stand up. And then he helps me rise up as well.

Do I really have the power to help people? I run a hand through my hair as Rider, Carter, and I walk to our new destination. "Carter, I'm on to you," I whisper as we walk. Carter touches my arm stopping me and chuckles.

"Hey, Addison," Carter says in a kind and happy voice.

"Hey there, Carter!" a happy, upbeat girl's voice says. Judging by the pitch in her voice, she is about thirteen years old.

"I brought someone you'll be happy to meet," he tells her, and I can hear the smile in his tone.

"Really? Who?" she asks him, sounding very excited. I wonder if she even knows who I am.

"Reece," he says in a softer tone, and I can just imagine him with a secretive smile.

"Reece is here? Carter, are you playing a joke on me? If so, I will be very upset," she says, and I can imagine a teenage girl crossing her arms.

"No, I'm serious Addison. Right, Reece?" Carter says, and I take this ask my queue to say something.

"Yeah. I'm Reece. It's great to meet you, Addison," I say trying to sound sweet because I am confused on how she did not know I was there.

"Oh wow! It is you! I am so happy to finally get to meet you!" the girl says very enthusiastically. How does she know who I am? "Carter has told me a lot about you! And I want to tell you, thank you so much for being strong and not giving up! You are a great inspiration," she says, and I am confused on how I helped.

"What's your story?" I ask her, running my hand through my hair. Hopefully, this question will tell me everything.

"Well, I'm Addison Michaels, and I am thirteen years old. Last year, I was showing my horse, just like I have been doing my whole life. And it was at night, and I running Poles. I take off into the show ring on my horse Saint, and it started to thunder and lightning. We did not know that she was afraid of that, and she ended up throwing me off. I being the idiot, I didn't wear my helmet, and when I fell, I landed on my head. I lost my sight that night and ever since I have been afraid to be near a horse, and I felt like I could never do anything normal people could do again. Then, Carter told me about you, and it has truly made a difference in my life. He told me how you're trying to run again and be independent. And to me, you are representing all of those who can't, whether they are blind, deaf, or disable. You have the chance to do what they can't. From what Carter has told me, you have what it takes to actually really run again. With that being said you have inspired me to get back on the horse, literally and learn to ride again. So thank you! I really hope you keep running because I know you could inspire thousands of people and not just me. You have everything it takes to be someone's hero, and I know you are mine. Don't give up," she says to me with a happy voice.

"I am glad I could help, and you shouldn't let being blind get in the way of anything," I say to her giving her a smile though I know she cannot see it.

Do I really have this power to help and change lives? Can I make a difference? Maybe, just maybe, there is actually more to all of this than I originally thought. What is the possibility that God did this to me to teach me a lesson? I am not a very churchy person, yet I still believe in God. So what if this was all a part of my plan, and I am supposed to run track again for all those who cannot? I am supposed to be a hero and role model for people. I really need to talk to my dad. He has always been the one to give me advice and help me. He has supported me and kept me in line. He is the person who will help me with this. *I am so glad that Carter brought me here*, I think as Carter, Rider and I go and talk to many other kids hearing their stories and even sharing mine. It felt right to share this with them and help them.

Chapter Fifty-Eight

Reece's POV

Lying on my bed, I wait for my dad to come in. I shot him a text when I got home, and he said that he would come in when he finished something. I run my hand over Rider's head as he lies beside me. Suddenly, the thought of Payton appears in my mind. God, I miss her! I miss hearing her voice and her touch, the feeling of her by my side. I miss it all. I love her so much. I know I may be able to live without her, but the thing is I don't want to! It would hurt too bad, and I enjoy everything much more with her by my side.

"Reece?" my dad's strong voice says as I hear him tap on the door.

"Come in, Dad!" I call out, and I hear the door creak open. Pushing myself up with my arms, I sit up and fold my legs.

"Hey, son, what's up?" he asks, and I can hear him near me and feel the bed sink down at his feet.

"I need your advice because it means so much to me," I tell him truthfully.

"Alright son, you know you can talk to me about anything, so let me hear it," he says, and I feel him reach over and touch my shoulder.

"It's about the surgery..." I trail off rubbing my face with my hands.

"I know about it. Your mom explained it to me," he says after a couple moments of silence.

"Good, because I'm sick of explaining it," I say, releasing a large sigh.

"What's troubling you, Reece?" he asks me with his concerned dad voice.

"I don't know if I should have the surgery or not. There is such a large risk, and the odds are not in my favor. I feel like I'm at the crossroad. One way could kill or make me normal again, and then there is the other road where I can stay the same and inspire people by getting to run again. I feel like if I chose the wrong one, I could be making a mistake. Dad, tell me what to do," I say ask I pull a hand through my hair in frustration.

"Son, I can't make this decision for you, but I will give you my opinion. You know we're not a very churchy people, but I believe in God and his reasons. I believe that you went blind for a reason. Bad things don't always happen for any reason. A lot of the times, there is a reason, and I feel that if God wanted you to see He wouldn't have taken your sight away in the first place or He wouldn't have given you such a small survival rate. Those are signs that you are meant to do more without your sight. You have the ability to inspire people and change lives. You have the ability to run again, and from what your brother have said, with some practice, you could be great again. Son, you have a chance to do things others never could! You have the chance to do great things, and I think you should take this. In the long run, if you want surgery later on, then you can. But now, I think it's better if you don't. That is just my opinion, though," he says, and everything he says is everything I think and feel.

"Dad, I know what to do," I say after I think for a second. In that second, I weighed my options. The benefits and effects of each choice I could make. The path I choose is the path that will decide my future... decide everything. I am starting to believe that this is all coming down to a few thoughts. When I die and leave the people I love and the people I knew, how do I want them to remember me? Do I want to be remembered as the boy who was blind for a while and then got his sight back? Or do I want to be remembered as the boy who died trying to see again? Or, and most importantly, do I want to be the person who was a role model and inspired and changed lives. Thinking about it like this, my choice became very simple.

"I'm going to need Conner, Carter and Jace's help with my choice, and most importantly, I'm going to need you, dad," I tell him, knowing for sure what my choice is, and I honestly believe that I am making the right choice for me.

"Okay, son, I will help you every step of the way with your plan. Just do one thing for me," he says, and I feel him pat my back.

"What's that, pops?" I ask my dad as I run a hand through my hair and feel Rider shift to where his head is resting on my lap.

"Go and make up with Payton already. You guys are being dumb and from what I have told, you need to apologize for not going to her when you had a problem," my dad says in a very stern voice like he is giving me a small lecture.

The worst part of all of this is that it's true. I am an idiot. I am jeopardizing my future with the person I love. There is no doubt in my mind that Payton is the love of my life. I am in love with her and want to spend the rest of life with her every day. Meeting her was a gift, and I really need to fix this problem because I am missing her so much.

"While you are at it, my boy, I think you need to lay your feeling and fears on the table," Dad tells me, and I nod my head. As hard as it is going to be, I know I need too. I need to be open and trust her.

"Thank you, Dad. I'm beginning to understand," I say with a smile. It feels as if a large weight has been lifted from my very shoulders. Finally, I believe this is the right choice, and I need to make everything right.

Payton's POV

"I like the way this one sounds," Lila says as she holds out a piece of paper to me. It is my valedictorian speech, which I really need to get finish with the graduation close. Since it is the end of the senior year, we aren't really doing anything in class, so we do not actually have to go.

"Are you sure? I don't want it to sound too cliché," I say as I sit at the foot of her hospital bed and look up at my sweet little sister. She has a hospital gown tied on her small, frail body and a red bandana covering her head. Her kind eyes are twinkling with happiness, and her thin lips spread in a smile. She is sitting cross-legged at the top of the bed. Lila is getting better, but now she is awake, it seems like we are paying more money. And my money is dwindling into nothing.

"I promise, sis, it's great," she says giving me a smile and I smile back.

"Let's go ask Ms. Rose," I suggest with a larger smile, leaving the room to fetch her, a wheelchair. She has been allowed to leave as long as she is in the wheelchair, from still being so very weak. Being a volunteer, I am allowed to get wheelchairs and do this kind of thing. Lila scoots over to the edge of the bed, and I scoop her into my arms and place her into the chair.

"Let's go!" she cheers with her large happy smile.

Pushing her out of the room, we make our way to Ms. Rose's room in silence. As we walk, I think about Reece and how much I am missing him. We haven't spoken since our fight, and I am now missing everything about him. I am totally in love with him.

"Hey, Payton. Hi there, Lila," Ms. Rose says. Her voice is getting softer and a little bit shakier.

"Hey there, Ms. Rose," I tell her with a smile as I push Lila over to the side of the bed.

"Hey!" Lila says smiling and waving at her.

"What brings you, girls, here today?" she asks as she tries to push herself up a little.

"For you to listen to Payton's valedictorian speech!" Lila tells her in a very happy tone.

"Okay, let's hear it," Ms. Rose tells me.

Pulling the folded paper speech from my pocket and unfold it. I begin to read my speech. I wish I could get Reece's opinion on this. Gosh, I miss him so much. I finish my speech, and a smile finds its way onto Ms. Rose's face.

"That was amazing dear! I know you are going to do great with it!" she tells me with the best smile she can muster on her face.

We sit around just talking about everything and all kinds of fun. Suddenly, her room door swings open, and May stands there. "Payton, will you come here? I need to speak with you," May informs me. I smile at Ms. Rose and Lila.

"I'll be right back," I say ask I touch Lila's shoulder. She just nods her head.

Walking over to May, we step out into the hall. "What is it?" I ask her as I fold my arms over my chest in discomfort.

"There has been a change in your sister's care," she says as she rubs the back of her neck.

"What do ya mean?" I ask her, raising my eyebrow in confusion.

"There has been a generous donor who is willing to pay for any remaining hospital bills and any future ones. They will pay everything in the hospital," she tells us.

"Everything?" I ask stunned. Someone is willing to pay for everything... For Lila and my family! Who would do something like that?

"Yes, everything!" she says with a big smile.

"Who? Who would do that?" I ask her in amazement.

"Anonymous and that's how they wish to remain," she answers with a shrug of her shoulders.

Tears begin to stream down my face while I think about it. Who is so nice to do this? This means the world to my family and me. I want to thank the person who did this. This is just so unbelievable, and at this moment, there is no one I want to talk to more than Reece, which just makes me cry harder.

Chapter Fifty-Nine

Payton's POV

Biting the last piece of my microwavable pizza into my mouth, I get up and walk to my kitchen sink. Dumping the plate into the sink with a thump, I turn on the water faucet allowing the water to warm up. Then, I snatch the blue sponge from the sink and run the warming water over it before squirting some dish soap onto it. I wash my plate. My dinners are normally microwavable because it's cheap, and tonight, my mom is spending some time with Lila before she heads to work. Leaving me on my lonesome, this leaves me nothing to do. Times like this, I miss Reece. Actually, I always miss him. It's just, right now, I wish he could be with me. I need a distraction because I hate being alone. That is when things I wish not to think about make an appearance in my mind.

So my plan is to wash this dish and go read a book or maybe sleep. I am even dressed for my plan. I have on a large t-shirt that covers my short pajama shorts along with my brown mess of hair contained in a ponytail. As I reach up to turn off the faucet, after I place the plate on the drying tray, a sound knock on the door captures my attention, and I snatch the dish towel from the sink, drying my hands. Another knock sounds, I drop the towel on the counter and speed walk to the door.

Who the hell is here at this time of night? Oh, my gosh, please don't be a robber.

Hey, dummy, I don't think a robber would knock on the door. You know it kind of contradicts the point. That annoying voice says in my head making a reappearance.

The sad thing is, the stupid voice is right! If it's not a robber, though, who is it?

Try answering the door and you'll find out smart one! The voice sasses me, and I groan rolling my eyes. I take the door handle into my hand and pull the door open.

I swear the one person I thought would never stand in front of my house was there. I feel like my wish was answered as I take in his appearance. How'd he get here? I glance over Reece's shoulder to see Conner waving from his car in my driveway and then backs out driving away.

Reece is standing in front of me, on my doorstep! His hands stuffed in his pockets of his dark blue jeans. My eyes travel to his DC shoes to his jeans, then onto his gray t-shirt that has "Washington High Track and Field" written on it with the winged shoes. The shirt hugged his amazing body. Finally, my eyes take in his face. His lips are in a tight line as if he's thinking, his eyes have bags under them, and the beautiful blue eyes looked glassy and filled with regret. His hair is short like it was when I first met him in the hospital, so he must have had it cut. It is still messy and totally hot.

After drinking him in, I remember I should probably say something. *Yeah, that'd be wise!* The voice says causing me to roll my eyes.

Shut up, voice! I tell it and then revert my focus back onto the man I love. "Reece?" I say. Yeah, that's my genius words after all this time.

"Listen, Payton, just hear me out. I am so very sorry for everything! What can I say? I'm stupid and made a mistake. I went to her because she was my best friend for a long time. I never thought she'd do what she did. I never ever would have dreamed of hurting you. And not having you hurts me. I am sick of all this silliness. I just want to be with the girl I am in love with and plan to spend the rest my life with. So I am so sorry. Please forgive me?" he says, and I can see his eyes water up.

I stand there as a couple tears slip from my eyes. Instead of responding, I leap forward and catapulting myself into his arms. I tangle my arms around his neck, and I feel his body stiffen in shock. Guess, he wasn't expecting that. After a minute, he relaxes and loops his arms around my waist. I bury my head into his chest, feel his warmth surround me and listening to the thump of his heart.

"You are forgiven," I whisper, knowing he can hear me. I could never stay mad at Reece.

"I love you so much, Payton," he whispers as he presses his lips to my forehead.

"I love you too," I say with a bright smile. I pull away from the hug and see his lips turned up into a breathtaking smile. Leaning up, I kiss him. It only lasts a few seconds, but it was perfect. "Come inside," I say as I slip my hand into his and pull him inside my house, closing the door behind us. Honestly, at this moment in time, I am slightly thankful he cannot see because I don't want him seeing my house.

"Okay, I need talk to you about some stuff," he says in a soft voice, and it is also a serious tone.

"Alright," I say nodding my head. I lead him into the living room and stop him at the couch, placing his hand on the armrest. Feeling around, he slowly sits down, and I smile sitting beside him. Shifting my body towards him, I take his hand and squeeze it in mine. "Talk," I say with a serious face as I take in his torn face. This only causes me to worry. Shit! What if something is wrong?

"Do you see us being able to have a future together with me, blind?" he asks me a serious look in his eyes. If only he could see the look, I'm giving him. It's a mixture of "are-you-serious?" and like he has three heads.

"That is a dumb question, Reece," I say, squeezing his hand and shaking my head.

He just sighs and moves his eyes away from me to face a different area. "Please just answer the question," he pleads, bringing his sad blue orbs back to me. There is a great part of the time I forget he cannot see.

"Reece, I can see a future for us. I will never leave your side unless you force me away. I can see us growing old, raising a family and having children and grandchildren. I can see all possibilities open for us. When I think about my future, Reece, you're always in it," I tell him frm the bottom of my heart. A few tears make an escape from my eyes.

"In your future, am I blind?" he asks, staring into my eyes even though he cannot see.

"Honestly, yes, you are, always," I state the truth without a single doubt. When I imagine us together, we are the same people we are now. "What's with these questions, Reece?" I ask holding his hand tighter, afraid he may slip away.

"I want to show you my trust I have in you, and I want you to know my fears," he says simply. I can see the water build higher in his eyes. This just shows me how much all this means to him.

"Fire away," I say and place my other hand on top of his arm and rub it.

"What if when we are together a robber breaks in, and I can't protect you because I can't see? I'm afraid you may get hurt, and it'd be my entire fault. The man is supposed to protect the women," Reece says, and I can see the fear in his eyes and hear it in his shaky voice.

"We will get a big dog, like the Great Pyrenees! And we will have Rider!" I reply with a smile, reach up with my hand from his arm, and stroke his cheek. I have always wanted a dog.

"What if, that does work?" he asks me with a completely serious face.

"I can shoot a gun," I say simply because it's true. I know how to defend myself.

Reece just shakes his head. "Alright, how am I supposed to find a job?" he asks with a concerned face.

"Well, Reece, blind people get jobs all the time! There is a lot you can do. You could even be an actor!" I tell him and smile at the thought of him acting. That'd be a sight to see.

"How would I get around our home?" he fires another question at me, and I sigh.

"We could have Braille around the home on things. You can learn it like you do the track, and you have a stick and Rider," I say, smiling since his fears are not that bad.

"How would I take care of our children and things like that? What if you're not home?" he asks, and I can see the worry and fear that live in his eyes.

"Reece, you learned Braille, you learned how to start running again, how to use your hands to make a picture in your mind, and how to use a Seeing-Eye dog. You will learn how to take care of them, and it'll become extremely easy. The kids will learn Braille, which you can teach them. You will always be there for them. And most of all, Reece, all that matter is that you love them and take care of them. That the most important," I tell him with a smile.

"We can do this, can't we?" Reece says with a smile.

I smile back. "We sure the hell can," I say and kiss him gently.

"I love you," he says as we pull apart, and I rest my head on his shoulder.

"I love you too," I reply with a big happy smile on my face.

"Payton," he whispers after a few moments of silence and enjoying each other's company.

"Hmm?" I reply breathing in his sweet aroma.

"I'm not having the surgery... and I'm going train for our summer track team," he says quietly.

Chapter Sixty

Payton's POV

Hearing him say that he is not going to have the surgery made my life. He is going to do the right thing. He is going to run again. Most importantly, he came back to me! He still loves me! I honestly still love him too. I am happy he chose not to have the surgery because I honestly feel that is the right thing to do.

I cuddle into his chest as we lie on my bed. He gently kisses my forehead. A smile makes its way onto my face. I trace small circles onto his chest. "I love you so much, Payton, and I would do anything for you," he whispers as he uses one of his hands to stroke my hair.

"I love you more," I say as I try to be closer to him because he makes me feel safe and happy.

"Payton, I don't know how I would have been able to do anything without you. You have saved me," Reece says in such a soft and sincere voice.

"No, Reece, that's where you're wrong," I say as I stop moving my hand and lift my head up to look into Reece's shimmering blue eyes. "Reece, I didn't do anything but be your friend. You, Reece, are the one who saved me. Before you came into my life, Reece, it was only made up of making good grades and trying to take care of my sister. I never knew anything outside of that. You came into my life and opened my eyes to a whole me the world. You helped me become who I am today. I have nothing without you, Reece. You brought the light back into my life. All I can do is thank you, yet that'll never be enough. I love you," I say as tears feel my eyes.

"Sweetheart, you are amazing, and I am honestly the luckiest man alive," Reece says wrapping his arms tightly around me. I cling to his chest.

"I love you," I say because it's all I can say. Squeezing my eyes shut, I fell asleep in Reece's arms with a smile on his face.

Reece's POV

My eyes pop open, and I am standing there in the hall that day, staring into the dark eyes of Erwin. His hand is shaking with the pistol in it, as his face is completely blank and cold. All that races through my mind is to keep him distracted and concentrate on me so that he does not hurt anyone else.

God, what did I do to deserve this? I ask Him. I have lived my life to be a good person. So why is he holding a gun to me?

"Please, don't," I beg, but it's useless. I stare into the last sight that is engraved into my mind. Erwin's finger pulls back the tiger and a loud boom sounds. Next thing, I wake in a hospital blind.

The images of the gun repeatedly flash in my mind and the darkness of his eyes. Why did he do that to me? Why do I get no answers?

Suddenly, as I once again return to the school's hall, I look around full of panic. Looking down, I feel my stomach drop, as I stare into the brown eyes of Payton, as they stare straight at the nothing. A puddle of blood surrounds her, and her brown hair begins clumping with blood. Her pale face was so lifeless. As I stood there staring down at her, I was shocked, and a scream escapes my lips.

My eyes shot open, and I am once again greeted by the pitch black. I feel a set of arms around my waist holding me still. Automatically, I know that it is Payton, so I don't want to wake her. I take a deep breath, trying to relax. I feel cool tears slip down my cheek. Squeezing my eyes together, I attempt to block the tears.

"Reece? Sweetie, are you alright?" Payton's sweet sleepy voice mumbles. She shifts lifting her body, I guess to get a better look at me.

"I'm alright, Angel, just a bad dream," I whisper back to her with a steady voice.

"You want to talk about it Reece?" she asks me still sounding tired.

"No, just get some sleep," I tell her as I use my hand to search for her head and kiss it.

"Okay, I love you," she whispers causing me to smile.

"I love you too, Angel," I say and listen as her breath becomes normal once again.

A soft whispering touch comes in contact with my lips, and my eyes pop open. For a second, I expected to open my eyes and see what it is, but that second was ruined by the reality. The soft lips on mine are removed before I could grasp what was happening and respond.

"Morning, Reece," Payton's happy tone brings a smile to my face. God, I sure have missed her.

"Morning, Angel," I say as I reach over feeling for her arm. Moving my hand up her arm, I guide my way to her neck, returning her lips to mine. The kiss heats up, and suddenly, I feel a stirring in the place below my waist. A groan escapes my lips as I realize that I am sporting a morning surprise. There are a few reasons why I am suffering this reaction. One is having the girl I am madly in love with on top of me, and the other is that I have not had sex for a while, and I'm horny.

Pulling away from Payton's sweet lips, I allow a few curse words to escape my lips. I shut my eyes tight knowing she is about to realize what's happening down there. The heat pumps to my face, and no matter how unmanly it is, I blush.

"Reece, sweetie, what's the matter?" Payton asks so innocently, and she moves away from me. She slips her hand into mine comforting me. Suddenly, I can hear a change in her breathing causing me to assume that she has spotted my problem. "Oh," she says trying to sound calm.

"I'm sorry Pay, I can't help it. It's been... umm... awhile since I, ya know?" I say reaching up and scratching the back of my head.

"Um... it's okay, Reece, you can't control it. I mean... I understand," she says, and I can sense the awkwardness in her voice.

"I am so sorry. I didn't mean to make you uncomfortable. It's just, having you so close to me... it just happened," I say softer, knowing how awkward this is and how much I am not helping my case.

"Reece, it's fine. Please just stop saying sorry! I should be the one being sorry for umm... You know... not fulfilling you," she begins to mumble, and I can imagine her cute face blushing.

As soon as those lips leave her mouth, I shot straight up turning to the direction that her voice was from. I run my hand up her arm, all the way to her cheek. "Don't... ever... say... that... again," I say placing a gentle kiss on her lips between each word. I take her face into my hands. "Never say sorry for that. It's nowhere near your fault. I can wait. I am in love with you and would never pressure you into it. I am fine with waiting till marriage or when you are ready," I tell her stroking her cheeks with my thumbs.

"Do you promise?" she asks me, and I can hear the sadness in her voice.

Shutting my eyes, I sigh before reopening them. "I swear," I tell her honestly.

Her arms wrap around me, holding me close and making me smile. We stay like this for a while, and I feel so comfortable. Once we pull apart, I can feel her rise of the bed.

"So what are you doing today?" she asks me with a smile present in her voice.

"Home, train, and hopefully, spend the evening with my beautiful girlfriend," I tell her with a bright, charming smile. Or that is what I hope it is.

"Oh, sounds like fun. Your girlfriend is pretty lucky," she kids, and I chuckle.

"No, I am the lucky one. So what are your plans for today?" I say with a smile.

"Drop you by your house, go see Ms. Rose and my sister, and then spent the evening with you," she says, and I smile.

"Sounds perfect," I state finding her lips once more to kiss.

"Lift your legs! Come on! We got to get the strength back up in them," Conner coaches me as I push my legs harder to lift them up with the weight on them. The pain was hell as it courses through my calves and thighs. It burns the familiar pain I was once so well used to. Like always, I push myself through the pain as I lift my legs. Sweat drips down my face as I do the exercise. My bare chest is sweaty too.

"You're at seventy-five now. You can stop or keep pushing," Conner informs me as he stands near my feet.

Shutting my eyes tight, I take a deep breath. *The only way to win is to work at it.* I say to myself, and I know I need more work. "I want to go to one hundred," I say as I continue the work out of my legs.

The pain becomes aching and killer. Every part of it hurts so badly. It was just a pain. I push my way through it. Grinding my teeth, I bare the pain as my breathing labors.

"One hundred!" Conner cheers once I lift my legs, which feel like rubber, up.

Placing my hands on my head, I cannot help but to breathe hard. "God, that... hurt," I pant. Conner just chuckle.

"I bet it did. Now, one to lifting weights," he adds taking a hold of my hand and pulling me to my rubber like legs.

I lift the weights until my arms feel like rubber too. "Bro... I'm done..." I pant, out of breath.

"Fine, only for now. After we get you refreshed, you're going to run," he informs me, and I shake my head, grabbing my stick to help guide myself away.

"Why am I the only one working out?" I ask in confusion as Conner, and I make our way to the kitchen.

"I am the coach, and you can't see and all. So you don't realize how in shape I am," Conner says in a very joking tone.

"Oh, boys!" my mom's voice says, and I take it as we made it to the kitchen as Conner helps me sit.

"Here's some water," he tells me sitting a glass in front of me.

"Gosh, you are so sweaty, Reece!" my mom points out the obvious.

"We were training," I say simply with a smile.

"That's great! I am so proud of you too! R—" the phone rings, cutting off my mom's sentence.

"Hello," she answers. "Yes, this is she," she continues, and then, I hear the sound of a gasp and phone hitting the floor.

I am so confused about what happened. Is everyone okay? Did someone die? My heart pounds against my chest. Please, God, don't hurt my family anymore.

Chapter Sixty-One

Reece's POV

The sound of shuffling and then my mom's voice again. "I'm sorry. I just wasn't expecting this." Expecting what? My mom pauses for a few causing my fear to rise. Well, she is not crying, I think, so that's good. "We never thought that we would actually be able to get answers, and this has come as a shock to me." Pause. "Yes, I understand sir. I will talk to him about it, and if he would like, I will bring him down." Whom is she talking about? "Thank you very much, sir," my mom finishes and after a few moments, I hear the phone being placed on the hook.

"Mom, what was that about?" I ask her as I rub the back of my neck. The sound of her walk lets me know she is coming towards me. Suddenly, I feel her touch my hand.

"Honey, that was the police station," she says calmly. If she is calm, then no one is hurt, right?

"What did they want?" I ask her a little worried about what her response would be.

"Son, it concerned the shooting. There has been a break in the case, and they have discovered a suicide letter explaining his reasons. If you want, we can go down to the station and go over it," she tells me squeezing my hand.

They found reasoning. They found out why he targeted me. He had a suicide note that holds all the answers. It's what I need. It's my closure. Of course, I want to hear it but not alone. "I want to go but I need Payton with me," I tell my mom in all honesty. Payton makes me stronger.

Payton's POV

"So, sweetie, how is Reece doing?" Ms. Rose asks as I sit in the chair beside her bed and lean my head back resting it.

"He is doing great. He is so strong and decided not to do the surgery. He is actually going to start running again. He's told me his dream to inspire people," I tell her as I gaze had her aging face. Since coming to her, I have notice Ms. Rose's weight seemed to disappear, and it's not due to her eating. It's her health.

"Honey, that's amazing. I am so proud of you for sticking by his side. I am proud of him for being strong. He is an amazing young man. Just perfect for the amazing young women you are. I know you two can make it through anything life throws at you. I am so proud to say I know you two," she tells me and smiles. It means so much to me to actually hear that.

"Thank you," I say as I think about how lucky I am. Suddenly, my phone rings, and I withdrawal it from my pocket.

"Hello," I answer not paying attention to the I.D.

"I need you," the voice was one that is engraved in my heart. Reece sounds so out of it and not himself, so I know something is wrong.

"Are you at your house?" I ask him as I take a deep breath to keep myself calm.

"Yes," Reece's reply was too short.

"I will be there soon," I reply in a hurry and hang up the cell phone. "I'm sorry Ms. Rose. Reece needs me, and it sounds serious," I tell her with a sad face as I shovel some of my things back inside my purse and place it on my shoulder.

"It's okay, dear, go!" she says waving her frail hand to me, and I nod my head. I walk quickly almost at a slow run, and my tennis shoes slap against the hard hospital floor.

Once I bust out the front doors of the hospital, I take off in a sprint to my car, not caring how crazy I look. Yanking the driver door open, I leap inside the car and start it, shutting the door and buckling my belt. My heart is hammering in my chest. Please let Reece be okay!

I drive away as quick as I possibly can. All I can think about is Reece and if he is okay. I swerve past some cars as I speed to the Collins house. All I know is that I need to get there and get there soon.

The Collins Mansion raises high above me as I near it. Switching the car to park in the driveway, I run through the grass and then up the steps. I knock on the door, or more like pound on it, as the banging in my chest continues and my heart thumps.

The door swings open, revealing and worried looking Conner. "Where is he?" I ask, still attempting to keep my voice calm.

"In the kitchen," Conner says and runs a hand through his hair and steps aside allowing me in. Quickly, I make my way past him and into the kitchen. When I step into the warm, homey feeling kitchen, I see Georgia leaning against the counter with her hands on her face and hair falling out of the hair bow. My eyes fall onto his hunched back, messy brown hair that looks like it was once sweaty and hands tucked in it. My heart sinks a little, seeing him so sad. Walking over to him quickly, I gently set a hand on his shoulder.

"Reece, what's wrong?" I ask, sitting down on the stool beside him.

"The police called," he says, his voice sounding distant. Why did the police call him?

"Why?" I ask taking a deep breath.

"They found a suicide letter that says why he shot me. I need you to come with me to read it. Please," he says, and his voice is so raw and heartbreaking.

A gasp escapes my mouth in shock. They found something. I know Reece still has problems relating to the shooting, and I think this is a gift to help him.

"Oh, Reece! Of course, I will. Let's go now, sweetie. The sooner is probably better," I suggest, gently taking his hand into mine and holding it. I watch as his amazing blue eyes flicker up as if looking for my eyes. Staring at them, I see how his eyes look glassy.

"Alright, let's go," he says as I stare into his blue eyes and hold his hand. "Mom, can you drive us please," he asks Georgia still with his face to me. Maybe, it's because he is not really sure where she is.

"Yeah, honey, let's go," she says, and I look up to watch her remove her blonde hair from the hair bow and then replaces it. Walking over to the table in the kitchen she picks up a black purse and a set of keys.

I stand up and tug slightly on Reece's hand. He rises up slowly, not moving fast at all. Everything about him just seems so sad, and it's like his mind is full of thinking. I hold his hand silently to support him and squeeze it to reassure him. Walking behind Georgia, we make our way out the front door. I follow Georgia to her car, holding tight to Reece's hand. Opening the driver's door, Georgia gets in, and she is oddly quiet. Reaching the back door, I open it for Reece and reach over, taking his other hand and placing it on top of the door.

"We're getting in the back seat," I say softly to Reece, knowing he could hear me.

He nods his head at me and feels his way around as he gets himself into the car, and I shut the door and walk to the other side to get in, scooting to the middle so that I can be beside him. Georgia starts the car and remains silent. Her face is masked with worry, and knowing her, I know it's hard on her to have to watch her son relive this pain.

Reaching over, I take Reece's hand in mine, and he squeezes it. I look up at his face to see his usual carefree smile replaced with a frown. His blue eyes are angled downward, and it looks like his jaw is clenched. "Reece, it's alright. I'm right here by your side. Try to relax a little bit," I tell Reece with a smile trying to get him to relax a little.

No matter what happens and no matter what this letter says I will always be here for Reece. This letter may just be a good thing to give us some closure.

Chapter Sixty-Two

Payton's POV

"Will you read it to me?" Reece's kind voice asks as we stand hand in hand at the police station.

How did I end up here? How did I end up standing beside the greatest person I've ever known? How did I become so lucky to be able to date this amazing person? How did he become mine?

"Of course," I say kindly, squeezing his hand to reassure him.

The police officer says, "This way you, two, then," and gestures us into a small room with a metal table and a chair on each side. A plastic evidence bag is on the table with a folded piece of paper inside. Leading Reece over to the table, I place his hand on the back of a chair as he feels his way to sit down.

Dragging the other chair to his side, I sit down and take his hand into mine. "Ready to hear this?" I ask him with serious, gentle tone.

"Yeah, as ready as I'll ever be," he replies after releasing a heavy sigh.

Extending my free hand forward, I remove the folded piece of notebook paper from the evidence bag. Then, taking a deep breath and preparing myself for what may lay on this paper, I begin to unfold it.

Squeezing tightly on to Reece's hand, I begin to read the messy handwriting.

Dear anyone who cares,

My life has been anything but perfect. It's that simple. I grew up without a mother. She died when I was three at the hands of some robber who shot her in front of me while my father would rather drink and smoke weed rather than getting to know his own son. Not to mention the nights when he'd stumble home wasted and look at me with pure disgust before pounding his fist into my body. One hit after another, the blows kept coming. The pain and abuse are too much for me.

At school, I'm just this weird freaky kid. I can't help it, though. It's who I am. No one speaks to me. Rumors spread about me. One person, throughout all the time I went to that damn school, ever spoke to me.

Payton Jennings. Payton was so kind and nice; she'd talk to me and acknowledge my presence. She didn't care because she is a loner like me. That is until the rumor of me being an "emo" spread. After that, Payton never spoke to me again. She just stopped as if it was nothing.

He said my name. My fingers grip tighter onto the paper, as I stare at these words, and my voice flutters a little bit causing my nerves to pick up. Am I the reason he did this? It's not like we were friends! I was just nice to the kid. Oh, my God! Did I cause Reece to get shot?

I cut myself one time! After that, I knew I didn't want to do it anymore. Why does that matter, though? No one cares about my side of the story! No one out there cares about me! I could die, and not one person would miss me.

What is even the point of me living? I wish I were dead every day of my life. Everyone acts so perfect and better than I do. I'm bullied at school and at my house.

You know, whom the one that everyone cares about? Reece Collins. Reece better known as Mr. Perfect is the most popular guy in school. His pictures cover the wall, girls fall at his feet, and he's smart. Everyone always talks about Reece. Reece this, Reece that. "Reece is the MVP for the football team for the fourth year in a row!" "Reece is going to run in the Olympics one day!" "Reece is going to be a Major League Baseball Star!" "Reece is going to attend Harvard Medical School!" "Reece volunteers at the homeless shelter!" "Reece spends his holidays helping others!" "Reece is so rich!" "Reece's family is perfect!" All the time everyone says all of this. Why can't I have that? Why the only thing people say about me is bad? Why is Reece freaking Collins so special? Why is everyone's attention on one single person? If he is Mr. Nice Guy, then why has he never spoke to me? He is no better than all of those other worthless people who attend that hell hole of a school!

As soon as Reece's name slips from my lips, I tense but so does he. His grasp on my hand tightens, and I glance out from the corner of my eye to see Reece's face become blank. My heart drops a little; I wish I knew what he was thinking.

They've had their times to shine; now, it's mine! If I'm going to go out, I'll go with a bang! I'll be someone they never forget! They will wish they had paid more attention to me. I'll become so well-known after I die. There is no point for me to live, but before I go, I am going to gain the attention of all those asses of people in school. How? First, I'm going to take out Mr. Perfect himself — Reece Collins; his life has been great so he can die because he has everything I didn't. Then, Payton Jennings; we are so much alike, but then, she ignores me! She starts treating me like the rest! She won't give me a minute of her day; then, I'm not going give her the rest of her life. Also, Jace Higgins is another who has lived long enough and can go. After that, it'll probably be at random since there is no one that I care to save. No one cared about me, so why should I care about them.

I would kill my father, but it'd be better for him to suffer. I hate life. I hate people, and there is no real reason for me to live. I am going to just do what everyone wants me to and kill myself but with a bang. My whole life has been silent and bad, so now is my chance to get attention and to die famous.

The last word I read hangs in the air like a bad aftertaste. He was just after attention! He did this to be famous! The worst part that is sickening, thanks to the media and constant talk about it, he is! People can be stupid. They can deny it, but the truth is they are to blame for giving him what he wanted. He won. I wish there were some ways that he could not win this.

A cool tear slides down my cheek as I fold the letter back up and place it back inside the evidence bag. More tears fall from my eyes as I realize something. Reece saved my life! If he hadn't been so brave and kept Erwin distracted, I would be dead. I was next. Reece saved my life in more than one way. Because of his bravery, I am alive along with hundreds of others. People should be giving him awards, not treating him like a black sheep. Squeezing tightly to his still hand, I bit my lip to keep myself from crying out.

The room is full of tension and silence. I wipe away my tears and sniffle slightly. Looking at Reece's eyes, I can see his pain.

"Let's get out of here," Reece says, and his voice is so monotonous yet still aches with emotion.

"Okay," I whisper, trying not to let him tell that I'm crying. With his hand in mine, I stand up and lead him out of the room. Georgia is sitting outside in the police station lobby. Her head is in her hands, and as I open the door, her head shots up in our direction. When she processes Reece's blank, emotionless mask and my teary face, her face becomes worried, and she jumps up from the chair as we walk silently to her.

"Are you all alright?" she asks and hugs Reece and then me.

"Yeah, let's just go," Reece says with no emotion.

Georgia looks stunned at her son, who seems so out of it. "Um, okay," she says simply. I can tell she is trying not to pry into his life. I know we are all thankful for that. Leading Reece out to the car, Georgia unlocks the doors, and I open the back door for Reece. He gets himself inside, and I shut the door before walking to the other side and buckle up.

The car ride back was long. It was silent, and there was this tension between Reece and me. It was strong, and I know it has everything to do with that damn letter. Is it because he was shot out of envy? Or is it me? Did something about me in that letter bother him? A million thoughts cloud my mind. Maybe, I should head home once we get back to Collin's house.

Georgia drives home silently, and all I want is for Reece to be happy again. It feels like sometimes something is always blocking us. I mean, I love him so much and do anything for him. Sometimes, I feel like he hides his feelings from me. I just wish he would open up to me for once.

The car slows to a stop, and I look over to Reece's face, still giving nothing away. I let out a sigh as Georgia climbs out of the car. Following suit, I get out, and by the time I reach Reece's side, he is working on getting out. Once he is, I shift on me feet.

"I guess I'm going to head home, Reece," I tell him, placing a hand on top of his shoulder and leaning in to brush my lips over his cheek.

"Alright, I'll talk to you later," he says as I pull away, and he forces a smile.

"I love you," I tell him giving him a sad smile.

"I love you too," he says, and I sigh and walk to the car as Georgia comes to his side.

"Bye, Payton!" she says, waving with a sad smile.

"Bye, Georgia!" I say, climbing back inside.

Maybe if I give him space, he'll get better instead of talking to me. Maybe if he processes it, it will help. I love him to death, but sometimes, he can be a butt.

Chapter Sixty-Three

Reece's POV

I didn't mean to push Payton away. I am not mad at her. It's just I am so confused, and honestly, I'm freaking out! If it weren't for me being there, it could've been Payton who was shot. Payton could have died, and I could have never met her. Life would not be like this. I could be gone. I was shot out of jealousy. I am blind now because someone was jealous of my life. Payton and Jace could have been shot! This is too much all at once. My brain begins to feel as if it is slamming against my skull.

Slumping on my bed with Rider stretched out at me side; I push my hands through my hair. Tears slide from my eyes. Hearing Payton read those things he wrote about her and wanting her dead is literally heart breaking. I am so mad at that kid for doing this! It all worked out, but still, it's so painful. If I weren't there, if I weren't able to stop him, then Payton and Jace would have been next. If it were not me, it would have been them and knowing this is eating away at me.

Knock, knock.

I lift up my head and wipe away my tears. "Come in," I call out to whoever is knocking on my bedroom door.

I hear the door creak open. "Hey, little bro," Conner says as I hear his footsteps near me.

"Hey," I say in a very sad tone. Petting Rider's soft fur, I feel the bed shift.

"Here, Reece," Conner says, and I reach out my hand that was on Rider and feel Conner place a cool glass in my hand.

Lifting the glass to my lips, I take a sip. A sour, burning taste enters my mouth and my throat. This causes me to begin coughing. "What the fuck is this?" I swear. Tinges travel down my throat as the liquid makes its way to my stomach.

"Liquor," Connor says to me as if it is nothing. Leave it to my fucking brother to give me liquor!

"Why in the hell are you giving me this? I don't drink, idiot!" I say angrily as I hold my arm out that has the glass in it as far from me as possible.

"Dude, chill the fuck out! Drinking for one night won't kill you. You have had a really bad day and for once since the damn shooting, need a break and to escape all this shit! So just fucking drink it!" my lovely brother curses. Damn, I can tell he already had a couple drinks.

Why does he want me to drink? It doesn't solve anything. Drinking only leads to more problems! So why is he trying to get me to drink?

"Conner, drinking won't fix anything! Getting drunk won't do anything for me!" I argue, running my hand through my hair with the hand that isn't holding the glass.

"Reece, drinking one night to loosen up and relax is not going to make you an alcoholic. For so long, you have acted like you had a stick wedged up your ass, and for one night, take it out and relax. After today, you need this. You are not going to be a drunk just for drinking one glass. So please, just drink. If it doesn't work, I'll never ask you to drink again. I cannot imagine what you're going through, but if I can give you a chance to forget for one night, I will," he says, and I sigh.

Squeezing my eyes shut, I raise the glass to my lips and take a sip of the bitter liquor. It travels down my throat and sends tingles through me. After I finish this glass, I can hear the sound of Conner pouring me more.

"Reece, do you want to talk?" he asks me as I sip some more. My body has adjusted to the taste, and it doesn't burn as bad.

"Well, I found out I was shot out of pure jealousy, and after me, he was going after Payton and then Jace. If it weren't for me stalling, then Payton could be dead! On top of that, I am afraid I may not be able to race track again. I just am so afraid," I tell Conner and drink some more. Damn, I am a girl when I drink.

"Shit, bro, that's bad!" he says, and I feel a movement on my bed. It sounded like he flopped down on it.

"Fuck, I know!" I say and drink some more. Suddenly, I remember I didn't talk to Payton! "Conner, can you hand me my phone?" I ask beginning to feel a little off.

"Sure," he says, and I feel him moving around on the bed and then a cool square object being placed in my free hand.

Lifting it up, I give the command to call Payton. The annoying ringing sounds play for a few seconds. "Hello," her sweet angelic voice says through the phone.

"Hay baby," I sat as I continue to drink.

"Reece, what's wrong?" my amazing girlfriend's voice says in a very concerned tone.

"Nothing, Pay. I just want you to know I love you so much. You are the best thing that has happened to me, and I don't care if we have a fight. I have been a total asshole for pushing you away. I was so afraid, angry, and shocked. I never want to think about anything happening to you. I am so sorry. I love you," I ramble on and on feeling so bad about it all. Like I said, alcohol makes me a total chick.

"Reece, what's up with you?" Payton asks me with a weary tone in his voice.

"I may have had a little to drink," I tell her, fibbing a little to prevent from hurting her.

"Ugh… okay. You're not alone are you?" she asks me as she releases a sigh.

"Nope, I'm sitting here with Conner," I say as I take another sip from the glass.

"Alright, good. Well, Reece, I'll see you in the morning. Be safe, please?" Payton asks me, and I can hear the caring tone in her voice. God, I am so lucky to have her.

"Okay, sweetie," I say to her, and a smile pulls onto my face thinking about her. "I love you," I add, taking another sip of the bitter liquid.

"I love you too, Reece," she says, and then the phone falls dead.

"Eww, so much love!" Conner fakes gag noises and then bursts into laughter.

"You're just jealous!" I shot back at him with a smirk.

"Man, you're right. I'd love to have a girl like Payton," he replies with a sigh, and this causes a smile to rise onto my lips. That makes me even more proud to be hers.

Flopping back onto my bed, with an empty glass beside me I shut my eyes. My whole body feels so numb, and the pain I hold has faded. I feel relaxed and calm.

"Rise and shine, sleeping beauty!" Conner's annoying voice sings as I feel his hand shake my shoulder.

Groaning, I feel for my pillow and pull it over my face. "No," I whine. My waking up is greeted with a killer headache. My brain feels like it is banging against my forehead.

"Yeah, now, get up! Time to practice," Conner orders and I groan. Why the hell would I practice? I have a freaking headache. God, I'm hangover, and he expects me to fucking practice!

"How in the hell are you not hangover?" I groan, pull the pillow off of my face and sit up. My head continues to pound.

"Dude, I've done this a billion times before, and I have gone to practice afterward. Just put on these shorts," he says as he shoves the shorts into my hands. I can tell by how they feel that they are basketball shorts. "Your shoes are beside your feet. Now, get ready," he orders and, I sigh, standing up and pulling off my shirt and shorts. Feeling around behind me, I grab the pair of shorts and pull them on. Sitting back onto my bed, I put my head in my hands.

"Take this," Conner instructs as he grasps my hand and drops what I'm guessing is pills in my hand and then hands me a cool glass in my other hand. I drop the pills into my mouth and then wash it down with the glass of water.

"Do I get a bite to eat first?" I ask him as I hold out the glass, signaling for him to take it.

He takes it, and I bend over feeling around for my tennis shoes. "Trust me, man, you do not want to eat first," Conner says, and I groan as I grab my shoes and pull them onto my feet.

Standing up, I run a hand through my hair. "Let's do this," I say taking a wary step forward.

"Here's Rider. I put his harness on already," my brother says as he places my hand on Rider's harness. "Now, let's go," he adds.

Five minutes later, Conner and I are jogging what use to be my everyday path. The whole time I run, I feel like shit. Then, my stomach twists and a stuff rises in my throat. I stop. Then I end up puking my guts out. Damn, I'm glad I didn't eat breakfast.

"Done?" Conner asks, not seeming concerned at all.

I stand straight again, wipe my mouth with the back of my hand and nod my head. We begin to run again, and the torture and puking continue as we run five fucking miles. I am never drinking anything ever again!

Chapter Sixty- Four

Payton's POV

"How are *ya* feeling, Lila?" I ask as I flop into the chair beside her bed.

Today, Lila has a blue bandana over her bald head, and she's still very thin and frail, but her skin is regaining color which is good. It was a very pale which is beginning to regain pinkness. She does look a little tired today given the fact that she has dark bags under her sparkling eyes. Her thin, still little chapped lips are pulled up slightly into a smile. Her hospital blanket is pulled up to her chest.

"I've been better," she says with a yawn. "The doctor says that in a couple months, I will go into remission and get to go home," she adds with a smile to me.

I take her hand in mine. "Why are you not feeling well today?" I ask her concern evident in my voice.

"My last treatment really wore me out, that's all," she says, and I can tell she's telling the truth. Squeezing her hand, I smile sadly.

"I can't wait for you to get to come home," I tell her. With my hand that is not holding hers, I brush some of my brown curls behind my ear.

"Me either, Pay-bear," she says, and I can see that her eyes are beginning to become droopy.

"You need some rest. I'll come back and see you later," I tell Lila as I stand up and kiss her forehead.

"Okay, can you bring Reece with you?" she asks me with a smile.

"Yeah, of course," I tell her with a smile. "I love you, sweetie. Get some rest," I add, and she nods her head.

"I love you too," she replies.

Walking out of the hospital, I go through the parking lot in search of the car. I already went and seen Ms. Rose this morning before I went to see Lila. She looks like her health is going downhill. I am hoping that she can pull through this.

Driving down the road, I head to the Collins' house to see my love, Reece. I know from the phone call last night that Reece was drunk. Yeah, I'm disappointed that he drank, but I'm trying to understand him.

I finally arrive and walk to the door. I reach out and use the knocker to knock. The door swings open, revealing a smiling Rayne. Her brown hair is pulled pack in pigtails with yellow bows. She is wearing a cute little green and yellow dress.

"Hi, Payton!" she says with a pig ole toothy smile.

"Hi' *ya*, Rayne!" I say, attempting to match her cheerfulness.

"Reece and Conner are in the gym," she says as she steps to the side and gestures me inside. Stepping inside of the very familiar home, I smile and watch Rayne as she shuts the door and twirls around facing me.

"Where's Juliet?" I ask, wondering what she's up to.

"Oh, she's with Jace... oopsy," Rayne says as she slaps her little hands over her mouth, and her blue eyes grow wide. "I wasn't supposed to tell anyone that," she explains, and I knee down smiling softly at her.

"It's okay, Rayne; it'll be our little secret. Pinky promise," I say extending my hand out to her. She sighs in release and wraps her small pinky around mine.

"Thank you so much, Payton! You are truly the best!" she says to me and wraps her arms around my neck hugging me.

"You're welcome," I tell her and hug her back. Once she let's go, she scurries off, and I smile. I walk through the house and to the gym.

As I push the door open and walk into the gym, I stop when my eyes fall onto the gorgeous man that is my boyfriend. Reece is laying on the bench press bench, shirtless and only in black basketball shorts. His body is gleaming with sweat, and I watch as his biceps flex as he pushes the heavy weight up in the air and then lowers it.

To be honest, I never really understood why girls fawned over sweat on guy's bare chest because to me that is disgusting. That was until now. Damn, he looks hot! I mean the perspiration make his skin shine and glisten which totally makes him look even hotter. How in the world did I ever get so lucky?

Conner is standing in front of Reece's head spotting him. Conner is wearing a gray shirt with the sleeves cut out and the sides of his shirt open with a pair of red basketball shorts. His blonde hair is messy and sweaty too. Conner looks up and locks eyes with me.

"Hey there, Payton," he says, and I watch as Reece's eyes pop open. Conner looks down and notices so he takes the weight from Reece's grip. Reece sits up and feels around at his side before lifting up a white towel which he uses to whip off his sweaty face. Placing it in his lap, he runs a hand through his sweat covered brown hair.

"Pay?" Reece says, moving his head around slowly and attempting to locate me with his ears.

"Over here, Reece," I tell him, and his head turns towards me. Smiling, I walk over to where my handsome boyfriend sits.

"You're here," he states with a big, shining smile.

"Yeah, sweetie. So what have you been up too?" I ask as I walk over to him.

Conner grabs a water bottle and places it in Reece's hands. He drinks from it. As he removes it from his lips, he leans his head back and swallows. "Oh nothing, just Conner making me puke up my guts every five minutes," he says in a grumpy tone, and Conner starts laughing.

"Hey, you finally stopped puking," he exclaims with his hands in the air.

"Yeah, after I almost dry heaved to death," Reece snorts, and I watch as he rolls his blue eyes.

"Will that be the last time you drink?" I ask him with a smirk and stand beside him placing my hand on his shoulder.

"Yeah, shit. I'm sorry I called you acting like such a girl last night," he apologizes rubbing face with his hands.

"Trust me, it's okay. It was nice to finally know how you are feeling," I say before I can stop my words. Shit! That probably just pissed him off. Conner's eyes widen in shock that I said that.

"Um... I'm just going to go take a shower," Conner says awkwardly, and I watch as he practically runs out of the room and the gym door slams behind him.

"I can't help it that I'm not always the best in sharing my feelings," Reece says as I sit down beside him on the bench. He holds his head in his hand.

"Reece, you can. It's like anytime you are close to opening up, you shut the walls and lock them. Then you push me away," I reply biting my lip. God, it feels good to get this off my chest, but it hurts facing it.

"I don't do that," he defends, lifting his head up and looking in my direction with watery, sad eyes.

"Yeah, you do Reece. You did it yesterday!" I argue, trying to open his eyes to what he does!

"No..." he starts to deny again, but I cut him off.

"You get upset and stop talking to me. You never tell me deep stuff about yourself," I say, and I have to keep myself from letting some of the tears out.

"I'm a guy. It's hard for me to express myself," he says and shrugs his shoulders.

I snort my laughter. Did he really just play the guy card? "You did not just say it's because you're a guy," I state and hopes he realizes how stupid that is.

"It's the truth," he says, leaning his head down, and his arms are lying on his legs.

"No, no, it's not, Reece. It's you. There are guys out there who show their true emotions," I reply. I didn't come here to fucking fight with him, so why am I?

"Why are we fighting about this now?" he groans, pulling at his brown hair.

"Because it's something we need to talk about, Reece! You won't let me in," I cry and feel warm liquid slip down my cheek.

"I do too," he argues, rubbing his face with his hands and then slipping them into his hair tugging at it.

"No, you don't. You blocked me out yesterday, and when it came to your surgery, you went to your ex rather than me," I say, wiping the tears from my eyes. "Is it me, Reece? Is there something wrong with me?" I ask softly and bite my lip. I rest my cheek on my hand and squeeze my eye shut.

"Shit, Payton, nothing is wrong with you," he says as his head snaps up towards me. His hands reach out and land on my legs as he shifts my direction. His one hand stays on my leg while his other finds my free hand. "You're fucking perfect. You are beautiful inside and out. You are the sweetest, nicest, most amazing person I have ever had the pleasure of knowing. You are absolutely the greatest person ever. I am so lucky to have you in my life. I want to spend the rest of my life with you because I am madly head over heels for you. You make me the luckiest guy in the world," he says. I stare into his blank blue eyes, and my heart melts. The tears cascade all the way down my face, and I ball.

"But why do you not share with me?" I beg, sniffing and squeezing my eyes.

"I guess because I don't want to out all my shit on you when you have enough to deal with. You have the whole world on your shoulders, and I don't want to add more weight putting all my problems on you. I'm sorry, it's just you've been through a lot with your sister and your father. I didn't want to add more to your lap. I'm sorry. I love you," he says, squeezing my hand and leg.

"Reece, we are a couple. We share each other's wait and burdens. I'll always be here for you. I'll be here forever by your side. I love you. You can always talk to me. I want you to talk to me!"

Removing his hands from my hand and legs, he pushes them into his hair and pulling he releases groans, shutting his eyes. "Fine, I'll open up to you. I'll work on it. I'll do whatever it is to make you happy," he states. His blue orbs pop open, and he sighs. "When I was standing there with the gun on me all, I could think about was making sure no one else got hurt. I figured if I stalled or distracted him that everything or at least, everyone would be okay. Then, I wake up, and I can't see my mom or family. I thought my life was over and snuck into a dark place. Why did God let me live and take my sight away? I thought I'd rather be dead than blind. My friends didn't come see me. Everyone dropped me or started acting differently. Then, you came walking into my life, and as soon as I started feeling sorry for myself, you told me how it was. You woke me up and lifted me from that dark place. You showed me a new way to see. You changed my life. This has not been easy, but you're always there. Thank you for that even with little struggles along the way and some choices I made. When I had the chance to get my eyesight back, I just wanted to protect you and didn't think about anything else. Yesterday, I was so angry and freaked out, thinking about you not being alive and you being killed. I don't express myself well, but I will change," he says as he holds my hand.

The tears silently fall down my face as a small smile rises onto my face. "Reece," I cry. Removing my hand from his, I throw my arms around his neck and bury my head in his neck. "Thank you for finally opening up!" I gush as I hold him for dear life, and his arms secure themselves around my waist. "From now on, please talk to me about anything. I'm here for you and want you to talk to me," I tell him kind of in a bossy tone, but I find it necessary for this situation.

"I promise you, Payton. I will from now on. I love you," he says into my hair which sends a string of chills down my back.

"Love you too. Now, onto a less serious subject, are you done practicing right now?" I ask as I pull away and look down at him as I wipe away the salty liquid falling down my face.

Reece chuckles a little, lighting the room's mood and shaking his head. "Depends on what you have in mind," he kids with a smile.

Placing my hands on his shoulder and standing in between his basketball short clad legs, I smile. "There is this little girl in the hospital who wants to see you," I explain with a kidding tone, hoping he'd get whom I was referring too.

"Lila?" he asks, raising his eyebrows.

"Yep," I say, popping the 'P' and running my hands up to his neck.

"Hmm… I guess I'm free and can go see her," he says simply with a smile. His thumbs are drawing circles on my waist as he holds my sides.

"Good, now, go get your stinky butt a shower," I joke as I go to pull away from him, but his grip holds me in my place.

"Wait, wait, don't I get a kiss?" he asks with a smirk. I couldn't help it but let my laugh slip from my lips. I lean down slowly and brush my lips against his set of perfect ones. I pull away, smiling big and step away to watch his blue eyes pop open.

"Now, go shower," I boss with a laugh, and he groans standing up. I slip my arms through his and escort him to his room.

"Alright, Payton, I'm good. I can handle it from here," he states moving around his room with such an awesome skill.

"You sure?" I ask watching him worriedly reaching up and messing with my messy brown hair.

"Yes, now, go watch TV or something," he commands me, and I sigh looking over at Rider who rushes to Reece's side.

"Fine! But if you need me, just holler," I tell him with a groan. Then, I turn towards the door.

"Yes, mom," he teases with a chuckle. I roll my eyes and shut the door behind me.

Leaving his room, I go to the den and plop down on the couch watching the TV. The sound of a door alerts me, and I sit up from my slouching position and look over my shoulder. Juliet's blonde head appears out of the hallway. She walks in smiling when she sees me.

"So did you have fun with Jace?" I ask her with a knowing smile, and her face turns pale white as she freezes.

"Damn, Rayne! I'm going to kill her!" Juliet swears angrily as she sits down beside me.

Shaking my head, I roll my eyes. "Calm your pants. She didn't mean to tell me," I tell her like it's nothing. "So you and Jace? Does Reece know?" I ask with a smirk, knowing the answer to that is "no."

"No, and you cannot tell him!" she says forcefully with an urgent tone.

"Fine, fine, at least, tell me about it," I tell her, and she groans.

Running a hand through her hair, she looks down at her lap with pink rising to her cheeks. "Well, after Reece lost his sight, my whole life changed because my family did. I wanted to be a bad kid, so I started smoking and drinking. Jace found me, one day, smoking, and he sat and talked to me. After that, he has been helping me heal and feel better. He is so sweet, and we like each other a lot, but Jace is afraid that Reece will kill him for liking his little sister," she explains, and huge smile forms on my lips.

I go to reply to her, but suddenly, my phone begins to ring. Pulling it out, I see the hospital number, and I begin to worry. Answering it, I raise it quickly to my ear saying hello.

"Payton, it's me, May. I have some really bad news, dear," her voice says so sadly, and my heart literally drops, and

I feel like throwing up. Please God, let Lila and Ms. Rose is okay!

Chapter Sixty-Five

Payton's POV

My body reacts while my mind is in shock from what I just heard and the phone slips from my hands. Inside my chest, I feel my heart clench and ache like a piece of it just died.

"I have to go to the hospital," I say like a robot to Juliet. Then turning around, I make my sprint to the door. As my feet take the step two at a time, I feel as if I am standing outside, watching my body react and feel nothing. I watch as the person running out a door and attempting to prevent herself from falling apart.

I jump into the car as the tears begin to fall down my face. I can honest not believe this has happened. I was just with her not too long ago and now… Pressing my foot down harder on the gas pedal, no doubt, breaking the speed limit, my entire mind is thinking about is getting to the hospital.

Swerving into the parking lot and into space, I then leap out the vehicle. I proceed to practically sprint into the hospital. The tears fall freely down my face as I rush through hallways and to the elevator. I can feel my heart slam against my chest. Panting a little as I wait inside the elevator, I lean against the wall to catch my breath for a moment. The large metal doors slide open, and I take off running off of the and through the halls. My running slows as I near her room and I see May standing there with a really sad look on her face.

"May," I choke out as I near her, and the tears are pouring down my face.

"Payton," her head snaps up and looks at me. Her face is grim and filled with pain.

"Please, tell me it's not true," I beg before I can stop myself. I feel like everything shattered, and I just lost my best friend. I never thought that this would hurt so badly.

"I'm sorry, Payton," she says softly and just wraps her arms around me. I cry softly into her scrub top. "If you want, sweetie, you can say goodbye," she tells me as she strokes my brown mess of hair.

"Okay," I say as I take a step away from May and use both of my hands to rid myself of the tears.

Taking a deep breath as if it has the magical power to make me strong, I walk into her room and bracing myself for what I am about to see. There, lying on the bed is Ms. Rose. Her eyes are shut, and her face looks so calm and at peace. Everything about her just looks at rest, and she doesn't look in pain anymore. Walking slowly to her side, the tears keep falling.

"Ms. Rose, know you're finally with your husband again, and you must be so happy, but I just wanted to say thank you. You were always here for me and were my best friend. You helped me through so much. I love you, and I am going to miss you so much. You were an amazing woman, and I know you are in a better place. I know you will be watching over me. I will miss you, but you will always be with me in my heart. I love you and thank you for being my best friend," I cry as I look down at her still body.

"She went in her sleep. It was a very peaceful death," May says calmly as she steps into the room and goes to the other side of the bed across from me. "She said she was tired after your visit and took a nap. I came into check on her a little later, and she had passed," she tells me, and I feel a little better knowing she died peacefully.

Slowly, May and I lift the cover and gently cover her head. "Excuse me," I say needing an escape. I walk out into the hall and lean against the wall, allowing my body to slide down it. I pull my knees to my chest and cry. Slipping my fingers into my brown frizzy hair and tugging at the roots, I continue to let out sobs. I knew this day would come, but I never expected to lose her so soon. She has been my best friend. I'm going to be so lost without her.

Suddenly, I feel an arm wrap around my shoulder, and I slowly bring down my hands to reveal the sad face of my amazing boyfriend. Instantly, I become confused on how he got there then I look at his side and see Rider laying there beside him with his head on Reece's lap. I notice that Reece's brown hair is still wet, and he's wearing his black sunglass along with a blue shirt and gray shorts. Taking a deep breath, I wipe away my tears. "Reece?" I ask with a raspy voice as I wrap my arms around his waist.

"Payton, what's happened?" he asks with a voice full of concern as he strokes my hair.

"Ms. Rose died," I say, and the sobs come rushing back. Reece pulls me into his chest, and I allow myself to cry.

"It's okay, Payton. She'll be in a better place now," he says to me as he strokes my hair.

I sniff as I hold onto him slightly and cry. We sit in the hospital hallway as he holds me while I cry.

I pull a black dress that Juliet lent to me. The black dress falls to my knees, and the waist up is tight and hugs me while the body is loose and flowing. The sleeve just barely covers my shoulder, and it has a heart-shaped neckline. Sitting in front of my mirror, I force a brush through my brown hair and pull the sides black out of my face. Using the make-up that Juliet is letting my use, I put on some mascara and eyeliner. I lean over and buckle the black high heels onto my feet, which Georgia lent me. Standing up, I feel super tall and look in the mirror, forcing a sad smile on my face.

It has been four days since Ms. Rose passed. These have been some of the hardest days in my life. Since Ms. Rose did not have any family, my mother, and I planned the whole funeral. This is so difficult, and it takes a lot for me to keep it together. Imagine losing your best friend or your grandma that is what it is like for me, and it kills me to think I will never be able to speak to her again. If only Heaven weren't so far away. She's in a better place now with her husband and God.

"Payton, are you ready?" Reece's voice sounds from outside my door. I swear if it wasn't for Reece and the Collins family getting through this would be impossible. If there were anything that needs paying, Georgia wouldn't take no for an answer. She insisted on helping because that is the kind of people they are. Even though Reece was the only one to meet Ms. Rose, they all are there and are going to the funeral.

I walk to my door and swing it open to reveal Reece standing there wearing a black Armani suit with black designer glasses. His brown hair is all styled back perfectly and his left hand resting calmly on Rider's harness, as he sits idly at Reece's side.

"Yeah, I'm ready," I reply as I take his right hand in mine. Holding his hand gives me all the strength in the world. As long as Reece is by my side, he gives me strength. The pain is still there, but thanks to him, I know I have someone to lean on. "You look very handsome," I tell him as I rest my head sadly onto his shoulder for a moment.

"Thanks, Pay. I know you look gorgeous," he says squeezing my hand. I heave out a sigh to sad to even attempt to argue with him. Raising my head off of his shoulder, I lead him to the front door. I can feel tears want to escape my eyes, but I force them back.

My mom appears in front of the door in a tight but classy black dress that falls to her knees. She is also sporting black heels hair in a bun, makeup is dark, and a silver necklace hangs around her neck with a cross on it.

"Ready?" she asks me.

"Yeah," I answer, holding tightly to Reece's hand. My mom nods her head solemnly as she walks past us and opens the door stepping out into the heat. The sun is high in the sky shining down with smothering intensity. A black Cadillac awaits us in our driveway. My mom leads the way to the car as Reece, Rider, and I follow behind. My mom climbs into the driver seat, and Reece puts Rider in the back seat and then slides in. I sit beside him. I hook our belts and take his hand while laying my head on his shoulder. The golden retriever has his head on Reece's knee.

My mom begins pulling the rented car from the driveway and to the church that the funeral is at. The car is silent, and I shut my eyes as I inhale the sweet scent of Reece. I don't know how to explain it but with him by my side, I feel safe, everything going to fine, and I feel loved.

The car finally slows to a stop, and I open my eyes seeing that we are at the church. Standing tall, the white church is big with a cross on it and a tall steeple. My mom parks the car in a parking spot, and we all get out. Reece shifts uncomfortable on his feet and adjusts his tie nervously.

"Are you okay?" I ask him quietly, staring up at his face which looks like he's having an inner argument with himself.

"Um... yeah. It's just I haven't really been to a church since the accident," he says seeming a little unsettled.

"Mom, we'll be in, in a second," I call to her as I pull Reece and Rider to a stop.

"Okay," she says over her shoulder and climbs the step going inside the church.

"Reece, will you be okay?" I ask him and rub his hand with my thumb.

"Yeah, I'll be fine Payton, it's just... hard," he mumbles, but I can still hear him and sense the sadness that is in his voice.

"Do you blame God?" I ask him, in a gentle voice trying not to make it so sound so hard.

"I used to. I use to wonder how He could possibly do this to me and what I ever did to deserve this. Now, I've come to realize that He has a plan for me and losing my sight isn't necessarily a bad thing. So I've come to understand it all, but what if God is still mad that I held a hate for Him at one time?" Reece rambles on about his feelings, which is a great thing.

"Reece, God is all about forgiveness I know He forgives you and understands. He doesn't blame you," I tell him as I squeeze his hand.

"You're right. I'm just being crazy," he says with a shrug.

"No, you're not. You've been through something major, and the feelings that you are expecting are normal," I tell him and lean up to kiss his check.

"Thanks, let's go inside," he sighs. I mumble an okay and begin to lead us to the church.

We walk down the church aisle to the first pew where my mom is seated. We take our seats beside her. A few minutes, the Collins show up and sit beside Reece quietly. Once the funeral begins, there are about thirty or more people there, some from the hospital, others may have known her before and seen her obituary.

As the Preacher goes up front and delivers the service, I cry the whole time. Georgia passes me tissues, which I use to try and keep my tears away. After the funeral, we travel to the cemetery for the burial. It's hard to say goodbye. One of the most painful things we do in life is to say goodbye to those we love.

After the burial and laying her to rest with a final goodbye, Reece, Rider, my mom, and I head back to my house. Georgia wanted us to come over for dinner. But after an emotional day like today, I just want to go home and curl into a ball. I told Reece he could go home with his family, but the guy refused. He said, "I want to be there for you." God, my boyfriend is such a cheese ball. A sweet, good one, though. I will never tell him, but I am really glad that he's insisted on staying with me.

Once we arrive at my house, we go inside and to my room while my mom disappears to hers. I show Reece to the bed so that he can sit down, and Rider sits at his feet. Reece quickly begins to loosen his tie from around his neck.

"I'm going to go get Rider some water," I tell Reece, and he nods his head as he takes off his black sunglasses, finally revealing his amazing blue eyes.

Moments like this, as I watch him take his suit jacket off, you'd never think he was blind. He has mastered being able to do this. It's amazing. There are many times when you can tell he can't see, but then there are moments like this, and you forget. I forget all the time, to be honest.

Leaving the room, I walk into the kitchen, grabbing a bowl, filling it with water and carrying it back to my room.

Entering, I find Reece on my bed in just his black pants. He ran a hand through his hair making it messy.

I set the bowl down in front of Rider, who happily begins to lap it. Walking to my dresser, I pull out one of Reece's hoodies and a pair of pajama shorts. "Reece I need to change clothes so can you... um... turn around or close your eyes?" I ask him, shifting my feet back and forth uncomfortable.

"Um... Payton, you do know that I'm blind, right?" he asks me and raises an eyebrow.

"Yes, but still it's weird to think you're looking at me," I attempt to defend myself against him.

"Why? I can't see you. Hell, I don't even know where you are standing," he defends himself and crosses his perfect arms over his chest.

"Still, Reece, please," I say with a soft voice.

He groans and covers his eyes. "You're crazy," he mumbles.

"Love you too," I shot back, taking off my dress and replacing it with the hoodie and shorts. I walk to him, and he lowers his hands from his eyes, allowing his blue eyes to meet mine.

I lean down, place a hand on his cheek and kiss him. He pulls me down beside him as we kiss. His tongue licks my bottom lip asking for entrance. I happily grant it. We lay back, entangling our arms together and our bodies kissing.

"Payton!" my mom yells for me. Reece and I pull apart.

"What?" I holler back.

"Someone is here for you," she calls back. I peck Reece's lip.

"I'll be right back," I tell him, getting up and walking to the front door. My body freezes as I see a man standing before me in a suit with a black briefcase. He had a solemn look on his face and looked like he was a very serious man. Why is he here?

Chapter Sixty-Six

"Are you sure you wouldn't like something to drink, Mr. Smith?" my mother asks as she nervously runs a hand through her hair while she stands at the kitchen sink.

"No, thank you, ma'am," he says with a southern drawl giving away that he is not natively from Indiana. My mom nods her head sighing and sits down on the seat between Mr. Smith and me at the kitchen table. Mr. Smith was a good looking man with his dirty blond hair and emerald eyes. I think my mom is smitten, and that's causing her to be flustered and nervous.

"I'm sorry about your loss, but Payton, I must ask you. Were you aware of Ms. Daylin's financial standings?" he asks as he sets his briefcase on the table before us and lifts the top of it up. I shift nervously crossing one of my bare legs over the other.

"No, sir, I'm not," I answer honestly. All Ms. Rose and I ever spoke of was our current lives, and sometimes, we talk about the past but never money. I hope Reece is okay upstairs all alone.

"Were you aware that her husband passed?" he asks me as he takes out a few papers and shuts his briefcase.

"Yes, sir, I was," I reply, Ms. Rose, and I talked about this before. At least now, I know she is happy in Heaven with her husband.

"Well, Ms. Jennings, Mr. Daylin was a very well off man, you could say. He was the CEO of Daylin's Restaurant which became a major chain restaurant throughout the country in 1996. Upon, the passing of Mr. Daylin a few years ago, Ms. Daylin became a widow and was left with her husband's business along with his fortune," Ms. Rose's lawyer explains to me, but I am lost to how this affects me. Plus, the fact that Ms. Rose owned Daylin's Restaurant. That place is amazing!

"As you may or may not know, the Daylin's only son was killed twelve years ago on September 11, 2001, in the Twin Towers. Ms. Rose has no other relatives," he explains, and I am bewildered to hear that Ms. Rose had a son, and he died in 9/11! Well, at least, her family is back together which is a great thing. I bet she is so happy up there in Heaven.

"Ms. Jennings, in Ms. Daylin's will, she left you her and her husband's entire fortune. She has it that half a million is to be set aside and be used for you college, a car, college books and everything you need for college. The rest of money was left to you to do as you wish. Ms. Daylin also left the Daylin Restaurant chain under your care. She encouraged me to tell you that the chain will provide a very steady and fulfilling income, but she wanted you to also go to college for your dream job," Mr. Smith explains, and my mouth falls open.

Ms. Rose left me everything. I stare up at the ceiling with tears in my eyes. How could someone be so kind? I can go to college now, for sure! I can pay the bills so mom doesn't have to work so much.

"Are you serious?" my mom asks in shock as she stares at the man that just changed our lives even more.

"Yes, ma'am, I am," he says, and my mom begins crying.

Mr. Smith finishes all the finalizing and signing of papers, and then, he shuts his briefcase, standing up to his 6'5" stature. "It's been nice meeting you all, and I hope you take care of this gift. If you guys ever need anything, you can call me here," he says and hands my mom his card.

"Wait, stay and have a cup of coffee," she offers to him. He pauses for a second contemplating the thought.

"Alright, thank you," he says, sitting down again and setting the briefcase at his side.

"If guys will excuse me, my boyfriend is upstairs, and I should check on him," I say politely as I stand from my seat. "It was nice meeting you, Mr. Smith," I say with a small smile to the man at the table.

"You too," he nods smiling.

I make my way back to my bedroom. As I push open the door, I find Reece lying on top of my crappy mattress that is on the floor. Reece is shirtless, revealing his amazing chest, and his black dress pants are just low enough to reveal his sexy V that leads down to a place that causes the blush to shoot into my cheeks. Rider is asleep at Reece's side, but as I step into the room, his head lifts up looking at me with his cute puppy eyes. "Pay, you back?" my amazing boyfriend asks me.

"Yeah," I respond as I rub my face, walk over to the bed, and lay beside him.

"Who was it?" he asks as he rolls over onto his side facing me. I smile at him as I stare into his heart-reaching blue eyes.

"Ms. Rose's lawyer," I answer him as I roll over onto my side facing him. Rider is asleep behind Reece. Because this bed is a twin, we are actually really closer together.

"What did the lawyer have to say?" Reece wonders and moves one of his hands out towards me. It searches for my hand laying in between us. Once he reaches it, he swiftly intertwines our fingers.

"Apparently, Ms. Rose Daylin was the owner of Daylin Restaurant once her husband passed. Ms. Rose had no family," Reece's face looks shocked yet also like he is trying to make sense of it all. "She left me everything," I finish and Reece smiles.

"That's amazing! Payton, I'm so happy for you!" he exclaims squeezing my hand.

"Yeah, it is! I can't believe it either. I never expected any of this to happen," I explain with a shy smile.

"I couldn't think of anyone who deserves this more than you, Payton," he says with such soft, gentle eyes.

I cannot help but be drawn to him, so instead of saying anything, I lean in and press my lips against his. He is caught off guard at first, not knowing I was about to kiss him, but he catches on very quickly, kissing me back. As our lips form together, and we melt into each other's kisses, I feel myself float into another world. His tongue fights with mine and eventually, wins. I roll over onto my back and pull him with me so that he is leaning over me.

My hands move from his neck to down his back feeling his nice muscles. He's using one arm to hold his weight off of me while his other hand is at the base of my neck. Out kisses become fiercer and more passionate. I move my hands around and run them down his chest, tracing his abs.

Reece's hand travels from my neck down my arm, leaving a trail of fire where his hand touches my skin, to my side to the hem of the hoodie. Gently, his hand barely slips under it and tease my bare stomach. As he shifts his hips, I become surprisingly aware of his "excitement" since I feel it rub against my leg.

His sweet lips leave mine only to leave small kiss from the corner of my mouth up my jaw, to my ear, and then down to my neck, using his lips as the guide. Reece kisses my neck and sucks sending tingles and bombs throughout my body. My breathing picks up as he continues assaulting my neck. I release a light moan as he blows his warm breath on my neck.

Then, he kisses his way back up to my lips, kissing me sweetly with so much love. His hand remains ideal the whole time on my stomach. Reece places a sweet, gentle kiss on my lips, and he pulls away breathing hard, and his warm, sweet breath hits my face.

"I love you," he says sweetly in a husky, sexy voice. Those three words— all it took were those three words to make the moment even amazing. At that moment, we didn't need to do more because that just makes me feel loved by a man, and that is something that I have never had before Reece.

"I love you too," I reply with a smile the size of Texas on my face.

Reece's POV

"Reece," a voice whispers in my ear like a warm breath fans it. "Reece, wake up," the cute voice says again, and I feel a hand squeezing my arm.

Being the non-morning person that I am, I grunt in response and shift around. "Reece, be careful, or you're going—" before the voice could finish what it's saying I roll over and hit the solid ground with a nice *thud*.

My eyes pop open to see the normal abyss of blackness. I let out a large groan as I sit up and rub my head. "Shit! That fucking hurt," I swear as I sit on the floor.

"I tried to warn you," says in an "I-told-you-so" voice, and she giggles a little.

Being the good charmer I am, I raise my left hand up and flip her off. "Sorry, but I don't take offers," she shoots back, and I just roll my eyes.

"Whatever," I grumble, reaching over for the edge of the bed.

"Damn, someone woke up on the wrong side of the bed the morning," Payton comments as I hear her move around.

"That would involve actually waking up on the fucking bed," I grumble irritated.

"Stop being an ass, Reece," she says in a dull tone as if she's scolding a child.

"Why were you waking me up, anyways?" I ask her once I am sitting on the bed again and repeatedly run my hands through my hair.

"Your brother called, says you need to be home in half an hour for practice because tomorrow is the 'big day,'" she informs me, and I grunt. Big day? What is that idiot brother of mine referring? Wait; today is Wednesday… oh shit! Tomorrow is Thursday and is the day I have a tryout with a summer track team. Then, Friday is graduation! How did I fucking forget?

"No," I groan, covering my face with my hands. "I don't want to practice," I complain. I don't want to practice. I won't tell anyone this, but I am scared shitless of tryouts tomorrow. What if I can't do it?

"Reece, honestly, I am fine if you stay. But Conner says if I don't have you there in thirty minutes, he is going to drive here, drag you out of the house by your ear and shove you into the car. Plus, he said that Jace and Carter will be there too," she says, and I hear her light footsteps walk over to me.

"Stupid brother," I mumble.

"Reece, Conner is trying to help. You should be grateful. He is standing by your side and helping you. He could very easily turn his back on you and say fuck you. He has stood by your side and helped you the whole time. Conner is just trying to be a good brother. So cut him some slack," she sighs as she gently runs her hand on my cheek.

"Yeah, I know. You're right. Sorry, I'm just being grumpy," I say with a sigh and run my hands through my hair, tugging lightly at my roots.

"Good," she says as she grabs my hands and places the fabric that feels like my shirt from last night. Then, I feel her soft, delicate lips press against mine. She pulls away, and I place a hand on her cheek.

"Now, put your shirt on. Your shoes are beside your feet. So we can go," she says softly, and I smile. God, I'm lucky to have her.

She steps away, and I take the shirt in my hands and pull it on over my shoulders. Then, from the top, I begin to button it and then bend over, slipping my shoes on. Sitting back up a sigh, I will be practicing today. My stomach shifts and does a flop as I think about tomorrow. Damn, I don't know if I can do it.

"Rider," I call and hear the patter of his feet as he runs over to me. I feel his head rest on my knee, and I shut my eyes to try to stay calm.

"Ready?" Payton asks, and I nod and stand up. Time to go practice, and then tomorrow is my big day. Friday is Payton's big day. I cannot believe this.

I can do this. I can do this, right?

Chapter Sixty-Seven

Reece's POV

Have you ever woken up one morning and realized this is the morning your life changes forever? That depending on how the day goes can change your future whether it's in the way you want it to or not. All it takes is that one moment. The moment that past events have been slowly leading up to, the moment my future will forever be changed. When I woke up this morning, that is all my mind was consumed with the endless possibilities.

Now, here I am sitting at my breakfast table and listening to my family's excited chatter.

"Reece, you are going to do great and make the team!" I hear my mom say excitedly.

I shovel some more food in my mouth, chewing and attempting to keep my overwhelmed nerves at bay. There's just so much pressure building on me. What if I'm truly not good enough anymore and look dumb out there running? Will people make fun of me then? I can imagine the disappointment that would be painted on my dad's face. What about Payton? Will she think I'm useless? Most importantly, what if I fail, can I handle that lost too? Not making the team would just add to another thing I cannot do. I'm unable to see, I'm unable to drive. I'm unable to basically do a lot of things. My girlfriend will have to take care of me forever. Having to be taken care of the rest of your life is awful. You lose your independence. You begin to feel like you are a burden on everyone around. This is my one chance— one thing I can do on my own and show I'm independent and doing what I love. There is also the pressure of those who look up to me. Those who see me as an inspiration and admire me because today if I fail and don't make the team I show them exactly what they've always believed— that we are different and unequal.

"Is Reece gonna run again?" my sweet, little Rayne asks in her adorable voice. No matter how long I've been blind, I still find an incredible desire to want and see her sweet face along with the rest of my families and Payton.

"Yeah, he's going to run again, Rayne," Conner says happily, and I can hear the proudness that is seeping through in his voice.

No pressure at all... *not.* I swear it's as if someone is laying all this pressure on you and then says "no pressure." Yet, somehow, there is always pressure!

My thoughts are interrupted by the sound of the doorbell ringing.

"I'll get it," Juliet's voice rings, and I hear the sound of a chair scraping against the hardwood floor, then the sound of retreating footsteps.

"What time is it?" Conner asks. I'm not sure whom he's talking to because I cannot see what way he is looking.

"Nine o'clock," my father replies in his casual, calm tone.

I have to be at my tryouts at eleven, and it's a thirty-minute drive to where the summer league is. So I have to be ready and leave here at ten fifteen at the latest. With this realization, I pick up the speed of how fast I eat.

As I stuff my face with food, I can hear the advancing footsteps. "Good morning, guys," the beautiful, angelic voice of Payton greets.

I hear footsteps near me as I take my last bite realize when my utensil does not bump into any more food. "Morning, sweetie," her soft voice says in my ear before I feel her soft lips press against my gruff cheek.

"Morning, angel," I reply with a smile. My nerves seem to shrink away as I am with Payton. "I need to go get ready," I say randomly.

"I'm still eating. Payton can do it," Conner says, and I can imagine him with a fork hovering outside his mouth.

"Um... Alright then, come on, Reece," Payton says, grabs my hand as I slide back and stands up.

"Let's go then," I say with a big smile. She leads me away to what I believe is my room.

"What do you need to wear for tryouts?" Payton voices ask by my side.

I really don't need her to get them for me, but then again, she can get them quicker. I release a sigh as I roll my eyes. "There should be a pair of blue track shorts in my dresser," I groan, and her hand slips from mine. I hear her walk away, then the sound of wood scraping against wood.

"Hmm... uh... ah," she makes noises as I guess she searches my drawers. And by that I mean my dresser drawers. "I found them!" she boosts in enthusiasm. "What about a shirt?" she adds, as she places the shorts into my hands.

"Just get me a zip hoodie from my closet," I tell her. I hear her walk away again and the closet door open.

Pulling my t-shirt off with one hand and tossing it to the floor, I then slip off my sweat pants. Running my hands around the band of the shorts, searching for the tag. Once I find it, I know how to put them on.

"Holy crap, Reece. That was fast!" Payton gasps. I cannot help the chuckle that escapes me.

"Did you get a hoodie?" I ask as I push a hand through my brown hair.

"Y-yeah, here you go," she says, stuttering slightly as I can hear her near me. Then, place the coat into my hands.

Laughing lightly, I take the zip hoodie in my hands and pull it on over my shoulders. "Are you checking me out? I cannot see, but I can just get this feeling that you are," I tell her with a teasing smirk. I was joking about feeling her eyes on me. It's like when you are in the dark but can sense someone looking at you or being near you. Plus, the tone of her voice and her stutter made me think so as well.

"What? No, of course not," she quickly denies, causing me to chuckle. I reach out my arm in search of her, and I finally connect with her warm body. I move my hand around until it rests on her hip.

"Aww, you are. I bet you're blushing and look so beautiful," I say with a husky voice as I step closer to her.

"Shut up," she grumbles and hits my shoulder lightly. Trailing my free hand up her arm and over her shoulder to her chin, I tilt it up.

"It's okay, Angel, this is all yours. You can stare all you want," I say in a light tone smiling down at my beautiful girlfriend.

Payton remains silent, and I can hear her heart beating fast and her breathing increasing. I lead my hand to her cheek and gently stroke it. Leaning into where my hand is, and I press my lips to her. Our lips move in sync. The kiss quickly heats up, and I begin to become very excited.

"Hey, guys you ready to— Whoa," Conner's voice says as I can hear him at where it sounds to be the doorway. Payton and I quickly part. *Talk about awkward.*

"I'm Coach King. It's nice to meet you, Reece," the man who will decide my future says as I stand in front of him. Rider is already attached to my waist.

This summer track team is in the city, just outside our town. It's about an hour drive away.

"It's nice to meet you too, sir," I say as I extend out in front of me. I feel his strong, rough hand grasp mine shaking it.

"So are you ready to show me what you got?" the man asks in his gruff voice. I imagine him being a big, muscled man wearing a track suit and a mustache, kind of the most cliché coach ever.

"Yes, sir," I confirm, nodding my head.

"Good luck, son. You can do this!" my mom says and kisses my cheek.

"Run fast, Reece," Rayne's sweet voice says next, and I smile.

"Good luck, bubby," Juliet adds, hugs me, and I recognize her familiar scented.

"Good luck, son. We know you can do this and no matter what, Reece, we are so proud of you," my dad says, resting his hand on my shoulder. It makes me feel so happy and glad to hear that.

"You can do this, Reece. No matter what, we are all so proud of you. You are amazing. I love you no matter what," Pay's gentle, sweet voice says, and I smile. She kisses my lips lightly causing sparks and heat to shoot through me. Unzipping my hoodie, I take it off reaching it out to Payton.

"I love you too, Angel," I say as she takes the hoodie from my hand.

"Alright, Reece. It's time," Conner says as he rests his hand on my right shoulder. He walks me over to what I am guessing is my starting point. "You're on the inside lane. The track is set up just like the one you are used to. You can do this, I promise you. Rider is right beside you. Now, show them what you got, bro," Conner encourages as he slaps my bare back, and I nod my head.

"Alright, Rider. It's our time boy. We can do this. Just like how we normally do, it's just me, you and running," I say to Rider but more to myself. Crouching down, I get in the running stance.

"Alright, ready," the Coach calls. "Set," here we go. God, please let me succeed. "Go!" as the word escapes the coach's mouth I push off and run. My eyes shut and my arms pumping at my side. I push myself running hard and faster. My body feels fine as I pick up speed and go faster. I round the last turn my energy still completely fine, and I feel so at peace and at home. Knowing the last stretch is ahead of me, I push myself, and I push myself hard. Using my mind, I will my legs to move faster and faster.

"Time!" Coach calls, and I come to a halt. Bending over slightly, I grasp my knees, panting lightly and just trying to gain my breath.

"Dang, kid, you have a talent. I'm seriously impressed," Coach King says. "This will be hard and difficult. You will face struggle and have to overcome anything that faces you, which I have no doubt that you will. But you did it, kid. You're on the team," the coach finishes, and I am honestly thrilled. I did it! I succeeded! I made it! The biggest grin was on my face. Finally, I have a piece of my old self back.

Payton's POV

"Juliet, Georgia, mom, I told you, guys, I just wanted a plain and simple dress to go beneath my graduation gown," I fuss at the women. We are all in Georgia dressing room, getting ready for my big day. Yesterday was Reece's big day, and he did amazing and made the team. We were all so proud of him. I never saw him run so fast. It was just an amazing moment.

Juliet holds up a mid-thigh length, hot pink strapless dress. I frantically begin to shake my head. Juliet is in a dark blue strapless dress. Her blonde hair is down in curls, and her makeup is lightly done.

Georgia is in a knee-length turquoise dress with small sleeves. Her blonde hair is up in a neat bun. My mom is wearing a gray knee-length dress that has thin straps. Her dark brown hair is in curls over her shoulders.

"Fine," Juliet groans, tossing that dress to the side. Georgia looks around at the dresses in search of one that I'll approve of. I've already vetoed a million dresses.

"How about this one?" Georgia asks me as she holds up a beautiful, simple, white, just above the knee dress that has about two-inch straps. I smile.

"I like it," I conclude, and they all let out a sigh.

"Praise the Lord!" Juliet cheers, sitting down on a leather stool.

"Take off your shirt and shorts to put it on," my mom instructs, folding her arms over her chest with a stern look on her face since she knew that I would try to object.

Groaning, I tug the shirt over my head, revealing my white, lace bra and then slipping off my shorts and showing my white lace underwear. I shift uncomfortably, standing in front of them. Georgia walks forward, slipping the dress over my head and then zipping up the back. The top of the dress hugs me and fits my body while the bottom flares out.

"Go sit in the chair," Juliet instructs as she stands up and points to Georgia's makeup chair that is in front of a vanity.

"Yes, ma'am," I mock as I salute her and march over to the chair, slumping in it.

I see Juliet roll her eyes in the mirror, causing me to smile. She walks to me, followed by Georgia. "Juliet, you do her makeup. Georgia, you can do the hair, and I will search for her some shoes and accessories," my mom says with a smile, and they nod.

Georgia begins pulling a brush through my hair. Juliet grabs some makeup and begins work on my face. "So is your speech ready?" Georgia asks as she grabs the curling iron to work on my hair.

"I hope so, Mom. She has to do it today," Juliet replies sarcastically. She begins smearing a cool feeling liquid on my face.

"Oh hush, Juliet," Georgia gripes at her daughter while curling my hair.

"Actually, I have it complete. I'm really nervous to say it, though," I explain nervously twisting my hands in my lap. Juliet rubs my face.

"You will do amazing," Georgia tells me and I smile. I can hear my mom shuffling through the shoes.

Georgia works had at my hair pulling it back, and Juliet works hard on my face. "Done," they both say just as my mom shouts, "Got it!"

My mother rushes over with a pair of white heels in her hands. She slips them on my feet and stands up, placing her hands on her hips with a satisfied smile. "Alright, look in the mirror," Juliet says excitedly. Standing up, I walk to the full-length mirror slowly because of the heels.

My jaw drops in shock as I stare at my reflection. Is this really me? I wonder as I raise my hand up to my beautiful blemish free face. My brown eyes pop out, and my brown hair is up in a curly bun with curled pieces at the front framing my face. This is who I've become. The dress fits me perfectly. My stomach does flip as the nerves set in. Can I do this? Will my speech go okay? Can I face my fear of speaking in front of people? God, please just don't let me throw up.

Chapter Sixty-Eight

Payton's POV

Walking slowly down the steps with my gown over one arm, the cap, and my speech in my hand, I make my way to the front door where everyone is waiting. At the foot of the stair is my mom in her nice dress, standing beside Juliet. At Juliet's side is Rayne who is wearing a cute blue dress with her hair up in a bow. Conner is standing beside his sisters and wearing a black tux with his blond hair nicely jelled back. Carter is beside Conner in a black suit, and his hair is neatly styled. Reece's parents are standing at the end with one arm around each other. Reece's dad is wearing a nice Armani suit, and his brown hair is neatly brushed atop his head.

My eyes then fall on the one who causes me to smile, Reece. He stands in front of all them casually looking around as if trying to locate which way I am entering. He is wearing a pair of black slacks and a navy blue button-down shirt.

Reece's brown hair has been cut a little shorter, and his sparkling blue eyes are glowing. His face is nice clean shaved. He looks absolutely gorgeous. His cap and gown are over his arm as well.

I reach the bottom and walk towards him. His head snaps in my direction as he hears my feet approach. "You look great," I say as I stop right in front of him and reach out my free hand for his.

Reece smiles his big, bright, white smile. "I'm sure you look absolutely stunning because you are the most beautiful girl in the world," he says and squeezes my hand causing me to smile.

"Aww, you, two, are too cute," my mom coos, and Georgia joins her. My cheeks heat up as the blush covers them.

"Hush, can we leave now?" I request, looking at the older women. Then, my mom draws a stupid camera from her purse.

"Not yet! First, we got to take some pictures," she says, raising up the camera to her face and snapping a picture. The bright light from the flashes and causes me to blink my eyes as I attempt to get rid of the bright circles in my eyes. Reece manages to wrap his arm around my face, smiling down at me.

"What?" I snap, elbowing his side.

"I heard your mom say pictures, so I'm posing," he replies and shrugs his shoulders.

"But I hate pictures," I groan with a pouty face even though he cannot see it.

"Oh well, do it for your mom. You're beautiful, and no matter what, you'll look amazing," he says, gently giving me a cheeky smile. I feel tears swell in my eyes at how sweet my boyfriend is.

"Fine," I groan, giving up the fight because I can never win one against Reece. Turning to the camera, I muster up my biggest, *fakest* smile for it. My mom snaps all kinds of pictures.

"Payton, move a little. Come on, do something cute," Georgia encourages, causing me to groan.

Reece chuckles a little at my side, causing me to jab him with my elbow. He grunts in pain. "Abusive," he scolds. Even though, I know that he cannot see I still roll my eyes.

"Don't be a baby," I reply then I stand on my tip toes and smiles as I kiss his cheek.

"Aww," my mom and Georgia coo. My cheeks burn as blood pumps to them once I settle back on my heels.

"Guys, we need to go, or they'll be late," Conner says, and I watch my mom heave out a sigh as she lowers her camera and places it back inside her purse.

"Okay, well, Reece, Payton, Carter, and Juliet will be in a car with Conner. Rayne and June will be in a car with us," Georgia instructs with gestures of her hand.

"Yes, ma'am," Conner salutes, and we all walk outside to the two vehicles in front of us. One is a large Chevy truck, I recognize as Conner's, parked idly. In front of it is a new blue Ford Focus.

Our parents head over to the Ford, climbing inside with Rayne at their side. I hold onto Reece's hand as we walk over to the truck behind Conner, Juliet, and Carter. Conner swings the driver's door open, and Carter gets on the passenger side.

The bright, early summer sun is beating down on our skin as it begins lower in the sky. Breathing in the fresh air, I try to relax my increasing nervousness that fills my tummy. Juliet opens the back door and slides inside. I help Reece get in, so he can sit in the middle. Laying his walking stick at our feet, I climb inside and shut the truck door behind me. Watching carefully, I see Reece fiddle around finding his seat belt and pulling it over his chest to buckle it. I smile at his independence and buckle my belt.

Conner pulls the truck to the road, and I slip my hand on Reece's lap, intertwining my finger with his as I rest my head onto his shoulder. "I'm so nervous," I whisper softly so that only Reece can hear me.

"Don't be. You will do amazing, Angel," he replies softly to me, causing me to sigh before lightly smiling.

Shifting uncomfortably on stage in front of my whole class and all their friends and family, I try to remain calm and not to make it look like I'm nervous. But I am so nervous. I am freaking out inside! I cross one leg over the over and fold my hands in my lap as I am seated uncomfortably in my graduation gown on a chair. On stage, the teachers and administrators sit on chairs along with the valedictorian.

I nervously twist my hands together as I grow impatient for my speech. What if I trip and fall when I'm walking to the podium? What if I stutter? What if I freeze? What if I throw up? What if I cry? What if—?

"And now, I am proud to introduce to you the 2013-2014 Washington High Valedictorian, Miss Payton Jennings," the principal says as he steps away and gestures for me. The crowd begins to cheer.

I swallow and take a deep breath, trying to calm my breathing. *Breathe in, breathe out*, I coach myself as I get up and approach the podium. I shake the principal's hands before turning to the podium and laying my notes out on top of it. Staring out at the crowd, I see many faces looking at me. My nerves become a whole new level of bad.

I clear my throat, and my eyes fall down onto the paper sitting in front of me. "Good evening friends, family, and honorable guests. Today's a day that we will remember for the rest of our lives, so thank you for sharing it with us. Most of you do not know who I am and those who do know me as the girl dating a blind boy. Earlier this year, our lives changed altogether. A fellow student who was struggling in life came in and opened fire in our halls. Reece Collins was shot blinded. After that, his friends turned their backs on him. This large moment of our lives dramatically changed mine and taught me many lessons. I was brought to Reece, and together, we learned to face both of our struggles. I learned not everything is what it seems and never judge anyone because we are all equals. I learned to accept myself and who I am. I've come to be in terms with my past, seeing that if it weren't for what I've been through, I wouldn't be who I am. Many times when we were young, someone would ask us what we wanted to be, and most of the time our answers were unrealistic. Over the years, our answers became more real and reflected our personalities. I was never sure and never thought that I could become who I am today. I never thought I could possibly be standing in front of you. Not because I didn't think I was smart enough, but because of the fear of standing in front of a crowd, knowing some may be judging you. This year, though, I learned a major lesson from two people in my life who have been close to death. As I watched Reece make the hard choice to face his fears of failure and run again for all of those who can't, my fears seemed obsolete. Even when Reece walked for the first time, he faced his fear of looking stupid and hitting something. Even though he got knocked to the ground, he got right back up. He never let fear keep him down. He never let his struggles and issues get the best of him. There were many times that he almost did; when he wanted to give up. Many of you do not know this, but Reece faced his biggest fear was when he came back to school since the shooting. He was terrified, but he did it, and he kept coming to school.

"Now, none of you may know this, but a few years ago, my sister was diagnosed with Leukemia. She was just a little girl. But as a little girl, she had to face something some people never do in their lifetime. That is the pain, fear, and ache of dying, and not just dying but dying without living. However, she never lost faith. It weathered a little, but she stayed strong. She never let the fear of dying wear on her. She remained happy. She never let the fear of chemo and losing her hair keep her down or make her sad. Instead, she faced them head on. She stayed strong. Maybe facing these fears and fighting for her life is what is keeping her alive.

"Because of these to people, I had to look at myself and think how silly I was to have fears like I do and be too cowardly to face them. I learned to face my fears head on and not hide in a corner. This can be applied to all of our futures. As we leave this safety and security of high school and our homes, we enter a whole new world on our own. It will be filled with fears we may have or face us with new challenges, but we have to face them. Don't let it stop you from doing what you want. The only thing to fear is fear itself. So face your fears and live for tomorrow. Know that no matter what you're going through, you're not alone. No matter what, remain true to yourself. So, class of 2014, I challenge you to live your life. Do not let fear get in your way. Go out and conquer your dreams!" I finish with tears falling down my face.

The whole crowd leaps to their feet in front of me, cheering. I smile brightly at all their faces as I reach up and wipe away some tears. Releasing a deep breath, I turn around and walk back to my seat, allowing the ceremony to continue.

As graduation continues, they begin handing out the diplomas. The principle calls the next name, "Reece Collins." I watch from the stage as Reece stands up and uses his cane to guide him to the stage. As he walks across to receive his diploma, the crowd roars in applause, and I cry watching him succeed.

There is truly nothing in the world that can stop us.

Two Weeks Later

Sitting on the metal bleachers in a pair of short, jean shorts and a blue spaghetti strap top with Converse and my hair pulled back into a ponytail, I stare out at the football field. Next to me are Juliet and Jace, whose hands gently wrapped around her. Carter sits alongside them.

Sitting to my right is Georgia while beside her is Leonardo. On his knee is Rayne with a great big smile in a flowery summer dress.

I look out at the field, and my eyes finally find what they were searching for. Reece is standing on the field in his cute track uniform with Rider at his side wearing a bandana that says "Guide Dog." Conner is standing with Reece, talking to him and helping him.

The sky is fair, clouds occasionally blocking out the sun. The field is cover with different track teams waiting for the event.

"Runners for the half-a-mile race report to the starting line," the announcer's voice booms over the speaker.

Conner leads Reece and Rider over to the starting line onto the inside lane. The runners get into their positions on the starting line. I watch as Conner walks away. Georgia reaches over and grabs my hand, squeezing it. Huge butterflies are flying in my stomach as we wait for the shot to fire. The stadium suddenly seems to be dead silent with anticipation. Then the silence is shattered by the sound of the gunfire, and the runners are off. Reece is running just like he always does, looking just like the rest of them. Rider runs at his side.

Reece is the fifth person back, and they finish their first lap. As they near their last lap Reece is still running in the same position. Then it is suddenly as if he was struck by a burst of energy. Reece pushes himself, and his legs pick up speed, passing the four in front of him. Leaping from our seat, we begin to cheer as he takes the lead and nears the finish line. We go crazy as we watch him break the red ribbon at the finish line.

"The winner of this race is Reece Collins!" the announcer announces over the speaker and Reece comes to a stop. I left the bleachers and through the gate onto the track.

"Reece!" I scream, and his head snaps my direction with tears falling from his eyes.

Running over to him, I leap into his arms and throw my arms around his neck to hug him. "You did it!" I tell him as I look down into his beautiful blue eyes.

"I can't believe it," he murmurs as more tears roll down his face. I don't care that he's drenched in sweat I don't care about anything, but this amazing man who is holding me.

I lean down, pressing my lips to his. "I love you," I say against his lips as I kiss him. We melt into the kiss, and I know that we are going to last forever.

"I love you too, Angel," he replies pulling back from the kiss and just hugging me.

Life isn't always fair. Life will give you struggles just to see how you can handle it. Life does not always go the way we want it. But as long as you make the best out of what you are given, your story will have a happy ending; even fairy tales have struggles. No matter what happens, God has a reason for it. When you are facing a hard time, remember that you are not alone. There is someone out there going through the same circumstances as you do. The next time you pity yourself and think that you are going through the toughest thing, remember that there is someone in the world who has it worse than you. Always remind yourself of the thing you have and use your struggles and issues to make you into a better, stronger person. Reece didn't get his sight back. Not everyone can get back what they lost, and it just makes them stronger. Never judge someone because they don't have something that you do. Count yourself lucky that you even have it. Just because someone doesn't have their sight, hearing, legs or anything, doesn't make them any less of a person than you are. They can still be independent. So next time you see someone like this, stop for a second and remember this before you judge them. Life always has a way of working out. It may not be as you planned it. But in the end, everything will make sense and work out for the best.

When you feel down, remember "Love is Blind;" it does not judge, and it does not see flaws, looks, disabilities. Love sees none of that, just the person within. And in life, that is what truly matters— who you are on the inside especially when you are faced with struggles.

Epilogue

Payton's POV

Ten years later

"Mommy, mommy," calls a little voice as I walk into the house. I set my briefcase down on the table beside the door and slip off my black heels. As I walk through the house to where the laughter and calls are coming from, I take off my black suit jacket, leaving me in just a white button-down and black skirt. Entering the living room, I find a blond-haired man sitting on the couch and laughing as he tickles the little, brown-haired girl's belly. A little boy with brown hair is climbing over the back of the couch like a wild man. Another boy with black hair is sitting on the recliner with a book while a baby girl crawls around the floor.

The brown hair boy looks up at me with his hazel eyes and smiles a toothy grin. "Mommy!" he shouts as he speeds over to me.

He wraps his arms around my legs, and he comes up to just below my hip. "Hey. Ander," I say as I lean down scooping my four-year-old up in my arms. I place a light kiss on his cheek. "Were you a good boy today?" I ask him with a smile as I sit him down.

"Of course," he says in his cute little voice. I laugh as I mess up his hair. He quickly runs back over to the couch leaping on it.

I round the couch only to have the little brown-haired girl leap at me from the guy's lap. Luckily, I catch the little brown hair, blue-eyed beauty. "Mommy, you're home," she says as she hugs me.

"Hi, Gardenia," I say softly as I hug my beautiful five-year-old daughter. "Were the boys good today?" I ask with a kidding smile. She scrunches up her face and shakes her head.

"I didn't think so," I reply as I sit her down. I look at the blond-haired guy with his green eyes and smile at him.

"Hey," I say before holding up one finger to say one second as I walk over to where the black-haired boy sits.

"Barrett," I say as he looks up at me with the lopsided smile like his dad's and stares at me with his blue eyes.

"Hey, mom," he says, looking back at his book. God, that kid got my personality; always has his nose in a book. For a seven-year-old, he is way too smart. Barrett is seven. I had him when I was twenty-one. I never truly meant for Barrett to happen even though I was married because I wanted to stay in college and wait till I was done to have kids. That worked out real well. I am so glad I have Barrett, and I was able to finish college and then went to law school which I completed.

With a smile, I walk over to the little one crawling around, scooping her up in my arms. Grace is two years old and has light brown hair and brown eyes, and she is so adorable. I hold her in my arms as the guy stands up.

"Were they good?" I ask him with a knowing smile. They are a handful all the time.

"Of course, they were, Payton," he says with a laugh. "I should head home, though," he yawns, picking his coat up off the back the couch.

"Way past your bedtime, old man?" I joke, making fun of him for being thirty-one now.

"No, I want to get home in time for my wife's cooking. But watch those old jokes, you're not that far away," he says pulling on his coat. I just laugh and shake my head.

"Alright, thank you, Conner, for watching the kids today," I say to him as I lean up kissing his cheek.

"It's no biggy. They're my practice for the one I have on the way," he says with a smile, and I laugh.

"Good point. Bye now. Tell Pen I said hi," I say as I walk with him to the door

"Will do, bye. Have fun with the kids," he jokes, and I roll my eyes as I hold Grace in my arms. The door shuts, and Conner is gone. I walk back into the living room and place Grace in her playpen.

Ander and Gardenia are on the couch, laughing as Rider has appeared and is now licking their faces. I laugh a little at them. "What do you, kids, want for dinner?" I ask, looking around at the messy living room covered with little kid toys and clothes.

"Mac and cheese!" Ander and Gardenia cheer with excitement.

"Mashed potatoes and gravy," Barrett answers and returns to his book. I nod and make my way to the kitchen.

As I complete dinner, I hear the front door open. "Daddy!" the two loud ones cheer, and I laugh as Barrett appears in the kitchen.

"Mom, do you need help?" he asks politely, setting his book on the counter.

"Yes, can you please set the table?" I ask him, and he nods, grabbing the dishes and silverware and carrying them to the dining room.

"Honey, I'm home," my husband's sweet voice carries through the house. I turn around to see him enter the kitchen. He takes off his black sunglasses, revealing his bright blue eyes, and his brown hair is cut short. He is wearing a t-shirt and shorts looking very casual and hot. I smile at him and see Ella, his new guide dog, at his side.

"Hey Reece," I say softly as I turn around, flipping the stove off and walk over to Reece, wrapping my arms around his neck.

"Angel," he says softly kissing my lips. "How was your case today?" he asks, and I shrug my shoulders.

"Okay, I guess. How was your day?" I ask.

"Good, got to help some kids," he says, and I smile kissing his lips. Reece is now a psychologist who works with kids going through tough spots and injuries.

"That's great, sweetie," I coo as I turn around and walk back to the stove.

"Daddy," I hear Ander say, and I turn back to see Reece pick Ander up. The two look a lot alike. I cannot help but smile.

Barrett returns to the kitchen. "Hey, dad," he says, looking at Reece.

"Hey, Barrett buddy," Reece's voice says, but he doesn't look exactly at his direction.

"The table's set," Barrett informs me with his normal gentle tone.

"Okay, you can get Gardenia and Grace to the table," I tell him, and he just nods. I begin to carry the dinner dishes into the dining room and set them on the table.

Gardenia comes running in and hopping into her seat. Barrett walks in, carrying Grace in his arms and places her into her booster seat. Ander runs into the dining room and takes the seat beside Gardenia. Reece walks in using his stick, finding his way to the end of the table. He sits down in the seat. I take my seat at the other end of the table.

"Reece, say grace," I say as my family bows our heads.

"Dear Heavenly Father, we thank you for this food and the roof above our heads. Thank you for keeping us all together. Thank you for blessing us with these four beautiful kids. Bless our food and hearts. Keep a watchful eye over my family as we go throughout our lives. Amen," Reece says, and we all say amen too.

"Dig in," I say with a smile. Barrett is sitting closest to his father and helps Reece get his plate, which is a usual routine. We never asked Barrett to help. He offered, and it filled our hearts with joy.

"Night, Grace," I say as I lay my baby girl in her crib. Reece wraps his arm around my waist from behind and kisses my cheek. I just smile as I turn my head meeting his lips with mine. Sparks shot through me like the fourth of July; the feeling never grows old.

"We love you," Reece and I say to Grace like our normal routine. Taking Reece's hand, we walk to the next room to put the next kid to sleep.

Our house is a large single story home covered with Braille and easily maneuvered for Reece. The home's set up allows Reece to be more independent than he would be in any other home.

Reece and I enter Gardenia's room which is a light purple color with a flower painted on the wall, a princess bed and toys everywhere. She is already lying in her bed, waiting to be tucked. We walk over, smiling at her. I lean over to tuck her in and then kiss her forehead. Stepping back, I watch as Reece leans down kissing her too. "I love you, princess," Reece whispers to her, and I smile. He is absolutely the best husband and father I could ask. Gardenia already has him wrapped around her little figure, and I know that it won't be before long that Grace will too.

With Gardenia asleep, we move to Ander's room next to tuck him in and lastly, Barrett's room to say good night.

Barrett told us a couple years ago that he didn't want to be tucked in anymore, saying he was a "big boy now."

Reece wraps his strong protective arm around my shoulder as I lead us to the den, so we can sit down and unwind. As we settle onto the leather couch, the doorbell rings. "I got it." I sigh, getting up and walking to the door with the two Golden Retrievers running to the door.

I pull the door open. On the other side stands my beautiful sister. Her face is thin and delicate, and her brown eyes are sparkling. Her skin is still a pale color due to her treatments in the past. She smiles at me.

"Hey, Pay!" she says happily, stepping inside and hugging me. I hug my sister back tightly too.

Lila had rough spots over the years after beating cancer. There were little scars coming back and some sickness. She pushed through it all, though.

"Hey, Lila, how'd the yearly checkup go?" I ask, letting her inside.

"Great, I am still cancer-free," she says.

"That's great!" I tell her and lead us to the den. "You can crash here tonight if you want," I tell her as we sat on the couch. I cuddle close to my husband.

"Alright, I will," she says, and I flip on the TV. I smile as I sit in my home with my children sleeping in their room; my sister is with us, and my wonderful husband at my side.

My life is not perfect. My relationship is not perfect. We have our fights and disagreements, but we always get through it. I would not wish for a better life.

In the end, everything does truly happen for a reason. Reece being shot brought him to me. Reece coming into my life helped me and made me a better person. Everything had a ripple effect and changed my life forever. Always be proud of who you are as Reece was. Always remember love is blind.

Can't get enough of Payton and Reece?
Make sure you sign up for the author's blog
to find out more about them!

Get these two bonus chapters and
more freebies when you sign up at
tara-declan.awesomeauthors.org!

Here is a sample from another story you may enjoy:

A UNIQUE KIND OF
LOVE

JASMINE ROSE

Prologue

Two light grocery bags in hand, she followed her dad to the bright, white family car that caused them many troubles as they struggled to find it in the middle of snow. The girl opened the front seat door and slipped inside the car, completely oblivious to the look her father was giving her.

He sighed. "Lena?" The girl froze because he never called her by her actual name, unless he was serious about something. He always called her Rosie. "We talked about this. On the way here, you'd sit in front. On the way back, you'll sit behind me."

"Daaad! Please?" Lena pouted and widened her eyes a little. He shook his head and pointed to the back seat. He refused to give in to her, not again. Lena groaned and held out a hand to her dad. He took it and supported her waist as she moved to the backseat. She huffed and put on her seat belt.

"Happy?" she asked.

He gave her a smile. "That's my girl."

The car ride was silent, until her dad put a CD in and played it. Lena grinned and sat up immediately. At the first notes of the song, she made jazz hands. Her ponytail swung as she swayed in her seat to the music.

"Love, love me do. You know, I love you. I'll always be true," they both sang loudly. The Beatles had always been their favorite band, even though Lena's mom didn't like them much.

"I love you, Dad!" cried out the girl, her chestnut-colored eyes shining in exhilaration and excitement.

Her father laughed. "You know I love you too, Rosie."

The next seconds were a blur. Between the music, their singing and the momentary happiness, there was a truck that had passed the red light and was heading towards them. Time froze—this was the moment that would turn the girl's life upside down.

Lena turned just in time to see the truck inches away from colliding with the car. Her dad noticed as well, and his eyes widened. She screamed. The car lurched and Lena was thrown forward violently, the seatbelt biting into her stomach and knocking the wind out of her. The sound of her dad calling out her name was the last thing she heard before the world faded away from her.

"Rosie!"

I could hear a vague sound in the background.

I felt myself crying. For a long moment my upper eyelid seemed glued to the lower one, because I couldn't open my eyes. When I finally could, they hurt from my tears.

My gaze settled on Mom's terrified expression, and I watched as her face slowly softened with relief. She wiped the tears on my cheeks, although that didn't stop them from falling again.

She patted my hand. "Was it a bad dream, honey?" she asked. I took deep breaths to steady myself. I nodded.

"I wish I turned earlier, so I could—I don't know," I whispered, watching as the invisible switch clicked in my mom's mind.

"I wish he was here," she said.

Me too, Mom, I thought. I miss him too. How often had I wished that he was still alive, and that I was the one who had died?

I closed my eyes again and felt myself drift away into another dream.

1

Wonder and Anxiety

"The best is yet to be."
~Robert Browning~

Lena Rose Winter

Sighing, I laid my head down on the unshaven grass. I smiled. Stars glimmered and gleamed at me, assisting the moon's job to light up the sky at night. It seemed to me that there was a snowfall sparkling in outer space and I felt privileged to witness it. With soft, soothing music blasting in my ears, I felt better than I had in a long time. Comfort was something I cherished more than anything. I could feel a slight breeze blow on my neck; it cooled the few beads of sweat that had formed earlier that night.

Mom and I had decided to do a Welcome to the New Home barbecue. We'd eaten until our stomachs were begging for a break. It was always a moment that embellished my relationship with her. She went to sleep about an hour ago, the wine easing the process. So I'd been lying here for what, an hour or two? In those moments, I witnessed the sun disappearing and permitting the moon to rise in the sky; it was a never ending cycle.

Except, of course, for people who lived in the North Pole.

I had come close enough once, though. A few years ago, when I was twelve, Mom's company gave her a post somewhere in Alberta, Canada. We lived there only for about two months, but my, oh my, we had gone there in the middle of January. I still recall fearing that my toes were going to fall off because I couldn't feel them.

Thank God that this time, we moved into a place that wasn't too horribly cold, hopefully. Albany, NY seemed like a pretty cool place so far. I took a walk around yesterday and there was a gigantic park, Ridgefield, where I was sure to spend more time throughout the year. Myrtle Avenue was a considerably calm street and I was content about the small house we rented for the year. Since it was senior year, Mom promised that we could stay here long enough so I could finish my year and do all of the senior celebrations.

I was never one to fear new beginnings, considering this was the seventh home I lived in. In the span of four years, I had gone to seven different schools, met different kinds of people, and lived in unique types of houses. I was aware of what was waiting for me tomorrow.

Pressure.

Questions would be asked and answers would have to be given. I'd have to walk away from the spotlight and fade away from the minds of students who loved the "new girl." I would go back into the turtle shell I built myself.

A particular star in the sky winked at me and it got me thinking about Dad.

I often wondered why life could be so fair, yet cruel. Growing up without a father for the past seven years was hard. I saw my mother cry on his birthdays and, of course, I also carried around the memory of my fellow 4th grade 'friends' practically engraving the idea that I murdered my dad in my mind. Mom often said that I wasn't to blame, that it was his fate to die. Still, it wasn't something anyone can just forget.

A shooting star shot through the sky, and I closed my eyes.

I wish that this year brings me happiness, I thought.

♥♥♥♥♥

I forced a big smile as I looked at myself in the mirror, my reflection looking ecstatic. Letting go of the strain I was feeling, my lips fell back into a straight line. I gave the rest of my features a cursory look. My long, dull chestnut brown hair flowed to my waist, and not even the sunlight hitting it could make it appear any more special than it was.

I wrapped a silver bracelet around my wrist. "Let's do this," I murmured.

"LENA! YOU'RE GOING TO BE LATE!" called Mom, disturbing the moment of peace I was having and making me jump in fright. I shook my head, chuckling absent-mindedly.

You'd think that after 17 years of living with her, I would've gotten used to her yelling that I was going to be late—which I never was—but I could swear that her screaming gets louder every time. I slipped my comfy, soft jean jacket on and hopped down the stairs.

I placed a kiss on her forehead. "Good morning," I said.

I mentally pinched my nose as I did so; I hated the smell of coffee. Mom gave me a small smile, sipping on her black, steaming drink. Her onyx black hair was in an elegant bun and she was in her business clothes, which meant that she was going to work.

"Good morning, sweetheart," she said, checking something on her phone. She looked up at me and gave me a small smile. "You ready?"

I nodded, pouring myself a cup of apple juice.

"Oh, I just remembered," said my mom, lifting her eyes from the magazine. "One of my co-workers' daughter goes to this school. Look for her. Stacy Hennings. Okay?" I noticed the familiar kindness and worry in her gaze. Noticing my absence of response, she prodded, "Okay, Lena?"

I rolled my eyes. Mom always had a fear of me being friendless. But what she didn't understand was that sometimes, I wanted to be alone. I'd gladly choose re-reading Looking for Alaska on a Saturday night than partying with a bunch of stuck-up teenagers. I was just that kind of person.

Saluting like a soldier, I replied. "Yes, mother." She looked at me, raising an eyebrow.

"What?" I exclaimed, feeling self-conscious all of a sudden. She walked over to me and stuffed a waffle in my mouth.

I immediately removed the oversized waffle from my mouth and glared at her, both of us extremely amused.

"I was just wondering what I've ever done to deserve a daughter like you." She winked, poking my nose.

I folded my arms over my chest and pouted. "Is that a compliment or an insult?"

"A little bit of both," she answered, putting her now empty cup in the sink. She pointed at it and I nodded.

"Hey! And I'll do them, I know."

After a few minutes of the daily teasing and fighting, I walked out the door, blowing her a kiss.

"Love you!" I exclaimed, taking a red apple and walking to our front door.

"Take care! Watch out for cars and don't forget to smile and be happy!" shouted Mom. I closed the door behind me and took a deep breath. I felt a smile appear on my face, making me feel just a little bit better.

Sure, it was autumn, but the weather was extraordinary. The sun was out, perfectly shining, but there was a breeze cooling the slight heat. The leaves of the trees surrounding my neighborhood were red, orange, and yellow, making the view breathtaking. I wished I had my camera to capture this moment. My dream has always been to become a photographer, to save every moment of every sunrise, sunset and every scene that takes my breath away.

I began my route to my new school, Albany High School. During the summer, I had walked by the school so many times—I knew the way by heart. I plugged my earphones on and put them in my ears. Lego House was playing, and that was because it had been on replay for a few days. I hummed its tune softly as I walked to the high school where I'd spend my senior year.

It was time to pick up the pieces and build a Lego house.

♥♥♥♥♥

After about 15 minutes, I arrived at my new high school. Unlike all those summer days when there was no one, it was now packed with teenagers. And seriously, it was chaos. As my eyes scanned the scene before me, all I could see were footballs being thrown around, making any path to the main entrance impossible.

Jocks these days.

There was a girl leaning her back against a giant tree, absent-mindedly smiling as she gently rocked her head. I could see ear buds in her ear and I figured she was listening to the music she loved.

A group of girls were gossiping about something, concentrating on that subject. I frowned upon seeing one of them dressed in underwear, or as they called them, short-shorts. It was autumn for God's sake! If you needed to get lustful gazes from guys, you should've done it during summer, instead of risking hypothermia.

I headed to the main entrance, eager to get my schedule. I muttered a few "Excuse me's" along the way. Some students looked at me, as if analyzing me with their eyes.

Why wouldn't they?

I was the new girl.

Out of nowhere, something hard hit the back of my head. Black spots clouded my vision and I felt my body fall to the ground as I lost consciousness.

Well, gosh diddly darn, what a great start to the new school year!

If you enjoyed this sample then look for A Unique Kind of Love on Amazon!

Introducing the Characters Magazine App

Download the app to get the free issues of interviews from famous fiction characters and find your next favorite book!

iTunes: bit.ly/CharactersApple
Google Play: bit.ly/CharactersAndroid

Author's Note

Hey there!

Thank you so much for reading Love is Blind! I can't express how grateful I am for reading something that was once just a thought inside my head.

I'd love to hear from you! Please feel free to email me at tara_declan@awesomeauthors.org and sign up at tara-declan.awesomeauthors.org for freebies!

One last thing: I'd love to hear your thoughts on the book. Please leave a review on Amazon or Goodreads because I just love reading your comments and getting to know YOU!

Whether that review is good or bad, I'd still love to hear it!

Can't wait to hear from you!

Tara Declan

About the Author

Tara is a 19 year old, college student, who first began writing at age thirteen after falling in love with books. She loves spending time on here farm with here many animals. Tara attends Concord University majoring in Social Work with a minor in Pre-law, to hopefully one day work at changing the lives and giving children hope. Tara first got her start on Wattpad, she was able to gain insight from her growing fan base.

Made in the USA
San Bernardino, CA
22 March 2017